The Book of Bob
Author: Gary Thomas Edwards
Cover Design: Gary Thomas Edwards
Editor: Calee Allen
Golden Shovel Publishing
© Copyright 2020, Gary Thomas Edwards, all rights reserved.
First Print on Demand: January 15, 2021 – First Revision: December 10, 2021
Contact: thegodscript@gmail.com
Social Media: www.thegodscript.wordpress.com • www.facebook.com/bookofbob

1

The Book of Bob

Gary Thomas Edwards

For Marianne

John 1:1

*In the beginning was the Word, and the Word was with God,
and the Word was God.*

*Know all things to be like this:
As a magician makes illusions
of horses, oxen, carts and other things,
Nothing is as it appears.*

The Buddha

A shooting star is not an uncommon occurrence in the waning hours just before sunrise. But a second, third and fourth streak of light were remarkable in their brightness and the length of time they remained suspended over the horizon where the morning's cyan met the receding black of night. The last two lingered with sparkling particles floating down like Fourth of July fireworks. Mesmerized, Aaron slowed down to stare out the windshield. The stars alone shone so brightly, framed by the snow-capped Sierra peaks, that with the light show, it rendered the scene surreal.

Headed to the Reno airport to catch a flight to Los Angeles, Aaron was not at all eager to attend the 2024 West Coast Data Transmission Conference. But he knew for his business it made sense. At least watching the sunrise on the high mountain lake would make the drive an enjoyable one. As he cruised near enough to see the beach, his thoughts, though momentarily distracted by the cosmic light show, were stuck in a loop. He couldn't shake the feeling of guilt for sneaking out of the house.

Cynthia's sweet smell still lingered in his thoughts, and he pictured her wrapped up in the covers on the bed. But there had been no soft kisses from a still-dreaming Cynthia this morning. No unintelligible murmurings of *Goodbye* and *Love you, Honey,* as her arms snuggled the pillow.

He shook his head from side to side. *Stupid. Stupid. Fucking stupid. I'm an idiot,* he thought. The evening's argument had been foolish. *The best way to cook rice, for God's sake. Rice!*

"Why did I say those things? Why?" he wondered aloud while slowly shaking his head. Blame it on too much wine or being tired, it mattered not. He had acted childishly and knew it. He had awoken late, not setting the alarm because he had been so upset. Ashamed, but in a hurry, he had left for the airport, stopping only to whisper an apology in her ear, hoping he would not wake her. He didn't have time to confess his stupidity right then. Now, with time to think, his heart ached because he had left without her being awake to hear his apology. *I am so stupid,* he thought again. *Stop thinking about it. Really, just stop it. Fix it when you land. Call and apologize.*

Aaron nodded at his plan with a slight degree of internal validation before turning his full attention back to the road.

The little Volkswagen Bug he had been restoring hummed along, heater scarcely working but working nonetheless. A rare thing for an older VW. In the higher elevation of Lake Tahoe, very little warm air manages to make the long journey from the rear engine to the front of the car. Barely enough to keep the windshield defrosted.

Glancing down at the dim dashboard lights to check his speed, Aaron noticed the gas gauge.

"Damn, I need gas!" he said, as if someone might be sitting next to him that cared. *An easy fix,* he thought, *I'll stop at Stateline. It's too far to the airport not to stop now.* He knew the station at Stateline would be open for the casino workers, even at this hour.

Swerving into the middle turn lane, he darted across the center lane to the station. Not a problem with little or no traffic this hour of the morning. He had to stay outside and pump and pay, as no one worked the stations this early. It was cold out, very cold, and in his hurry this morning, he had forgotten his jacket. He shivered as he slid his debit card on the pump's console and only put fifteen dollars in, enough to bring the VW's aging gauge up to show almost half a tank. A gauge, he knew, not to be trusted. While driving, the little pointer danced back and forth like the hula dancer on the dashboard.

Pulling out once again onto the main road, Aaron found himself next to another VW Bug almost identical to his. What were the chances of seeing another fifty-year-old car the same make and nearly the same color in the wee hours of the morning right next to him? His glance only took a second, before he returned his focus to the road ahead. But in that second and dim light, he clearly saw a man in his forties or early fifties, wearing a bright-colored, floral, short-sleeve shirt.

The man returned his glance, smiling broadly as they made eye contact. Then he too returned his attention to the road ahead. Aaron noticed that, like himself, the man was not wearing a jacket on this cold early morning.

Odd, he thought, as he knew this old guy's VW and its heater weren't worth a shit either. *Must be a Bug thing,* he thought and laughed.

As both cars cruised next to one another, slightly askew with the VW next to him ahead by a bumper, the sound from the two engines started to harmonize. It was a rich, wonderful sound, music to anyone who had spent hour upon hour restoring old VW engines. For that brief, fleeting moment, Aaron, who, in fact, had spent hour after hour working on his VW, reveled in it.

From his self-induced engine harmonic euphoria, Aaron noticed a peculiar pattern within the harmonic sound. He had never heard this before in his engine or any other. It sounded like the engines were picking up an external frequency, making a sound like an old-fashioned telegraph. He quickly deduced it must be interference from the flashing lights of the casinos.

Aaron's lights flashed off then on, startling him. *What? What's going on with my lights?* The dash lights and headlights continued to flicker, dimming on and off, then on again. *Was the generator going bad? Maybe the voltage regulator?* Over the years, his father had impressed on him the principle of Occam's razor: The most obvious solution is usually the correct solution. *It had to be the wiring. Something is shorting or coming loose under the dashboard where I just worked.*

Then as quickly as it started, the lights returned to normal, as if nothing had happened. "What the hell?" Aaron said, returning his attention once again to the road in front of him. It was then adrenaline rushed through his body.

The early morning stars that had dotted the darkness were gone. The flashing casino signs were gone. Instead, it was already late morning with the sun well over the horizon.

Unsure what to do, he continued down the road. Wide-open, high desert with dry, sagebrush-covered mesa spread out in front of him under a postcard-perfect, brilliant blue sky.

He retraced in his mind what had just taken place. He had not felt so much of a hint of a bump, and there had been no noise to warn him.

My lights flickered, he remembered.

Aaron tried to discern where he was. Why did it now look like he was on the road heading into Las Vegas? The lake and the snow-covered Sierra had been replaced by desert in the blink of an eye.

His vocabulary was reduced to three words: "What the fuck?" which he kept repeating under his breath as he rubbed one eye with one hand, then, switching, rubbed the other. *I've had a stroke. I have been driving for hours, totally unaware. Yeah. Yeah, I read about that, mini-brain strokes.*

He instinctively looked down at the gas gauge, which still danced at the half-full mark. He looked to the left for the VW that had been next to him harmonizing so beautifully, but it was no longer there.

Welling up from deep within came the nightmarish realization that this wasn't okay, that something terribly wrong had just taken place.

Up ahead, a sign indicated only a half-mile to the turnoff for the Last Hope Truck Stop. With no other logical option, Aaron took the offramp, his mind in a state of disarray, unable to fully take in what his eyes were seeing. billboards, highway signs, other vehicles. His mind, reeling over the fact that only moments before he was leaving Cynthia safe and sleepy, snug in their bed, was jolted back to reality by a loud horn blast. In his anxious distraction, he had inadvertently cut off a very unusual-looking big rig attempting to leave the truck stop.

Aaron waved his hand, mouthing, "Sorry, sorry," but he wasn't. He was too panicked to feel anything but dread. As he pulled up to the store, muscle memory slid the VW into neutral, pulled up the emergency brake handle and turned the key to shut off the engine.

He turned the key back on, checking the gas gauge once again. It still read half full, which made no sense. *How could I have driven this far and not used any gas?* he thought. Biting his knuckle as concern contorted his face, he turned the key off as shock began to overwhelm him.

Slowly, with great trepidation, he got out of the car and walked into the store like one would walk to the gallows. At the moment, the truck stop was not very busy. The front portion of the store, near the registers, offered basic convenience store necessities, snacks, drinks and mud flaps with graphic females in various compromising positions. To his right, he saw a lit opening that led to a bar with slot machines, bright lights and a headache full of ringing noises.

Aaron turned as the woman at the cashier's station asked, "You okay, hon?" Through the fog of panic still rolling in over his senses, he could make out she had shoulder-length black hair with grey highlights and a very bright, royal blue shirt. Her name tag read, *Dancer, from Nevada.*

"I'm fine, thank you. Maybe a tad confused; I don't know. Tough drive." He added the last line so as not to sound too out of place. "Do you mind if I ask you, and I know this is going to sound really weird, but, uhm, where am I? You know, what... what town is this?"

Dancer had heard it all over the years, and it took a lot to surprise her. But this young man and his manner were odd. He didn't quite appear to fit in. Cocking her head slightly to the left, she thought to herself, *Is this guy just being funny, or is he drunk?* Aloud, she answered, "Well, hon, we are 'bout a mile out of Flagstaff. Are you sure you're okay?" Dancer watched, concerned, as the man before her seemed to melt at her words.

"Where did you say? Flagstaff? Flagstaff, as in Arizona?" Aaron's whole body went cold, and his voice shook.

"Yeah, hon, you are in Arizona on Highway 180 that comes down out of the Grand Canyon. You want to maybe sit down?"

"No. No, I'm alright," he answered automatically, then thought better. "Okay. Yeah, actually, maybe I will sit down, just for a second. And could I have a glass of water, please?"

Dancer reached out, putting one arm around his shoulder and her hand under his elbow as if he were an elderly gentleman she needed to assist. She then tried to lead him toward the bar. Aaron resisted slightly, wanting to protest what he felt to be unnecessary assistance, but as he started to turn away, he was blindsided by a digital advertising board mounted to the wall behind Dancer. Over and over, it flashed a brightly glowing ad boasting this year's *Energy-Efficient Ford Trucks—New for 2040.*

Unable to catch his breath, Aaron looked around the interior of the Last Hope, his eyes exposing his fear. It seemed to be your average truck stop, cleaner than most. But at the same time, it appeared out of place, too modern. He could feel his knees buckling, desiring the security of the floor where gravity held less authority over his body. *How the hell can it be 2040?*

His stomach churned uncomfortably, and his mind leaped from one moment and event to the next. *How did this happen? How will I get back to Cynthia, to home? Where am I? Where am I going to spend the night? Where am I going to eat?*

Despite everything else racing through his mind, Aaron's frontal cortex took over, allowing basic responsibilities to creep in and add to his already overburdened mind. *Shit, how am I even going to pay the bills, the house, the insurance?*

Alarms were going off in his brain, warnings running rampant through every muscle, every cell in his body. The brain is a funny animal, for in the midst of this overwhelming deluge of unexplained fear, he found himself remembering an old movie he had seen years before: *Dragnet,* and the detective in the movie telling a hysterical woman, "Just the facts, ma'am." It made him smile for but an instant, long enough to get his mind to reset. He needed to sit, catch his breath and start over at the beginning. He also knew, like finding yourself lost in the mountains, that he needed to take care of basics first. First, make-a-plan for the evening: a place to stay, something to eat. Then he could go over the details of the day's events and try to figure out just what the hell had happened.

He turned and looked at the lady helping him. "Your name, it's Dancer?" Aaron asked, searching for words, something in the form of normal conversation, knowing he had to stop drawing attention to himself. He really didn't want to have to explain what had just happened. He was still rational enough to understand that no one in this town would believe him. They would just lock him up and throw away the key.

"Yes, hon, and you would be?" Dancer replied with a smile. It was a pleasant smile, and nurturing. Dancer possessed a wide array of pleasing expressions, like shoes in a woman's closet.

"I'm sorry, my name is Aaron. I'm, ah from the Lake. I mean ah, Lake ah, Tahoe. Lake Tahoe in California. I apparently have managed to get myself very lost." Aaron tried to chuckle but felt like his efforts to look normal were only making him stand out more. Panic reared up again, heat spreading throughout his body and directly into his throat. His voice started to falter. "Dancer, that's an unusual name, pretty. I like it. You know, I think—I think I will go sit in the bar and get something to drink, maybe something to eat. You serve food in there, yes?" Aaron fought the tremble in his voice as he felt himself slowly establishing purpose and direction for his immediate future.

Dancer blushed at Aaron's compliment, but her concern grew when he said he lived in Lake Tahoe. Still, she mustered a smile, her bright-white teeth standing out in sharp contrast against her dark-red lipstick as she replied. "Ah, thanks, hon, that was sweet. I'm originally from Reno, and I did spend a few years in Las Vegas before escaping to here. I loved Lake Tahoe; I really miss it. I visited there many times before—well, you know—"

She stopped, looking down for a second, then continued, "But in answering your question, yes, they have a pretty damn good menu at the bar. C'mon, let me get you a table."

Gently taking Aaron's arm, she directed him over to a bright blue-and-black neon-lit archway that led into the bar. Once inside, the only real light emanated from the slot machines beaming up from the bar and against the wall. The room was filled with background music that could barely be heard over the cacophony of bells, voices and sirens emanating from the slots. A handful of people were propping up the bar like a bunch of masonry grotesques supporting an old cathedral roof. The bartender, a young woman maybe twenty-five, wiped the bar in front of an older gentleman. The man, hunched over a beer, didn't move a great deal and seemed either lost in thought or drunk. Or maybe he was mesmerized by the flashing lights of the slots.

Dancer pointed to a table at the opposite corner of the room. "Here, sit there. I'll go get you a menu, hon. What do you want to drink? Aaron, right?"

Aaron replied, "Yes, it is Aaron. A beer please?" Feeling a touch of tangible reality returning, he stopped Dancer before she turned away. "Excuse me, can you make that an IPA? Do you have an IPA on tap?"

"Wow, I gotta tell you, hon, I haven't heard the term IPA in a long, long time. I used to drink a lot of IPAs back in my day, but no one has been making them since all the little micros were bought up by the big boys. But I do have on tap what I think will be damn close, what with you being an IPA sort and all. You just sit here and relax, I'll be back with your beer."

Aaron sat, his posture uncomfortably straight and every atom in his body screaming at him that there was something wrong. Sitting there alone, left to his own thoughts in the cozy, somehow familiarity of a truck stop bar, he relaxed a little.

It didn't last long. His attention was redirected, caught by the old man at the end of the bar. The man held a small, well-worn, leather-bound notebook, which he rhythmically tapped on his thigh. His faded, but still brightly colored, oversized Hawaiian shirt bounced with each tap.

Aaron took a moment to study the man. He was bony with pronounced features and deeply tanned skin. A thick, long grey ponytail hung down his back, and he tapped the book on his thigh out of time with the overhead music but somehow in sync with the random noise of the slot machines.

14

It all seemed to Aaron like watching a movie that focused in slow motion, the camera zooming in on the odd details you're supposed to remember for later on. The odd man was enough of a distraction to offer Aaron's muscles a chance to let go, to relax again. He sank ever so slightly into the deeply padded, faux leather booth. He was still staring at the man, the long-haired barfly, who then turned and stared directly back at him. The man's gaze was intense, and Aaron quickly turned away, realizing his rudeness.

Aaron felt his face flushing from embarrassment and was surprised he was still capable of such a normal response. For the second time that evening, he smiled and laughed to himself, though his laugh carried a note of fear.

Dancer approached with a beer in a frosted pint glass, the foaming head doing its best to escape and run over the edges. She set it down gently so as not to further encourage the advance of the foam. She then handed Aaron the menu, a blank sheet of what appeared to be black plastic about ten inches long. Puzzled, Aaron looked up at her to suggest that the menu must have fallen out, but when he touched the sheet, it lit up, displaying the bar's menu. Familiar enough with touchscreen technology, he instantly understood its use and thanked her.

Dancer spoke reassuringly, "You take your time, hon, I'll be right back." She turned toward the old man at the end of the bar and nodded, then walked over to wait on him.

Aaron, thinking nothing of the nod, watched for a moment. Then he glanced down at the menu, using his finger to slide through the pages. But after hastily perusing the entire menu, he realized he really wasn't all that hungry. He was scared and wanted answers, not food.

But maybe eating something would do me good. It will help me think. Returning to the appetizer menu, he browsed through the deep-fried finger foods. They all seemed to be titled after the establishment, 'Lost Hope' this or that. Finally, he settled on the Lost Hope Fish and Fries.

Dancer walked over and then slid in next to Aaron.

"You don't mind if I make myself comfortable, do you, hon?" She looked Aaron directly in the eyes as she spoke. He noticed she seemed to think nothing about closing that natural 'keep your distance' gap everyone possesses to protect themselves against strangers. He realized that was probably something Dancer could do effortlessly, making you feel as if you had been friends your entire life.

Needing a friend and beguiled by Dancer's natural ability, Aaron replied, "No, by all means." He had felt his unease returning—*Did that sign really say 2040?*—but her presence helped him relax again.

"Good," she said. "I know it's not the biggest menu, but what there is, is really just good old-fashioned stick-to-your-ribs kind of food. What did you want?"

"The fish and fries, and some malt vinegar if you have it. Please."

"Whoa, such a polite young man. You're a rare one. The truckers that come through here aren't much on niceties." She reached over to touch the menu. "You just select what you want and hit the order button at the bottom. There ya go, and good choice. That's real fish. Frozen, but real. None of that 3D-printed crap. Can I get you anything else?"

"Not unless you know a good psychologist," Aaron sighed.

Dancer cocked her head. "Okay, hon, tell you what. I'm going to go pick up your fish, get you a bottle of malt vinegar, and then I'll be back to hear the rest of this story. I'm no psychologist. But I damn sure know when someone could use an extra ear. Which, by the way, I have years of experience providing. You've got me for fifteen minutes, hon, then I'm off. That is if it is okay with you? Besides, I'm not the waitress. She's on break. I just work the front counter selling quick charges of Juice and beer, making sure no one skips without touchin' out."

Aaron felt embarrassed by the attention. "Actually, Dancer, it's okay. I'm just having the mother of all bad days, I think. My world at the moment is just not playing by the rules."

He sighed at the thought of opening up and communicating with someone. He knew very well he couldn't even begin to tell her what had transpired in the last hour. She would surely believe him certifiable and call the cops. Still, he was desperate for someplace to start. Some way to figure out what had just happened. "Wait, you know what? On second thought, yes, that would be excellent. I could use the company and the extra ear. Thanks, Dancer."

"Damn, hon, this story is getting better by the second. You stay here, I'll be right back."

Aaron let himself settle further into the seat, then glanced over at the old man in the flowered shirt. The man at the end of the bar was still gently keeping time to the slot machines, tapping his book while staring in Aaron's direction.

Aaron snapped his head back and shivered. *Shit, that's creepy.*

Dancer returned with Aaron's fish and fries, malt vinegar and another beer. "Here, I thought you might be ready for another beer to go with your chips. It's on me, hon."

She set the food, bottle and pint down in front of the dazed young man, who had by this point managed to push himself as far back into the darkest area of the booth as he could. Aaron leaned forward and sat up as she spoke to him.

"Thank you. Thank you. Yeah, I need it. I may need a few more before this evening is over. Can you sit down now?"

Before the last word could leave his lips, she was already sliding in next to him.

"Okay, guess that's a yes." Aaron smiled as he said it. "This is really odd to say right now, but I have to tell you, I'm impressed. Fish and chips, sorry, I mean fries. You guys at least call 'em what they are. But wrapped in newspaper. I thought they only did that in England."

"Yeah, well, it's a nice touch and all, that and the basket, but I always thought it a bit odd, since I haven't seen a printed newspaper in, must be twenty years. It's all marketing, hon, the printed paper to look like a newspaper and the basket. Okay, hon, so what brings you to the Last Hope here in beautiful Flagstaff, Arizona? If you don't mind my asking, that is?" Dancer socialized with enough strangers to know how to get them to open up. And she kind of liked this kid.

Aaron was about to answer when he realized the old man at the end of the bar had gotten up and walked to the other side of the room to a small stage of sorts set up with a podium, video monitor and a microphone. The sign just behind the podium on the wall read, "You're Our Last Hope Karaoke Night."

Realizing what the old man was about to do, Aaron looked over at Dancer in disbelief. "Can this get any weirder?" he said under his breath.

Following Aaron's gaze and hearing his mumbled words, Dancer placed her hands on his cheeks. "This is no dream, hon. You are not going to believe this. That gentleman there is Bob, and he is about to blow your mind."

Bob was fiddling around with the machine when the music came on, replacing the background music and almost drowning out the sounds of the slot machines. Instead of ringing, chiming and cheap sound bites, music lofted through the room as the old man pulled a microphone from its plastic holder on the side of the cabinet. Aaron noticed that though he was an older man, he was by no means frail or out of shape. In fact, he stood up at the podium proud and strong.

Then, with a pop of electricity, Bob's voice filled the room. It was clear and powerful, a perfect Italian tenor's pitch. Aaron recognized the song; it was one his mother played often called "Time to Say Goodbye." Mouth agape, Aaron looked again at Dancer as this odd, older man continued a performance worthy of a much bigger stage and audience.

"Told ya," Dancer said, grinning and giving him a soft jab to the ribs with her elbow.

Bob didn't miss a single note or lyric. He moved around the stage like a seasoned professional, the microphone in one hand and tapping his book on his thigh with the other. As he hit and held the last note, Bob quietly bowed his head. Then after a moment of silence, his head popped back up with the microphone closely following. Using the hand holding the book, he deliberately messed up his hair as he began to sing, "You shake my nerves and you rattle my brain—" gyrating around the podium as if possessed by Jerry Lee Lewis himself.

Aaron stared in complete disbelief, but when Bob dropped almost to the floor in a split and bounced back up like an eighteen-year-old gymnast, he stood up and screamed his approval.

"Oh my God! Oh my God," he said, leaning into Dancer so she could hear him. Dancer just smiled her wide, toothy grin.

Bob finished the song and the music retreated. He then gingerly replaced the microphone in its holder, triggering one last loud, resounding pop. Then, as the casino sounds poured back into the void, he returned to his seat at the bar. Both Aaron and Dancer clapped enthusiastically.

Dancer then turned back to Aaron, who was still looking dumbstruck. "Okay, hon, where were we? You were about to tell me about the exciting adventure that brought you from what used to be the beauty and serenity of the Sierra to the middle of the desert." Then she stopped suddenly. "Shit, I'm sorry, hon, I didn't know Bob would steal all my time to talk to you. I have to do my rounds again and make sure no one is stealing the store out front. Fortunately, for me anyway, since all the truckers started using 'Cloud Trak' to pay for their Juice, I really don't have to do much except smile. And I do that pretty damn well." She tilted her head back with one hand on the back of her head, posing like an old movie star from the Golden Age of Hollywood.

She did have a charming smile, he thought. A beautiful, creamy-white toothy grin that exposed an extremely askew left lateral incisor as she spoke and filled Aaron with a minute moment of happiness.

"So let me get you to touch out," she said, handing him her black pad. "I'll make some quick rounds and come right back. Hell, you know what? I'm off in fifteen minutes, so let me make it up to you with another beer."

Still trying to figure out what she meant by *touch out,* Aaron assumed it was slang he did not understand and that she meant for him to pay. He reached for his wallet, but before he could retrieve it, he felt a hand on his shoulder. Out of nowhere, Bob had stepped in, smiling at Dancer.

"I have this, Dancer," he said, and swiped his hand across the pad's glass. Dancer seemed to think nothing of his sudden generosity and simply smiled. "Aaron, I would like you to meet Bob. Bob, Aaron." Dancer held out her hands toward each of them in a show of introduction.

"Well, thank you, sir. Bob. But really, I have it," Aaron protested.

"No, you are too late. I have already touched you out," Bob said matter-of-factly. Then with his hand still on Aaron's shoulder, he motioned with his book to the empty seat across from him. "You wouldn't mind if I join you?"

Dancer spoke up, "Good idea, you two get to know each other. I'll be right back. Aaron, don't worry. Bob's docile." She paused. "Well, for a crazy old coot. Bob, stay in this universe, okay? I'll be back in a flash." She turned and walked off toward the registers at the front of the store.

Aaron, still shell shocked by the events, turned to Bob, searching for something to say. "That was really beautiful, your voice, your singing. Are you a singer?"

"I am a good singer, am I not? But to answer your question, I am an engineer. A very educated and experienced engineer. Music, singing—they are tools. Something that helps me turn off the constant stream of information my brain is trying to process. Always trying to solve everything," Bob replied.

Aaron realized then that, because of Bob's singing, his mind had momentarily slowed. He was calm.

Bob continued, "I do not know a great deal of songs, just a few. Real music, none of today's synthesized digital bullshit. Mostly opera—Lanza, Pavarotti, Bocelli, and Callas. As well as, of course, the early days of rock and roll. I do know a few of the great crooners classics, too, the works of Sinatra, Dean and Sammy. Well, those are before your time," he said, chuckling lightly to himself.

The momentary mental reprieve allowed Aaron to respond unconsciously. "Actually, I know all of those artists and their music. In fact, I still have most of them on vinyl. Well, except Callas. I've never heard of him." Aaron thought about his collection at home, many of his own vinyl 33s, as well as his father's. He would carefully play them on a turntable old enough to have a setting for playing 78s.

"She!" Bob corrected him loudly. "Maria Callas is the most amazing female singer ever. She had the most incredible strength of voice. Vinyl albums, did you say? You do not look as if you are that old." He chuckled to himself. "I haven't seen an old record like that in—" Bob stopped, thought, then continued, "For some time. So, it is Aaron? I am correct, yes?"

"Yeah, it's Aaron. Aaron Hodges."

"I am quite sure that I have never seen you here, or even around town. You are from out of town?" Bob inquired.

"Well, I am most certainly not from around here or now." His normal resting face, thoughtful with a half-smile, returned as he replied with a sense of humorous indignation. His plight and these strangers talking to him like it was just another day made no sense. They didn't have the slightest clue what he had experienced. "I live in Lake Tahoe, on the California side."

"If I might be so rude enough to ask..." Bob said, and then paused once again before continuing. "Everyone tells me that all the time. That I am rude. I am not rude! I know what I know, I know what I want others to know, and I do not mince words. I believe they are just angered that they cannot keep up with me."

"Rude? No, no, go ahead," Aaron managed, wondering again at this strange man he was talking to. But, after all that had happened, Bob seemed normal in comparison.

"What is it you do, and why are you here?"

Aaron pondered his answer for a second, not really knowing how to reply. "Well, to tell you the truth, Bob, I don't know. I feel like I am in a really bad dream, and I keep hoping that any second I'm going—" But before he could finish, Bob broke in.

Okay, that was rude, Aaron thought.

"You know, Aaron, dreams are a favorite topic of mine. A topic that I have pondered since the very first time I optimized a fragmented Macintosh hard drive." Bob became animated as he talked, as if he were addressing a classroom full of students. He seemed oblivious to the fact he had just monopolized the conversation.

"Back when there were PCs and Macs, before the Cloud, before Infinite... Hmm, I should explain better, so you will understand, Aaron. My computer had reached a point of running slower and slower and crashing at the drop of a hat. A friend introduced me to a program that would 'optimize my hard drive,' as he put it. Imagine my surprise, which we know does not happen often. I became mesmerized when he ran the program. A window popped up, displaying a graphic of how the drive's data was fragmented into hundreds of different colored blocks. My friend explained that when a computer writes information to the hard drive, it does not always write a contiguous line of information as one would in writing a report. Instead, the systems back then looked for any available space to write segments of this information to. It then assigned each segment, regardless of how small it was, an address for retrieval at a later date.

"It is a rare occurrence, but Carl—yes, that was his name. Carl insisted I run this program, and it proved to be enlightening. And if I might add, significantly applicable to what I was working on at the time. I watched, intrigued, as the program ran its optimization function, creating a steady stream of different colored segments. Little squares were being subtracted from the larger fragmented pile of data and rearranged so that they ran together in a single file. A horizontal line moved right to left, creating a pile perfectly grouped with all colors matching on the other side. It was much like watching an old-fashioned filmstrip. The kind that used to go from spool to spool, passing in front of a lightbulb that then projected the image onto a screen." Bob became more and more animated as he spoke, waving his book right to left in the air as he tried to describe his ideas.

To Aaron, it became apparent that a serious disconnect in Bob's brain existed between him and the rest of humanity. Bob was no longer really talking to him. Rather, he was talking to hear himself, turning side to side and sweeping his arms to mimic the motion of the filmstrip.

"At first, like everyone else, all I saw were the different colored segments, each representing a small chunk of information from individual files stored on my computer. They were now moving in one line. Because these random pieces of information were now attached to each other like a filmstrip, it was creating what I thought would have taken one half of a movie. Well, if you could watch it, that is." Bob paused, lowering the book to his thigh. "And then it hit me. It hit me like a zettabyte of data. So blatantly obvious."

He stopped waving his hands and the book, wiped his lips with his wrist, then turned to Aaron and asked, "Why do we get tired and have to sleep?" He paused for the desired effect, but before Aaron could answer, he continued, "Because our little pea-pickin' brains are so chock-full of fragmented bits and bytes of information taken in during the day that we need to be optimized so as to function better, clearer, quicker." A small amount of spittle had escaped along with the words pea-pickin', and Aaron looked at the glistening drops on the table with a slight sense of disbelief. He shuddered. *Am I really here, listening to this old man with a grey ponytail in a flowered shirt discuss computers and dreams in a truck stop of the future?*

"Now, Aaron, if I am right." Bob chuckled. "Though, of course, I am—then what is occurring in dreams is this: as you sleep, your brain runs its own diagnostic and optimization program. As that steady stream of fragmented bits and bytes of information flows across in a filmstrip-like progression, the subconscious, your subconscious, with nothing better to do while the conscious snores away, reads the fragmented information as real-time and translates it. Most likely, our subconscious ad-libs a bit—okay, a lot—so that the stream is a cohesive story. A story that, when you wake up in the morning, you wonder how that weird dream could have seemed so real."

Bob had talked for nearly fifteen minutes without so much as pausing to take a full breath, a drink or even blink. Aaron had simply sat there, his own dilemma moved to the back of his mind as he was simultaneously astounded by this man's knowledge and lack of regard for his audience's participation.

Dancer returned, allowing Aaron to breathe a sigh of relief for her rescuing him from this odd man's rambling dissertation. Still, as that thought rolled across his mind, he also felt genuine intrigue. What Bob had just said about dreams made tremendous sense.

This guy is incredibly intelligent, like an idiot savant. And he can really fucking sing.

"Well, I hope you boys have gotten to know each other," Dancer said. "See, I told you he wouldn't bite. Bob and I go way back. He helped me out when I first moved to this town. He took care of me, and now I take care of his old coot ass." She gave Bob a gentle shove as she said it.

"I believe, Dancer, I am quite capable of taking care of myself, and rather, it is you who needs looking after. You, of course, know that I am correct. I always am. Seems I am the one always bailing you out of one predicament or another that you have managed to somehow blindly stumble your way into." Bob pulled Dancer toward him, giving her an awkward-looking shoulder hug, before straightening himself and taking a step away.

"Wow," Dancer muttered, startled by Bob's unusual, almost but not quite there, affectionate hug.

Aaron spoke up then, changing the subject back to something he felt of much greater concern. "Where can I find a cheap motel for tonight?"

answered instead. "Aaron, you still owe me a story, and quite frankly, I'm not at all sure why I trust you already, but I do. Sooooo, I have an empty room at my place you are more than welcome to use. You can tell me your story, I'll supply the beers tonight and coffee in the morning, and then you can be on your way. Besides, like Bob says, I am always finding a way *blindly*"– –she held her fingers up in quote symbols to emphasize the point—"to get myself into some sort of trouble. What do you say? Want to get in some trouble, honey?" she asked in her best Mae West imitation, complete with the sarcasm.

"Well, that's better and cheaper than any ideas I can come up with," Bob stated. "You know I am a great judge of character. I believe Aaron here will not get you into too much trouble."

He turned to Aaron. "Young man, you should not pass an offer like that up. I should, however, warn you. A word to the wise—she is trouble, be careful."

Bob nearly fell over laughing while Dancer shot him a mock look of disgust. She turned to Aaron with a smile and said, "He's right, honey. Still want to come?"

Aaron couldn't help but wonder about how normal and comfortable he felt, at that moment, in the presence of these two strangers. It felt like he had known them for years, and for a moment he had mercifully forgotten the reality of his present misadventure. He also realized Dancer's offer was indeed the very best thing he had going for him. He didn't know where he was—or when he was—and had nowhere else to go. Here were two people he could at least talk to, and maybe he could even confide in this woman who had so quickly befriended him.

Besides, he thought, *I can't sleep on the street.* He turned toward Dancer, knowing a good thing when he saw it. "Dancer, that is very generous of you. But are you sure? I mean, I'm a total stranger to you." He let out a soft unconvincing laugh, then added, "Of course, so are you to me as well."

"You can't be any stranger than Bob or me, for that matter. Yes, I'm sure. I'm off now, so why don't you just follow me home? Let me go finish closing out, and I'll be right back. And Bob, try not to talk his other ear off." She turned to Aaron with a laugh. "When you've known him as long as I have, you learn to let it all go in one ear and out the other," she said as she walked away.

"Indeed," Bob said after Dancer had left. "Well, my new and good friend, I am afraid I cannot stay and use my verbose vocabulary in such a way as to remove either of your ears, as

Dancer suggests. I do have to get back to an experiment that is running as we speak, back at the Cave—Sorry, my lab. I am quite certain you have found it a pleasure to meet me. I hope I get the opportunity to see you again soon. You are, in the meantime, in great hands. Dancer is a unique, genuine person and a lady. She mothers me far too much, so be careful. Have a good evening."

And with that, he turned abruptly and walked off, head thrust back and ponytail hanging down, looking up as if there were something on the ceiling. All the while, keeping perfect cadence to his gait, he bounced the little book he had never let go of.

~~~ ~~~ ~~~

Aaron placed the directions Dancer had sketched to her home on the passenger seat of his Volkswagen. "Just in case we get separated in traffic," she had said. He settled into his seat with a sigh, finding a comforting familiarity in the worn tan vinyl. Right now, it was the closest thing he had to home. He sat there not moving, just breathing with eyes closed for several seconds, until a dull whine and bright multi-colored lights brought him back.

He peered through his rearview mirror at Dancer's car and what he assumed were the headlights. The lights were very odd, though. Two sets of lights consisting of three thin, horizontal slits shining brightly from the car's front, each one a different color: a blue light on top, a red light in the middle and a green light at the bottom. Although the lights were bright, the three different colors were quite easy to look at, not at all like looking into the typical headlights of a car. But in front of the vehicle, where the three lights shone onto the ground, they combined to create volumes of white light. It was like daylight in front of her car.

RGB, he thought to himself. *Of course. How clever is that!*

As he stared, mesmerized by the lights, Dancer pulled around. Poking her head out of her window, she said, "You comin', hon?" Then she paused as she took her first real look at Aaron's car. "Where on Earth did you dig that museum piece up? Wow, and it runs." She smiled and waved to him. "Come on, hon, you can tell me about it at the house. See if you can keep up. Besides, I'm off and don't want to spend my free time here when there is a perfectly comfortable house full of food and cold beer."

She tossed her hair, then pulled her head back inside her car, motioning for him to follow.

Aaron slid the key into the ignition and turned it. The little engine roared to life, sounding more like an oversized sewing machine with flatulence issues. He pulled out the little knob on the all-metal dash, and the lights blazed to the glorious, pale-yellow, comforting light that he knew. Seeing the pavement dimly lit in front of him, he considered just how remarkable the lights on Dancer's car were. He would have to ask her about that when he got to her house.

He let the clutch out slowly and headed into the night, his mind filled with foreboding wonder.

As he'd feared, just after they pulled off the freeway, Dancer disappeared into a hundred sets of taillights that all looked the same. Aaron grabbed for the piece of paper she had given him with the directions on it. With not enough light and too much engine vibration to be able to read it, Aaron chose to head through the intersection toward a small parking lot in front of a well-lit shopping mall. Suddenly, the back of his car and rearview mirror were bathed in blindingly bright red-and-blue flashing lights.

"Shit! Shit, shit, I'm not speeding, what?" He knew all too well what the colorful array of lights meant: the police. He pulled into the parking lot, his original destination, and parked directly under one of the tall lights, shutting off the Bug.

Where the hell did he come from? I mean, what, did he drop out of the sky? He rolled down his window and waited. He could hear the deputy's radio, but the lights were too bright for him to clearly see the vehicle behind him.

After what seemed an eternity, and knowing Dancer must be halfway home, the silhouette of a deputy climbed out of the passenger side of the cruiser. He walked toward the rear of Aaron's car, white-hot lights blazing behind him. Aaron watched the haloed silhouette approach, adjusting his belt and hat. He stepped up to the side of Aaron's car, shining his light first into the rear of his car and then directly into Aaron's eyes. He paused, then lowered his flashlight and bent down so he could look Aaron in the eyes.

Aaron instinctively asked the same question asked a million times over the years by people being pulled over. "What did I do, Officer?"

The deputy smiled and asked, "Where did you dig this relic up, and where on Earth do you get fuel? Pretty cool, though."

A little surprised, Aaron replied, "It's kind of, well, sort of my hobby. I have been fixing it up, you know, restoring it."

"I haven't seen one of these things on the road in fifteen, maybe twenty years. Amazing you can even find parts for it. Nice, kid, nice. But you have to know, I pulled you over because of your headlights. They're not legal. Actually, neither are your taillights. And I tried to run those plates. We have no record of them. Besides, they're not legal either. Not even for an antique classic like this. So, sorry, kid, I'll need to see your registration and get a quick scan."

"Sure." Aaron leaned over to dig through the glove box. His hands were shaking badly, but he quickly located the registration and handed it to the deputy. The deputy reached over and took the piece of paper, staring at it with a bewildered look.

"What's this?" he asked, as Aaron was pulling his wallet out of his back pocket. Aaron's hands shook so hard that when he withdrew his license, it flew out in front of him, bouncing off the windshield and then dropped to the floor.

"You seem kind of nervous, kid," the deputy observed, starting to realize this wasn't going to be a simple traffic stop.

"Yes. I'm sorry, I am nervous, sir. I have never been pulled over before," Aaron lied, trying to buy some time and sympathy.

"Okay, kid, take your time."

Aaron bent down, retrieved the license and handed it to the deputy. The deputy, looking even more puzzled, took the small plastic card, then said, "May I please see your right arm?"

Aaron's heart sank at this request, believing he was about to be arrested. "Why? Are you arresting me?"

"What? No, I am not arresting you. Just please stick your right arm out of the window so I can scan it." The deputy was still polite, but firmer, using a far more authoritative voice.

Puzzled, Aaron complied. He feared not doing exactly what the officer told him. The deputy pulled a small device from his belt and slowly scanned the top of Aaron's arm. Then, releasing Aaron's arm, he returned the device back to his belt and said, "You sit tight, I'll be right back."

Aaron watched in his side mirror as best he could through the bright lights. He could make out the deputy in the patrol car hunched over talking to... no way.

Aaron strained, peering more closely through the bright glare, doing his best to discern what the shape was. It looked like a robot.

Again, after some delay, the deputy returned to the side of Aaron's Bug. Standing back a few feet, he looked at Aaron and said very officially, "Please step out of the car and put your hands on the roof of your vehicle."

"What the fuck? This can't be happening," Aaron muttered under his breath. He slowly got out of the safety of his car—the last remnant of his other life—and turned, putting his hands on the roof. He had never been arrested before but knew with absolute certainty that he was going for a ride in the back of that patrol car.

It was then he got his first clear view of the patrol car.

It was a drone. A drone-like sedan with a myriad of flashing lights, including the same RGB slit headlights he'd seen on Dancer's car. Rectangular and flat in shape like the wing of an airplane, the dark-grey drone appeared to be made of carbon fiber. On top sat a clear dome, split at the middle with half opening toward the front and the other half blacked out. Large fan blades were spinning in housings molded to the front and rear corners of the drone. The housings, painted white, were smoothly rounded at the top and about three feet in diameter. On the back were two smaller fan housings that were mounted upright from the body and rotated to control direction.

The deputy pulled Aaron's arms down to cuff him by wrapping a long strip of material around his wrist that then filled with air. The 'cuffs' were not uncomfortable, and Aaron could still move his wrists—though not enough to free himself. The deputy led him over to the rear portion of the drone's pod and motioned for him to step on the side, where clearly marked bold white letters read, "Step Here."

Aaron stepped up and then into the rear compartment, all the time staring at the motionless robot that sat in front where a human driver should be. It seemed right out of a cheap science fiction novel, molded out of shiny, beige plastic with a semi-human appearance.

The deputy spoke to the robot, "Fifty-four, secure the rear," and then climbed into the passenger seat. "Okay, then. Fifty-four, let's take this one back to the station. And request a tow for the kid's vehicle to the impound yard."

The robot nodded, and as the whine of the fans increased, they lifted straight up into the air about ten feet. "Merge lane plus ten at ten," said Fifty-four.

"Really, Fifty-four. I told you, you don't have to tell me every little detail. I know how it works," the deputy replied to Fifty-four with a certain amount of sarcasm mixed with irritation.

"I am sorry, sergeant," Fifty-four answered. "You know my protocol for flying is set to comply with standards set by the Department of Drone Transportation. I find it annoying and redundant as well, but I must comply."

Aaron thought the robot showed a disturbing amount of personality.

The deputy gave the robot a friendly slap on the shoulder and smiled. "Whatever. Let's get this Scab to the station."

Aaron watched his Bug disappear below him as the police drone rose to about two hundred feet. Aaron could see the surrounding desert and city, which was astonishingly beautiful. He was quite familiar with seeing the city lights from twenty thousand feet in a commercial airliner and was surprised by how different the view was at this altitude. There was more depth and focus to the lights. And as they rose and moved forward, it produced an odd illusion of multiple layers below them, with each layer having independent motion of direction and speed.

~~ ~ ~~~~ ~~~~

"Nate, sorry to bother you. We think we might have a hit on that Mandić guy, the hippie professor you've been chasing since dinosaurs were still roaming the earth." Miles shot Nate a smug smile, then continued, "The guy who stole all of the equipment and plutonium from that lab in Livermore."

Nate turned, no longer interested in the boring and basic sandwich he had thrown together in the morning before walking out the door. A mundane pile of bread that now lay lifeless in front of him.

"Really? But that *might* part. Ya know, that shit just scares me when you back up a fact with *might*. It's like that damn word *except* that renders all absolutes open to discussion. So give me something I can chew on and spit out. Not *maybe*, and most assuredly not *might*."

Miles hesitated. He was an intelligent and up-and-coming detective with an odd combination of confidence and insecurity--a result of his youth and quick rise through the ranks of the United Incorporated Investigative Bureau, the UIIB.

Stammering slightly, he said, "Sorry, Nate. It seems a Scab got picked up last night driving what, as described by the arresting deputy, has to be an antique Volkswagen Bug. And, the Volkswagen matches the description of your guy's car, the one he was last seen in. What is it with these Scabs? They're idiots. Why would anyone in this day and age not want to have their PIC? I mean, come on, you can't do anything, go anywhere, buy anything—it's just stupid, if you ask me."

Old enough to not give a shit about PIC technology, Nate motioned with his right hand, circling in front of him that he wanted the young detective to get on with his story. "I didn't ask you for a lecture on the use or nonuse of Personal Identification Chips. Now, tell me how a young kid in a VW Bug puts Mandić back on my radar. What's the connection?"

"Well, it's kind of good news and bad news. He is much younger than your guy Mandić. I believe they said late twenties. But, get this, he had a 2018 California Driver's License. The kind you used to put in your wallet. The kind that had your picture on it. The Bug the kid was driving has old-style plates from 2018 on it. The bad news, the plate numbers and VIN numbers don't match those of the VW Mandić drove when he disappeared. Kid must be good with cars to still have that car running. Where the hell does he get fuel for it? I mean, it's really hard to get the special permit for that explosive shit. Anyway, a VW Bug, 2018, the year Mandić went off radar. I don't know, seems like a pretty big red flag to me."

"You don't know, that's right," Nate tossed back at him. "What you have is a lot of coincidental bullshit, if you ask me." Nate returned his stare to the lifeless sandwich staring back at him. Not the least bit excited by the prospect of lunch, he asked, "Where did they find this twenty-year-old-something runaway?"

The detective straightened, smiling. "Arizona. Flagstaff, Arizona."

Nate turned his gaze away from his less-than-beckoning sandwich to look at Miles. "Where?"

"Arizona. And one more thing; he was bailed out by an old geezer named Bob Kesey, whom the sergeant described as—and these are the sergeant's exact words—'an old hippie fruitcake.'"

Nate flew out of his chair, grabbing his coat and bag. Then, spinning his finger in the air and pointing it toward the door in one quick gesture, he said, "Get us some air!"

~~~~ ~~~~ ~~~~

Aaron had been quiet for some time. Riding in Bob's car through this part of the country at night left everything to the imagination. He could make out the top of the San Francisco Peaks, silhouetted by the city lights beyond, but still had no idea where he was. Dancer had pointed to the peaks earlier in the Last Hope's parking lot. She tried to explain where they were and where her home was. She had also told him how the Navajo considered it to be the *Sacred Mountain of the West*. But she had cut the story short, telling him she would finish it back at her house.

At the moment, Bob was in control of Aaron's world. He was grateful that Bob just happened to have a friend at the police station who thought to call him about the young drifter who kept mentioning his and Dancer's name. Pleased, Bob had come and picked him up, a total stranger. *I must appear so strange to these people. Why on Earth do they have any interest in helping me?*

Aaron shook his head and glanced out the side window. They were climbing as they left the lights of town, and he watched as the high desert, dark-red rock plateau formations, sage and silhouettes of an occasional tall, saguaro cactus flew by his view like an old black-and-white movie. Aaron had not seen another car in some time, so he knew they were headed out into the backcountry.

"Bob, do you mind my asking, where exactly are we going?"

"Fortunate, yes, very fortunate they found me. This time of night, I am most always in the Cave..." Bob paused, then continued, "My shop, that is. You will love my shop. I have been building it for years, since the Eight-Year War. The Federal Government has been so kind as to allow me to acquire the materials I needed for my projects from slightly used leftovers of older projects I once worked on. And that, my new friend, is exactly where we are headed. It is at my home. I like to live far

appreciate my solitude. No salesmen or religious zombies trying to convert me to their flavor of the month. Just me, the marmots, the deer and coyotes. Did I mention rattlesnakes? Except for Dancer, there are few people who even know I exist, and I like it that way."

Aaron watched and listened, again recognizing Bob was talking more to himself and at the little book he held in his left hand than to him. *Creepy*, he thought. As Bob took a second to breathe between words, Aaron jumped in. "I have to thank you again, Bob. You don't know me. You don't know anything about me at all, and you are willing to bail me out of jail and take me to your home. I'm—well—just really, really grateful. I am worried, though. Dancer is expecting me at her house, and I sort of disappeared. Something I seem to be doing involuntarily all too frequently of late."

"I already spoke with Dancer," Bob said. "I told her the police did not like your little car, which I do have a great affinity for, by the way, and that they believed you to be a Scab. I told her I would bring you home with me tonight, and in the morning, she can pick you up to return to the police station and retrieve your car. I will print you out a special Classic Car permit, and then you should be able to drive it in the daytime as you will not need your headlights—which, by the way, is what got you pulled over. Those types of lights were outlawed many years ago..." Bob paused as if catching himself. "They were outlawed in this city, forcing everyone with older vehicles to buy the new RGB slit lights. They were a brilliant idea, and mine, of course. But enough of lights. You have no interest in lights, though I could tell you much about light and how greatly misunderstood the entire concept is. Dancer will pick you up and take you to get your car in the morning. Being around the police station is, well, let's just say we have history." Bob ended with an odd little chuckle.

"What is a Scab?" Aaron asked quickly, for fear Bob would just keep talking. But asking a simple question, he would soon learn, was not the best way to get Bob to talk less on any given subject.

"Sorry, yes, you might not have heard of a Scab from when you are from. It is a derogatory term that refers to someone who has removed their PIC, a corporate-mandated information chip that is inserted at birth. It is supposed to be voluntary, but really, it has been required of everyone since those stupid fucking terrorists blew everything all to hell!" Bob emphasized the word "hell," speaking much louder. A shift from his normal tone, Aaron noted. "The chips are supposed to make it easier to spot terrorists. It carries all of your basic personal information, like your Corporate Security Number, medical alerts, and as you get older, your right-to-drive number, also your bank account numbers. All the things you do not want others to know. Well, to be fair, they do contain your medical information, and that's good. *They*—" he said with great emphasis, "the Corporates, require you to have it so they know the where, when and the why about everyone. There are many who do not think it is right, that it has gone far past protection from terrorists. So they resist. When someone removes the chip, it generally leaves a small scab, then a scar. There is an entire underground movement whose desire, like mine, is not to be on anyone's radar. I have one, but it is of my own design. I can set the tracker in mine to make it appear I am somewhere other than where I am. I also filled mine with false information, should they be so lucky as to hack into it. As I said, it is not illegal to remove them, as the chips are technically voluntary. But when they catch someone without one, it is grounds to bring them in. Those headlights and you not having a chip or a scar, well, you must have seriously baffled the crap out of them. I will bet they thought they had a career criminal in their custody." Bob paused, feeling an uncommon need to reassure Aaron.

"You do not have a scar or a PIC, you have a car with headlights that attract cops like flies to feces, and you are, so far, willing to listen to my endless babbling and self-absorbed lectures. I know I talk too much and talk to myself, but I am the only one capable of understanding everything I say." Bob chuckled. "So you see, Aaron, I signed a Mandate of Responsibility for you at the station. I am bringing you to my home because I have a feeling about you, a good feeling about you. I trust you enough to give you a hand because—well, Aaron, my boy, if I might be so blunt, you are out of place here." Bob turned his gaze from the road and looked straight at Aaron. "I know that look. You do not have to tell me anything about your world until you are ready. I know a thing or two about being scared and not trusting anyone. You should, for now, sit back and rest assured you are in the hands of an excellent driver, and know you are, at least for the moment, safe."

Aaron had been patiently waiting, and now sat up straight in his seat. "Did you say, *when?* When I was from?"

Bob's face flushed like a child being caught red-handed, but without missing a beat, replied, "Aaron, you, like Dancer, will learn not to listen to half of the things I say. All sorts of nonsensical things, things that are always correct, mind you, do tend to find their way out of my mouth. Ask her."

They pulled off the paved road onto a dirt road that appeared to be of the barely traveled variety. The turnoff was very hard to see, especially at night and surrounded by large rocks and cactus. Bob stopped the car and hurried over to a metal gate with a large "No Trespassing" sign on it. He pulled a ring of keys from his pocket and opened the lock, letting the chain and lock drop as he pushed the gate open. Once through, he hopped out to close and lock the gate.

"I like old fashioned key locks; you cannot hack into and open them. Only a few still possess the ability to pick a lock." He slid back into his seat, and driving off, the car bounced down the rough dirt and gravel road. Aaron guessed they had traveled maybe five or six miles before the road ended and they pulled up in front of a modest, adobe-brick style home. It appeared in the darkness to be a light-tan building with a low, gable roof covered with terra cotta tiles.

Bob pulled around the circular driveway where two large Shamel ash trees grew in a rock-lined area at the center of the driveway. As they exited the car, Aaron saw in front of him a thick adobe wall that stood six feet, maybe more. At the center was an archway with two ornate wooden gates, decorated with old Spanish decorative trim around the edges. Aaron's attention went to the hand-carved depiction of Quetzalcoatl in the center, split between the two gates. Aaron recognized the Aztec's Feathered Serpent God responsible for creating mankind from a college course. Below the sculpture were two large, rusted iron rings to pull the gates open. Once opened, they led into a patio area covered with terra cotta paving stones.

A single, small light attached to the house illuminated the area, and he could make out a wrought iron table and chairs and what looked like a barbecue sitting back further in the dark corner. Bob unlocked the door, which Aaron noticed had three separate locks, all requiring a key. He opened the door, gesturing for Aaron to come in.

The lights came on automatically as soon as they passed into the entry, and a female voice spoke. "Welcome home, Bobby, all is nominal." As she spoke, a display screen on the wall lit up with colorful fractal designs matching the inflections of her voice.

Bob addressed the screen, "Thank you, Miko. Do I have any mail or messages?"

She replied rather seductively. "No, Bobby," the voice purred. "I thought you and I would be alone this evening. But, I see you have brought me a guest. I've run a scan and note our guest has no PIC. Would you enlighten me, please?"

"Yes, Miko, we do have a guest. This is Aaron, and he will be staying with us for a few days. I will have him give you more information later," Bob explained.

"Welcome, Aaron. It is a pleasure to meet you." The display responded with fractals again, though in different colors and patterns than when she spoke to Bob.

Aaron turned to Bob and whispered, "Bobby?" lightly mocking the greeting.

"It's her programming," Bob snapped back, embarrassed. "Now, if you will follow me, I will show you your room."

Bob opened the door to a small but pleasant room, and Aaron took a step inside. Suddenly, he once again felt the weight of his situation. He had no luggage, as it was supposed to be a quick trip. He had only an overhead travel bag with one change of clothes plus those on his body, a toothbrush and his electric shaver. He had keys to a car now illegal to drive and a wallet full of useless money and cards. He had nothing.

In the calm and temporary security of Bob's home, the realization of his situation came crashing down on him. He felt his knees grow weak, begging to buckle. He tried to fight the tears, but they streamed down his cheeks as his knees and hands reached out for the floor. Finally letting it all surface, there on his hands and knees in a complete stranger's house, he sobbed uncontrollably. He wanted to be with Cynthia. He wanted to open his eyes and have this nightmare be over.

Bob, unable to comprehend this type of emotion and in unfamiliar territory, being at a loss for words at Aaron's raw display, stood back for a moment watching with strange fascination. Finally, he mustered up enough of what he believed to be compassion to walk over and lay his hand uncomfortably on Aaron's shoulder. "Aaron, I need to know if you are okay. You may not believe me, but I do understand more than you know. I can see, even feel, that you are dealing with a major traumatic issue. I believe I have some insight as to what that might be."

Aaron, feeling Bob's presence, wiped his face with his forearm and slowly stood up. His head was hot, feverish, and he felt great embarrassment on top of everything else. Though never tested like this in his life, Aaron dug deep within, grabbed hold of his emotions and forced the infelicitous thoughts to the back of his consciousness.

"Thanks, Bob," he said. He took a deep breath and nodded. "Yeah. Yeah, I'm okay. You're right, I have been through some traumatic shit in the last twenty-four hours. Things you wouldn't—things nobody would believe if I tried to explain. Sorry for losing it there. It won't happen again. And, Bob, I would completely understand if you would rather I just head out and down the road."

"Oh, no. No, no, Aaron, it is not often I get someone willing to listen to my endless rants about the world and our universe. You will tire of me far faster than I of you. Come, make yourself comfortable. If you need anything, just ask Miko. Tomorrow I will show you the Cave.

~~~~ ~~ ~ ~~~~

Cynthia had been up for several hours. She'd had time to make and sip a cup of coffee while taking in some news. Then she jumped into the shower where, without remorse, she drained the hot water until the water turned cooler, making her shut it off. She had hesitated on taking the shower as she knew the day would be spent covered in sawdust, concrete and paint. But after all, she told herself, *First and foremost, I'm a lady.* She felt more creative when fresh and had taken the time to put on a little makeup.

It was just the way things unfolded in her world. She knew it, and Aaron knew it. It was why she loved him, because he understood and loved her in spite of her eccentricities.

She glanced at her phone, wanting to see if Aaron had texted. She could always count on some sort of silly, loving message on the phone before she awoke, but not today. It didn't worry her, knowing he must have run into several fires from his work that he would be consumed trying his best to extinguish, all the while dealing with airports and airplanes. Cynthia knew Aaron encountered daily emergencies brought on by unreasonable clients and unfathomable interference from nature and humans. Getting away from his office at home did not lessen these intrusions; it would only increase his work while away.

She glanced over where Half Dome was sitting, patiently waiting for his morning attention and biscuit. Half Dome, their four-year-old English bulldog who bore some obvious pug DNA that had snuck in somewhere along his not-so-AKC registered linage, just looked at her. His speckled white, black and grey color and unusually flat, black face made him resemble the famous peak his name was derived from.

"Sorry, Half Dome. Come on, boy, let's get a cookie." Her words had Half Dome up and trotting toward her, tongue out, showing his endearing wide grin.

She gently handed Half Dome his cookie and rubbed his back, then smiled and turned her attention to the table she had been working on for several days under her own deadline. Cynthia's clients, wonderful people, were not as much unreasonable as they were at times painfully demanding of designs that made her teeth grind as she did her best to steer them toward something better. The life of an artist, she had to remind herself almost daily, was very much like an old west gun for hire. Others hired her and her creative talent to do what they could envision but were incapable of making into reality. There were times, though not enough, when she created just for herself—fine art. They were small chunks of time, but chunks she cherished.

"He will call..."

~~~~ ~~~   ~~~~

Bob walked over to the south wall, where a collection of small, framed photos of various sizes and shapes was neatly hung. The wall seemed to be constructed of adobe, with a natural sienna color, and looked as if it had not been dusted in years. The photos, every one of them level, were arranged with an odd symmetry. The photos were of groups of men and some women, mostly in white lab coats and posing in front of or working on large contraptions that consisted of wire harnesses and tubing ranging from small pipes to cylinders as large as a commercial airliner's fuselage.

Bob carefully counted the frames from the left and up, pointing at each one as he did. It was a ritual for him, as he knew which one it was from the start. Then, with a show of faux recognition, he grabbed one photo and removed it, exposing a small numeric keypad. Bob looked suspiciously behind him, as if about to commit a crime, then turned back and quickly punched in a code of six numbers. Aaron smiled now, knowing the combination as Bob telegraphed the information by hitting his book on his thigh the number of times represented by the number he punched into the keypad.

With that, Bob stepped back and turned to Aaron, smiling. "I built this wall because, one, I want everything in here to be a secret, and two, because as a kid, I always wanted a secret passageway behind a wall." As he spoke, the entire wall, molding to molding, started folding upward and back into darkness.

Aaron stood motionless, amazed and impressed, as Bob continued, "I knew you would like my wall. I built this entirely by myself—I do not need to brag—quite easily. Simple, simple mechanics, though I doubt few could do this. You, Aaron, you and Dancer are the only two people I have ever allowed to see the inside of my cave, my laboratory."

"Why me?" Aaron asked. "You don't know me well enough to trust me with a secret like this." As he spoke, Aaron felt the hair rise on the back of his neck. None of this made sense, not that anything in the last twenty-four hours had. The thought ran through his head, *Great, I'm about to be slain and eaten by a psychopathic mass murderer,* and he let out a nervous chuckle.

"Aaron, I bought this house many years ago, just after the end of the war. I came here in part because of the abundance of sunlight that provides me free energy. But the main reason is, I knew of this spot from an unfortunate time in my childhood. I knew about the abandoned mine that goes deep into this mountain. I knew it would be the perfect place to build a laboratory off the grid. I require privacy, and the power usage I require would be like waving a huge red flag. Others simply do not handle me well in social circles, their loss, of course. And, I will be honest with you, Aaron, there are individuals who seek out my knowledge. People I do not wish to share my genius with."

Bob's last words struck a chord, something Aaron understood from his own past. He seized the opportunity as Bob took a breath. "You're hiding from someone," Aaron boldly stated, nodding firmly and repeatedly. "Yeah, I'm right. You did something that has someone after you. I'm right aren't I?"

Bob stood still, caught off guard. Even the tapping of his book against his thigh stopped. For a moment, all was silent except for a distinct hum emanating from deep within the darkness beyond the wall.

Then, finally, he answered. "Yes, Aaron. Yes, there are elements of the law who would like to talk to me, take away my equipment, shut down my work. I cannot allow that to happen. I can never let that happen!" His voice was angry, but also filled with resentment.

For the first time since he had arrived unceremoniously against his will in the future, Aaron no longer was thinking about it. His thoughts now were that he very much wanted to see what was inside the cave. To see what a man of this intelligence could have built that the police—or someone— wanted so badly. And then it hit him. He smiled at his recognizing that it wasn't the cops or the local police. *No,* he thought, *this is bigger, much bigger, like maybe the FBI.*

"Bob, please show me what you have created!" Aaron blurted out, with the first real feeling of excitement since his arrival.

But Bob's mind at that moment was stuck like a skipping record. "Yes, this is my creation. No one else has been involved. They would only screw up what I am creating anyway. Not one of those self-righteous idiots from LLNL and JPL could build this. No, here, this is my world. We do it my way, period!" The resentment in Bob's voice was clear.

Recognizing this, Aaron instinctively switched gears. He wanted to ensure Bob would not compare him to those from his past. "Bob, I understand this is your doing, yours alone. Please, show me. Please explain what you are working on, what you are creating."

But in the blink of an eye, Bob withdrew like a child whose feelings were hurt. He turned. "No, we will go back inside."

Aaron was astonished at how quickly Bob had switched personalities. He realized he was dealing with a genius on the level of Einstein on the one hand, but also a man with the social skills of a five-year-old. Aaron was right at home dealing with immature individuals. He had spent time volunteering to work at the prison print shop while attending college. He thought maybe it might be best to practice what salespeople refer to as the *takeaway*. He shrugged his shoulders and, putting on his best, nonchalant, I-don't-give-a-shit-attitude, said, "Yeah, that's okay, Bob. It would probably bore me to tears, and you wouldn't be able to explain it so I would understand anyway." Aaron turned and headed back toward the living area of the house.

It was textbook. Bob stopped in his tracks with a look of astonishment. He could not believe someone would not be interested in something he created. His greatest creation, his collider, his particle accelerator. "No. No, Aaron, you will see. You will like it, and I can explain it. I am very good at explaining my work."

Bob turned back toward the entrance to the cave. "Miko, lights on." The room behind the wall became dimly lit, exposing racks of dusty wine. In front of the wall were arranged a small table and two chairs. On the table were several wine glasses, a couple of corks, an empty wine bottle and a corkscrew. The entire table, its contents and the chairs were covered in a thick layer of dust.

Aaron smiled to himself, pleased his ploy had worked so well. He turned back toward Bob, a bit confused, as he'd been expecting some sort of lab. "So ah, Bob, no maid?" he asked sarcastically, and started to pick up one of the wine bottles.

"Stop! Do not touch anything in this room. You will remove the dust. I want it to look like a wine cellar no one ever uses. Come, come over here." Bob walked over to the far corner. "Miko, open vault one."

Aaron stared as a portion of the wine rack and wall opened, exposing a small set of rickety old steps heading down into darkness. "Bob, if Miko can open all of these hidden doors, why didn't you just set it up so she could have opened the wall?"

"Diversity, Aaron, diversity. Now, follow me. Miko, stair lights, please."

The entire room lit up brightly. Aaron had to look down and squint, allowing his eyes time to become accustomed to the sudden deluge of light. Still squinting, he raised his head and looked down the staircase into a cavernous room. At the bottom of the staircase was a machine shop inside a naturally formed cave. The floor appeared to be concrete, but in the light, it looked rough and uneven. The walls were clearly formed ages ago, cooled magma with no signs of being scraped or shaved by digging machinery. On the far side of the room was a long workbench with various pieces of electrical testing equipment. To the right of the workbench were three upright toolboxes, all of them red with various sized drawers. On the other side of the cave sat a lathe, a bandsaw, and on the bench, a chop saw and grinder. Beyond the bench were welding tanks and hoses, and what looked like a huge press. A strong smell of cutting oil with a hint of ozone filled the room.

"Nice." Aaron nodded. "I've always wanted a shop like this. Well, maybe not this big, and for woodworking. I would love to come into a shop like this every morning, coffee in hand, and be met by the sharp, tangy smell that only comes from fresh-cut pine." Aaron spoke with a true appreciation for what Bob had built. "Nice hobby." *This is it? This is what he thinks he has to hide from the cops?*

To the left, he could see a tunnel that disappeared into blackness. "Where does that go?"

"It goes to a small living area. In case I need to stay down here for an unsolicited, extended period. Past that is my means of escape," Bob replied.

"Escape? What do you mean escape?" Aaron asked. "Wow, you're really freaked out about someone coming to get you. Where does it escape to?"

"I do not get freaked out as you suggest," Bob protested. "I have survived a great many things by being careful and thinking ahead. Thinking of all the possibilities. But then, of course, I am very good at protecting myself from those who wish to interfere with my work.

"If you follow the tunnel, which has no lights, by the way, about three hundred yards in, you will come to some hand-hewed stairs that take you up a shaft to another tunnel with a metal door. That leads to the outside on the other side of the mountain. There is another dirt road there that will eventually come out to the highway," Bob said, still bristling from the suggestion that he could be freaked out. "As I told you, I am good, very good at protecting my work. The escape tunnel is a misdirect for those who might make it inside the cave. They will, after seeing the shop, follow the tunnel and discover I have eluded them." Bob became increasingly excited as he spoke, his small leather book rapidly bouncing off his thigh. "You see, Aaron, this wonderful shop, my cave, has been my home for many hours of my life while I design and make reality of my dreams. But there is more, much more. Come with me."

He grabbed Aaron by the sleeve and tugged him toward the other end of the cave, to a wall past the end of the tools and bench.

"Miko, lights on." A new set of lights came on, exposing the end of the cave—a shiny black molten rock wall. "Here, Aaron, this is where my genius becomes reality."

Aaron looked at the wall and then looked back at Bob.

"Bob, am I missing something? It's just a wall," Aaron said, thinking this guy—as brilliant as he seemed—might well be ready for a straitjacket.

"Just wait," Bob said. "Miko, open sesame." Suddenly, where there had only been a rock wall, a perfect rectangular fracture appeared. Bob slid his fingers into the fracture and pulled out a large stone door. He opened the door only enough to allow one person in at a time.

"Go ahead, Aaron, go in. I will be right behind you."

Aaron looked at the dark opening. "Open sesame, seriously?" he asked, trying to delay stepping inside. He did not wish to find himself alone in the black hole in front of him.

"Open sesame," Bob laughed. "Yes, yes, I know that no one would ever try that. It is too silly, too obvious. Besides, only Miko recognizes my voice." He nudged Aaron's shoulder. "Go in, Aaron, I am right behind you. You are going to like what you will see."

With great apprehension, Aaron cautiously walked into the dark space. It was void of all light, except for a ray of light bleeding around the edge of the opened stone door. He could hear and then feel Bob slide inside and stand next to him, and then came the sickening sound of the stone door closing and sealing behind them. It was now pitch-black, and Aaron felt goosebumps rise on his arms.

"Should someone get in this far and not know the second password, they would be locked in this darkness until I found them and freed them," Bob said quietly, almost whispering. Then he spoke. "Nikola."

A new door opened with the sound of escaping air, and they were instantly bathed in brilliant, blue light. Aaron had to shade his eyes yet again until they adjusted to the illumination. As they did, his first thought was, *Whoa, I am on the set of a sci-fi movie.*

He was standing in a cave, or maybe a tunnel. Like the room before, the walls were natural, not man-made. It did look like a film set, with blinding arc lights on tripods, wires and cables taped to the floor, and an ominous-looking, dark-blue cylinder raised up four feet above the cave's floor. It was about the width of both Aaron's arms outstretched, and ran parallel to the cave wall, curving until it disappeared with the curve into the tunnel. To Aaron's left, he could see the configuration remerging from the curvature of the cave.

The cylinder was divided into segments, each atop a concrete riser and delineated by a black and white checkerboard pattern that wrapped completely around it. At the segment directly in front of Aaron, the tube separated, exposing in greater detail the pipe's interior.

Coming out of the center, continuing across the span into the other side, was a seamless, stainless steel tube about two inches in diameter. Parallel to the tube were seven equally spaced, half-inch finned copper cooling coils. The exposed area inside the pipe, between the much smaller tube and the main tube, was filled with magnets, each wrapped in gold foil with a small circuit board attached to it and a neatly wrapped set of wires that went into a larger wire harness held above the cylinder with a green oxide, metal truss connected to one side of each concrete riser.

Aaron had never seen anything like this before in his life. There were literally hundreds of small LED lights flickering on and off all around the room in a myriad of colors.

Yup, aliens. This guy is one of them, and I was abducted.

Then there was the hum. The sound he had been hearing in the background since Bob opened the Cave's door. Though not overly loud, its low electrical bass was powerful enough that he not only heard it, he felt it in his bones.

"Aaron, this is my greatest achievement," Bob said. "It is the culmination of all my great work, all of my combined knowledge. This, Aaron, is Pandora." Book in hand, Bob pointed to his baby.

Aaron could only summon a "Whoa." He paused, then continued, "Bob, I am no physicist, but Pandora, a collider? Really? I mean, come on. I studied the Hadron Collider, the one at Cern. They had to use some kind of superconductor material that had little or no resistance and required that it be kept at some absurdly cold temperature. I mean—I'm not sure what I mean, but do you have your own nuclear power plant in another cave to power this thing? And how the hell did you get all this stuff down those old steps to build this thing?" he said, spreading his arms to indicate the collider. "Wouldn't maybe an elevator have been a good idea?"

"First," Bob glared, "I did have an elevator. I took it out when I finished and put in the steps to further disguise the possibility of anything of significance further down in the cave. It is all my extremely well-planned ruse.

"Second, I am quite impressed by your limited understanding of colliders. But you still do not, as yet, understand whom you are talking to. I have to point out what I have built here functions very much like a collider. It uses the same principles, but—and this is a huge *butt*." Bob giggled to himself like a child who just said a bad word for the first time as he grabbed his own bottom, giggling even more.

Aaron could only smile and shake his head.

"You see, my young friend, it does not produce a collision. Rather, the neutrinos, elements of radiation decay that I introduce, continue to circle, accelerating to a nanosecond faster than the speed of light. But that is just fast enough to warp time. So, in essence, Pandora is not a collider but an accelerator.

"You see, everything modern science does, they seem to over-exaggerate in both size and complexity. But, as I always do, I solved it by creating my own version of metallic hydrogen, the material you mentioned. Well, sort of. You see, for true superconduction, it is only necessary to create maximum coupling between the conduction electrons of a material..."

Bob ceased talking when Aaron held up his hands, waving them across each other, signaling him to stop.

"Bob, you forget who you are talking to," Aaron said, chuckling. "I have no idea, nor do I care to know. It would take far too long for me to learn how superconducting works. Let's just suffice it to say, it does." With that, Aaron gracefully bowed, gesturing to Bob for him to continue.

"Yes. Yes, I do often forget no one else thinks like I do. So yes, Aaron, suffice it to say, as you say, I have created a means of simplifying and miniaturizing the superconduction so as to use less space and far less energy."

Aaron nodded. "Fine, let's just forget for one second no one else on Earth can do this. Where do you find the time, and more importantly, the money to do all of this? What, did you finally figure out what all the medieval alchemists tried to do and create gold? Bob, there is enough gold foil in there to build a second Temple of Sripuram."

Bob didn't hesitate to respond. "You know of the Golden Temple in India?"

Then quicker than a speeding electron, he returned to his usual nature, almost bragging and said, "Before I left—" He paused for a second. "Before I voluntarily departed ways with Livermore, I held, I still do hold, five hundred and eighty-seven patents for many types of hardware, motherboards and software. Money that I, of course, being smart, invested in places I knew I would be able to retrieve from at a later date should normal accounts become frozen as they so often do in matters of proprietary disagreements such as this. And no. No magic gold."

Aaron laughed, mostly under his breath but still obvious enough for Bob to detect. "Bob, where the hell do you get this shit? *Proprietary disagreements*? Bob, you stole a fucking collider from Livermore Lab, didn't you?" As the words left Aaron's lips, he felt his face turning red as he remembered the old adage, *Don't bite the hand that feeds you.* He was lost; Bob had found him and was taking care of him.

Bob replied with a boyish grin, which surprised Aaron as he was expecting an agitated response. "I did not steal it. I borrowed it, temporarily procuring what I needed to complete the project. A project, mind you, I tried to create for them in the first place. I was going to give it back once I finished. I really was. Who knew a stupid war would come along and turn the entire world upside down? And well, after that, I just didn't believe they would be interested in me or the outdated equipment."

Aaron shook his head, smiling at Bob. "I am without words, Bob. You are some kind of amazing. And this cave, where the—no, how the hell did you find this place?" Aaron quizzed. He realized he was becoming more and more relaxed and interested in his new world. *Perhaps,* he thought, *the strangeness of it all had simply overwhelmed my nerves.*

"That is a very long story, Aaron. I will tell you in much greater technicolor detail another time. Suffice it to say, I knew of these caves from my childhood. There is a somewhat famous park nearby called the Lava River Cave. That cave is several miles long, formed some seven hundred thousand years ago by volcanic action. These caves, the one we are in, only I and two other people know about. Well, and now you. They were, of course, formed at the same time and are much, much bigger, not to mention apparently undiscovered. There is no light, and there are times the caves fill with gases that can suffocate you. Anyone venturing down here needs to be prepared."

"Note to self, important safety tip, always carry matches," Aaron joked.

"No! No, Aaron, never light a match down here. If there is gas present, it could very well ignite, and the resulting explosion would most certainly kill us." Bob was both serious and excited, as if Aaron were about to light a match that very second.

"Bob, relax, really, I was joking. Cigarette?" he said, pretending to hold out a pack toward Bob.

"You are not funny."

"Sorry. Sorry, I apologize. What you have created here, Bob, is the most amazing thing I have ever seen," Aaron stated. *Who knows? Maybe I met this guy and his machine for a reason. Maybe he can help get me back home.*

~~~~ ~~~~ ~~ ~

Dancer arrived late morning the next day to take Aaron to the police station for his Bug. Bob had retreated back into his lab after breakfast, claiming he had some work to do.

The sun was already high enough to be baking the cactus and Mexican feather grass, while undulating waves of heat rose from the desert floor. They sped down the highway, the quiet, cool air streaming from the dash keeping them comfortable.

Aaron, thinking over the past day's events, stared out the window, saying little. An odd-looking sign ahead just off the road caught his attention enough to make him turn his head to read it. "EcoGold Landfill Mining Operations. What the hell? What, they dig through old garbage?" Aaron scoffed.

Dancer looked at him quizzically. "You're kiddin' me, right?"

"A mining operation in a landfill? Sounds like they're looking for precious old plastic and glass," he joked.

Dancer's quizzical look changed to an expression of concern as she looked over at him. "You are yankin' my chain, right?"

"You're serious? They're mining old garbage?" Aaron asked, confused. "Why the hell would—" He stopped to consider her words and what the sign said. "EcoGold... oh, you are serious. They're digging through old landfill garbage to find materials to recycle. Got it, wow!"

"Duh, do you know how much money that shit is worth? It's gold!" Dancer said.

Aaron sat back in his seat, continuing his ponderings while he stared out the window. Finally, he looked again at Dancer. "How long have you known Bob? What do you know about him?"

Dancer paused for a moment before answering. "Long enough to know half the shit that man says is just, well, sometimes I wonder if he shouldn't be locked up. The things he says, regardless of his pompous, holier-than-thou, I'm-always-right attitude, are just out there. I swear sometimes I think he is from another planet."

Funny, I've been thinking the same thing, Aaron thought.

"Don't get me wrong, I love the man. We have taken care of each other for so many years, folks around here think we're married or lovers. But Aaron, sometimes... sometimes the man says things that are just wow. I mean, really, wow," Dancer said, gesturing like her head was blowing up. "Fact is, he may well be from another planet." With that admission, she laughed.

"What about that book? He always has it, sometimes bouncing it off his thigh or tapping it with his finger, or both. What is in that little book?" Aaron asked.

Dancer's head dropped in mock surrender and she looked back, smiling. "I have never seen the inside of that book. In all of these years, I can count on my one hand the times it did not occupy his left hand. I've asked what's in it, and it's always the same answer: 'Everything I know.' He did actually elaborate a bit more one time when I got him really drunk. That was fun." She bent forward and slapped the steering wheel, reliving the moment. "He said, and I quote, *This is the contents of my mind. It contains every idea I have ever dreamed about. If I lost this book, I would be lost as well.'* So knowing Bob, and I do, I have gone out of my way over the years to watch out for both him and that book."

"Wouldn't you love to peek inside that book for just a minute, and read some of what he has written down?"

Dancer looked at Aaron. "Nope, I would feel like I was reading his personal diary, his innermost thoughts. I am not sure I could do that. I know what you mean, though. You can bet there is some bizarre shit in that book. But, if he wanted to share the contents, he would. Of course I would like to read it, though with my simple mind, I'm sure I wouldn't understand the first thing in it." She laughed. "He is one smart—screwed up, yes—but very smart man."

"Why does he constantly tap it on his thigh? Does he have some sort of nerve disorder? You know, a Tourette's thing or Parkinson's?

Dancer, still smiling, shook her head. "I think it's just his internal metronome. It keeps time for him, keeps him going. I can tell you this, for a man who can sing like he does, he can't keep a beat to save his life. Whatever beat is playing in his head, it does not match any form of music known to man."

~ ~~ ~~~~ ~~~~

Deputy Stenson handed Aaron a tablet to sign, which he did. Then, holding Aaron's keys in the air just above his outstretched hand, he asked, "Where on Earth do you get parts for that antique? It really is a true classic. You must be really into restoring old cars." Finely, lowering the keys into Aaron's hand, he added, "You know you can still get a special exemption license for this baby that will allow you to drive it using conventional gasoline and the old-style incandescent lights."

Aaron wanted to question Deputy Stenson further, but decided it best to avoid asking anything that might only get him in more trouble. Instead, he nodded. "Thanks, I wasn't aware of that. Where do I apply for a permit like that?"

"Just visit the DVA orbit, and you will find everything you need there."

"Sorry, DVA? Orbit? What's that?" Aaron asked, then scolded himself for perpetuating the conversation.

"You're really not from around here, are you? It's the Department of Vehicle Authorization on the collective, the web. One more thing. Before you go, I have to give you this citation to appear. You are going to have to explain to a judge why you have no chip or no scar where you took one out. Actually, kid, I would really like to know as well. You don't seem like the Scabs I've met."

Aaron recognized he would not be able to satisfactorily answer the question for the Deputy. He muttered, "My parents, you know, they were hippies and didn't believe in that kind of thing."

Deputy Paul Stenson, an astute man, instinctively knew Aaron wasn't the criminal type. He nodded with satisfaction, accepting the explanation for the moment. "Okay, kid, be careful."

Seeing the perfect opportunity to retreat and get out of there, Dancer grabbed Aaron's arm and said, "Come on, hon, we need to get on the road. I have to get back to work. Thanks, Paul. See you around."

Aaron felt an odd mixture of uncomfortable normalcy in what had become his new reality as he drove, window down and sunroof pulled back, down the highway following Dancer back to Bob's property.

~~~ ~ ~~ ~~ ~

Cynthia sat down on an upside-down, crusty old plastic bucket, covered with layers of concrete from years of creative endeavors. She stared for a moment at her latest project, trying to decide if she loved it or hated it. She had been working for several hours with power tools that required all of her attention for detail and safety. As she sat, sipping on a room-temperature energy drink, it dawned on her Aaron had still not called. She got up and walked over to the workbench to look at her cellphone. *Maybe I didn't hear it,* she thought. But there were no texts, no messages, no missed calls. For the first time, she worried. Aaron had never gone this long without sending at least a simple "I love you."

She picked up her phone and dialed his number. It rang once and went immediately to voicemail. "Hey, honey, where the heck are you? Call me when you get this message. Love you."

She took another sip of her energy drink and shuddered. *Yuck, these things suck when they're warm.*

Where the hell is he?

~~ ~ ~~ ~ ~~~~

Dancer got out of her car to open the gate, but first she walked back to Aaron's Volkswagen.

"Did you see that?" she asked, referring to the huge rattlesnake crossing the road in front of her.

"See what?" Aaron asked, leaning out the window.

"I'm showing you right now."

"Showing me what right now, where?"

Dancer leaned in the Volkswagen's driver's side window and asked, "You can't see what I'm showing you, can you?"

Aaron shook his head and repeated, "Showing me what?"

"You don't have *Nipples*, either, do you?" she asked, frowning. She couldn't put her finger on it: his clothing, the way he talked, or how little he appeared to know about everyday life. *This boy*, she thought, *acts like he just appeared from another time.*

"I can only assume you're making fun of me, as of course I have nipples, but what has that got to do with if I can see what you're seeing. I have no idea what you are trying to get me to look at. You're just messing with me, right?" Aaron responded, a bit agitated. So far, he had been doing very well coping with this new reality, but his endurance was faltering. *This just isn't fair.* He couldn't tell anyone what had happened. He didn't want to find himself locked up in the local hospital's top floor, filled full of Thorazine. *Nobody, not this nice lady, not the weird old guy,*

no one has a clue as to why I am here or where I came from. Shit,
I must look so out of place to them.

He looked out the VW window directly into Dancer's eyes.
"Dancer, I have no idea why you are being sarcastic, with *nipples*
or what you think I should be seeing. But I am pretty damn sure
we are not talking about the same things. I gotta tell you
something. I'm scared. Something is terribly wrong in my world.
I feel like I'm on a really bad acid trip that won't let me come
down."

Dancer held up her hand to stop him. "Hon, I know
something is not right in your world. I knew it the day you
walked into the Last Hope. Why do you think I asked Bob to
come over and meet you? I really thought he would be able to
offer you some help. Then you got your sorry ass thrown in jail,
and, well, I haven't had time to process all the events. Nor have
I really had time to talk to Bob. I did notice that when I pointed
you out to him, he became very, I mean *very*, interested in you.
And, for Bob, that is unusual as hell. I knew your car didn't fit
in, your clothes don't fit in. You have a credit card, for God's
sake, and you have a cellphone. Who the hell has a cellphone
anymore? And, you don't have a chip. So, it's not a big jump for
me to assume you have no *Nipples* either. I'm not the prying
type, though, hon, so let's just forget everything else for right
now. When you're ready, you'll tell me, and I'll listen. Fair
enough?"

Aaron nodded, grateful and speechless.

Dancer laid a hand on his shoulder. "Let me explain
about *Nipples*, dear boy. You don't mind if I call you boy, do you?
I mean, you're old enough for me, hon." She laughed and winked,

breaking the tension. "*Nipples* are the implants you should have received when you were eight years old, if your parents could afford it. They place an NBPL—It's a sembio... glass... Shit! I know this. I've said it a thousand times to memorize it." Dancer closed her eyes, took a deep breath and started tapping her foot. Then, foot still tapping, she looked up and half sang, "It's a Semi Perm-a-nent Nano Bio-tic Poly-mer-glass Lens. I have to sing to remember it." She laughed. "They put one over both of your eyes. The NBP—Bob and I think it sounds like nipples, so that is what we call it—anyway, it talks to a nanochip that they place in your neck, which somehow communicates with your ventral and dorsal visual pathways. It is all magic to me."

She stopped long enough to shake her finger in the air. "Don't let the fancy words have you be thinking I'm smart. Trust me, I'm not. I had mine done only a few years ago when I could afford it. And, I might add, only after I did a shitload of research. I didn't want them messing up my already messed up brain." Smiling, she let out a sigh before gathering a full breath of air.

Aaron, still processing what he was hearing, could only return a nod.

Dancer continued, "That nanochip—Hell, that chip, it's a whole friggin' computer the size of the nail on my little finger. It works on Lightwave technology, sending and receiving signals from other people's chips. Did I mention it is also connected to my hearing and my speech? I can take phone calls in my head if I choose to accept them."

Quite unable to speak, Aaron stared at Dancer, his mouth open.

"Like the PIC, they started pushing for everyone to have one of the other. If you have Nipples, you don't need a PIC, and neither are required by law. But they really do the hard sell with both. They said it was to make it easier to spot terrorists, resolve potential legal issues, crimes, and to make it safer for women and children. But in all reality, it's a damn Bodycam that's recording everything you see, say and hear. The law guarantees all of the information recorded is for your eyes only and that only a subpoena from a court of law can force you to turn over specific requested timeframes. But I gotta tell you, I have always been afraid the Corps could hack into my Cloudnet account. Hack, hell, they don't even need to—they control them. If they choose, they can see what I've been doing and even what I've been thinking. The point is, I can look at things and mentally take a photo or a video and send it to you. I can even pull things from Cloudnet that I recorded ages ago and allow you to see them too." Dancer stopped and looked at him, "You don't have a clue what I am talking about, do you?"

"Can Bob—does Bob, um—can you talk to each other when I'm in the room, and I don't know it?"

"Well, in a word, yes! Though people get certain facial expressions like when talking on the phone, and you can guess they are sharing. And yes, Bob does, and we do talk and share photos and stuff. Bob has already reprogrammed his own chip so that he can't be tracked and added a firewall that won't allow anyone from the outside to see what he sees. He wants me to let him do mine, but I don't know. I'm not entirely sold yet."

"And that cop, Deputy Stenson and his Bot—they could talk to each other?" Aaron slowly asked, the reality starting to sink in.

"Yes, hon, you think of the name you created for your implant. Mine, I named Rock, after an old actor I had a crush on. I just think 'Rock' and a transparent display shows up in front of me with menu items to choose from." Both amused and scared, Dancer watched the expression form on Aaron's face. *How the hell could he be so clueless? He either has amnesia, or he really did just step out of a time warp.*

Simultaneously, Aaron's personal humorous thought he hoped was a joke ran through his head. *Aliens—yup. Aliens, it is the only logical—no, it is the only plausible answer. I was abducted—I wonder how long I was gone?* Returning to the moment, he asked, "So my cell, it won't work here?"

Dancer couldn't help herself and broke out in laughter. "Hon, there is some service still available for those who simply refuse to give up their antiques and beliefs. But I saw your cell, and it belongs in the Smithsonian."

Taking in all of this new information, this new way of life, he asked, "So, everyone who now has Nipples is what, instantly a genius? They know everything about everything?"

"You know, funny you would put it that way. Damn boy, under what rock have you been hiding? Sorry. I said we wouldn't go down that road until you're ready. There was a time when this first started becoming popular, replacing cell phones and such, that many thought it would be just like you said. That it would create a world of geniuses, and no one would need to go to school any longer. Geniuses that, in reality, would be completely ignorant if Cloudnet were to go down. They feared as well, with the world now on an even playing field of intelligence and technological advancements, that it would seriously slow down work ethic, normally learned from childhood. Competitive nature would die, and with it, the advance of society and technology. You know, yada, yada, yada, said the so-called experts. But, as I see often being the case, they were wrong. Nothing much changed. We had been a society bent over our cell phones with access to all of the world's knowledge for some time, and the only thing that noticeably changed was a lesser need for chiropractors and surgeons fixing carpal tunnel and bad necks. No, even now, there are simply those who don't wish to use the technology versus those who can't get enough of the drug to satisfy their quest for more knowledge. Or those who need mindless entertainment. Really, most of the salt of the earth folk just want to live their lives without interference. They'll look when they need to, but then it boils down to those smart enough to ask the right questions versus those who are not. And, of course, then there is the whole can of worms of interpreting what they read from Cloudnet."

She stopped and looked at the bushes where the snake had slithered away. "Come on, let's get going. Follow me. I know it's just his driveway but try not to get lost and arrested again." She chided, giving his shoulder a light rub before turning to head to her car.

~~~ ~~ ~~ ~~~

71

Dancer closed the gate after Aaron drove through, then they both headed up Bob's driveway. Aaron followed close behind. There were no other houses for miles, so the driveway, more a long, winding road, became solely Bob's responsibility to maintain—which he didn't. He liked it that way. The less traveled it looked meant less unexpected visitors showing up at his doorstep. In the daylight, you could see the holes, large rocks, cactus, and other obstacles.

Dancer looked back at Aaron in her rearview mirror just in time to see him repeatedly hitting his steering wheel with his hands. She stopped her car in the middle of the road, figuring it was high time she dug a little deeper into the roots of his behavior. Now was as good a time as any, as Aaron appeared to be at the end of his rope, and she wanted to talk to him without Bob around in hopes he would open up more.

She walked back to Aaron's car. "Aaron, why don't you get out and come here for a second? Get in my car and cool off before we head further up the driveway. I need to ask you something important before we get to Bob's," she said as a ruse to lure him into her car.

"I'm okay, Dancer. I just can't shake something out of my head that I said to Cynthia the night before." Wanting to change the subject, he asked, "So I noticed you have your own keys to the gate back there."

"Please, hon, I love Bob, but don't go there." She laughed. "Yes, I have keys mostly because I am the only human being on Earth Bob trusts, and he knows he needs me to take care of his sorry ass." Again she laughed.

Aaron looked around at the rolling strata of red rock covered with golden grass, low sagebrush and small succulents. He could see the snow-capped San Francisco mountain still far off in the hazy and purple distance under a blue sky filled with puffy white clouds. He took a deep breath then sighed, overcome with sadness and concern for Cynthia. *What is she thinking? She has to be seriously freaked out. She must have called the police by now. How can I call her, let her know I am okay, that I am sorry about what I said? I'm fucking Alice down the fucking rabbit hole!*

"Okay, hon, hop in the car. I recognize that sigh, having let out many of my own on this very road, headed toward Bob. I'm guessing that exclamation had little to do with Bobby boy. You wanna talk? No, you need to talk," she said, nodding her head emphatically.

"No, I just miss Cynthia. I'm pretty sure she is missing me by now, and I have no way to tell her I left or where I am. So I am betting she is freaking out or really pissed off."

"Aaron, come on, hon, sit down and talk to me." She was much more insistent this time.

Aaron, shutting off his VW, reluctantly got out and then into her car. He slid back into the seat. "Wow, it's really cool in here." A comfortable smile grew on his face as he settled back further in the soft, plush seat.

"You see, Aaron, I can read people better than they can read themselves. And you, you are truly overthinking something. And driving in that Bug, cute or not, in the Arizona sun is not helping. So relax for the moment, if you can, enjoy the coolness and start with telling me why you didn't tell Cindy—

no, wait, that's not right. Cynthia, right? You didn't tell Cynthia you were leaving, did you? I mean, I know it is none of my business, but, well, did you have a fight or what?"

Aaron sighed as his last night with Cynthia flooded his thoughts. "Okay, shit yes, we had a stupid childish fight. Childish on my part," Aaron admitted, followed by another sigh. "A very stupid quarrel, and I'm totally to blame. I love her with all that I am. And well, I—ah—I—ah—well, I didn't know I would be coming here. I didn't know I wasn't coming back. I have no idea how I am going to get back."

"Ah hell, hon, no need for you to worry. I can fill your tank up with gas, they still have a pump out back, and I can give you some traveling money. You can head out of here tonight. Where does she live?"

"Dancer, I really appreciate that, but I couldn't take your money." Aaron desperately wanted to tell Dancer everything: how he didn't know how he got here, that somehow, he magically arrived in the wrong time. "She lives in Tahoe, Lake Tahoe."

It was Dancer's turn to be shocked and confused. "I'm sorry, did you say Lake Tahoe?"

Aaron nodded. "Why?"

Dancer put both her hands at the top of the steering wheel and, looking deadly serious, staring straight ahead, said, "Engine off." And with it went the cool air pouring out of the vents. She then looked over at him sternly. She didn't like being lied to. "Look, hon, I have been nothing but nice to you, even watching out for you. Yeah, a bit motherly, but that is how I am. And I don't like to be repaid with lies. You are obviously in some kind of trouble. It is time you fess up and tell me what the hell is going on."

Aaron was stunned by the abrupt change, her sudden anger. He swallowed hard. He desperately needed to be able to confide in someone, and recognized the time was now. "Dancer, I'm not lying to you. I swear to you, I swear to God." He paused and took a deep breath. "If I tell you what is going on, what I think is going on—and honestly, I don't know what is going on—you are going to think I am lying to you or that I am out of my mind, crazy, or both."

"Well, we aren't moving, and that air is not coming back on until you do tell me something that adds up."

"Shit!" Aaron said heavily, like a boulder hitting the ground. He shook his head back and forth and then continued, "The real truth and the best answer is that I have lost my mind. But, the second-best answer that makes any sense, and it doesn't, is that..." He paused, grimacing before continuing, "I think I have somehow traveled in time, gone through a time warp! I don't know how, but I did. The only other plausible idea is aliens abducted me, and when they decided to return me, they missed, leaving me here instead of Lake Tahoe. And, it's fifteen years, maybe more, in my future." Aaron looked Dancer straight in the eyes, showing no emotion. And then, like he had been holding his breath underwater for several minutes, he let out a huge sigh.

Dancer was speechless. She lowered her gaze and took her hands off the wheel. Switching roles like some twisted black comedy, it was her turn to shake her head slowly side-to-side. She started to speak, raising her head, but stopped, thinking to herself, *How can this be? He really believes what he is telling me, but he has got to be lying.* Her anger left as she realized there was something in his voice, and she clearly remembered the way he looked the night he came into the Last Hope.

"How can this be, Aaron? I don't understand. And, really, aliens? We both know Tahoe has been in radioactive quarantine since the beginning of the Eight-Year War. You can't be from Tahoe. What the hell are you running from?" she asked, her tone raised slightly, starting to feel anger again.

It was like watching a pinball machine with their heads and minds being the bumpers. Aaron could not speak. His eyes were wide open, and his breaths grew short.

"Are you okay, hon?" Dancer asked, frightened by the look on his face. She felt sure he was going to pass out or stop breathing any second. "Aaron, can you hear me? Nod if you can hear me."

"What do you mean, radioactive quarantine?" Aaron managed.

"Okay, wait, are you telling me you don't know about the quarantine? You don't know Tahoe got nuked?"

Aaron, from deep within an ever-growing pit of horror and despair, opened up and spent the next ten minutes explaining everything that had happened since the night the lights flashed on and off while he drove in the early morning hours in front of the Lake Tahoe casinos. Dancer did not say a word. Instead, she listened, amazed, knowing all the time this young man had, real or imagined, just been through the most mind-bending experience of his life. A life she had become involuntarily an integral part of.

But he can't be telling the truth. What he is saying is impossible. Aliens—fuck that shit. she thought to herself. "Holy Mother of God, Aaron, that is the most amazing story I have heard in my life. But really, you think I'm going to buy any of that, time travel, alien abductions... You're hiding something. I'll tell you what, since you want me to believe your story, then you won't mind me doing a quick search." She paused, thinking. "I know; what high school did you go to, and what year did you graduate?" she asked with a smug smile, figuring she got him. He would squirm now.

"Martin Luther King High in Auburn, California, class of aught-four," Aaron answered without hesitation.

"Um, okay. Engine on. Air on. Search," she spoke toward the dashboard.

"What would you like me to search for, Dancer?" the car's computer responded.

"Search for Aaron. Wait, Aaron, what is your last name again?"

"Hodges, Aaron Wayne Hodges."

"Search for Aaron Wayne Hodges, Martin Luther King High in Auburn, California, class of zero-four, please," Dancer said again, facing the dashboard.

"Yes, give me one moment. There. I have it." And on the small dashboard screen, a yearbook page popped up with a very young-looking Aaron. His name and a caption with courses he majored in—Computer Science, Marketing, Yearbook Staff and Most Likely to Get Lost—were next to the photo.

"Most likely to get lost? Seriously, if they only knew." She laughed, but the ramifications of what she was looking at were hitting home, hitting hard. "Well, I'll be damned," Dancer blurted out.

Aaron smiled apprehensively.

"I have no idea why I should believe you, but there it is. I have to, that's you. Maybe because I have seen far too much shit in my life that simply does not make sense, but it happened anyway. I don't think you're crazy, you seem as sane as me, but then that really does not bode well for you." She laughed lightly. "And yeah, right now, my money is on alien abduction, kid. It's the only thing that makes sense."

"Oh God, thank you for believing me and not just asking me politely to get out of your car. I'm scared, Dancer. I don't have any answers. I have thousands of questions I fear no one on Earth can answer. Worse, I am scared I will never get back to Cynthia, to my life with her, all our hopes, our dreams, our plans."

Dancer took a moment to compose herself. "Aaron..." she started to say, and then paused to move over close enough to grab both of Aaron's hands, holding them tightly and pulling them to her chest. "Aaron, you are a good guy, and your Cynthia is a lucky woman, but this is not the end of the story." Maintaining a firm hold on Aaron's hands, she started to cry, then sniffling, but with a calm voice, explained what she did not want to. "The war starts at ten-seventeen a.m. on October 17, 2024."

She paused to allow Aaron's brain to process information far more frightening than the ordeal he had experienced so far, then continued, "A powerful, splinter terror group called Allah's Revenge led by a wealthy extremist from Uzbekistan took control of a city once held by the old Soviet Union. When they took control of the city, they apparently stumbled upon six Cold War-era nuclear warheads. They had been misplaced at the end of the Cold War and sat hidden and forgotten in a bunker until discovered by the cleric Akbarjon Abdullayev and his Fighters of the Jihad. More spoiled brat than religious zealot, Akbarjon's true niche was marketing. He rattled his saber for some time on social media trying to gain attention. But at that time, after so many years of the same violent shit, everyone had tired of the constant background noise of terrorism and become complacent. Terrorists were like mosquitoes, a nuisance. Very dangerous, but each new cell was short-lived, always disappearing only to be replaced by some new, over-zealous religious group proliferating some new atrocity trying to outdo the horror of the last. Trying to make the world gasp a little louder than the last time. But, like I said, the world—you know, you were there during that time—they didn't pay enough attention. They just ignored him, and that put him over the edge. He had the money, the resources and worse, he faced an ambivalent world that no longer tried to keep its guard up. The group, in the name of Allah and now in a position to finally start a Jihad, couldn't be ignored with their find. A Jihad, as he put it, that would rid the world of the unclean, all us non-believers. And get this, the biggest irony or betrayal. He paid, many say threatened, a Jewish American physicist to ensure the bombs were in working order. They then smuggled and placed the nukes in New York at the site of the 9/11 memorial, Los Angeles, Moscow, Paris, and Jerusalem. All points they thought would cause the most turmoil and draw the western world into their Jihad."

Aaron pulled one hand free and gestured for her to stop. "Oh my God. This is the start of the Eight-Year war you've been talking about? Whoa! But wait," he said, not yet putting all the pieces together. "How is Cynthia in danger? She is in Lake Tahoe, hundreds of miles from LA."

Dancer gently pulled his hand back down. "You didn't let me finish. They did capture Akbar the Mass Assassin, as he became known, alive, and the little chickenshit cried like a baby telling everything he knew. Apparently, many years before as a younger man, he spent a great deal of time in the States, being shipped off by his parents to college in the U.S. He went first to Yale, where he washed out, and then Berkeley in California. The little turd, more immature than a child and with more money than brains, thought himself quite the desirable bachelor, a jet-setter. He developed a great weakness for gambling, alcohol and a following of women, his harem, interested in living the great life. The free-flowing money that trickled off of him did just that, and they blindly followed his trail of breadcrumbs. He spent much of his time in Las Vegas and Lake Tahoe. Story goes, while in Lake Tahoe, during one entire week, he went on a gambling and drinking binge that cost him millions of dollars. He made such a stink and a scene they eighty-sixed him from all the casinos. He swore he would someday get even. So, in yet another uniquely twisted human irony, in trying to start a religious Jihad, he sent the sixth nuke to Lake Tahoe for no other reason but to exact his childish revenge. On the morning of October 17, while everyone drank their coffee, watched the news, and was getting ready for work, he ordered to detonate the first of six nukes. Los Angeles first. It turned out to be a sick but brilliant move on that little shithead psychopath's part. He had it flown across the Mexico/U.S. border in a small plane. Jets intercepted, but they didn't want to shoot down a plane over downtown Los Angeles. As they hesitated, the pilot detonated the bomb a couple of thousand feet above the city. Then, and this is the sick, brilliant part; in the ensuing panic they were able to bring the rest of the nukes across the borders into New York, Moscow, Paris, Jerusalem and Lake Tahoe. One-by-one, they were detonated over six days. All those beautiful cities ceased to exist in a flash of white light. Except New York. For some odd reason, that nuke didn't go off, and New York, which had suffered so greatly from terrorism, escaped annihilation. Sadly"—Dancer stopped and put her hand on Aaron's shoulder—"with it, Cynthia perished, as would have you, if you were still there."

Aaron sat stunned, speechless. His heart rate slowed, and his blood pressure dropped. He was on the verge of going into shock.

Dancer, not seeing his face go white, continued, "Confusion and chaos were instantly the new reality of the entire world. He and all terrorists finally had their Jihad. And, of course, it took the civilized world several months to pull their collective shit together, banding as one entity with but one sole purpose, to erase off this planet, once and for all, the cancer of terrorism. The UN declared worldwide martial law, but was then disbanded. Still, it took the next eight years to surgically cut out anyone or thing who even appeared to have a connection to religious extremism. It got ugly, Aaron, real ugly. The world you and I knew disappeared, gone forever, and with it the freedoms we once took for granted—gone. We are lucky some very intelligent and well-meaning men and women have since restored much of the old democracy. But I am sure by now you have seen it is more a business than government. Shit, I am talking to you like you really are from sixteen years ago. Well, Aaron, if you're crazy, so am I."

Aaron sat, lost in his own thoughts. *Cynthia is dead.* Suddenly, his head fell backwards, hitting the passenger's side window with a loud thud.

Dancer reached in a late attempt to catch his head, believing he had passed out. "Aaron, Aaron!" She brought one hand to the side of his face to stabilize his head. "You okay, hon?"

Aaron blinked and then straightened up with a startled look. "Thought I was going to pass out."

"I thought you did. I'm sorry. I don't know any other way to say it. I don't know what is going on. You shouldn't be here. How the hell did you get here? I want this to stop for you. I know it isn't going to, and I believe that somehow you are telling me the truth. A truth that's gotta be way harder for you to comprehend than me."

Dancer held both sides of his face and stared directly into his eyes, thinking, *This, cannot be happening. Time travel is not real.* "You, poor man, I am so sorry."

"She could have gotten out. A nuke wouldn't have taken out the entire lake?" Aaron asked desperately.

"Yeah, well—here, listen to this," she said and turned toward the computer screen on the dash. "Search for witness account of Lake Tahoe blast."

The computer responded, "There, I found it. The nuclear explosion that atomized the once-famous Lake Tahoe was witnessed by three survivors who had been climbing nearby Pyramid Peak at sunset. The survivors told reporters it looked like someone picked up the entire volume of Lake Tahoe's water a hundred feet in the air before it vaporized."

Dancer continued, "Some water did drain back into the basin, but for some time, aerial shots showed a giant valley void of anything. Just a big puddle. Photos today show it filled up again, but nobody can visit the area. There is nothing to see. There are no buildings, no casinos, just forest and water."

She lowered her head. "I'm sorry, I am so sorry. Aaron, your Cynthia is no longer. You would be too if whatever the hell brought you here hadn't brought you here." She paused and then continued, "I can't keep saying that. It is simply is not possible."

"Welcome to my world, Dancer."

"Aaron, I have an idea. I think we should go visit the spot you say you reappeared. See if there is any evidence of, I don't know, burn marks, or maybe crop circles in the sagebrush."

Aaron, still reeling from what Dancer had told him—and that Cynthia might no longer be alive, just nodded.

"Come on, hon, get back in that cute little Bug and let's go up to Bob's. Maybe later, we can take my car and head out to the spot you said you first appeared at."

Aaron got out and made his way back to his Bug. In a daze, he followed Dancer the rest of the way to Bob's house.

Bob was outside at the sound of their approach. As Aaron pulled up, following Dancer, Bob waved his book, pointing to an open gate. "Aaron, drive your car up that road. At the turnaround, park there. Then walk back; it is only a bit."

Aaron robotically obliged without question, but soon discovered the walk back, a *bit* as Bob suggested, to be more like a quarter of a mile.

~~~~ ~~~~ ~~~

The three of them traveled together for the first time, albeit only to ride into town and pick up food at the Amazon Pick Up Center: The Puc, as Dancer explained to Aaron, was how the locals affectionately referred to it. Bob said he also needed to visit the Scrub Brush, an old, local's favorite, small-town hardware store he frequented. He liked buying items he needed the old-fashioned way, not having to shop online, and it was his favorite spot to pick up tools or other odds and ends that he needed for Pandora. He was acutely aware that the peculiar nature of many of his purchases would most certainly raise unwanted attention.

Earl, the store's proprietor, was a crusty old curmudgeon, bent over with age, who wore his signature suspenders and well-worn, dark grey pleated welder's hat every day—the kind, with heavy red stitching. He was a man very much like Bob, in that they shared the same way of thinking, not trusting the new order of things. They also shared an unspoken understanding that allowed Bob to order unusual items without any questions.

As the trio walked in, Bob turned the corner of the first aisle, nearly knocking down a tall, gangly man. The man was unusually dressed for the heat this time of year in a full-length, dark-red satin robe with bright-red piping. It was open at the top, exposing a black clergy shirt and collar with a red satin tab where one would normally wear white. His black Quaker-style hat, now on the floor, had fallen in the shuffle.

Completely startled, Bob stepped back, staring up at the man in disbelief with his mouth wide open.

After regrouping and retrieving his hat, the man rose to full height and then carefully tucked his purchase under his arm. The man looked down at Bob. "Many pardons, sir." He paused, staring at Bob with the same surprised expression. His stare was deliberate, with dark, deeply sunken eyes that loomed from his pale skin.

"Robert, Robert Mandić?" he asked.

Bob could only stare, shaking. Dancer, seeing Bob's distress and being his societal buffer for so many years, jumped in. "I'm sorry, sir, I fear you are mistaken. This is Bob, Bob Kesey, do you know him?" Before he could answer, Dancer turned to Bob. "Bob are you okay?"

The tall man slowly turned his attention to Dancer. "My apologies, ma'am. I thought surely, I recognized this gentleman from my childhood, but I suppose not. Sir, are you okay? Did I hurt you?" The tall man's voice was raspy and shallow, with a hint of southern dialect.

Bob finally responded, "No. No, you should be more careful. I am fine. I was startled. Not paying attention, just startled, okay?"

Dancer pushed Bob toward the inside of the store as she apologized to the man. "He's okay. I got it. Thank you for asking, have a good day." With Aaron in tow, who had been watching, they moved onward into the store. Dancer glanced back to see the tall man slowly turn, watching them until they disappeared behind a row of displays. He then walked very slowly out of the store.

The ride home was quiet, too quiet for Dancer, who finally spoke up after a couple of miles, "So Bob, if you don't mind my asking, who the hell was that?"

Aaron scooted forward from the back seat, as he, too, wanted to hear. Bob stared straight ahead out the windshield as the desert flew by on either side. Finally, he turned to face Dancer.

"Like seeing a ghost, Dancer. The ghost of a most terrifying and horrific man. The ghost of the Reverend Skythe." Bob took a long deep breath. "The Reverend I had hoped died years ago. A death I can assure you I rejoiced over, danced over. I am not terrible for saying this; he was a very evil man. When I saw him, just now, in the store, it was like being electrocuted. I could not think, I could not speak, I could not breathe!"

"That wasn't him, Bob, it couldn't have been. We both know that, so who could it have been?" Dancer asked as Aaron pushed even closer to listen.

"Logic would dictate that it could only be one person." Bob paused, shaken by the ordeal. "It had to be the Reverend's son, Judas."

"What kind of sick parents would name their kid Judas?" asked Aaron.

"You are quick to see the evil this family represents, my good friend," Bob replied. "As a child, I played with Judas, the only one who would play with him. He and I were the two kids brave enough to resist the Reverend and the Elders' warnings not to leave the compound in search of adventure. When exploring with Judas, I discovered the cave my shop is now built in. I lost touch with Judas when still a child. But many years later when looking for the perfect place to build my laboratory, I remembered the caves. And, knowing better than the realtor who wished me to buy elsewhere, I bought the property. I knew only a short distance as the crow flies, on the other side of the mountain, is the old compound." Bob stopped to shake the shock out of his head. "He is a clone of his father. He looked every bit as frightening. Pure evil, I could feel it. You could feel it too, yes?"

Aaron sat back in his seat without so much as uttering a sound. *Great, the characters in my nightmare are having nightmares.*

They returned from the Scrub Brush, dust settling around the car and them as they pulled into the driveway a bit too quickly. Dancer waited for some of the dust to settle while Bob already had the door open and was halfway out, waving his book to try and clear the dust before walking toward his house. Aaron got out of the car and stood, uncertain of what to do.

Dancer stepped to the back of the car, where, after a moment, she popped her head up with a smile. "Aaron, I hope you don't mind, love. But, well, I am a thrift store shopper from way back—and how do I put this politely? You see, ah screw it.

I'll be blunt. That's the real me, and I'm sure you're growing to love it anyway. You see, your clothes, the way you dress, looks like my grandparents. Worse, maybe their grandparents." Dancer laughed and looked back into the trunk. "My point being, I took the liberty to pick you up something a bit more stylish. If you know what I mean?"

Dancer finished the sentence rubbing her hands down the length of her body in a slow sexual dance, mimicking Mae West in a way that did not escape Aaron's attention. Then, laughing, she held out both arms with a load of folded clothes.

Caught completely off guard by Dancer's taking it upon herself to look out for him, Aaron quickly realized that looking like everyone else around him would help him to keep a low profile—something he very much wanted since his incarceration earlier. "Oh my God. Dancer, you are so awesome. Thank you. I'm glad you possess a sense of style, if it weren't for Cynthia, back home—" He had to stop as the unavoidable lump in his throat rose just uttering her name. Then, with an exhale and sigh, he continued, "If it weren't for Cynthia, I would be wearing clothes from when I was in high school. She's a thrift store junkie too. It's a once-a-week ritual going to what she calls 'the dead people's store.' Creeps me out. But who am I to complain as she buys all my clothes, even if she apparently likes grandma and grandpa's clothing." He shot Dancer a sarcastic smile. "Sorry, thanks, Dancer. I have no doubt they'll fit, as I'm betting you're a lot like Cynthia in that department."

"Not just Cynthia, sweetie, it's a woman thing. We know how to dress our men." She laughed. "Now come on, let's go see what trouble the curmudgeon is getting himself or us into now."

As Dancer and Aaron walked toward the front door, it quickly became apparent that Bob had not yet resolved the encounter with Judas in his head.

"Bob, come on, let's go inside and open some beers. It wasn't the Reverend, it wasn't..."

Bob cut her off, swinging about, waving a yellow piece of paper. "They know I am here. Shit—shit—shit, how could they know?"

Dancer walked toward him, reaching for the paper that Bob wildly waved about. She could see the fear in his eyes. Unaccustomed to seeing him in hysterics and scared to death, almost crying, she asked wide-eyed, "Who knows you are here? Who cares?" She grabbed for the paper again and missed. "Let me see that, Bob, what is it?"

"It's a summons, a summons for me, me!" he said with an indignant air. "They want me to report in at the police station. It's signed by your new friend Deputy Paul Stenson." He pointed the book at Aaron.

"Whoa, wait a second. He is not my friend. Maybe your spooky-ass-looking friend at the hardware store tipped off the Deputy," Aaron shot back defensively.

"Both of you hold on for one gosh darn second. Bob, why do they want to see you? What is so important that you're freakin' out like this? It is not like you. You're actually scaring me, Bob." Dancer finally grabbed the paper out of Bob's hand after following it around like a dog after a treat. As she started to read it, she instinctively backed up, knowing Bob would now try to grab it back. Her forethought and quickness paid off, leaving Bob groping for air with his one free hand. She continued to read, finally looking up at Bob,

"Who is Robert Anderson Mandić and who the hell is Nate Brewster? And why on Earth does the UIIB want to talk to you?" she asked poignantly.

Bob's head dropped like a shot of sodium pentothal had just kicked in. Even his hand holding his book was motionless. The only sound was the buzzing of insects around the flora on the sunlit patio.

Aaron, remembering his earlier conversation with Bob, had to chime in. "These wouldn't be the same guys you told me about earlier, ah, would they? How did you put it? Oh yeah—*Elements of the law, who would like to talk to me.* I think it's time maybe that you let us, certainly Dancer, in on your little secret." Aaron flashed an *I know what you did* smile, not knowing just how correct he was, nor the degree of seriousness involved.

Bob motioned. "Follow me. Let's go into the Cave so we can talk in private. Just in case they are already listening, or Nate decides to show up." Bob walked toward the front door, head down like a kid walking to the Principal's Office. "Damn it. I knew he was around. I could sense his presence. Come, I will tell you what I know, tell you what I fear Nate has planned for us, for me."

Downstairs, Dancer and Aaron sat near the computer desk, Bob's control center for his mini-collider, Pandora. Bob walked to the other side of the room, turning to face them, taking in a huge breath of air as he did. The book went motionless. "My real name is Robert Anderson Mandić, not Bob Kesey as you know me. It is a long story I have kept to myself. I am sorry,

Dancer! I did not do so to deceive you. I changed my name long ago to vanish. I rarely think of the past or that name. In fact, when I hear it, it sounds like someone else. I had to. But Dancer, everything else you know about me is the truth. Really!" He looked directly at her, unusually concerned for what someone else might think about him.

"His name is Nathaniel Brewster. He has been on the force since long before they created the UIIB. Back to when they were the FBI. Today, so many years later, I believe he holds a great deal of seniority, and with that, power. I am really quite surprised he has not retired. But, at the same time, I understand him. He could not retire. He had to find me."

Dancer wanted to say something. In truth, she wanted to smack him upside the head and cry. He held his finger to his lips. "Shhhh. Please, just hear me out. It is a long, sordid journey I have been on. Many years ago, long after I had run away from the family, and after I had graduated from Berkeley, I found work at Lawrence Livermore National Laboratory facility, Livermore Labs. The other engineers were immediately threatened by me, by how brilliant I am. As such, we did not get along. They were fools; they would not listen to my ideas. So I chose to pursue my ideas on my own. The only problem, I could not afford the type of equipment I required, nor can one just go to the local hardware store and buy it. The obvious solution, was of course, that over many years, I procured what I needed piece by painstaking piece. They were so insecure about how much more intelligent I am than them that they turned their collective heads so as not to have to socialize with me. Really, perfect for me and my plan, as it was all I needed to sneak out under the tightest security in the world at that time. I walked out right under their stuck-up noses with everything I needed to build my collider. My baby, Pandora." He waved his book in a slow arc toward the huge piece of machinery in front of them. "Then, trouble. About six months after I quit—they said they fired me, but I quit—they took a closer look at the inventory and, well, they not only figured out what disappeared, but where and with whom it walked out."

Bob stopped to take several deep breaths, calming himself before continuing to talk. "Enter one very young hotshot FBI agent, Nathaniel Brewster, 'Nate.' Nate is good. He is very good at what he does. But I am better. He quickly got wind of what I was up to and where I most likely would be. He chased down leads that put him in uncomfortable proximity many times. In fact, he got close, so very, very close to figuring out this location. Just before he could close in, the war started. So much has happened, so many years have gone by, that I hoped he had given it up to the unsolved case files. After all, there was a new government in place, a new police agency with more important and timely cases to solve. Who wants to chase an old mad scientist with equipment nobody uses anymore, or even wants? Still, I took no chances building into my lab, here, every possible means of avoiding the authorities should I have to." He stopped talking, leaving the room silent. Dancer and Aaron could only stare, waiting with bated breath for the rest of the story.

"I cannot allow them to stop my work. They do not understand the importance. They didn't before, they certainly do not now. It has been so many years. I really, like I said, had hoped they had just given up, as they would think the equipment so old and obsolete that it was of no value to them any longer. Thus it would not have any importance compared to their current load of legitimate crimes. The real criminals they need to bring in."

"Ah, Bob," piped an astonished Dancer, "you just admitted you stole an entire collider, albeit piece-by-piece, but still that is kind of a big deal that they don't take lightly or forget about."

"No! They owed me those things. Finishing my work was imperative. Then and only then would they see their error and then understand my brilliance. It is that Nate asshole. He has a vendetta against me. He is only angry because he could not find me. He is ignorant and unimportant."

"Well, it would appear, even if he is a dummy, that he is one tenacious son-of-a-cop and has made himself very important in your life and work at the moment," Dancer said, looking Bob squarely in the eyes. *He doesn't think he has done anything wrong,* she thought to herself. Dancer had become Bob's mother, his sister, his friend, and she knew she had to take care of him. She loved him, and he certainly wasn't going to pull this off on his own. "Bob, I know what to do."

"You do? Good because I have work to finish, I have to solve—" Bob stopped, knowing he shouldn't continue the sentence. "That is good, Dancer, thank you."

Dancer and Aaron stared at him with a bewildered, wanting-to-ask-a-thousand-questions look. Dancer, whose mind was already laying the groundwork for what needed to be done, spoke. "Bob, your lab, the Cave is self-contained and pretty damn well-hidden, at least for now. And you have a bathroom in here too."

"Yes," Bob said, annoyed anyone would think he had not thought of everything. "Of course, even a sonic shower."

"Perfect, here is what we are going to do."

Like a couple of kids waiting for a bedtime story, Aaron and Bob moved closer to listen.

"Bob, you are going to go upstairs and pack your luggage, just one bag, like you're leaving for a trip. Pack clothes, toothbrush, shaving stuff and then bring it back downstairs and lock yourself inside. Aaron, you are going to drive Bob's car and follow me to the airport where we will park it and then come home. When and if anyone comes asking for you, Bob, we just tell them we're housesitting while you went to visit relatives."

"But I have no relatives alive, Dancer."

"Really, no cousins on your dad or mom's side? A long-lost illegitimate brother or sister, maybe?" Dancer quizzed.

Bob thought for a second and then looked up. It was easy to tell when Bob was in heavy thought, as the normally slow and steady beat of the book glued in his hand would pick up tempo the deeper into thought he would go. "You know what, yes, my mother's brother had several kids. One girl, Carrie, that I very much liked as a child. I think she is still alive and living in Canada."

"Well, then Bob, I guess you just headed off to look for long-lost cousin Carrie in Canada—perfect! So, what say you get your stuff packed, and then we get you set up in the Cave. I'll need to make a list of what you might need when your old buddy shows up, ya know, in case you are in for an extended stay."

"Why would I go look for my cousin in Canada?" Bob asked, perplexed.

"Bob how can someone be so smart and so oblivious at the same time?" Dancer asked rhetorically. "Never mind, I already know the answer. Bob, when your buddy Nate shows up, you are going to run downstairs as fast as you can and disappear. Aaron and I will then tell your shadow a bit of fabricated story... okay, a fucking-bald-faced-lie about you going off in search of your long-lost cousin. Got it?"

"So, uhm, Dancer? Just what is a bald-faced-lie anyway?" Aaron tossed out sarcastically, just being difficult.

"Oh my God, really?" Dancer said, stomping her feet and throwing her hands to her hips. "You too?"

"Sorry, sarcasm just kind of slips out of me like bad gas," he said, grinning. As he spoke, for but an instant, he felt just the slightest amount of normalcy, of being himself.

Dancer looked at Bob. "It's just too bad with all the shit you have invented that you didn't invent a cloaking device and we could all just hide."

"You know, Dancer, it is funny that you would mention a cloaking device. I am sure you have both heard the term 'things are not as they appear.' Well, and as you know, only I could do this. I have, in fact, in my spare time been working on what, for all practical purposes, is as you refer to it, a cloaking device. I am using something akin to the magician's concept of sleight-of-hand, only in my case, I am using dimensions." Only Bob could segue to another subject so quickly and so far off track. Dancer and Aaron looked at each other smirking, knowing they were about to hear a mini-monologue.

"Maybe I can best explain it like this." Bob smiled innocently before taking a very deep and deliberate breath, and then went on. "The dimensions that make up our reality have since early man been conceptualized as being three. Height, width and depth. And it is pretty easy to see why—everything around us is. There is simply no way of escaping the reality before us. I know, you know all of this, but bear with me for a second. This is a story based on the old adage, 'You cannot see the forest for the trees.' If we have height, the first dimension, you still have nothing, for without width or depth, there is simply nothing there to see. Keep in mind, seeing isn't everything. So we know we have height, we just cannot see it. So let's say we have twelve inches of height..."

"Yeah, I wish," chuckled Aaron.

"Why did I know your childish mind could not help but go there, Aaron. Please, do keep in mind, we are dealing in reality here." Bob continued now chuckling to himself. He moved over to the wall to mimic drawing on a chalkboard, while Aaron hung his head in mock shame. "We know there is something there, we just are unable to see one dimension. Imagine that, knowing something is there without being able to see it, would that not be faith? So, we will call the first dimension Faith."

"That's good, Bob, I like that, that's really good," Dancer said, smiling and listening though she was tapping an impatient foot, wanting to get on with her plan. Still, biting her tongue and biding her time, she kept quiet.

"Well, of course, I thought it pretty cool myself. Okay, now let's add width, call it half of an inch. Suddenly there is a visual, a wide line or rectangle. Now, another thing to keep in mind is that each dimension needs to carry a visual descriptive, like say, color. But I will cover that further in a second."

Stretching his right hand vertically above his left hand to indicate the line, Bob continued, "Here we have a black line, nothing fancy, but we can see it. It is within our perceptive reality at this point with only two dimensions. Thus, I call the second dimension the Cornerstone. However, turn it sideways"––Bob turned sideways and sucked in his chest to appear thinner—"and poof, it is gone. Vanished into thin air, a magician's dream. There is a great, very short novel called *Flatland* by..." He trailed off as he had to think about who wrote it. "Abbott. Edwin Abbott, that's it. In his great book, he discusses this very topic. You really need to read it, Aaron."

He walked over to the bookshelf behind his desk, and thoughtfully, moving his head and the book back and forth and up and down, he surveyed the books' spines. Suddenly his hand darted toward a thin book, which he pulled off the shelf and dusted with his right hand. He then turned and offered it to Aaron.

"It is so short and so thin, it is almost a two-dimensional anomaly onto itself." He laughed. "Please, when you have a moment, read this. I think, no, I know you will love it."

Aaron nodded a thank you. "Thanks, Bob. I mean, I got nothing but time."

"Yes, yes, I know. I am not sure what to say to you, Aaron, except I, for one, am glad you are here. I know you would rather be home with your girl, your lady, Cynthia, right?"

"Yes, Cynthia." Aaron took a painfully long, deep breath, letting out a sigh. "Wait, how did you know about Cynthia?"

Bob, obviously caught off guard by the question, was quick to respond. "Um, Dancer mentioned her to me." Pausing for a second, he continued directing the conversation elsewhere. "You have a uniquely odd appreciation for the same things that fuel my fire, my passion, and Aaron, I am grateful to be able to share what I understand of this universe with you. I have this feeling you are not the only one who is going to learn much from this encounter, you and I—" He stopped to rethink what he was about to say, only to finish with, "Life, our journey, it's pretty amazing isn't it?"

With that, Bob slowly walked back to the wall he had moments before been using as an imaginary chalkboard. He stroked his chin in deep thought, then slowly shaking his head, he continued, "Back to the depths of reality—that is exactly where we are on depth, the third dimension. If we add depth to our line of height and width, suddenly we have an object we can walk around, and it stays visible in our reality from every vantage point. Thus, through the ages we have learned that our world, our reality, is made of these three dimensions regardless of what name you give them. But there is more. It looks like it is there, but is it? Wave your hand through it." Bob waved his hand through the air to illustrate. "Guess what, there is nothing there. It's a ghost. You can see it, but there is nothing there. You cannot touch it, you cannot pick it up, it's just not there. This is why I call the third dimension the *Ghost* dimension. If there are ghosts, paranormal activity of any kind, and I know there are,"––he held up his hands like a ghoul, making ghoulish noises before continuing—"then they, or it, must occur within the third dimension."

"Okay, then what the hell is missing?" Aaron asked. "There are no other perceptible dimensions. I mean, okay, *Time* has always been considered the fourth dimension, but that is debatable and quite clearly is not going to help out here. We are missing solid, substance, the shit you can hold in your hand." As the words left his lips, he trailed off in thought. You could see the synapses firing. He smiled at Bob and started to speak, but Bob, not able to contain his excitement, interrupted.

"Yes. Yes. You understand. I can see it in your eyes, you've got it. It is mass! The fourth dimension is Mass. That which gives weight, color, and solidity. That which allows us to interact within our reality. The single most important factor of all is the fourth dimension: Mass, the Reality dimension. It has always been there, but it was so obvious we have just blindly accepted it. We could not see the forest for the trees. The Reality dimensions, the Mass dimension, the fourth dimension is what separates us from the ghosts—it makes us alive!" Bob stopped, drew another long breath, and said, "Take away any one of the dimensions, and whatever it appears, or should I say does not appear—that is, it becomes invisible."

"So your cloaking device can hide one or more dimensions?" Aaron asked.

Bob pursed his lips, slightly glancing down. "Well, no. Not yet. As I clearly stated, I am working on it."

"Well," Dancer said, having heard enough, "now we'll get started on packing that bag for you. Since you don't have a cloaking machine yet."

~~~~ ~~~~ ~~~~

Nate and Miles's United South West Shuttle landed at New Pulliam. Waving their badges under the scanner, they were able to bypass Mandatory Security Screening and head through the security office and directly outside. A deputy, a patrolbot and patrol drone from the local police station waited for them. As they lifted off in the drone, Miles and Nate in the back found conversation limited to polite greetings and talk of the weather, until Nate leaned forward to speak. Pulling himself closer, his fingers poking through the holes in the carbon fiber shield that separated passengers in the rear from the officers in the front, he asked the passenger, Deputy Paul Stenson, "Do you know of an old codger out in these parts that goes by the name of Bob Kesey?"

"Crazy Bob?" he responded without hesitation. "An old hippie-type guy, short-sleeve Hawaiian print shirts, sandals, grey ponytail?" Paul stopped to look back for a reaction. "We don't see him very often, but you might catch him on a Thursday evening at the Last Hope doing his karaoke thing. I had to break up a fight a year ago between him and some trucker who had too much to drink. Old Bob—I mean, the guy has to be late eighties or ninety-something—kicked the shit out of the truck driver over what music to be playing. That truck driver was so embarrassed, when he sobered up, he refused to press any charges and slithered out of town with his tail between his legs. You mean that Bob Kesey?"

Nate smiled and settled back in the hot, vinyl bench seat, listening to the hum of the fan blades. "Yeah, that Bob Kesey."

~~ ~ ~~~~ ~~~~

"Bob, warning, this is a first alert. Drones of unknown origin are approaching, eight minutes out." Miko was no longer using her not-so-subtle, sexy siren voice. Instead, a deeper and somewhat ominous authoritative voice sounded the warning, one of many voices Bob had programmed for Miko. All three turned to look toward the speakers as if they were looking at a person speaking to them.

"Miko, how many drones?" Bob asked.

"There are two approaching, following the driveway."

"Can you identify them?"

"The first vehicle with two occupants is from the Flagstaff Police Department. The second vehicle has Corporate tags but is not identifiable. There are two occupants in it as well."

"Here they come. It's Nate and his gaggle of college cop preppies." Bob stood, but it was apparent he did not know where to go or what to do.

Dancer did, however. She had an innate ability to take charge in a tough situation. She reacted without allowing her emotions an equal voice, taking immediate control.

"Okay, here we go, boys and girls. Bob, you know the drill. Everything you need is in the Cave. Go lock yourself in and do not, I repeat, DO NOT come out for any reason. Aaron, ever want to do theatre? Well, regardless, here is your chance to see if you can act. Just sit back, relax and look bored. Remember, we haven't seen Bob since we took him to the airport, right? What was that, two days ago? No, make it yesterday. I almost forgot he picked you up at the station." Dancer spoke quickly as she headed to the kitchen to get a beer. Slipping into character, she tried to set the stage for Aaron.

"Hon, you want a beer?" she asked calmly.

Miko announced, "There are visitors at the door."

Dancer got up, and as she slowly walked toward the door, she felt a surge of adrenaline pump through her veins. *Oh crap, I hope Miko listened in on our plan about his being gone.* Dancer pulled her shoulders back, then straightening up, composed herself and continued toward the door. *I got this,* she told herself, and opened the door as though expecting to see a friend.

"Oh, I thought you would be Margaret," she said, using the first name that popped into her head. "Can I help you gentlemen?"

"Ma'am, are you the owner of the property?" the older detective asked.

"Well, no, that would be Bob, but he's not here. Can I help you?"

"No, ma'am. Can you tell us when he will be back?" Nate was old school, standing firmly, weight balanced on both feet and standing slightly closer than he needed to. Close enough for Dancer to smell the peppermint gum he was chewing.

"Well, to be truthful, Officer, I am not sure. We dropped him off at the airport yesterday. I know he was going up to Canada. Something about following up on a lead about his cousin, Carrie. She apparently is his only living relative, and he wanted to visit her. You know, before it was too late." Dancer spoke from a very relaxed position, weight on one foot and hips to the side, but not budging an inch from her personal space. Space that Nate was deliberately encroaching upon.

"Hmm, I thought her name was Gina."

"Pardon me?" Dancer replied, surprised by the answer.

"Nothing, sorry. Ma'am, can you tell me what kind of car he was driving?"

"Yes, I can. He drives an older, metallic grey Tesla Mars Trekker."

"I apologize, ma'am, for not asking first. You are?"

"My name is Mary, Mary Madeline Murphy. But you can call me Dancer as I wouldn't even hear you if you spoke the other name. And you, you are?" Dancer countered, staying cool in the cat-and-mouse exchange.

"Ma'am, sorry, Dancer, I'm Detective Nathaniel Brewster. I'm with the UIIB. You can call me Nate, since we are now on a first-name basis. The young man sitting so quietly over on the couch, he would be?" he said, pointing.

For the briefest second, Dancer flinched, not prepared for that question. But, before she could answer, Miko spoke. "Dancer, another vehicle is approaching." Dancer was caught off guard again. First, because Miko had used her name as if Bob were not on-premise, and second, that there was another vehicle coming up the drive.

"Thank you, Miko, that must be Margaret," Dancer quickly responded, knowing full well there was no Margaret coming up the drive.

"Oh, that would be a couple more of my boys, routine, ya know, ma'am—sorry, Dancer. They are in-ground cars, slower," Nate said, and then turned to where the sound of Miko's voice had come from. "Computer, where might I find Bob, the owner of this house?" Nate smiled at Dancer, knowing he had just made a chess move that surprised her.

"I'm sorry, sir, I do not know the exact whereabouts of the home's owner at this moment. I would direct your question to Dancer as she is housesitting right now and would know more than I," Miko answered calmly.

The smile left Nate's face and he turned back to Dancer. "Hmm," he snorted under his breath.

Dancer smiled at Miko's blatant lying to the detective. Still in character, Dancer responded to the detective's question. "Oh, in answer to your question regarding the young gentleman on the couch, well, Detective—sorry, Nate—I have to tell you, you have hit the jackpot on that one. His name, as best we can all tell, is Aaron." Aaron sheepishly waved at Nate. "You see, he walked into the Last Hope, where I work, looking very disheveled and disoriented. Bob was there that evening. And best we can tell, he is suffering from some sort of amnesia. So we took him in to help him until he remembers something. Heck, Paul—sorry, Deputy Stenson here picked him up and brought him down to the station because his car is so old it broke every law on the books. And, he has no chip, but really, he doesn't appear to be a Scab. You remember that night, Paul?"

Nate turned to the deputy. "Ah, this would be the one that triggered our little trip, got it. Do you know what flight he took to Canada?"

"Actually, no, can't help you there. Bob does his own thing when it comes to travel, especially airfare."

The young detective, Miles Edger, standing just behind Nate said, "We can find out which flight he is on. He can't board even if he tries to use an alias." He smirked.

"Don't be too quick to bet your paycheck on that," Nate warned. "Who the hell do you think originally wrote the software they use? Dancer, I have to say I am a bit concerned that you have not asked why we are looking for him, as that would indicate to me you already know. Do you already know?" Nate looked at her with a questioning smile.

Returning his smile, she said, "You, sir, are trying to put words in my mouth, to get me to say something, to spill some sort of beans. Sir, Nate, let me tell you, sweetheart, I have been around the block more than once, and I already know what your answer would have been, had I asked."

"Really. What's that?" Nate responded, surprised by her bravado.

Dancer raised her shoulders, puffed up her face and in her deepest voice, pretending to be a male detective, said, "Ma'am, I am afraid I am not at liberty to disclose that information." She relaxed back to her weight-on-one-foot stance with a sarcastic grin.

Nate returned her smile, nodding. "Okay, you got me there."

"But, since you brought it up, why exactly are you looking for Bob?"

Detective Edger spoke. "Ma'am, his name is Robert Man..." but Nate held up his hand in a gesture to silence him and said smiling, "Dancer, what I can disclose to you is we have some outstanding warrants we would like to question him about. When you do talk to him, or see him, please have him call me. Thank you, and you both have a good day."

Nate handed her his card, turned and walked onto the patio and out the gate. Dancer slowly closed the door, watching their retreat. When the door closed, she turned to Aaron. There was fear in his eyes and a *what the fuck* sort of smile on his face.

"Well, that was fun, eh?" she said, smiling at him.

~ ~~ ~~~~ ~~ ~~

Cynthia was awakened by her phone ringing. She had just fallen into deep REM sleep after being awake most of the night crying. The worst part was, she didn't know why she was crying. She could only feel a great loss but not what that loss might be. She had to wrestle herself out of the twisted and turned sheets and blankets held firmly in place by a cinder block of a dog, Half Dome, whose weight pressing down on them made it nearly impossible to reach the phone. Free at last, she answered out of breath.

"Hello?" she asked, struggling from deep within that painful place, trying to drag her unwilling consciousness from the depths of the euphoric fog. From the blissful sleep she had worked so hard to reach. She hoped it might be Aaron finally calling from LA.

"Cynthia, turn on the news! Oh my God, Cynthia, they have gone and done it," her obviously upset mom responded, nearly screaming into the phone.

"What? Who? Mom, is that you?"

"Yes, yes, dear. Turn on the news. Oh my God, my God. Turn it on right now. A nuclear bomb just went off in Los Angeles!" The horror and tears in her mom's voice made her words difficult to understand, and Cynthia hoped she had heard her wrong.

Cynthia's consciousness instantly broke through the fog ceiling upon hearing those chilling words. "What? What the hell? No way. Okay, okay, hold on."

On the TV, two newscasters were talking, looking unusually distraught. In the background was the very clear icon mushroom cloud of an atomic blast, still rising into the heavens, with the famous "Hollywood" sign visible in the distance on the hills to the left.

"Oh my God... Aaron!"

~~~~ ~~~~ ~~~~

Aaron stared out the window as the scenery scrolled by. They were headed into town to the Puc to pick up some shelter in place groceries for Dancer's plan. Still reeling from the encounter with Bob, he turned to face Dancer, his voice tense.

"Is Bob safe? I mean, with the police and all looking for him. He's just so odd. I guess what I mean is, how well do you really know him?"

Without saying a word, Dancer pulled off the road into a small turnout with two small but wide-spreading trees at its edge. The gravel crunched under the turning tires as the car came to a halt. "All windows down," she spoke toward the dashboard. "Engine off." Silently, her command was carried out.

"Sorry, hon," she said, turning to face him. "you need to know about Bob's past to understand Bob. I, too, just discovered with you what his real name is. I am not shocked, I know him too well, and his heart is true. He's a good guy. He really is. It's cool enough in here with the windows down, yes?"

"Yeah, I'm fine."

"Good. Seeing as how neither of us has anywhere important to go at the moment, let me try to explain Bob." She smiled, then looked directly into his eyes. "You know you can ask me anything, and you can tell me anything, right?" She slid her finger gently under his chin and slowly pulled it toward her as she spoke, then paused for an answer.

"Yeah, I know, I know." Aaron looked down for a second, his mind heavy with thought. A gentle breeze found its way through the shade of the trees into the car's window. Aaron relaxed and settled back into the seat. "Yes, Dancer, I know, and

I am grateful beyond words for the kindness you have shown me. Thank you. Yes, please explain Bob. This has got to be good."

"You see, sweetie, when life dealt him his hand of cards, he got a real mixed bag. He has Asperger's syndrome. Not super severe, but enough to make him a real pain in the ass, as you have witnessed. Thing is, it turned out to be a double-edged sword. It amplified his genius, but it hurt those who cared about him while pissing off everyone else. He's incapable of carrying on a conversation with most people, and it affected and shaped him growing up. Not just with kids or wanting to date girls, but worse, with the very men and women he needed to work with, other scientists and engineers."

Aaron thoughtfully returned her gaze. "Okay, that makes things a bit clearer. Much clearer, actually. That had to be tough for him."

"Well, actually, no. Bobby—oh shit, don't ever let him hear you call him Bobby and don't ever tell him I call him that. His head gets all purple and he gets really, really pissed off." She laughed. "Bob does not need other people. He does not need their approval; he does not need their companionship. He only needs, in most cases, the raw materials they possess to pursue his totally self-absorbed goals. He's not even aware of the pain and anguish he causes other people. He is simply unaware, detached from others' emotions."

Aaron started to say something, but Dancer held up her hand. "This is why I had to stop the car. I need to finish this in one thought." She smiled. "Bobby boy might have been just fine. Who knows where life would have led him had he been raised in an environment that nurtured him, helped and guided him. But there was one more card in that mixed bag of a hand, a really shitty card. Dealt by his parents, actually. Though in the scheme of things, it mattered not who. He was still dealt the card by that ever-so-grand universe of ours that just keeps unfolding as it wishes, with little or no say on our part. Bob's parents, if you can imagine, were a little odd themselves. I know, imagine that. They were taken in by the teachings of a religious cult before there was even such a thing as religious cults. After only a few encounters with this group, his parents sold everything they owned—their house, their cars—and gave all the money to one Reverend Desmon Skythe and his 'Unity of the Heavens' family."

Aaron looked at her, face scrunched up like he was watching a horror movie. "That's the scariest name I think I've ever heard. I've no idea what you are going to tell me, but I already know it can't be good. Shit, that's the guy Bob thought he saw in the hardware store, right?"

Dancer nodded. "Yup, that would be the one, and yes, it should scare the hell out of you. But no, that wasn't him. You saw the Reverend's son at the hardware store. They *are* scary looking men. I remember years ago, before I knew Bob, seeing an article about the reverend and his cult. A bunch of the elders had been arrested for child molestation, and several, including the Reverend, were up on murder charges as well. I saw the photos on the news. He was a tall man, near a head taller than the sheriff deputies who had arrested him. Tall and skinny, with dark sunken eyes, crooked teeth, and long, thin hair stuck to the sides of his head like it was wet. And those eyes were piercing. His red get-up made him look like a cross between a Catholic priest and the spawn of Satan. Spooked the shit out of me just looking at him in a photo. The Reverend and his family owned a growing spread of property near the foothills where all the caves are and the forest starts. Bob told me the reverend told everyone he had a special line to God himself. He said that the Elders ran it like a dictatorship. A bunch of middle-aged to older men who had been with Skythe for many years. Bob has explained in far more detail than I ever wanted to know that every night after dinner they would gather, and the Reverend would go on and on about the importance of compliance to touching and dominance by the elders. I gotta tell ya, the stuff Bob told me curled my pubes tighter. These motherfuckers were some sick, twisted excuses for human beings. The elders, he said, had all the children brought to the center compounds to perform the *Rights of Adulthood,* which of course was nothing less than child molestation and rape. The women had little or no say in any matters outside the kitchen, the laundry or the gardens. The women also endured being made to wear early Americana Puritan clothing at all times. I mean, what the hell, why is it all the cults seem to want to dress their women in old wool blankets? Have they no imagination at all?"

"I think if they had enough brains to have an imagination, they would not be in cults in the first place," Aaron said.

Dancer nodded approval. "Bob said, during the touching rituals, entire groups of young women and boys were made to strip to nothing, allowing the elders to touch them however they desired while all other members of the families watched. He said his own mother felt grateful when they considered her too old to be allowed into the *Touching Ritual.* Instead, she gladly herded the younger girls and boys, the children, into the center of the theatre, only to watch." Dancer paused as tears were now streaming down her cheeks.

"Are you okay?" Aaron asked, scooting forward to reach up toward Dancer's face to wipe the tears. But she quickly caught his hand and brought it down to her lap. "I'm okay, Really."

"What's the matter with people? How can they allow one man to control them like that, their families, their children?" Aaron asked, still leaning in close to Dancer. He gently tried to free his hand, but Dancer held onto it firmly.

"It happens over and over. I mean, for crap's sake, look at what Hitler and the Nazis did to millions of innocent people while the world watched, allowing them to do it. I don't know, Aaron. I don't know. I wonder quite often these days if there is a God. If there is, he is either blind or really mean."

She sniffed hard, wiping her eyes with her sleeve, then continued, "They had many other odd, really odd rituals and laws. Crazy shit, like there were certain names that were forbidden. They were not allowed to speak or write names like *Dave* and *David*. Which makes no sense to me as those are biblical names. They were just freaks. Very scary freaks." She stopped to take a breath and wipe her eyes again. "Bob said many of the kids he had to live and sleep with disappeared, never to return. So I have no doubt many children died on that property in the hands of the Reverend and his elders."

She sat up, finally releasing Aaron's hands. "Now, here is the interesting part, if there can be an interesting part in this true-life horror story. This is one of the times in his life, Bob's

Asperger's proved a blessing. Because of it, Bob simply could not socialize with anyone, so he just up and ran away one evening, never looking back. He made his way toward the west coast, doing odd jobs, accepting handouts, even stealing. But by the time he reached his early teens, he had earned his GED and then put himself through college, finishing at Berkeley in California. Which is where he met Timothy Leary, but that is another story for another day. And, oh God, trust me, you will hear the story of Timothy, over and over and over," Dancer said with an eye roll.

"Wow, I had no idea. I mean I really had no idea the man had suffered through something that dramatic. Those events alone would be enough to make any man act the way he does. Thanks, it helps put things into a clearer perspective. Who knew Bob was so—so—I don't know, so complex, so resilient. And, Timothy Leary, wow..." Aaron said, trailing off as he turned again toward the open window.

"Actually, Aaron, the reason I tell you this story is the amazing gift he received because of this evil. It gave Bob an empathy and understanding he would not have received in that day and age from any of the so-called professionals, or even just good people with kind intentions. No one tried to help him; no one understood Asperger's. But somehow, in a unique ironic twist, this unspeakable evil was able to penetrate Bob. It gave him empathy for other humans. He witnessed and felt such great pain at the hands of these sadistic animals, it stuck in his mind, and he did not want to perpetuate that evil on anyone else."

"So this reverend, did they convict him? And, hopefully, fry his ass on low voltage for a while?" Aaron asked, turning back more alert.

"Yes, they did. They convicted him and sent him to death row at Florence. But, it was after the Eight-Year War, and security in the country was still half-ass. There was a nasty prisoner uprising that took weeks to shut down, and the Reverend escaped with one other man. They later caught the man he escaped with, but no one has seen or heard from the Reverend since."

"But surely his son must know where he is, right?" Aaron asked, and then stopped as he realized the implications. "Okay. I understand why Bob freaked out at the store."

~~~   ~~~ ~~~~

"No, Bob, you can't leave," Aaron said. "Dancer is absolutely correct. You need to stay out of sight. There is no question those guys have some sort of twenty-four-hour surveillance on us. I love Dancer, she's good, but those detectives didn't buy her story for a second. You know it, I know it, more importantly, they know it."

"Yes, as you say, I do know it. I have feared this day for so many years, and then when it never came, I allowed myself to relax, to let my guard down. We need to start searching for options other than the emergency escape route I originally built. I want to look deeper into parts of the cave I have not been in for some time. There are endless tunnels and hiding spots deep in the caves. As you have made it abundantly clear, I am on lockdown, against my wishes, I would like to note, so, I will need you to go to the garage for me. You need to find a gauge we will need. It is in my toolbox in the garage up the side road in front of the house, the gated one, up where you parked your VW. When you get there, there is a lock on the door. The combination for the lock is very easy, but no one would guess it. It is 'TESLA56.' The most brilliant man in human history, and the year he was born, of course. Inside there is a large red toolbox against the back wall. In the second from the bottom drawer, you will see a bright-yellow handheld device on the right-hand side that says Honeywell Gas Alert on it. It will detect most of the poisonous gasses we need to be concerned with in the caves I wish to explore."

Aaron approached the garage with some degree of trepidation after his own warning to Bob about the cops watching their every move. *Don't look around. Just look where you're going and don't look suspicious,* he told himself, thinking about the cops watching them.

The garage was detached from the house so that it would appear to someone just driving up to the house that no one was home. Bob had then gone on to explain—more as an excuse, Aaron thought—that garages fit perfectly within one of his personal set of laws. A *Bobism,* as Dancer referred to them. In this case, *any unused area of a garage or storage area will be filled; build it and it will be filled.* As such, he explained, he could no longer park in his own garage.

Aaron walked to the side of the garage, well out of sight of the house, following a dirt path lined with yellow thistle stickers. He entered the combination Bob had told him and then opened the door and reached for the light switch. The illuminated garage was filled edge-to-edge with a multitude of garage-type objects stacked on top of each other. *Yeah, build it, and it will be filled, he thought. Holy crap, the man is a hoarder.* He laughed and pushed aside some small boxes, an old bicycle and various yard tools, making his way to the red toolbox, then opened the second drawer only to be greeted with the work of someone with severe OCD. All the tools were clean and precisely positioned.

"Well, I'll be a son of a bitch," he said out loud, laughing as he did. *Okay, Bob, you have Asperger's, you're a hoarder, and you have OCD, of course.* He grabbed the yellow gas alert, exactly where Bob said it would be, and shut the drawer. As Aaron turned, he saw the outline of what could only be a car under a very dusty canvas tarp. He waded in and pushed his way over to the front corner of the tarp, carefully lifting it—then stopped, amazed. It was something he was getting uncomfortably used to these last few days.

There, in front of him, sat his VW Bug—or very nearly so. It was the same year, same condition, and close to the same color. Aaron had painted his dusty eggshell white, and this VW seemed a stock, light grey. On the dash sat a hula dancer identical to his.

The hair on his arms and the back of his neck tingled. He had seen this car before.

Aaron made his way back to the Cave after covering the car and locking the garage. He handed Bob the yellow gas detector without saying a word, as he looked for the right way to phrase his next question.

"Thank you, Aaron," Bob said, wanting very much to continue his explanation of Pandora. "Pandora is..."

He stopped as Aaron, visibly shaken, could no longer wait and cut him off, stating, "There is a VW Bug in your garage. A VW Bug that is exactly like mine."

Only silence followed except for the hum of Pandora. Bob froze, the book motionless and frozen to his leg. Bob mentally punished himself for being so stupid as to forget the VW in the garage. *But it has been years since I put it there*, he argued with himself.

"That was you in the VW next to me. Wasn't it? What the hell did you do? Do you know how I got here?" Shaking, Aaron paused, considering his next words. "Are you..." he asked in a slow, matter-of-fact tone, pointing his finger towards Bob's face, "are you in some way responsible for my being abducted? For bringing me here?"

Bob stuttered, stopped, then continued, "Uhm... uhm... Aaron, I do not know where to begin. You are, in fact, correct in your assumption. Indeed, it was a much younger me in the VW you saw the other night, and yes, it is the same VW that you just now saw in the garage and has been sitting there under that tarp for over sixteen years." He looked down, eyes closed, shaking his head back and forth before returning his gaze towards Aaron. "And yes, I might know something." He paused, drawing in a deep breath. "No, not might—I do know what happened. Well, let me clarify that a bit. I know what happened; I know how you came to be here. I just cannot really explain right now how it happened."

Bob, biting one side of his lip, was obviously nervous and unprepared to explain. The intensity and speed of his book beating against his thigh increased enough to leave a bruise. "We have shared much in the last few days, and it has been difficult for me not being able to explain this to you. I didn't know where to start. I knew you would be angry with me."

Aaron stood statue-still, taking in everything Bob said. The perplexing puzzle that had haunted him since his arrival was now fitting together, and he felt a growing sense of nausea in the pit of his stomach. For three days, he had lived under the impression he was either crazy or had suffered a stroke. Unable to communicate with Cynthia to tell her he was okay. Unable to talk to anyone, for fear of being put in a straitjacket, and living in constant fear of where he would stay, how he would survive, how he would get back.

The puzzle was solved; he now understood. He was standing in the laboratory of the man responsible for his abduction.

"Why? Why did you bring me here? What possible fucking thing motivated you to steal my life from me with your sick experiment? You're insane. Look what you've done!" Aaron vented his anger, the veins in his forehead pulsing as he did.

Bob motioned with his book toward Pandora, then brought his hands to the sides of his head like a small child caught in a lie. Bob completely understood his implicit involvement but only seemed alarmed at being scolded, revisiting the terror he had not experienced since his days in the cult. "Aaron, this was an accident, so help me God!"

"You said you don't believe in God!" Aaron fired back. He paced in disbelief between the door to Pandora and the main computer station's desk. "How the hell could this be an accident? How could you pull me, solid matter, out of my time to here? How? That simply is not possible, Bob. What you are saying cannot happen." Aaron, overwhelmed with anger, tried his best to come to terms with the implications. This old hippie in front of him somehow was responsible for his being there. He had thought the man who had taken him in was his friend, when actually he was his abductor. "Why on Earth did you create this thing, this machine? Certainly not to abduct people."

"I created Pandora to explore the possibility of communicating with myself in the past. You see, the idea was to create a sort of black hole or skinny wormhole to transmit information into—"

"Whoa. You created Pandora to create black holes, or wormholes, and you fucked up, didn't you? Bob, even I know black holes and wormholes are so powerful that light cannot escape. Anything sucked into them is crushed to microscopic space dust, then it is spit out the other side somewhere else in the universe or universes. So why wasn't I crushed to the size of an atom when you dragged me, and my Bug, I might add, through your mini-fucking wormhole?" he snapped at Bob.

Being typically Bob, quite incapable of diplomacy, he responded with unsympathetic calmness. "To be accurate, Aaron, skinny, not mini-fucking, but skinny wormhole. And of course, for me, this is really quite easy to explain, as I have been trying to for some time, apparently on deaf ears.

"We, you, I, everything, are the product, an illusion created by a data script for which we have processors—our souls, if you will—that read the script alluding to us in this reality. In reading this quantum script, our reality is best described, well, like a *video game.*" Bob's voice took on a defensive tone as he explained, "It is a game of reality, created with God-like complexities. What I have discovered, what I have actually known my entire life, is that script, data, code, the Godscript, whatever you wish to call it, has no mass. It is not even energy. Rather, it is a pattern of on and off again energy fluctuations."

Bob's voice rose for greater emphasis. "It, the script, can travel through a black hole or a wormhole and survive intact because it has no mass. Once it has passed through a skinny wormhole, the code is moved forward to this time, as did you apparently. The code is pasted back into the pages ahead in the script or story to where we exist now and thus appears to be time travel. So you see, your physical body did not pass through the skinny wormhole; it does not even exist. The script that creates the illusion of you passed through the wormhole."

Bob, who had remained unusually calm in trying to convey how incredible all of this was, now became very excited. "Once I figure this out entirely, and I will, I will harness it, learn to control it. Then things will get really exciting."

Aaron stared at Bob, dumbfounded. Only because, for the moment, as he grappled with the understanding he had, in fact, been accidentally abducted and by whom, he clearly grasped the enormity of what Bob had accomplished.

He knew he had to remain calm and wrap his head around what Bob had just told him. But the same questions just kept repeating, with new ones multiplying, pouring into his mind as he simply could not yet grasp Bob's explanation.

"Bob, I want you to know I'm trying to get this straight in my head so that I don't pick up a hammer and beat you over the head with it," he said, hands raised, pretending to strike with a hammer. "So, you just sort of plucked me, sorry, you just sort of plucked my code, the script, the what-the-fuck-hell-ever from where I was, and then when you un-plucked it, or pasted it back, I reappeared here, in the future, in your world. And instead of being a thousand miles away from here, back in Tahoe, I found myself driving way out in the middle of the desert. And—and—and—" Aaron paused to steady his voice. "And how did you know I would be at the Last Hope?" Aaron's hand and finger trembled as he pointed toward Bob.

Bob smiled, thinking to himself, *It's a good thing you didn't land in the same area. It would have been a very rough landing.*

"Aaron, you will just have to believe me when I tell you, I did not know I had brought you here. I was only trying to send a message to myself using simple, old-fashioned Morse Code and utilizing Pandora to do so. You see, I knew where and when I was exactly because of a watch I had just purchased that afternoon. The watch could sync with the atomic clock in Switzerland. A clock, I might add, that is accurate to within one second over thirty million years. I set the coordinates to transmit at the speed and time required to reach back in time to that exact moment. It was all working perfectly. It was beautiful, oh, you should have smelled the ozone and heard the music, the singing, the harmony of Pandora as she came up to speed."

Aaron remembered being transfixed by the soothing harmony of the two VW engines. He smiled for the briefest of moments, his anger temporally subsiding as a second wave of memory rushed over him like a chill, the odd pattern-like noise he'd heard in the harmony of the two engines. *The noise—the Morse Code.* He looked up at Bob. "What kind of message did you try to send yourself?"

Bob continued, ignoring Aaron's question. "Then pop, the lights went out and bolts of blue lightning arced back and forth like a Tesla experiment gone awry. The beautiful music of the collider made the oddest sound as it faded while shutting down. It sounded like it was being sucked down a drain. The battery lights kicked on for but a moment, then the normal power returned with the bright lights filling the cave. A mist of blue smoke rose to the ceiling, filling the room with an acrid, ozone smell. I was so upset, I turned everything off in the cave and drove to the Last Hope to see Dancer. She somehow can always make me feel better. There, I tried to drink away my confusion and disappointment. I was furious with myself that I did not have the proper protection and backup in place to support the collider. Then what do I see? What appears to be my old VW Bug pull up and you get out and stagger toward the door like—well, like as you said, like you had been abducted by aliens. I knew at that very instant, I had inadvertently stumbled upon—by serendipitous error, as all the greatest scientists like myself do from time to time—the proof of what I had always believed. I knew where you had come from and why. And I knew you were now my responsibility to take care of and guide. At least until you understood and could deal with your new reality. You, Aaron, you are my greatest mistake!" Bob put one foot on the chair, head back, seeming very proud of himself.

Aaron was quite unable to speak. Which mattered not, as Bob continued, "I believe Aaron, when the wormhole collapsed, it somehow, and I will figure out how, ripped your script data from then, and sucked it back home to the collider through the collapsing wormhole to where you are now. Well, where you are in this timeframe of reality, my present, what was your future. You know Aaron, once I figure this out in its entirety, how to read it, harness it, learn to control it, and maybe even write it, we will be able to travel through time and reality at will. The old paradox associated with the effects of the speed of light on mass will quite simply become irrelevant."

Aaron was astonished at Bob's cavalier segue and total disregard for anyone else's feelings but his own. *He's fucking crazy,* he thought to himself. But, at the same time, it was quickly becoming clear to Aaron that if this crazy old man could bring him here, he was the person to be able to send him back. "Bob, how can you just cut a bunch of script out of thin air and paste it here, in more thin air?"

"Well, this is awkward, Aaron. I do not know yet. You see, I assume that when the collider's Wormhole shut down and then came back online, it cut the portion of the script it was focused on—you—and pasted it here into the present that is mine and Dancer's script. But, and this is a very real possibility, quantumly speaking, you could have very well continued on to your way into work. That is to say, I may have only copied the portion of the script that is you. You may, in fact, exist in both realities at the same time. Which, of course, is entirely possible because of the quantum nature of things. I assume, that I cut your portion of the script." He stopped to bring the book to his forehead. "Hmm. What if by copying, the two of you are still conscious of your surroundings? You here are confused as to how you got here, but the you back there would not know anything has transpired. I need to give this a great deal of thought. So many new paradoxes," he finished with a peculiar chuckle to himself.

"Wait, how can I be in both places and still be me? Suppose there is another me out there now, or infinite 'mes' as you suggest with quantum physics. In that case, they must all be individuals with their own individual thoughts. Therefore, they cannot be me; they are them... right?"

"Aaron, there is an infinite number of you, and of me."

"That's a scary thought!" Aaron sarcastically chided with as much bite as he could.

"Yes, yes, as I was saying. There are infinite quantum 'yous' out there, and they are all connected as one entity," Bob returned.

"How the hell is that even possible?"

"You are most likely not familiar with the spooky particle theory..."

Aaron cut in, feeling a hint of excitement. "Actually, Bob, I am very familiar with the spooky particle theory. We studied it in college. When you separate two particles, they will remain entangled to the point of being able to perform action at a distance."

"Yes, impressive, Aaron, a very memorized recital of textbook quantum entanglement," Bob answered dryly. "What we have here—wait—let me be blunt, answering your question is far more complex. You see, we are entangled with all of our quantum selves, though each of us is on an individual journey."

"Bob," Aaron laughed, "how on Earth, or in the universe, can we all be hooked together? I mean, come on, wouldn't we all go insane with that much incoming information loose in our brains? We would be like the schizophrenic peo—" Aaron paused, head tilted as he considered what had just come out of his mouth, and then slowly continued, "People. And if everything is based on the script, your Godscript, then nothing is real, and there aren't even any particles to entangle." He trailed off, losing his train of thought, still thinking about schizophrenia parallel.

Bob smiled. "Isn't it wonderful when you answer your own questions? Now, Aaron, I am quite aware of how much you and Dancer loathe when I go on at length doing my best to impart on you the vast knowledge I have accumulated. Still, your questions deserve an answer that, prepare yourself, requires more than a couple of words to explain." Bob patted himself on his shoulder, book in hand. "You see, my boy, when dealing with life, the complexity of the entanglement buffers our ability to sense those attached or entangled. It is very subtle, but it is there. And as you guessed, schizophrenics are proof. They have a greater degree of sensation, an ability of picking up more information from their entangled counterparts, and thus are considered insane because they hear voices. The reality, I believe is, they simply cannot process all that loose information pouring in from who knows where. Now, as far as the script not being material enough to be entangled, nothing changes in physics by our better defining how reality is perceived. Early man believed everything around him to be solid. Little did he know that it was an illusion, that his entire reality was really an infinite sea of molecules and atoms that were quite fluid. When it was discovered we were made up of atoms that came with written instructions in the form of DNA, the world as they knew it did not end. It did not suddenly change their reality. Reality held up under this new scrutiny, and no one sank into the abyss of atoms and molecules. So you see, the Godscript is the same. We merely now have a better understanding of the depth of our reality and one more piece to the puzzle of how all this works and why."

Aaron pondered Bob's words. "So you're telling me Cynthia doesn't even know I am gone? Some version of me is there for her right now, even though I'm here, right? Wait, how do I know I am me?" Aaron asked, feeling a chill at the thought. "This is just all fucked up!"

"You make a good point. It would mean A, Cynthia does not yet know you are gone, and everything is normal for her, or B, you are gone, and you have been erased or are fading from her future memory due to the potential for self-healing of the script. Or C, you just disappeared with no logical explanation. That is the thing with quantum physics; it is all possible. Of course, even if I did, in fact, copy you, creating two of you, there would only be one of you left now, as the you in Tahoe was vaporized sixteen years ago."

Aaron felt the epiphany rise up through his body and, with it, great anxiety. "Um, Bob, if as you say, you cut or ripped this code, not copied, removing the script from one part of reality, from its rightful place in space and time, that is. Do you know if you have created a wound in the fabric of space and time or your script? Shit, would the wound heal? Do the people where you removed the script react? Do they feel it? Will Cynthia forget who I was, forget I ever existed, forget how I loved her, held her, wanted to be with her forever? What have you done, Bob?"

A long uncomfortable silence ensued, allowing the hum of Pandora to seem louder. Even Bob's book moved so slowly that it made no sound.

Bob spoke like a doctor telling a patient bad news. "Aaron, first, I do not know if it, your portion of the Godscript, was cut or copied. Further, I do not know, if it was cut, what the ramifications to you, to reality, would be. Suffice it to say, it happened, you are here, and you are alive. Let me try and explain it to you using another analogy." Bob stiffened, standing up straighter. Taking a deep breath, he moved his arms behind him, stretching them and his neck. "You understand DNA. Deoxyribonucleic acid contains the code that makes us who we are, what we look like, sound like, even smell like. DNA is a code, a script, whose programming allows it to combine with another set of DNA and create similar but unique human beings. Yes? Well, let us take a quantum leap past the concept of DNA to a place where things are much, much smaller, but in their smallness, they comprise greater detail. Imagine, if you will, something akin to DNA that is the script for how DNA itself is to behave and function. A script that tells even DNA where and how it will perform in this reality. There, Aaron. There, you will find the Godscript, as I have chosen to call it. It is not printed; it is not digital. In fact, it is, ironically, more analog in nature. It exists as patterns within patterns that define our very reality."

Bob lowered his book and looked at Aaron. With each day, each unsolicited Bobism, Aaron was becoming an unconscious but willing and wanting student. The revelation materializing in his brain had his eyes wide open. He just smiled, understanding, returning Bob's gaze, and could only say, "Wow!"

Bob, recognizing Aaron's comprehension, went on. "This is how I can move you from there to here, from then to now. Quite simple, really. I moved the portion of Godscript that defined where and when your DNA was to here. What I am now processing, and honestly finding difficult to understand, is how reality functions because of the Godscript. Is it self-healing? How does it reconcile all of the entangled relationships of people, places, memories, history? Somehow it does, and I think it might be something very much like the concept of entangled particles. You melded into this *Now* very well, do you not think? I am assuming—yes, even I make assumptions, though they are near always correct—that the *You* from where you were just disappeared. Your Cynthia will almost immediately forget who you were and or will suffer some sort of an acute repetitive déjà vu disorder. She will most likely fear she is becoming paranoid with delusional thoughts, memories that seem so real but are about a man she cannot remember ever existed. And eventually, even those will fade as the Godscript self-heals."

"She really might forget she ever knew me?" Aaron asked quietly.

"Your concern is to be expected. It is possible. But there is, of course, a second possibility. That you were cut and pasted, to here, and you simply disappeared without a trace until the spot in the script where you are pasted back in. She will have no memory of you being here, as she does not exist here yet. Her new memories moving forward, however, will be that you vanished without a trace, an unsolved mystery. Further, and to dispel any paradoxes, if we looked here now, for an older duplicate version of you, we would find nothing. The older you would not be alive today because, well, because you would have vaporized in the nuclear explosion, or because when I brought you forward, you ceased to exist back then and thus could not continue to grow older." Bob stopped long enough to smile, pleased with himself for understanding the effects of his work.

Aaron's thoughts focused. *If there is going to be—has been—a nuclear explosion in Tahoe, then—*"You have to save Cynthia!" he blurted out. "I don't know whether to hate you or depend on you. But I guess I know the answer; I need you to save Cynthia..." His voice trailed off, pleading, "Save her!"

"Well, actually, not that it is any consolation, but for you and me here now, Cynthia already died in the nuclear explosion and thus is feeling no confusion regarding your disappearance," Bob said nonchalantly without concern for the anguish it would cause Aaron. "Now, it is getting late. I think it is time you go find Dancer and get yourself something to eat and some sleep. I need to work on deciphering the code further before I go to bed. Goodnight then, Aaron." He turned and walked away.

Aaron, shocked at Bob's nonchalant dismissal, spoke up loudly in an attempt to continue the conversation. "Whoa, wait one second, I'm not finished yet with..."

Bob looked back toward Aaron. "You know, Aaron, you are a bit of the Connecticut Yankee, in reverse. To be factual, not fictional, you are, in fact, now in remarkable company with the likes of Columbus and Neil Armstrong. You, Aaron, are the first human being to successfully travel in time!"

Aaron stood, his lips still frozen in the position needed for the last syllable he had been about to speak. He didn't know if he should scream or hug him. But as always seemed to be the case with Bob, his logic instantly changed the paradigm of the discussion.

"Again, goodnight, Aaron. We can continue in the morning."

~~~~ ~~~~ ~~~~

"Good, you are both here now," Bob said, walking over to the small table against the cave wall where Aaron and Dancer were drinking wine.

"Bob, can I interest you in a glass of wine? Some crackers and pesto, some cheese?" Dancer smiled as she held out a glass of red wine to him.

"Thank you, I do not mind if I do, Dancer," Bob said and grabbed a cracker, which he promptly buried in the pesto dish, drawing it out with a mound of pesto that required some degree of balance to keep it from falling off.

Mumbling slightly with a mouthful of pesto and cracker, he went on. "Aaron, I understand your great level of animosity toward me for what has transpired. I know you also see that it was an inadvertent accident that was out of my control. An accident that has brought you here, saving your life."

Aaron started to protest, but Bob stopped him, holding up his half-eaten cracker. "Please, Aaron, let me finish. I think, no, I know you will be very pleased with what I have to say and what I have planned."

Aaron nodded. "Okay, I'll listen. Like I have a choice," he added.

"Thank you. Dancer, I know you will be impressed as well." Bob took a sip of wine. "Ah, pesto and red wine, food for the Gods."

Dancer shook her head. "Yeah, let's see what you have to top the last twenty-four hours, Bobby," she said with the obvious emphasis on *Bobby*.

"Dancer, why do you torment me? You know how I despise being called by that name," Bob replied, irritation in his voice.

Dancer was subconsciously still venting at Bob's deceiving her all these years. But she was wise enough and knew his heart was in the right place. It always was, even if his social interactions weren't. Dancer had risen above her negative feelings and had prepared one of his favorite late-evening snacks as a treat to encourage him and keep him upbeat. She knew all too well only Bob's brilliance could bring Cynthia to safety.

"Well, I know how to save your girlfriend, Cynthia," Bob said, looking at Aaron, pausing and waiting for an

131

acknowledgment. Both Aaron and Dancer turned, giving Bob their full attention. "I've worked out how to duplicate the conditions and the shutdown sequence that cut you, your code, and brought you here. I am going to start running some tests today to confirm the validity of what I have learned. I will first attempt to bring an item from the past, the last couple of days—nothing too big to start with."

"You can bring Cynthia here?" Aaron asked, not really listening to anything after, 'I know how to save your girlfriend.'

The irony was not lost on Dancer, who watched as Bob, not hearing a word Aaron had said either, continued without responding to the question. "There is an empty beer bottle that is still sitting on the table on the patio from several days ago. My first experiment will be to bring it forward from before, prior to it being opened, still cold. The goal is to not only bring it forward, but to also change its position so that it reappears in the Cave." He finished looking up at the ceiling, almost as if waiting for applause.

"But you can do this? Is it safe?" Aaron quizzed, sounding hopeful.

"Yes. Yes, of course. I succeeded in figuring out the sequence required. But, and this is why we are testing, I have not begun to understand the script enough to only grab the bottle and not the table. We do not want to be bringing only half of Cynthia back." Bob smiled as both Aaron and Dancer gasped in horror.

"You're damn straight you're not going to attempt this until you can do it over and over without any mistakes," Aaron said strongly.

"Aaron, I apologize; that was insensitive, but let's be realistic. Number one, your Cynthia has already passed on. She died in the nuclear blast. Further, should there be an error and she is killed in the process, we only need dial back mere seconds and try again. I am completely confident we will bring your Cynthia to now, safe and sound."

Dancer looked at Bob, shaking her head. "My God, Bob, you know, I love you, but sometimes you can really be an asshole."

Aaron just stood there with a mixture of fear and hope on his face.

"I thought you would both be pleased with my announcement. I do not understand. Why are you both angry with me? I can do this!" Bob said emphatically.

Aaron had been trapped in this nightmare long enough. He was tired of being afraid, and something snapped in his mind. "Okay. Bob, do it, just fucking do it! What can I do?" Aaron knew this could be his only chance to ever see Cynthia again.

Bob nodded. "Excellent, we will run the experiment first thing in the morning. I need the rest of the day to work out some logistics. You both should find something else to do for now. Tomorrow, Aaron, we start."

~~~   ~~~~ ~~~~

Dancer brought Aaron a tray with a thermos of French roast coffee and a plate of bear claws. She had purchased them earlier at a bakery near the Last Hope. They were another of Bob's favorites, filled with extra almond paste and dripping with melted butter. Dancer smiled as she handed the plate and cup to him. "Didn't know if you like cream, so I added a touch. I can get you more or make you another cup," she offered.

"Wow. No, this will be just fine, Dancer, thank you."

"Come on, kid, we need to get into the cave or we'll miss the big show. Bobby is a very early riser. In fact, I don't think he ever really sleeps. Get dressed and I'll wait for you in the living room."

Dancer had nailed it. Bob had been up all night and Pandora was running as well, generating the familiar hum. As Aaron and Dancer approached Bob, she held up the tray with the bear claws and coffee so that Bob could see and smell them. His head abruptly swung around in search of the source of the delicious smell.

"Oh, yes, thank you, Dancer. Thank you," Bob responded, excited as a child at Christmas. He twisted back and forth in his chair, unable to grab for both the cup and plate with the book in one hand. Dancer, seeing his dilemma, rescued him by placing the tray on a small side table. She knew Bob would blow a fuse if anyone were to put a drink or food on the table where his keyboard sat. "There ya go, Bobby boy."

Bob was so eager to partake of the pastry, his favorite treat of all time, that he missed Dancer calling him Bobby, which made her smile.

While Bob greedily dug into the bear claw, Aaron spoke up. "I was awake most of the night thinking about all of this. Bob, you said everything is code, like computer language? Our reality, even though it seems real, is actually a sophisticated, multidimensional, holographic illusion. Your Godscript is the ultimate video game of which we are participants, correct?"

Bob wiped his mouth and responded, "Yes, that is it exactly. You see, it took even me a long time to believe this. I knew that if we looked long enough, we would stop seeing smaller and smaller particles that were the building blocks of our reality and discover a pattern that could only be described as an intelligently designed code. It was in front of my face my whole life and I could not see it. But I found it." Bob stood up, bear claw in one hand, the book in the other, and started pacing.

Aaron and Dancer looked at each other, knowing what was coming.

"I was watching a stupid video posting, something I really never do. Never," he repeated to emphasize the statement. "I was looking for something entirely different when I stumbled across it. Looking back, I feel stupid that I watched it as long as I did. Go ahead and laugh now, but it was a unicorn, a stupid cartoon unicorn dancing around singing some obnoxious childish song, and rainbows were streaming off his back, looking more like they were coming out of his butt," Bob said with an extra undignified emphasis on the *T*. "I finally had enough and hit pause. Then the miracle, as providence often does, upended my thinking. For suddenly, in front of me, I saw the most basic principle of Astral Physics. Magically appearing before my eyes were black lines, spaces in between the individual colors—the black line patterns that are the spectral signature of everything. I know this, every physicist knows this; it is the signature of what powers the electrons orbiting an atom's nucleus. But I had never looked at it in this way. For the first time, I saw what it really was, a pattern, the one I had been searching for my entire life. There in that stupid cartoon was the answer. The code, the script, the Godscript, it was in the light. It was so obvious, light is the delivery system of the code. It tells the processors in our brain how the atoms and their electrons are to behave. The light creates the reality not by shining on an object but by feeding our processors what our reality looks like, feels like, smells like." He pounded the book on his thigh and waved his other hand, holding what was left of his bear claw in the air like a Greek dancer.

Aaron uttered a "Whoa," under his breath as he understood! Bob had almost sat down, his muscles already flexing to access the chair below and behind him, when suddenly, as if he'd sat on a tack, he shot straight up, even more excited than before. "Oh! Oh! Oh, do you know what else? I do!" Bob said excitedly but stopped to grab another bear claw and take a huge bite.

Dancer and Aaron, both laughing, waited for him to finish chewing. "Has either of you heard of the double-slit experiment?"

Dancer looked over at Aaron holding a finger to her lips. She'd learned long ago it was best to just see where Bob was going with his thoughts. Aaron nodded, understanding. As long as he could save Cynthia, he was all ears.

Bob took another bite, and mumbling something, continued, "It is the experiment done many years ago where they shoot a stream of electrons through a double slit. When not observed, that is, no one is looking, the electrons act as particles and waves simultaneously. However, and this is the beauty, the mystery of this great experiment, when a source of observation, a measuring device or camera is applied, the electrons act as individual particles only. I now know why the electrons act differently! When we fixate on something, I now realize it is light that is directing the scene. Therefore, the electrons suddenly become fixed because they have passed through what I call the IQRES field or Infinite Quantum Realities Existing Simultaneously. They become locked into the observer's memory, into their past. We literally have taken a quantum photograph. It is quantum reality real-time." Bob turned and deliberately fell into his chair with a loud flop.

"It is not a theory or an answer. No, it is, in fact, proof of IQRES and the Godscript. The double-slit experiment verifies that there are infinite quantum possibilities for us to choose from. The IQRES is that portion of the script not yet looked at. As soon as we look at any portion of the script in front of us, it becomes reality in the form of our past, our memory. It's actually quite brilliant."

Aaron jumped in. "Gee, imagine that, something written by God being brilliant." Aaron bent over in a mock laugh, slapping his knee, then straightened up, still smiling. "Sorry."

Bob let out a rare smile, then continued, "Many years ago, I was playing with an idea, experimenting with various filters while using the electron microscope at Lawrence in Berkeley. It was, at the time, the most powerful microscope on Earth. Mind you, obtaining time on it was highly sought after and was carefully regulated. I was fortunate enough to be working on another project that required I use the scope with a specific set of parameters. And, quite unable to help myself, I entered a defined parameter of my own, making for an experiment. Upon setting things up, I immediately noticed a pattern consisting of light globules repeating in a *four-four-four* sequence. The light, while being bent, actually slowed enough to allow a distinct change in the visibility while viewed through the series of filters I had chosen. Each globule consisted of a series of three smaller groups with four of the round glowing orbs. There it was, the pattern I had been looking for, the proof of the code, of the Godscript. The light was the conduit by which the code was being delivered." Bob gestured like Moses parting the Red Sea, with his hands in the air doing his best to look all Alpha and Omega-like.

"So, what happened? How come it never came to light, was never published?" Aaron asked.

"An interesting point you bring up, Aaron. You see, it was about that time my personal experiments required I leave the employment of Lawrence Livermore National Laboratory. As I explained earlier, it seemed we no longer saw eye to eye on the procurement of resources for pursuing my work at home."

"Bob, just admit it, you stole their shit," Aaron stated. "You dog." He laughed. "And now, we have your friend Nate and his goons chasing after you, after us."

"My mind is a great resource for this world. They were obligated to let me have that equipment, so I could further pursue my revolutionary ideas. It would have been of the greatest benefit to them. They did not recognize it, so I left. Then with the onset of the Eight-Year War, it all worked to my advantage. They no longer had the time or resources to chase after me. I simply was not important enough. So I disappeared. I wrote over my own chip, giving myself this new life. But Nate! Nathaniel Brewster, he is one pit bull of a detective. He just will not let go. It became personal for him. And though he and I have never met face-to-face, I will be the first to admit the man is good. Every time I think I have sent him chasing down the wrong alley and lost him, he pops up again. As your inadvertent arrival here has done. You set off all of his alarm bells."

Aaron resisted reminding Bob that his arrival was Bob's doing in the first place.

"I do miss that microscope." Bob sighed. "But, I have compensated using software that I wrote to mimic the code based on what I saw and learned. I have drilled many layers deeper. What I find astonishing is that with every layer, it just keeps holding to the *four-four-four* pattern. The depth of the code and its intricacy are infinite. Which, of course, one would have to expect from a code capable of generating reality."

Bob grabbed his pad and wrote on it. Then he turned it so Aaron could see what he had drawn: three groups of four dots. "Obviously, it looks different than this. It is always a series of what, for lack of a better word, are dots. Always in groupings of three sets of four dots. Imagine it like folders on a computer," he said as he turned the pad around so he could draw again. "The next layer, inside a four-dot grouping, looks like this." He turned the pad once more for Aaron to see. Under the first group of three sets of four dots was a new series of three sets of four dots. "These, I have discovered, are the descriptions of an individual object in terms of height, width, depth, mass and color—what it looks like."

Bob paused to take a breath and ponder his next statement. "What I surmise is these are all some form of three-dimensional layers that allow individual autonomy for each object, so it can operate without necessarily having to interact with another object. It repeats infinitely, defining things smaller than the overall object itself, like a cell being a part of the body, for example." Bob paused. His breathing and Pandora's hum were the only sounds.

"After several days of looking at what seemed like endless layers of dots in every possible configuration, I noticed a pattern. Except, and you know it could only be through my keen eye and perseverance that I found this—yes, of course, you know this."

Aaron's head dropped as he bit his knuckle, thinking, *Let it go, he's a genius. It's what geniuses do. He is saving Cynthia.*

"You see, between the repeating, identical patterns, I discovered an empty space. Millions and millions of dots and in the same repeating sets of unique patterns and suddenly an anomaly." He stopped to draw another series of dots: one, two, blank, three, four, space, one, two, three, four, and space, one, two, three, blank. "What this meant was quite simple. I had proof this was indeed a script. Something obviously written, not just an accidental pattern born out of the random luck of chaos. No. No, it is a script. We are a script. Do you understand? No accident, this was written!" Bob looked at Aaron and Dancer. "I have no doubt as I get deeper into the code, drill down far enough, I will find the very signature of the author or authors."

"Bob," Aaron said with a bit of a smirk, "you're scaring me. You're starting to make sense."

But before he could continue, Bob jumped in, "No, Aaron, my brilliance is as unique as the universe itself. I know it, you know it, Dancer knows it. No one as yet has made sense of what I know. If they did, they would be as smart as me. And no one else is."

"Well, actually, Bob, I think you are a bit over the top right now ego-wise." Aaron laughed. "You see, I merely wanted to draw a similarity to a funny thought that occurred to me."

"I am sorry, Aaron. I am sure you have good ideas too."

Aaron's shoulders and head dropped. Lightly shaking his head back and forth, he had to laugh to himself. *How the fuck can he be so brilliant and so incapable of communication?* "Bob, you are the master of the wet blanket. What I was trying to say was, it occurred to me that what you have discovered, what you are now playing with, is the same thing they used to do back in my time, well, yours too, back in the '70s into the '90s. There was that television show called *Star Trek*. You have to remember it. They had the ability to transport people or things wherever they desired. At the time, we all thought they were talking about dematerializing someone at the atomic level and then reassembling them where they were transported to. But you, you're doing exactly that. You did it with me. You have moved me on the digital code level from one place to another. I was going to tell you, Bob, you are a certifiable, one-of-a-kind genius."

"Yes. Yes, as I was saying," Bob continued, and Aaron smiled, looking down and biting his knuckle again so he wouldn't laugh.

~~~   ~~~~ ~~~~

Try as he might, be it the dry air, the horrific dreams, the anxiety of all that he had gone through in one big ugly collaboration of unsolicited events, Aaron simply could not sleep. He lay awake all night, in between nightmares and thinking about the myriad of things that could go wrong trying to duplicate what Bob had accidently done to him. He was scared to death Cynthia would be maimed or killed. Bob's words kept echoing through his mind: *She is already dead.*

He finally gave up and sat on the edge of the bed listening to the silence. He thought that before heading down into the Cave, he might go for a walk, explore his new surroundings a bit more. Maybe the brisk morning air and watching the sunrise over the mesa would help alleviate some of the anxiety.

Aaron headed through the kitchen, slowing to inhale the glorious aroma of freshly-made coffee. A smell that meant Dancer was about. Dancer had become his safe haven, his rock through this nightmare.

But at this moment, Aaron wanted to be alone, to not have to talk to anyone, not Bob, not Dancer, not Miko. He just wanted to escape outside and attempt to regain some of himself, his old self. He needed to take back some degree of control of his life and come up with a plan that didn't just depend on Dancer or Bob. He knew he needed to make a plan as to what he and Cynthia would do once she was safely here. And, as much as he did not want to consider it, he needed to make contingency plans in the event Bob was unable to bring Cynthia here. He shuddered thinking about it. *Maybe I should seek outside help? Talk to the cops? Hmm, no, bad idea.* Aaron gently opened and closed the rear screen door hoping not to alert Dancer.

It was still cool outside, and he stood for a moment, taking in the brilliant orange overpowering the mesa. In the distance were long, salmon-colored clouds giving way to white before fading into the coming blue of the morning sky. He took several deep breaths and, for the shortest of moments, found peace, filled with hope he might once again see Cynthia. Short-lived, the peace quickly gave way to anxiety. He headed up the trail behind the house, quickening his pace with each step as if he could outrun the turmoil in his mind.

He had traveled nearly a mile as the trail switched back and forth, quickly gaining elevation heading toward the top of the mesa. He stopped for a moment before a steep, sharp turn in the trail that would take him above a small gathering of Joshua trees. Looking around, he felt some semblance of serenity brought on by endorphins from the exertion. He scanned the entire horizon. It was easy to be positively distracted amidst such beauty.

Breathing heavy, he continued stepping up to make the turn. The steepness of the trail made him turn his gaze from the horizon to the steps he needed to take. As he did, he found himself staring at a startling vision directly in front of him. There, not ten feet in front of him, sitting on a wide flat rock that overlooked the lower mesa floor and valley below, where Aaron had just scanned and found such incredible beauty, sat Bob. Bob, in the cool morning air and completely au natural. His hair was neatly pulled back in a ponytail, and his eyes were closed as he sat in a yoga position with legs crossed and his feet neatly tucked in. He sat quietly with perfectly straight posture, hands in front and palms out. The book was balanced in his outstretched left hand.

Aaron stood staring not so much at the naked man in front of him, who for his age appeared to be in phenomenal physical condition, but at Bob's tumescent member. Bob just sat, humming a steady mantra, eyes closed.

Not moving so much as a muscle, he spoke. "Aaron, you have found my sanctuary. Welcome."

Faced with yet another unwelcome and unsolicited surprise, Aaron tried to catch his breath to speak. "Yeah, um, hi, Bob," Aaron stammered, not knowing quite what to say or how to act, but finally turning his gaze upward to meet Bob's now open, blue eyes.

Before he could get another word out, Bob started talking as if he had been standing there all morning. "Maybe you have noticed"—Aaron was sure he was about to say *my erection,* but didn't, leaving Aaron able to breathe a small sigh of relief—"but I am a bit on the introverted side. It is because my mind is always going at the speed of light, covering many diverse topics simultaneously."

Aaron let out a snort at this understatement. *A bit of an introvert,* he thought, still keeping his eyes on Bob, and laughed to himself.

Bob continued, "I am driven by an internal inquietude I cannot define. But it does just that. It drives me, it exhilarates me, excites me. I have had many professional people over the years try to tell me my many problems, but I know my mind, the way I think. It is a blessing that allows me to understand more than they will ever be able to comprehend. I see things and understand things that no one else does."

Aaron stood there thinking to himself, *I'm listening to an insanely brilliant naked man with a hard-on, sitting on a rock, in my future, and, for some odd reason, I'm not running around screaming for help.* Aaron knew he was a victim of circumstances that, at the moment, were beyond his control. But at this, he took a breath. "Bob, stop! Just stop. What the hell are you doing out here? The cops are watching us. And, ah, I gotta leave. I—I—I can't stand here and pretend to talk to you normally. Not in front of you, all naked and shit like that," he said, waving his right hand in a circle, outstretched towards Bob. "What are you out here doing, some kind of Tantra? What the hell? Please get dressed or pull a towel over yourself. No, never mind, I'm just going back to the house."

Aaron stopped talking, dropping his hands to his sides in exasperation and surrender. "I just can't do this." He turned to walk away.

"Aaron, please, do not run off just yet. I apologize if my personal self-confidence overwhelms you. It does many. It is not as you would think. I have the ability to sit here and meditate, visualizing a licentious experience on a metaphysical level, without the need to touch."

"Yeah, that really just falls into the *too much information* category," Aaron protested with a grimace.

Unable to understand Aaron's apparent prudish behavior, Bob continued, "Aaron, I am not pleasuring myself as you might suggest. It is through my meditation I am able to release a cocktail of chemicals in my brain: norepinephrine, serotonin, oxytocin, vasopressin and—"

"I don't care what you release—" Aaron covered his face. "Oh God, did I just say that?"

Missing the unintentional innuendo, Bob continued, "—nitric oxide. It is a wonderful way to remove all the stress and anxiety from my body and mind. It is the body's perfectly natural sedative. I have always been very comfortable being naked around others, whether those with me were naked or not." As he spoke, he rose slightly, enough to pull out the towel from underneath himself to use as a cover. "There, that will put your modesty more at ease, yes? No one knows I am out here. And, I have another way to get in and out of the Cave. It is well hidden. We are far enough away from the house, and no one would look for me here in my Shangri-La."

Aaron turned back to face him, relieved to see him now partially covered with a towel, though it now looked more like a circus tent.

Bob readjusted and continued, "You asked earlier what I was trying to accomplish by contacting myself back when you decided to drive into the middle of Pandora's sphere of influence. The unforeseen act that inadvertently brought you here. You see, as I said, I wanted to send myself a message, using Morse Code via the skinny wormhole I created with Pandora. I know you will not understand this, as only I can really grasp it. Even Einstein, who predicted it, had difficulty as he felt them to be unstable. I, on the other hand, with, I admit, some help from the studies of the legendary Kip Thorne regarding Casimir Energy, successfully predicted—and obviously implemented—a hole, a skinny wormhole, that could be held open long enough to transmit fluctuations of radiation in the form of Morse Code. At the other end, I in my Volkswagen, and you in yours apparently, picked it up as static. And I did hear it. I so clearly remember being completely astonished I had to pull over to write it down, so I could decipher it. Which is when you, well, your script became attached into the retreating Wormhole. I didn't even see you disappear."

"What message did you send?"

"I did not get the entire message at the time. I could only make out, *It's me, you, in the...* I, of course, thought it to be some sort of practical joke. I headed back out onto the road on my way to a new life here. How funny, do you not think? If you figure, based on our ages at that moment, you beat me here, but I arrived here first." Bob stopped talking long enough to adjust his position on the rock. The sun, now much higher in the morning sky, made the area much warmer, and sweat started to roll down his forehead. He wiped his head with a small towel and laid it back down. "It is now too warm out here."

Aaron pondered the last part of that statement: *I beat him here, but he was here first.* He understood Bob's riddle; it made sense.

"As you have so effectively interrupted my seeking solitude, and as you have pointed out there are eyes about seeking my whereabouts, let us head back to the Cave. Follow me, I will show you one of my secret entrances."

~~~   ~~~~ ~~~~

After being up all night working, Bob finally succumbed to sleep. The video monitors on the wall, where Miko so often communicated, were programed by default to match the outside time and weather. A nice touch of Bob's that made the interior of the Cave a little more comfortable. With the faux morning light streaming in, and Bob out cold in his chair, Aaron, who had ventured down to check on Bob's progress and found him fast asleep, couldn't help but notice Bob's book lying on his lap. His hand was completely off, exposing the entire cover. It gave him his first real chance to look closely.

It was simple, yet complex, made from dark, burnt umber leather, smooth with a slight goosebump texture to it. There were no designs or embossing, having only one line of heavy thread stitching around the edges. Very well worn from years of his carrying it at all times and bouncing it off his leg, it was still in remarkably good condition. The leather was stained darker where the palm and fingers of his hand almost always held the precious journal. A small book, it couldn't have been more than about six inches tall and maybe five inches wide. Aaron looked but was unable to ascertain how many pages there were, glancing at the stained edges of ivory-colored paper. The complexity was in the binding and latching. The hemmed leather cover wrapped all the way around and back so that it covered half of itself again on the front. There was also a one-inch-wide strap that slid through a latch of leather cut into the front cover, sealing it closed.

Aaron wanted so badly to be able to look inside, but Bob was asleep, and to touch that book would be a breach of trust and surely bring the wrath of an awakened dragon. As Aaron turned to sit and wait for Bob to wake up, he inadvertently hit Bob's chair with his foot.

"Wha—What? No, I am not sleeping. Oh, Aaron, it is you," Bob said. He rubbed his eyes with his one free hand as the other instinctively found its rightful place on the book.

"Good morning, y'all," Dancer announced, her smile bright even this early in the morning and holding what seemed to be a perpetual tray of coffee in her hands.

"Oh my, yes, I can use some coffee, with extra caffeine would be nice. No treats?" Bob asked, looking a bit dejected.

"Bob. Sorry love, not today, unless you want some 3D donuts!" she responded.

"Cardboard donuts, I think not," Bob responded. "I spent last evening working on some very deep details," Bob said as he reached for some coffee, "mapping the portion of the code I believe contain the beer bottle on the table outside on the porch. But, before I start this experiment—" Aaron cut him off so quickly, Bob, still reaching for his coffee, drew his arm back.

"Bob, how do you access this script? I mean, where is it? You can't just plug a monitor into the air so that you can then cut and paste. Or can you?" Aaron asked, becoming far more invested, wanting to understand and know more.

"Aaron," Bob smiled in an uncharacteristically fatherly way. "Aaron, what you have not yet come to realize is what is

149

the most fantastic part of my discovery. I find it actually beautiful in its simplicity for being able to organize such an incredible and vast array of information. We are all accessing, reading from and writing to the script as we speak. Everything you have ever done is permanently recorded by you onto the portion of the Godscript that defines you. Your folder, if you will." He stopped to see if they were following, then went on. "The beauty is how the information, though totally unique to each one of us, is all linked together."

"Sounds like the Internet!" Aaron nodded.

"Yes, yes, Aaron, that is a very good, very archaic, but still a very good analogy. It is, however, at the same time, a bit like comparing a grain of sand to the entire beach. The Godscript is data collected and connected in depths even I cannot as yet fathom. The three of us standing here, communicating with each other, is proof of its existence and magnificence." Bob finished and looked up toward the ceiling with a smug smile.

"That still doesn't answer my question. How do we, no make that, how do you access the code to actually touch it, affect it? I mean, I am pretty sure you don't go up to sit on your rock in a yoga position, God forbid, and mentally access it. So how?" Aaron asked with both sarcasm and concern.

Dancer, standing there quietly and listening the entire time, was thinking to herself, *yoga, rock?*

"How can you be exact enough to know where Cynthia will be in relation to where she is now in both time and space at the moment you throw the switch? How the hell can you figure that out? I assume you are counting on my telling you Cynthia is a creature of habit, and I know where she always is at that same time every moment since I have known her. Well, I don't. So how can you?"

Bob glanced down, then looked up from the computer screen. He calmly, almost nonchalantly spoke. "Aaron, it is like this—"

Anxious, Aaron yet again stopped Bob. "Bob, please. Experience has taught me if I ask you what time it is, you are going to tell me how to build the mother fucking clock. I can't even begin to imagine what you are going to explain now. But I know damn well it is going to take longer than either of us have. I need to know the short and quick of it."

Bob let loose a big smile. "Fair enough, Aaron. Fair enough." He slowly turned back, glancing down toward the screen. Then he rotated, standing up straight, and pointed the book toward Aaron. "Just let me say—and I will be quick; I do not want to bore you with my explanations and ideas. Heaven forbid, I explain anything in detail so that you might grasp and understand it," he said with a hint of aggravation. But he quickly switched back to his self-absorbed nature, talking more to hear himself. "It is not about time and position. There is no time or position outside the reality of the code we are in. They do not exist. Rather, it is more like turning the pages of a book, searching back through the script to the point that chronicles that moment—such as your Cynthia's location. Then I use my IQRES software, positioning the Now Membrane on the page I want, and then is, well, then is now. Where will Cynthia be exactly? As we do not possess a crystal ball, I, we, will have to use our best-educated guess. There, I explained that very well, didn't I? And quite quickly, I might add. Quick enough for you, Aaron?" Bob smirked, reeking of sarcasm.

Aaron was not entirely pleased with the simplicity of his explanation, as it did not quell his fear. He still wanted to know more, to understand where and how Bob connected so he could access the code. Seeing he was not going to get further, he nodded questioningly. "Thank you, Bob, that does sort of help, I guess. And thanks for being honest."

"I cannot read the script yet. I only know it is there. It is in the light, the patterns, the endless repeating *four-four-four* patterns in the light. Pandora sees the patterns, but I am still working on the software that will allow Pandora's computer to show the pattern's hierarchy. Actually, it is when Pandora comes up to speed, very, very close to the speed of light—"

"Lightspeed? You are talking about time dilation, that stuff, and you are going to lose me here. This is way out of my pay scale. Can't wrap my brain around it," Aaron stated, shaking his head.

Bob took a sip of coffee, which Dancer had placed next to him, then went on. "Aaron, you are not alone. The greatest minds have struggled with the concept since Albert proposed his Theory of Relativity. Not me, of course. I understand it with all of its subtle implications. I think I have complicated matters for you proposing that light is the perception of reality. That is, well, that it is the conductor of the code, the delivery system for the Godscript." Bob was in his comfort zone, where he felt admired when asked to play the role of teacher. He had a much softer than normal demeanor, talking slower, more deliberate and concise, warmly like a father to his son. "Light, a force, an energy with a constant speed of six hundred and seventy-one million miles per hour, is the measure of our reality. Think of it this way. You are trying to get on a freeway behind someone who is scared to death of the fast-moving cars. As they approach the on-ramp, they slow and almost come to a complete stop. They are scared. They watch in horror the horde of cars whizzing by at eighty miles per hour. You behind them, you can scream, swear and flip the finger at them, but it matters not. All that driver sees is that there is no hope of mixing with what appears to be a solid blurred line of color. But you and I know if you accelerate in the transition lane and approach the speed of the cars on the freeway, something magical happens. They stop whizzing by. They become individual cars, with individual colors and shapes that, relative to you, are not moving fast at all. It is where you came from that has changed. From your new vantage point, the stationary objects to the sides of the freeway, buildings, trees, and people are now the blurred, solid line of color that appears to be moving extremely fast in the other direction. You have virtually crossed from one reality to another. Now my young friend, apply this to light. Once you reach the speed of light, when you are traveling at six hundred and seventy-one million miles per hour, the photons themselves will become individual elements that have stopped in relation to you. They will no longer define by reflection of shape the world you came from. And the world you were in is now the solid blur of color whizzing by you in the opposite direction." Bob at this point actually giggled, smiling with great satisfaction at his explanation.

Aaron, too, smiled, then asked, "That was awesome, Bob. But, not to rush you or anything, but can we get back to saving Cynthia?"

"This is all about saving your Cynthia. You see, I do not yet understand fully how only your code was cut from the script and brought here. I do not yet understand why when your code was added back into the script further along its timeline, you weren't suddenly driving on roads that no longer existed since the war. Why you landed on a road at all just outside of town is a mystery to me. But I will figure it out, I will not only understand, but I will be able to reproduce the events and elements so that we can first experiment bringing non-life forms from the past to the present.

"I will employ the oldest and greatest method for invention known to man: trial and error. However, Aaron, right now I do not have the answers you want to hear. I know what parameters I set up when I was trying to communicate with myself. I know exactly what occurred when Pandora's power shut down, and I know exactly how long it took before she came back online. I also know when the data package—you—dropped. But that is all I know.

"Today, I will recreate the Shakespearian play that brought you, Aaron, to us. But I will do so with a new script that is deliberate, not accidental." Bob squirmed, reluctant to admit he was not in absolute control. "I will use my best guess as to what portion of the *four-four-four* pattern holds the code for an area that encompasses about the size of the table the beer sits on. I will, of course, need to use the broad stroke of the brush, as I do not yet know exactly which folders delineate only the table and beer. Time will be based on the speed of the collider. Obviously, we do not need to go far back, just to four-thirty yesterday afternoon, precisely when there was a cold beer sitting on the table."

Bob tapped his chin with his book, a sure sign he was in deep thought. "Right now, I must work on the premise that when Pandora comes back online is when she drops the packet of data, and that is based on speed and the distance between where the packet originated from and here. Beyond that is exactly why I am experimenting, yes? Shall we get on with it then?"

Dancer spoke up, "I would offer to go make some food, but I don't know, I don't think I want to miss this. Somehow, the thought of seeing history happen in front of my eyes is pretty enticing. And I'm glad you decided to start with the simpler test of replacing the old open bottle with the unopened cold one. You know, see if it works first." She smiled, knowing it would ruffle a feather.

"If! You doubt for one second that I am capable of bringing Cynthia here, to now?" Bob retorted. "I give you Aaron as proof I can and have done this."

"Ah, last time I checked, Bobby, Aaron here was an accident."

Bob started to say something but stopped, slouching a little when he did. Then, straightening himself up, he protested, "Some of the greatest discoveries ever made were accidents. It is my ability to recognize the potential and be intelligent enough to capitalize on it that will make history." He crossed his arms with the book firmly in one hand, finishing with a light snort to make his point.

This shocked Dancer, who was not expecting him to take it so hard. "Bob, I'm sorry. I really mean that. I did not mean for you to take offense. I was just poking fun at you. You know damn well how much respect I have for you. Your intelligence and your ability to create anything you set your mind to are beyond reproach. I love you for that. Don't be mad, please." She finished, giving Bob her best big-eyed puppy face.

Bob cared more for Dancer then any human being he had ever met. She was the only person in his life whom he actually listened to, though she was most likely not aware to the degree that he did. He looked at her eyes and melted. "Okay, but do not call me Bobby."

No sooner did the words leave his lips than Miko's voice interrupted them. "Bobby, I have a first alert warning. There are three ground vehicles headed toward the house. They are seven minutes out."

Dancer and Aaron, who had at first started to laugh at the timing of Miko saying 'Bobby,' quickly changed gears. Dancer, without a second thought, took charge. "Bob, park it where you are, lights out, no noise. Aaron, you and I need to get in the house and slip into our bored, there-is-nothing-to-do-around-here look. Actually, when we get inside, you just sit on the couch, find a book to read, or no, wait. Miko, turn on some sports on the living room monitor. I will start preparing some food. Let's go!"

"As you wish, Dancer, is golf okay?"

"Perfect. Let's do this."

"Wait, Dancer," Bob protested. "I want them to wander around the property without talking to anyone. Follow me, we need to go back into an area of the cave where their scanners will not be able to pick up our life signs."

"Scanners? They have scanners, like Tricorders?" asked Aaron.

"Yes, they do. It's more like a Bicorder, a motion and infrared heat detector. They are only good through rock to a depth of about two feet. I know this, of course, because I am the one who worked out the original algorithms and designs. But here, we are below them, and they will be scanning horizontally. We must be still and quiet. We can talk, but quietly."

"What about our cars?" quizzed Dancer, miffed that Bob had taken charge and changed her plan.

"You could be out hiking," said Bob.

"Yeah, well, we know you do," chided Aaron. Dancer glanced at him quizzically, recognizing the sarcasm in his voice but not the meaning.

Bob walked over to his computer desk as he motioned for Dancer and Aaron to sit down, pointing to one of the older dining room table chairs set against the wall. "Obviously, if we sit, there will be less chance of us making a mistake like tripping or knocking something over, which I admit, I do often. A loud sound would create vibrations they can detect. This man is very good at what he does. He does not give up or let up. But I am better." Bob turned to the computer and, quickly using his unoccupied right hand, made a few keystrokes, putting Pandora in rest mode. Then he looked toward Aaron and held up a finger to his lips. "Shhhh."

They sat in the near dark with only the lights from Pandora and the computer screen lighting the room. The screen showed several different surveillance camera angles of the outside and inside of Bob's house. The third camera showed movement, and Bob recognized Nate as he stared almost directly into the camera. He and two officers turned and left the front area heading around the side.

All three sat motionless in the dark and silence.

"Reminds me of the Sensory Deprivation Rooms back in San Francisco," whispered Dancer. "We just need some incense."

They sat for nearly fifteen minutes, watching the movements of Nate and the other officers search in vain, trying all the doors, staring in all the windows, before Bob quietly spoke up.

"I knew it. I knew Nate would return here today. They will continue looking outside for a bit longer, and then I am quite sure they will cut the lock off my gate and will follow the old road up to the garage. I put that gate there on purpose, to lead those away from the house. A locked gate is just too inviting. They will find interesting artifacts, garbage of mine, get bored and leave. You watch, I know this."

"What are you, a psychic, too?" Aaron whispered.

"Psychics and prophets are not feasible," Bob quickly replied. "They are charlatans seeking only to relieve a fool from his money and his pride."

"I only meant, how could you know the cops would come out here today?" Aaron asked, leaning forward and whispering. "I am with you, Bob. I think the psychics and prophets thing is bullshit."

"No, Aaron, not bullshit. Ninety-eight percent of them are wackos and crooks. However, as is with everything in this universe, there is always an element of truth. In this case, a truth misaligned thousands of years ago. But there is no question there is a handful of those that know something. They are privileged to something the rest of us cannot see. In fact, they are one of the greatest sources of proof I have for the Godscript."

"How the hell is that?" Aaron asked in a normal voice.

Bob and Dancer responded with a collective, "Shhh!"

"I told you of the time I spent with the Unity of the Heavens family at their compound. The Elders required I read the Old and New Testament many times. Then and now, I found those portions about the prophets quite interesting. Especially in Revelations when the End Times were predicted. Let us assume for a moment that they were indeed prophets who could see the future. Thing is, if they could see exactly what happened in the future, then the entire religious concept of man having free will is baloney. How can you have free will if the future is predetermined? I pondered this question whenever I read from the scripture. What intrigued me was a developing theme of the religious prophets who were close with their prophecies. They could hit on the basic occurrence, but none seemed to have ever nailed it right on the head. The only plausible explanation was that our reality has to be part of a prewritten script that has infinite possible individual choices written into it to satisfy the quantum rules and thus the outcome." Bob paused to watch this realization sink into his fledgling prodigy. "It must have a basic storyline that we can all exist in, not knowing our individual outcomes even though the basic premise will not change and is, well, written in stone."

"Let me simplify this for you," Bob said, pretending as if he were holding a controller and playing a video game. "Imagine you pull up a chair to sit down and play a hypothetical child's video game. It is easy, and you play it a few times until you get the hang of it. Now, before you start the next game, I want you to tell me exactly how the game will end. You cannot, can you? You do not know if your skill, even on this easy game, will get you past all of the challenges and obstacles the same way each time. Your individual outcome, live or die and how you achieve it, will be different every game. Especially when you play it for the first time. Now, tell me about the basic storyline of the game. This. This you can do. You can tell me what it looks like, what to expect, what the future looks like, but you cannot see the outcome. You have to participate in it. You are suddenly a prophet."

"A bit like driving to the same job, day in and day out, to the same office, same stuff, just a different day. You can tell others exactly what your day will look like and how it will unfold with great accuracy, but you can be surprised when something new happens. Yes?" Dancer asked.

"I was thinking something very similar, Dancer. And Bob, the comparison to a video game, that really helps me visualize what you're talking about. Wow," Aaron said.

"Indeed, both of you, indeed. Now consider what you have just said. But as you roll those little tidbits of possibilities around in your mind, fitting them together like so many puzzle pieces, think in terms of the computer geeks or nerds who might have written such a script. Consider that they would be a hundred thousand years more advanced than us, maybe millions." Bob was only adding to the ether in the room. Dancer and Aaron were both riveted, wanting to hear more.

Bob went in for the close. "Now, our prophet would have to be privy to a similar scenario. He or she would have to be aware of the script and its general purpose and destination. That is to say, they could say with great certainty when certain events would occur as they would be hard-written in the script, while not being able to predict in any way the outcome for any one individual. I do not believe they were prophets or psychics. I think they were intelligent life forms interacting with us, teaching us, molding us. Intelligent beings, aliens, if you will, who would have to be aware of the Godscript to prophesize!" Bob finished wearing a very satisfied look.

Miko broke the spell, "The officers have returned to their vehicles and are departing the property."

~ ~~ ~~~~ ~~~

Another night, hammering out his calculations till the sun's rays filtered in from the video monitors. Bob sat sipping coffee he had Miko make for him. He was ready, like a college professor, waiting to talk to his students.

"Before I try this, let me, in the simplest terms, explain what I am going to do." Bob stopped and took a sip of the coffee after lightly blowing the rising steam off the surface. Dancer and

Aaron looked at each other, knowing no such thing as simple existed in Bob's toolbox.

"Bob, simple would be a refreshing change," teased Dancer, smiling at Aaron.

Bob continued to watch the steam rising from his coffee, his mind subconsciously looking for patterns. Unaffected or unaware of Dancer's statement, he went on. "I know you are both incapable of seeing all that I see. I can see so much of the construct of the universe, even I cannot consolidate it all into one working theory. Einstein's Unified Field Theory is mere fodder for children's books in comparison to what is really going on. But today, let us concentrate on simple. Simple, like how to lock on to the table and bottle's script, cut it and then paste it into now. Basically overwriting the existing script with what I bring forward from the past, the full, cold bottle of beer."

"Yeah, well, don't miss. We don't want it to materialize in the middle of a tree. Or worse, one of us," Aaron said, realizing as he spoke the disturbing significance of his statement.

"Yes, that would be bad. I will try to avoid that. I have broken the code. That is, I have drilled down into the *four-four-four* folders far enough. I now know where the front porch is. I am setting my coordinates as a small sphere or net, if you will, of the area within those packets. I will direct the collider to focus on that area when I know the bottle was sitting on the table full of cold beer. Pandora will, at the moment I have set it to, run a hard shutdown and reboot, matching what happened the night I inadvertently brought you here."

"Yeah, did I thank you for that enough today, Bob?" Aaron joked.

Bob shot a stern, piercing look at Aaron. "You would be dead now had I not. Your petty emotions aside, I have decided to keep the first test even simpler. I am not going to move the table. I set the restart to focus on exactly the same place so that when it does bring the code forward, it should hypothetically write over the old code, and there will be a full bottle of cold beer where now is a warm, empty bottle. Yes?" Bob asked, looking at both Dancer and Aaron. "Any questions?"

Both Dancer and Aaron silently shook their heads. But as Aaron thought about it, he considered what this meant in terms of Cynthia. "I can only guess what all that means. But, if it will bring us closer to bringing Cynthia here alive—do it!"

As Bob turned to the computer keyboard to start the sequence, both Dancer and Aaron instinctively took two steps back as if that might help in some way should something go awry. Bob bent over the keyboard, glanced at the two of them, and then confidently pushed the return key. Dancer and Aaron took another step back, which made Bob smile. The hum of the collider picked up in intensity, and they could feel the acceleration as Pandora came up to speed.

"It will take about ten minutes to the hard shutdown sequence," Bob said.

The Cave's lighting dimmed slightly as arcs of blue light rode the static in the air, produced by the acceleration of radiation through the collider. They leapt off points of the collider, hitting the cave wall.

"Fifteen, fourteen, thirteen, twelve, eleven, ten." Bob glanced wide-eyed and smiling at them, like a child playing with his chemistry set's Bunsen burner. "Nine, eight..." At this point, both Dancer and Aaron joined in the countdown, "Seven, six, five, four, three, two, one..." in unison. As they all said *one*, the lights went out, followed by a screaming, screeching sound that made the entire cave shake. Then, with one lurch that nearly knocked all of them down, it stopped. In less than a millisecond, the lights came back on and Pandora started her windup again.

"Come on, come on," Bob said excitedly. "Let's go look." Bob pushed away from his chair, still looking like the wide-eyed child but filled with intrepidness.

They all scrambled toward the door but found themselves stacking up against each other as Miko, not matching their excitement, methodically went through the motions of unlocking it. Finally in the house, the three continued to bump into each other like Keystone Cops trying to get to the front door. Reaching the door at the same moment, Dancer put up her hand. "Stop. This is Bob's doing, his genius at work. It is his right to see it first."

Bob smiled and slightly bowed to her, then turned and opened the door. At which point, all three bolted out the door with Aaron and Dancer climbing over each other and Bob despite Dancer's chivalrous speech.

Outside they stood side by side, gazing star-struck at the table. The table now lay on its side with broken glass everywhere. It looked like something had taken a big bite out of the table and the tile it had been sitting on and then spit it out on the ground. Their faces went to shock, then dismay, until Aaron noticed the broken amber beer bottle lying in a puddle of beer.

"Bob." He paused, still looking, processing. "Bob, look, I think you did it. You did do it—you brought it back, the bottle of beer. That bottle of beer was full when it broke," he said, pointing.

Bob and Dancer both looked down, following the line of his pointing to see the pool of spilled beer. A grin crept over Bob's face that, for the first time, betrayed an insecurity that he hid well.

"Yeah, I am tingling all over about the beer bottle making it back, but, ah, bit of a rough landing, eh?" Dancer's words hit Aaron's consciousness like a rock between the eyes as he realized had this been Cynthia, she would be dead or horribly maimed.

Seeing the look on Aaron's face, Bob said, "Aaron, I know what you are thinking. Remember, it's only a test. All good inventions and creations have to be tested and retested. Then tuned, fine-tuned and then more tests. That is why we used a beer bottle. Aaron, the fact is, you can now see—I can do this. I just need to perfect the script, and I will."

Aaron stood motionless as the tension and the anxiety left his body. Where hope had been a distant shore, Bob had returned them within sight of it. He also clearly understood at that moment just how lucky he had been to have survived the night of his reassignment to now.

~~~ ~~~ ~~~

"So Dancer? While we wait for Bob to figure out how the universe will unfold at his bidding today, maybe see if he can totally disrupt someone else's entire life, what about you sharing a little more of your life? You know, how did you end up in Flagstaff, Arizona, working at the Last Hope? And how the hell did you meet up with and become friends with the likes of Bob?" Aaron asked, staring out the real window in the kitchen where he and Dancer had retreated after cleaning up. Bob had disappeared into the Cave, requesting privacy to continue working on the code. "Seriously, I mean, if you don't mind sharing."

"Whew, there's a horse trail with a whole lot of road apples to avoid. But wow, where to start. Well, first I have to tell you about Ruby's," she said and took a sip of her water, holding the glass with both hands while trying to get comfortable in her chair. She set the glass down and got up. "Water just ain't going to do it. This will require a beer. It's not too early, is it?" she asked, grabbing herself a beer from the refrigerator. "You want one, hon?"

"Yeah, please," Aaron responded.

Dancer handed Aaron his beer and then twisted off the cap on her bottle, releasing the carbonation and taking a quick, big drink to catch the foam. "Ahhh! I needed that. Where was I? Oh yeah, Ruby's."

"Rubies, like the deep-red precious stones?" Aaron asked, intrigued by her opening line.

"No, not the rocks, hon. Ruby was a wonderful grandmother-like lady. Well, okay, maybe more like a Madam. She owned and ran Ruby's. It's about four miles north from the

Last Hope up old Highway 180. Best Silicones in the business, and trust me, they can fulfill anyone's strangest fetish or deepest desires."

"Sorry, Silicones?" Aaron responded.

"Yeah. A.I.s. Sexbots. Females, males, any race, any color skin, hair, eyes. Pretty kinky shit, way kinkier than when I worked there trying to survive." She paused, then quickly went on. "But I do have to say, despite anyone's protests or objections, of which there are plenty, they are a whole lot safer for the Johns and Janes."

"Safer?"

"Yeah, cleaner, they don't do drugs, they don't drink, no drama, and no worries about pregnancies, no STDs or old jealous boyfriends showing up with a loaded twelve-gauge. Oh yeah, and they work for free."

"Dancer, I am sorry. Did you just say you used to work at Ruby's? You were a, ah..."

Dancer cut him off. "A prostitute. Yes, darling. I did indeed, just now, let that slip out. I was hoping you would just kind of glaze right over that, lost in visions of silicone boobs. Yeah, Ruby, awesome lady. Gentle, kind and very strong-willed. I owe her a great deal. After the war, my home, my family, everything was gone. I ended up in this little town with a trucker who, bless his eighteen-wheelin' heart, picked me up on the side of the road just outside of Las Vegas on Highway 93. I was in bad sorts. Suffering from radiation sickness, dehydration, starvation. I really wasn't too much longer for this world. I didn't know who or where I was. It was just pure survival instinct that had me on that road with my thumb out. Hell, I was as good as dead. So it wasn't like I put myself in any danger. Ralph—who the hell becomes a truck driver with the name of Ralph?" she said, letting out a sigh. "Ralphy, my nickname for him. He hated it but took care of me anyway for about six months. He had a little house in Bellemont and let me stay there while I recovered. He would head out to pick up and deliver God only knows what. Then, one trip, he didn't come home. Days went by, then weeks, and I knew something had gone terribly wrong. I had no way to communicate with him, but I knew if his heart was beating, he would have come home." Dancer's head drooped with the weight of her memories, betraying just how much she cared for the man.

"Dancer, I'm sorry. I had no idea. I mean, since I have been here, my only thoughts have been about me. You know, woe is me. I never stopped to consider what you and Bob and everyone else went through during that war." Aaron stood up and pulled Dancer out of her chair toward him, holding her tightly, stroking her hair. They quietly held that embrace for several minutes, not saying a word, until Dancer gently pushed him back and raised her head to look into his eyes.

"Thank you, Aaron, that means more than you will ever know." She wiped a tear from her eye with her sleeve. "He never did come home. To this day, I have no idea what happened. But I am sure he is dead. News was difficult to come by at the end of the war, and tracking people down was near impossible. Finally, I had to do something when I ran out of food. I had been to Ruby's a couple of times with Ralph. They were friends from way back. They weren't in a relationship, and he didn't go for the girls. I think they just helped each other out now and then, no questions asked. Well, Ruby liked me from day one. She was a sweetheart.

She told me if I ever needed anything to come see her. So I did. At first, I worked at the bar serving drinks to the Johns. One thing led to another, and after seeing how much money the girls made, well, I couldn't pass it up." Dancer stood up this time and leaned over to give Aaron a quick kiss on the lips and then turned away.

"Another beer?" she asked. "Have you ever been with a Silicone, an A.I.?

"Ah, no," he stammered. "They really weren't all that real looking in my day." *Am I really talking about sex with a robot and referring to back in my day,* he thought, shaking his head.

"Well, you wouldn't say that now, kid. I am the first to tell you they are amazingly real and, well, damn it, damn good. They even carry on a good conversation, if you're into that. They're warm, and whereas back in my day you never kissed a John because it gets too personal, now kissing is encouraged, as it is a big part of the menu. With a Silicone, you can do anything, and I do mean anything." She laughed. "Ruby hated them. She purchased a few early versions as a new attraction, not realizing they would be sought after by so many. After she passed away, two of the girls took over and were smart enough to see the way of the future for the oldest profession. Within a year, they were the only human ladies working. The rest of the stable was all Silicone. And for the record, Aaron, Ruby's is where I met Bob. And no, not for the dirty-ass reasons running through your sick little male brain right now." She stopped and shot Aaron a mischievous smile. "Why, Aaron, I may just have to take you over to Ruby's for a visit."

~~~~ ~~~~ ~~

Bob had been working all night, every night since Aaron's arrival, and it showed on his face. "I know you are both eager to learn of my progress. I have tracked down what happened and how to reconfigure the sequence script for Pandora. You see, in the first test, I had successfully copied the portion of the Godscript that defined the table and beer bottle. I have since discovered it copied, not cut, that portion of the script, so when it reapplied forward into the present script, it did not overwrite it. Rather, it added to it, and the two were forced to become one. However, the bottle and the ground were not capable of coexisting as a new configuration of mass and they—well, for lack of a better word, transformed into what we witnessed." Bob finished and looked at his two subjects for approval.

Aaron and Dancer just stared at him.

"Fine, then as I was saying, I believed I had to reconfigure my request algorithm so as to cut the script so that object no longer exists. Thus, when it is applied in the present, there will be nothing there for it to mix with. Before I started to change the sequence script, it hit me. I do not have to change the algorithm, well, maybe a tad, but really all I have to really do is go move the table to a new spot. Thus, there will be nothing in the present script to convolute the application of the copied script from the past."

Aaron, catching on, spoke up, "But, what about the ground, the tile and dirt? They were part of the last grab, so won't that still be an issue?"

"Aaron, my boy, you are sharp this morning. Yes, that would have been a problem, but as I said, I still need to adjust the request algorithm a tad. You see, in looking further at the configuration of the *four-four-four* folders, I discovered how to single out one object from another. This time I will grab, oh, I love that, *Grab*. I think I will use that from now on. I will grab the table and beer bottle only. I need to spend another hour or so on the new sequence script while the two of you go move my newest example of modern art, the table." Bob quietly laughed enough so that some coffee decided it no longer required sanctuary in his cup. Setting his cup down and wiping the errant coffee off himself, he continued, "Move it far enough so it is no longer in the way. And this time, I want Dancer to stand outside and video the event."

"Well, actually, Bob, the table, what was left of it, is already moved to the garbage," said Dancer. "Come on, Aaron, let's go check the area to make sure nothing else is in the way. Besides, I have wanted to rearrange that patio for some time." She laughed and headed for the stairs.

"Dancer! You are not to disturb the carefully arranged balance, the feng shui, of my patio."

"I think you have beat me to that," she blurted out as they were leaving. "Sorry, honey, sorry."

Aaron and Dancer returned to the cave after a bit more cleanup. Aaron had done his best with a shovel to return the patio floor to its normal state. However, many of the tiles were

171

uneven and broken where the first grab had scooped out a sphere-like portion of ground.

Bob was fully engaged rewriting and fine-tuning the sequence script. Dancer had headed back upstairs to make something to eat, allowing Aaron the time to let his mind wander. *Where is she? Is she freaking out? No, she's dead, and I will never get to see her again, or Half Dome.* Tears formed in the corner of his eyes as he forced himself to take several deep breaths. He had no option; he had to believe Bob could accomplish a miracle. It was his and her only hope. But, it was, he reminded himself, hope nonetheless.

Aaron allowed himself to drift further, to the possibilities that arose from Bob's discovery. *Time travel and quantum parallel realities. I am simultaneously dead and alive. Shit, I was vaporized, and yet here I am now. There really are infinite quantum universes.*

"Were there infinite Big Bangs, all with different outcomes?" he wondered out loud, eliciting a response from Dancer who had just shown up with snacks.

"You know, hon, you will think I am crazy. Well, Bob, you will for sure. In high school, I was required to write a paper on the Big Bang and its origins. It was really the first time I had heard about it in detail." She set the snacks down on the table in front of Aaron and went on. "That evening, I had a dream that was so vivid, I had to get up and write it down. I envisioned a Super Universe, where our universe is nothing more than a white dot among infinite other universes. Very much like our own night sky filled with infinite galaxies. And our universe and everything in it was contained in an ever-expanding balloon, ever since what they call the Big Bang. The balloon, like a giant helium party balloon, had reached the point that it was so expanded, tiny micro-holes were developing in the skin, or the membrane, take your pick. I was so far away in viewing all of this, the stuff that makes our universe at that scale was little more than gas, and it was escaping, propelled out and through the little membrane holes. Funny, I remember someone in my dream kept yelling, *those are Black Holes.* So when I actually wrote it for school, the point of my paper was that our Big Bang wasn't a Bang at all, but instead was the sudden opening of a micro-hole in the membrane of another, much greater universe that simply started expelling or leaking its matter and universe-like stuff into a new balloon, creating a baby universe. Like how, you know, soap bubbles can create new bubbles. It created what we know as our universe. And we, in turn, are now creating millions of new universes on the other side of our black holes." She held up her hands to convey an expanding balloon. "I remember so clearly the loud *psssssssssssss* sound of the escaping matter through the holes developing in our universe's overstretched membrane, and in my dream, as I pulled back even further away, I could see thousands of little jets of escaping matter, creating new baby universes. Bottom line boys, black holes do not suck—they blow!" Dancer slapped her thigh, laughing.

Bob stopped to look back over his shoulder smiling, as did Aaron.

"You know about the Marangoni Effect, about surfactants, Dancer?" Bob, still looking over his shoulder from his position in front of the computer, asked incredulously.

"Is that the soap bubble thing?" Dancer asked. "Kind of."

"What did you get for a grade?" Aaron asked.

"You know, I remember that too. I was very proud of myself for that paper. Mr. Conrad, that bastard, he wrote on my paper, 'Very imaginative!' and the asshole gave me a C plus. What a dick," she said, laughing.

"Imaginative indeed, Dancer, quite brilliant actually," Bob told her. "But if you both please, I need to finish this."

~~~ ~~~ ~~~~

"If everyone is quite ready, I am prepared to engage my next test. Dancer, if you would be so kind as to go out to the patio to record it. I will have Miko give you the signal when to start. Aaron, you can just stay in here and watch," Bob instructed, standing in front of the computer and keyboard, smiling with an odd, mischievous grin.

Noting the grin, Dancer thought it best not to ask any questions and headed out of Pandora's Box, as Bob liked to refer to the room. She waited outside, finding a spot as far away from the area where the table might suddenly appear but still be able to record. She stood in the shade of the roof overhang and patiently waited.

After standing there long enough to settle in and get comfortable leaning against the side of the house, Miko spoke from directly next to her, "Bob informs me you may start the sequence now." Dancer, startled, jumped but fell forward, tripping over the bushes at the side of the house as she did. Regaining her stance and standing up, she saw Miko standing in the shadows. "Where the hell did you come from? You scared the living crap out of me, Miko. That wasn't funny."

Miko stood in the shade wearing white shorts and a top that nearly matched her porcelain white skin. Her obsidian black eyes and long blue-black hair glistened in the bright sunlight as she swept the shining hair back over her shoulder, out of the way while helping Dancer back up. "I apologize, Mary Madeline. I certainly never intended to scare you. I don't very much like standing in the direct sunlight. It is very bad for my outer layer," Miko replied while helping Dancer dust off.

"Jeez, Miko, you sound more like a girl than me. And it shows, as you're certainly a lot prettier than I am." She laughed. "That's okay, apology accepted. Why are you out here in the silicone, anyway?" Dancer asked.

"I had some chores that required the use of my physical body to complete. I was in the middle of them when Bob asked me to come to the patio and inform you it is time to start your video sequence."

"Oh shit, the video." Dancer turned, hitting the record button as she did. She aimed her camera at the spot the table and beer should appear and waited. After ten minutes, she asked Miko, "Miko, can you ask Bob if he has completed the Grab? Because we got nothing out here."

Just then, Bob stepped outside into the light, holding the book up to shade his eyes, and spoke, startling Dancer yet again.

175

"No need, Miko. I can well see we are missing a table and a bottle of beer. And yes, Dancer, we did finish what seemed like a perfect sequence."

As he finished, Aaron too stepped out onto the patio, covering his eyes as well with his outstretched hand.

"So, where the hell is it?" asked Aaron, as surprised as Bob there was nothing there. Bob held the book between his two hands, almost as if he were praying.

"I must return to my chores," Miko said, without the emotion required of the moment, and started to walk away.

Hearing Miko's voice, Aaron looked to see her for the first time. "Wait, whaaa—" he said, dumbfounded, unable to finish his sentence.

"Aaron, you seem surprised. I am glad you finally get to meet the physical me," Miko said in a very sweet, Asian voice. She smiled, then bowed.

"Wow. Miko, you're beautiful! Dancer was telling me about the Silicones at Ruby's. I guess in my mind, I pictured Silicones in the stereotypical brothel, that I have never been in, I want to add, underdressed, overweight, smoking a cigarette in one hand and holding a shot of whiskey in the other while waiting for the Johns to make up their minds. But you, you're stunning! Elegant and delicate even, every bit the lotus blossom I imagined when I first heard your voice. I am honored to finally meet you in the flesh," he said and bowed slightly in what he imagined to be the correct response.

"Silicone, not flesh," corrected Miko, returning his bow with both hands together in front of her.

Still distracted by Miko's appearance, Aaron turned toward Bob. "Maybe we should go out and look on the highway where I popped into this nightmare. Sorry, your experiment," offered Aaron with emphasis on *your experiment.*

Bob nodded. "Actually, that is a good idea. A very good idea. Dancer, would you and Aaron please drive out to the spot Aaron believes he first arrived here and look around."

"Are you serious, Bob? You think that table could be sitting in the middle of the road?" Dancer asked.

"Yes, that possibility does indeed exist. There could, in fact, be a default built into the retrieval algorithm. That would be good, actually, as it would help me better understand the sequencing and code required to have objects land where I want, not where they want." He lowered the book to his thigh, where he started his usual metronome-like tapping, then turned and headed back to the Cave. "I have much work to do, apparently."

"Well then, Aaron, what say you and I go for a little drive? Wouldn't want some half-asleep driver to meet up unexpectedly with our table. And besides, getting out of here for some fresh air and new views will do us both good."

Aaron nodded, unable to hide his disappointment with this recent test.

"Aaron," Dancer said gently, "I know nothing short of your girlfriend standing safely in front of you is going to help, to make you believe. But trust me, Bob can do this. Let him do his thing and let him do it his way. He will anyway, but we all will suffer a great deal less grief if you just let him bounce his book on his thighs and think. So, come on, let's check it out, and I'll buy you a burger and a beer after we look."

Aaron looked at her and smiled. "Okay, Dancer, now you're talking my language. Let's go find ourselves a table."

The spot was no more than ten minutes up Highway 180, not far from The Hope, as Dancer commonly referred to it.

Aaron, looking keenly out the window, started waving his hand, pointing. "Here, here, this is it. Right there. That speed limit sign, bent over, that is the first thing I remember seeing when the lights came back on. Before I realized I wasn't in Kansas anymore." Aaron was excited. The odd occurrences in his out-of-place world offered him a memory, his first in this new life. Dancer laughed at the Wizard of Oz reference.

"Appropriate, Aaron, perfectly, utterly appropriate." She looked over at him, grinning with the epiphany, "Oh my God, Bob is exactly that isn't he? Oz the Great and Powerful."

"So, then that makes me what, Dorothy?" Aaron chuckled.

They drove another ten more miles until Dancer saw an area large enough to turn around. "Well, apparently our missing table is somewhere else that it doesn't belong. Imagine the surprise on the faces of those who are right now staring at it, wondering what the fuck." She laughed. "I'll turn around and we can head back, give it one more look."

Silence filled the car. *This isn't working*, Aaron worried.

Dancer read his thoughts. "Aaron, he did bring you here, and he did bring half the table back, well, kind of." As the last words left her lips, Aaron shouted excitedly.

"There! Shit, there it is. Right there! Look, right there, the table." Aaron pointed up the road, where off to the side on the shoulder sat the table, sans the beer.

Dancer pulled the car off onto the shoulder, and they both hopped out to look.

"Well, will you look at that," said Aaron, pointing to the legs in the dirt and the obvious drag marks. "It did land in the middle of the road, and someone dragged it over here so no one would hit it. I'll be damned, he did it. The table is in one piece, but where's the beer?"

"Ha," Dancer scoffed. "An unopened cold beer in Arizona. My guess is whoever pulled the table off the road felt that bottle, noted it was ice-cold, wondered why the hell not, and drank it figuring it their just reward. Wouldn't you?" Dancer asked with a cross between a snort and a chuckle. "Well, that thing is not going to fit in my car, so let's get out of here before someone shows up and starts asking questions we don't want to answer. I'll next Bob and let him know. Then, hon, I know the perfect little spot in town for that burger and beer I promised you," she said and headed back to the car. "You comin'?"

At the diner, Dancer picked up her beer and took a long draw of it before setting it down. "It's nice to get away from the Hope and from Bob. They have become my entire life. I forget sometimes about my other life, before. You popping in out of nowhere has reminded me of that. In fact, there is a lot about you that reminds me of my past. I really can't put my finger on it, but you do. My life is safe and comfortable now, though. Bob, no, he is not a lover, and well, let's face it, the man is a couple of sandwiches short of a picnic in every category but physics. And, even on that note, the man can stretch reality way beyond what I care to know is true or not."

Dancer gave Aaron more of a grimace than smile as she laughed. She took several more sips of her beer. "I'm not complaining. I'm satisfied, I'm happy. The war took so much out of me—all of us. We all lost a great deal. But mostly, we lost an innocence we didn't even know we had. The world has changed so much in the last sixteen years. I thought I would have a man, a family, live in the mountains and live happily ever after. You want another beer? You look like you need another beer. I want another beer. I'll go get us a couple more and be right back."

Dancer got up, and though she didn't stagger, Aaron could tell by her gait that she felt the three beers she'd already had. He sat back and finished off the last of his beer while pushing his last French fry through a pool of ketchup on his plate. As the fry fell satisfyingly into his waiting mouth, he wondered what he would say to Cynthia when she suddenly found herself standing in front of him in the Cave. She was a strong and intelligent woman, but he knew firsthand nothing can prepare you for the realization that you have just traveled in time to the future. He knew he would have to quickly come up with some pretty convincing logic to calm her, explaining he had no other choice; he couldn't let her stay behind and die.

Her mom would be okay, she lives in San Francisco. But all of her friends, my friends, they're all gone, vaporized. Better she's alive and freaked out than vaporized with the rest of Tahoe. We can start over here, now. Alive and in this future.

Dancer walked back, two more beers in hand. "The Samplers are here," she said with a hint of disgust as she set the beers down, tilting her head toward a table near the kitchen entrance.

It was an unintentional but well-timed statement that snapped Aaron back to the present. "Samplers? What are Samplers?"

Dancer shook her head, then sarcastically replied, "What rock have you been hiding under, boy?" She laughed, but thought to herself, *my God, so much has happened in sixteen years. He has so much to learn!*

"Like I had a chance to hide under a rock," Aaron joked back.

"Yeah, things have changed so much in the last sixteen years, and these Sampler guys, they scare me. They work for Corporate Monsanto. They're the ones gathering statistics for a visual and taste catalog for SGFP. No, wait, you don't—"

Aaron could not contain his laughter. "Are you shittin' me? Really, SFGP?"

"They had 3D printers when you were, well, back then—" She stopped. "Sorry, Aaron, I am so sorry." Getting up, Dancer walked around the table and, bending down, hugged Aaron. Squeezing him tightly, she kissed the side of his face while repeating, "I am so sorry, so, so sorry."

Aaron thought to himself chuckling, *I'll be damned she can't hold her liquor.* "I know you are, Dancer, me too. And I am scared to death about bringing Cynthia here. What are we going to do moving forward? A house, jobs. I mean, I know we'll figure it out. I am just grateful I ran into you first."

With that, Dancer leaned in closer and kissed him on the lips. Standing up, she said, "I love you, hon, you are family, and don't you ever forget it." Then, noticing the effects of the alcohol herself, she promptly plopped back down in her chair. Picking up her beer, she continued, "So then, SFGP, Solid Graphic Food Printing, is 3D-printed food. Food printed from paste; I think they use six different kinds for their recipes. The paste contains everything our bodies need to survive. They're having food professionals all over the country taste their recipe samples of SGFP foods, so they can determine which of their fake-ass foods"—she grinned as she said it, lisping the 's' like air escaping a tire—"taste and look the closest to the real thing." Dancer's voice clearly carried her disdain for their endeavor.

"Why?"

"Well, that's a good question," she said, continuing with a noticeable slur. "I read an article about them. They are preparing for the future when real food is simply no longer available. Real food, as you and I have known it, what we grew up with, because it is not practical from a financial or nutritional sense. When that day comes, the article said they wanted to have cataloged what those real foods not only looked like, but tasted like, so they would be able to maintain the diversity of taste we have been accustomed to since the beginning of humankind. What really pisses me off is that it makes sense; it actually makes sense for the future." She reached into the side pocket of her pants and pulled out a small flask. She deftly removed the cap, took a swig and held it up to Aaron. "Want some?"

Aaron now understood why the woman he believed could drink any man under the table was having such a reaction to only three and a half beers. "Dancer, I have never seen you drink like this. Why?"

"Oh, hon, maybe you haven't noticed, but a lot of weird shit goes on at Bob's." She laughed at her obvious remark. "I really needed to get away from everything. It is all reminding me of the past. Today is the anniversary of Ralphy's disappearance. I just needed to escape for a bit. Haven't you ever needed to escape?"

Aaron nodded. "I am so sorry. I'm betting Ralph must have been one hell of a guy. I'm really glad he did stop and take you in, very glad." Aaron got up and walked over to Dancer, bending down to hug her. "Dancer, I'll drink with you anytime, anywhere. But let me remind you, one of us needs to drive."

She laughed. "No, my car, she can take us home," Dancer said with a broad smile.

"Of course, *she* can," he replied, and thought to himself, *I am in the fucking future with fake food, cars that drive themselves, and robots. I have been dragged into a science fiction fairy tale that's a cross between Oz and the Jetsons.*

He paused, grabbed the flask from Dancer, took a breath, and took a shot. "Bwawawa," he mumbled, lifting his shoulders and shivering. "Dancer, that just may be the craziest and sanest thing I've heard since I got here," Aaron said, obviously astonished by the concept as it settled in.

Aaron picked up his beer and held it up to Dancer. "Here's to the last real burger."

~ ~~ ~ ~~ ~~ ~

It was far too quiet outside. The light streamed in between the slits of the blinds, illuminating the floating dust particles seeking a home. Half Dome lay on the bed next to Cynthia, who was trying her best to get some sleep. But even with the television and lights off and the blinds down, she was unable to stop thinking that Aaron might be gone, blown up in the nuclear explosion in Los Angeles.

God, if only he would call, she thought.

Acutely aware of her stress, instinctively doing what he did best, Half Dome pushed his flat face up and under her arm closest to her head, making sure he left enough drool to be cutely annoying.

"Shit—ew, Half Dome, stop," she said, burying her fingers into the thick nape of his furry and folded neck and massaging him. "You know, don't you, Half Dome, Mommy is freaking out. I am so scared your daddy is gone from us forever." As she spoke, she couldn't help but break down, sobbing so hard she struggled to breathe. Half Dome just took this as a sign to snuggle in even closer until his big, glistening brown-black eyes were only inches from hers. Half Dome then proceeded to change the subject back to him, letting out a huge sneeze complete with jowls slapping back and forth, sending high-velocity impact drool-splatter across the bed and Cynthia.

It worked. Cynthia instantly stopped crying and started laughing. Half Dome's antics had her sniffing back the tears as she laughed, hugging him even tighter.

The phone rang, startling her, bringing all the stress and tension crashing back down on her. She reached over, hoping it would be Aaron, even though she knew by the ringtone it had to be her mom.

"Hi, Mom," she said into her cellphone, the sound of disappointment heavy in her voice. She knew instantly, simply by the slow response of her mom and by the sound of her breathing on the other end, that another shoe was about to drop.

"What, Mom? What?" she almost screamed, feeling the panic rising up in her throat like a clenched fist from the pit of her stomach.

Silence is not always golden. Sometimes it is unbelievably, devastatingly painful, intensifying with the slow passing of time. Cynthia waited, feeling her pulse pound in her neck, sure her mom would tell her bad news about Aaron.

Finally, Rosanne spoke. "It happened again. Oh my God, darling, they did it again. They just blew up Paris. They blew up Paris. It's gone, gone just like LA. Millions of people gone. The news is telling everyone not to panic, but how the hell are we not supposed to panic?"

The mind plays horrific tricks, for Cynthia's first reaction at this horrid news was, she was happy. Happy that she hadn't just heard bad news about Aaron. But, in a flash, the gravity of what her mom had said sank in.

"Who is doing this, why, why?" Cynthia's mom tried her best to talk, but found it very difficult, sobbing hysterically on the other end of the phone.

Cynthia herself was unable to utter a response. Seconds ticked by as they each held onto their phones tightly as if trying to pull each other closer for comfort. Half Dome retreated slightly but still lay on the bed, front legs out in front of him, as straight as a bulldog can get them. He watched her with his head slightly cocked, knowing her posture was caused by something bad. He instinctively knew she was going to need far more of his best work.

"Honey, I want you to come to San Francisco now, today. Pack up whatever you need and come here where you will be safe with me," Rosanne finally blurted out, doing her best to be the mother.

"Hold on, Mom, I want to turn on the TV. I need to see what the hell is going on."

In a sadistic repeat of the news from but a day ago, behind the two anchors excitedly talking, was the unmistakable iconic mushroom cloud rising up into the air. And as if choreographed by Hollywood, still standing, silhouetted in front of the rising mushroom cloud was the Eiffel Tower. She turned the sound off and watched in horror.

Her heart sank and she felt nauseous, realizing even if Aaron had somehow survived, right now, she had to get her mom to Tahoe.

"Mom, you need to come here, to Tahoe. The two bombs have been in big cities. San Francisco is a big city, a big target. Don't pack anything; just get in your car and get out of there right now!"

~~~~ ~~ ~ ~~~~

"You didn't bring back my table? You said you found it. Where is it?" Bob asked with an incredulous gasp.

"Welllll, no." Dancer held the sound of the "l" on her lips while she danced back and forth, searching for a good answer to a question she was not expecting. "First, who in their right mind would try and stuff that nasty old table into their car? Second, you already have that very table. Well, what's left of it, sitting, sorry, laying on the porch. Oh, wait, sorry, laying next to the trash." Dancer responded. She tried to keep a straight face, but then started laughing at the thought of the tragically morphed table, laying like a Doctor Moreau vivisection experiment gone awry. "Seems to me, Bob, if you really want it that bad, you can just grab another and bring it forward."

Silence fell as all three started thinking, considering the possibilities suddenly presented by this statement, simultaneously realizing anything from the past could now be brought forward to now, to here.

"We must be careful with this. This is obvious to me. I have discovered a way to time travel. No, I have discovered Quantum Travel, which preempts all of the former insurmountable paradoxes. We are now walking in completely uncharted territory. I must give careful consideration to every move I make going forward. For now, regardless of whether I copy or cut the code, I can have a duplicate sitting here that is perfectly at home in this reality, as it is also now in its own reality." Bob bounced the book on his thigh at an accelerated rate. "I believe what we have here is actually unbelievably simple. Wherever the code is, there it is, and that is reality. No paradoxes; it is what it is. No self-healing of the script, so yes, there can be exact duplicates. And if you go back in time and kill your father, it will only matter in that reality stream, which will have then taken on a new direction. Back here, your script, streaming along, will still contain you as is, because in this stream, you have always been here. You see, the quantum pool, IQRES from which we draw, is quite infinite."

"So, Bob," Aaron asked, interest piqued, "you're saying you could do something like, I don't know, reintroduce dinosaurs or even a Neanderthal here, now?"

Bob stopped bouncing the book to look at Aaron. "Well, yes, if I can figure out, and of course I can, how to target an animal or object that far back in time," he answered with a certain smugness.

Aaron's mind filled with possibilities. "So, if I needed an organ transplant, a new heart, let's say, I could bring a duplicate of me forward to harvest his heart? Shit, Bob, you may have resolved the paradoxes, but the ethics of all of this is going to get really messy."

"Indeed, Aaron, indeed. You then see my need to be very, very careful moving forward. And I think now is a good time to say this. I know you are both smart enough that I should not have to say this, but I will anyway. None of this, absolutely none of this, under any circumstances ever leaves this room!" Both Dancer and Aaron were nodding in complete agreement.

"Great! Quantum Travel, the paradox-free way to travel," Aaron joked, doing his best to imitate an announcer's voice.

"Yes, I am sure that is funny, but first things first. And first, Aaron, we must figure out how to bring your Cynthia here safely." Holding the book to his breast, Bob gently grasped

Aaron's shoulder with his other hand in an odd gesture, for Bob, of empathy. "I need to figure out why objects copied and pasted will come here as I have instructed in my algorithm, and those that I cut and paste end up in the middle of the road miles from here. You know, of course, what this means? Because you landed on the highway, you were cut and pasted. A duplicate of you does not exist back where your Cynthia was. The good news is, where there is consistency, there is repeatable and identifiable reason. Please, if you both could entertain yourselves, I need to run some calculations so that I might replace the table in my patio."

"In that case, I'll go round us up some sustenance. Snacks, anyone?" Dancer asked.

Aaron didn't answer, lost in the far reaches of his mind, going over the possibilities of what had just transpired.

"Fine, sandwiches, it is," laughed Dancer to herself as she headed up the stairs.

~   ~ ~~~~ ~~~~

Dancer returned with a tray full of sandwiches, some oranges and several beers. She sat them down on the little table next to the monkey wood bowl and then went to grab Bob.

"Come on, honey, you need to take a break and feed yourself." Dancer tousled his grey hair.

"Don not do that, Dancer. You know I hate that," Bob said, perturbed by her actions. Standing up, he pulled the hair tie off his ponytail, being overly dramatic. He then pulled a small brush from his pocket and carefully ran it through his hair, twisting it back into a ponytail and replacing the tie.

"Works every time. The shit I have to go through to get you to listen to me," she laughed.

Bob just grumbled as he turned and followed her to the food.

Beers open and mouths full, the only sound to be heard over the hum of Pandora was the clicking of Bob's jaw as he chewed. Bob finally leaned back into his chair, brushing some crumbs off his face. As he did, Aaron, who had been pondering much of his current situation while they ate, looked over at Bob and asked, "The code, your Godscript, the digital script or whatever it is, it is not solid. It is just space between the light. It is fluid and without mass, yet here we stand or sit upon it. We only see and touch what it tells us we can? Am I saying that correctly? Does that make sense? But how?" Aaron's inquisitive side was taking over, truly wanting to understand.

Bob smiled at his question. He got up to walk around the table. Aaron noticed his arm with the book hung still against his side, not moving. He had learned that the best way to read Bob's emotions, his moods, was to watch the book. This, he knew, meant Bob was either calm and happy or visibly shaken. He hoped for calm and happy. Bob stopped next to Aaron, gently grabbing his shoulder.

"Aaron, my young inquisitive friend, every once in a great while, someone asks that perfect question that fires me up like

190

a furnace on a cold morning." He let go of Aaron's shoulder and walked over to the virtual window, gazing out at the open prairie with beams of light that lit hovering insects, adding to the illusion he was looking out a window. "Even though what you see here is not real, it is only digital, it is still real-time of the reality you know. What you see out this virtual window is what is really happening outside looking in that direction. I have thirty-five cameras along the perimeter of the roofline that feeds Miko a complete synchronistic, three hundred and sixty degree view all day and all night." Bob then returned to the table where Dancer and Aaron were sitting. Bob reached down into the monkey wood bowl filled with whole shelled walnuts and the large navel oranges Dancer had brought down. He picked up one of the oranges and turned to face Aaron.

Oh, shit, what have I done? thought Aaron, knowing a lengthy Bobism was in store.

"This orange, it's real. At one time, the belief that the Earth was the center of the universe and that everything revolved around us was just that, only a belief, but very real to them. The ball of fire in the daytime sky, the ground they walked on, and the night sky that revolved over and around them, they were written in stone. It stayed the prevailing belief until a brilliant young man by the name of Aristarchus first thought up the idea that maybe, just maybe, it was us that revolved around the big yellow and very hot ball in the sky. I do not even know if they understood the concept of orbit until Copernicus and Kepler developed a workable theory that backed up Aristarchus's idea. Finally, Galileo proved them correct with his wonderful little invention, the telescope. They did not dwell on it or overthink, trying to understand this new revelation. But, oddly enough, to no one's surprise or concern, everything stayed exactly as it had been before they learned of this revelation. The seasons came and went, all seemed right with the world." Bob tossed the orange into the air for added effect, almost dropping it.

"Are you sure? Apparently, oranges are affected differently?" chided Aaron.

"Yes, that is funny. I was trying to make an impressive gesture before diving into the rest of my very worthwhile diatribe, thank you very much," Bob snapped right back, and then continued, "So along comes this guy in puffy shirts and pants, pointy shoes and a strange hat trying to convince the world that the world was not flat as had been believed and unchallenged since the dawn of man and fire. No, he said, the world is round, like an orange, a sphere." Once again, Bob tossed the orange into the air for effect. This time he missed completely, and it, bound by gravity, found its way to the floor with a thud.

Bob shook his head, bent over and picked the now oblong orange off the floor. "I will assume Columbus had better luck when he met with the Queen to present his idea and request funding to prove it," he said, giggling at his own humor. "As we all know, he did prove it by not sailing off the edge of the world into the universal abyss. Again, armed with this new knowledge, humankind did not suddenly start falling down because the Earth was now round and spinning. No, once again, everything stayed as it had been, spinning right along." Bob smiled, pleased with himself, loving being able to command the moment.

"The world now revolved around the sun. It was round and solid!" Bob continued. "Nothing left could truly shake up conventional thinking and logic. Well, except—" Bob paused, as he so often did for effect when about to segue into something else seemingly unrelated. "I have to say my two favorite words, and at the same time most irritating, are *except* and *infinity*. Except can creep into a conversation at any time to disrupt anything thought absolute. And infinity, well, talk about self-deprecating. Its meaning opens up the door that everything is incorrect, as there will always be more knowledge to outdate what people previously thought correct or absolute. The two words just always get in the way."

Bob, becoming annoyingly proud of himself, bit into the pulverized orange, then peeled it back with his long fingers at the point of incision made by his teeth. "There is, of course, more, as there always is."

"Imagine that," chimed in Dancer.

Bob shot her yet another look of being perturbed but smiled and went on. "The early Greek philosophers first envisioned the possibility that our solid world could actually be composed of small indivisible particles. Still, it was much later an English gentleman, one John Dalton, and later an Italian named—oh shit, what was his name?" Bob rubbed his forehead with his book. "Oh, oh it is there. Right there on the tip of my tongue—Amedeo, Amedeo Avogadro, yes. Amedeo proved the concept that our solid world might really be made up of a very fluid sea of atoms and molecules moving around each other, well, very much like Copernicus's concept of our solar system. They had proven our world, the very ground we stand on, was not only round and spinning, but that it wasn't solid at all. Rather, it was composed of an infinite sea of moving particles. And guess what?

Nobody fell off, over, or through the world. Humanity now understood far better how the world, our reality, worked." Bob's voice slowed, trying to make his point.

It worked, for suddenly, hearing this argument for the second time, Aaron's eyes opened wider, the expression of discovery written all over his face. "So, what you are saying is, the idea of a digital world, a script of data, is just another layer of depth in understanding how our reality is created. It is peeling back the onion to expose more knowledge. This is a script; it is a code that tells everything how to work together so that we see, feel, taste and experience our very lives!" Aaron paused, drawing in a deep breath and then slowly letting out a "Whoa!"

Bob, glowing with himself and his presentation, popped an orange slice into his mouth.

~ ~~ ~ ~~ ~~ ~

"I am ready to commence with the next phase of testing," Bob stated as he walked into what had become the lounge area of the Cave. The room provided plenty of space for the one table and several not so comfortable chairs. "Dancer, I am going to need your assistance, please."

"Oh my, I feel like the magician's assistant when you talk to me like that, Bob," Dancer teased. "But I will gladly assist you with anything, Bobby," she added, rubbing up against his side in a provocative manner.

"I need you to drive to the landing area, as we now apparently refer to it, where the items I have successfully cut and reintroduced into the script arrive as they are intended to, in one piece. I believe, however, this time I will be able to cut the script that is this table and paste it back in the script so that you will not see it appear in the middle of the road. A bad thing," he added, then took the monkey wood bowl off the table, setting it in the chair nearest him. He pulled it slightly away from the wall, toward the other side of the room. "Aaron, if you would be so kind as to grab the other chair and bring it over here."

Aaron complied, picking up the chair and bringing it over to where Bob placed the first chair. "You're going to move this table? Where are you going to try and move it to?" asked Aaron, concerned.

Dancer, running her fingers through her hair, spoke up, "Okay then, on that note, I'm glad I will be way the hell out on the highway. God only knows where you will have the table reappear this time. Aaron, hope I don't see you when I get back as the table version of a centaur, half table, half man." She laughed and turned to head up the stairs.

"Do not be silly, Dancer. I am only going to move it a couple of inches over to here," Bob said, pointing just to the right of the table.

"Yeah, thanks, Dancer. Like I have some idea where a safe place might be to hide," Aaron said jokingly but with honest concern in his voice.

"You are both generating some degree of anger in me with your childish chiding. Aaron, you stand over here with the chairs, just in case," Bob said without so much as missing a beat or understanding his own concession as to not being completely sure where the table would end up. "Dancer, I will give you twenty minutes and then run the sequence. And please bring back the table should it land there."

"Aye aye, captain," she said, saluting and smiling from the stairs.

"Twenty minutes exactly. Here we go," Bob said, and left to go into Pandora's box. "Aaron, please stay here and watch the table."

Aaron took a deep breath. "Got it, I'm good. Let's do this."

Aaron could hear and feel the intensity that can only be described as pure acceleration as Pandora started coming up to speed. He kept his eyes fixed on the table, anxiously hoping to see it disappear and reappear. Aaron knew it took nearly ten minutes for Pandora to come up to speed but standing there watching it felt like thirty. The lights blinked off for a mere second. Aaron could not see a thing as his eyes were not accustomed to the dark, and then the lights came back on. For a moment, it did not appear the table had moved at all. Then, as the rods and cones in his eyes came back into position, he could see the table had moved. Not to the right, where Bob had pointed, but rather toward the wall it had been up against. The table had become the wall, or at least part of it. Three-quarters of the table protruded out of the stone wall as if it had grown there. One leg had been completely embedded, while another embedded only partially in the wall hung in the air, no longer touching the floor. Instead, it was about a half an inch above the floor. The other two legs sat squarely on the floor.

Aaron squinted looking at it, thinking, *It looks so comfortably normal, like it has always been that way.* The table listed because of the one leg not being squarely on the floor. Not enough for a cup to slide off, but a pencil would roll off. Aaron looked at the table in complete amazement. But he realized that Bob had actually come very close to doing exactly what he hoped. With it was still the realization of what could happen to Cynthia.

"I don't think Dancer is going to find the table this time, Bob," Aaron said, doing his best to clear his mind of the disturbing picture in his head. He turned in time to watch Bob come to a sudden stop upon seeing the results.

"Hmm," was all that emanated from Bob. "Hmm," he said again. "It would appear I should tell Dancer to return. Hmm."

~~~~ ~~ ~ ~~ ~

Even after another long night in front of the soft glow of a computer screen, listening to the steady hum of Pandora, Bob, who had not slept but for the briefest of moments, appeared different. Younger, alert and energetic. So much so that both Dancer and Aaron looked at him curiously.

"How can you be alert and happy after being up all night?" Aaron asked, gripping his coffee like it were the last life preserver on a sinking boat. "I mean, don't get me wrong, Bob, no one is happier that you can work all night and still be raring to go at first light."

Dancer, with a firm grip on her coffee as well, nodded.

His verve, undaunted by their lack of enthusiasm, showed in his childlike grin. "I have decided it would be far more prudent to try a simpler approach until I can master removing the code from a location in the script that precedes us and reintroducing it into the script where we are at present. I am going back to my original plan, slightly altered, mind you, to copy the code that represents this box"—he set down a small black enameled box with no visible hinges or handles—"and reintroduce the code representing the box so that it will appear as a duplicate but appearing here, near the original."

The black box sat on the three-quarter table embedded in the rock wall. It almost felt somehow natural now, like an art piece protruding out of the rock wall. He pointed to the other end of the table. "To there. I am doing this so that it will make the amount of code I need to deal with much simpler. And I do not wish to fill up the Cave with unwanted tables, beers, or boxes."

Dancer added, "Let's not forget inadvertently killing some poor bastard with a table that suddenly appears out of nowhere, right in front of him on the highway."

Aaron cringed as Bob spoke in a sour tone of dismissal. "Yes, Dancer, thank you for that important safety tip. But do keep in mind I did just bring it back to here." Both Aaron and Dancer shot a quick glance at the table now jutting out of the wall, then returned their gaze toward Bob, who continued, unaffected by their sarcastic grins. "I have yet to discover the anomaly that when I cut the code, not copy it, it always lands intact on the road. Whereas with the copied code, I can bring it to where I want, but I have obviously less control over exactly where. Working with the box will be easier. I am thinking the code being in two places simultaneously is behaving similarly to what we see with spooky entanglement. And yes, Dancer, safer."

Miko's voice, pleasant with no hint of urgency, filled the room. All three instinctively looked up toward the ceiling like she might be up there. "I'm sorry to interrupt you, Bobby, but it would appear your favorite detective is coming up the entrance road. As far as I can discern, he is alone this time. There are no other ground vehicles. However, he is accompanied by a model 3700 Halliburton military-grade surveillance drone. The detective has just passed the gate, and his drone is currently directly overhead. I put him, at his current speed, at eight minutes, thirty-seven seconds out."

Bob, no longer looking up, addressed her, "Miko, has the drone detected us down here?"

"Please give me a moment to access their data. No, at present, the drone does not recognize any lifeforms on the property."

"Excellent, thank you, Miko."

"Wait. Can Miko hack into a military-grade drone?" queried Aaron.

"I am right here, Aaron, you know you can ask me directly. I'm not a wall, though I do understand I appear like one at times, like now?" Miko laughed as she spoke. "I have an update. I am now able to access their onboard cameras. I can show you what they are seeing, if you wish."

"Why is she in such a good—sorry, Miko, why are you in such a good mood when we are about to get raided by the police? And for the record, Miko, I don't think of you as a wall, well, not anymore," Aaron said grinning, thinking of his earlier encounter with Miko on the patio.

"Thank you, Aaron. I am not alarmed because the detective would not travel this distance alone to attempt anything forceful. Statistically speaking, he is most likely here seeking information he does not want the rest of his staff to know about. I would advise that one or both of you, Dancer and Aaron, head to the house so the drone does pick up two lifeforms before the detective pulls up."

"Good thinking, Miko, but I gotta tell you, I don't know, I think sure as hell this can't be for anything good," Dancer said. "Aaron, I think you should come with me. Bob, please stay put and be quiet. Don't be firing up Pandora and spooking his little spy drone," Dancer instructed, slipping into her, *make it happen* voice.

Aaron looked at Bob, who shrugged his shoulders, being quite used to her various demeanors. Bob turned to head further into the cave as Aaron followed Dancer up the stairs.

"I think the same routine as before; you go find something to watch that has you bored to the point of falling asleep on the couch. I will head into the kitchen and make the best use of time making us something to eat."

"Two minutes out," said Miko.

"Shit, let's do this." She quickened her pace up the stairs to the kitchen with Aaron right behind.

Nate sat in his car for close to fifteen minutes. He watched his monitors showing the property being scanned from above for life. While he watched, he fiddled with three small yellow pieces of paper he had pulled from his shirt pocket, until the overhead drone completed its scan with the infrared camera and motion detection sensors. Satisfied, he stuffed the pieces of paper back in his shirt pocket before slowly and methodically opening his door to walk the short distance through the patio to the front door. He hesitated at the door while he scanned the front of the house, looking carefully at the door and windows. He stopped when his eyes came across the disheveled table and broken glass, still laying in a pile waiting to be taken to the dump. Making a mental note, he then turned and knocked on the door.

Like any good chess player, Dancer, who had Miko keeping her posted on Nate's whereabouts, calmly contemplated her next move and took her time to answer the door. She wanted Nate to think they were up to something, that they would be out of breath and worried answering the door. She hoped it would catch him off guard that they were just hanging around the house being homebodies.

Slowly she tied on an apron and walked to the door, smiling at Aaron, who had found something to watch. She couldn't see what it was, but did note he looked like he had been there for an hour or more. *Perfect,* she thought to herself, and then opened the door to the smell of peppermint gum and the mocking smile of Nate Brewster.

"Well, what a surprise, Detective Brewster," she said, wiping her hands on her apron like she had been cooking all day. "Would you like to come in?"

"Well, yes, ma'am. Sorry, sorry, I mean, Dancer. I would."

Dancer stepped to the side and waved him in. Which on cue, Nate did, walking directly into the main room where Aaron, now standing up, had been sitting watching the monitor.

"Hi, Detective," Aaron uncomfortably offered.

Nate waved his hand. "Sit down, my boy. I'm just here for some information."

As he turned back to Dancer, he noticed a tray of sandwiches on the top of a small cabinet near the entry. Sandwiches Dancer, surprising herself, had been able to make because Nate had taken so long in his car.

He thoughtfully studied the sandwiches before looking Dancer in the eyes. "That is a whole lot of sandwiches for just the two of you, ma'am," he said, not correcting himself this time to make the moment more significant. "I'm not here to mince words. I know Robert did not leave the area. He did not go to Canada. I am quite confident he is still in town, and more than likely, judging by the prolific amount of food you have prepared, he is somewhere very nearby. Would I be correct in that assumption—" again pausing for effect "—ma'am?"

Dancer quickly and with some degree of guilt glanced toward the tray of sandwiches, realizing without thinking she had made extras for Bob. She felt a sudden queasiness in the pit of her stomach and thought to herself, *damn it, I'm such an idiot.*

Gathering her naturally quick wits without missing a heartbeat, she took a small step toward Nate. With a cute, almost flirting movement with her head and shoulders, she looked him squarely in the eyes and replied, "Detective—I am so sorry—Nate, Miko let me know you were outside when you first pulled up. I thought it only proper that I make enough so as to be able to offer you some."

With that, she turned just enough without having to step so she could reach the tray. Turning back, she offered up her best, toothy white grin and the tray which she held up to the detective, asking, "Can I offer you a sandwich? Aaron, why don't you grab the detective"—she coyly looked down, still smiling—"Sorry, Nate, a soda."

Nate knew he had been outplayed. "No, Dancer, I already ate, but thank you."

"Well then, if I may, what sort of information were you hoping to obtain today?" she asked with a tinge of Southern Belle accent added for effect.

Switching gears and demeanor, Nate decided to cut to the chase, the real reason he was there. "Let me be real honest, Dancer. I need to talk to Robert alone, privately. I have some questions only he will be able to answer. Please, when you do see him, tell him I came alone and what I just told you. And thank you, I think I will take a sandwich for the road." He reached down and picked up a single sandwich, which he immediately took a bite of. "These are good, Dancer, really good. Again, thank you." And without another word, he left.

~~ ~ ~~~ ~~

Bob protested, both arms and the book up in the air then coming down against his waist, like a child stomping his feet. "Dancer, I really do not care what that man wants or says. He is evil. He has pursued me like I was a criminal."

Aaron looked at Dancer, then back at Bob. "Ah, Bob, you stole an entire collider from the federal government. In some circles, they consider that criminal."

"I did not steal anything. I temporarily procured what I needed to build this, to show them my theories were correct. It has always been my intention to turn over what I built to them, but with Nate hounding me, then that stupid war, suddenly many years had passed, and it became pointless to even show my face." Bob's tone became even more petulant. "Besides, while you two were up there playing with my archenemy, I figured out what I have been doing incorrectly," Bob said, enlisting a bit of elite snobbishness.

"We were not playing with him, damn it, Bob. We were doing our best to protect you from him," Dancer said, pointing her finger at him.

Before she could continue, Aaron cut in, "Wait! Whoa, Dancer, that can wait. You figured it out? How? What? Can you move something here safely now?" asked Aaron excitedly.

"Yes, Aaron, but as I expressed earlier, we are going to start small, with the box. First, I will copy and paste the code to create a duplicate placed just to the side. Once that is successful, I will cut the code of the duplicate box and paste it back in so that it will appear here, just in front. Once I am confident with that scripting, I will try something a little tougher. Like returning to our beer bottle, while still cold and not opened as it sat on the table before meeting its tragic end on the patio during my earlier attempt." Bob was a bit too smug in his description, which worried Aaron. Still, far too excited to contemplate all of the things that had gone wrong prior to this moment, he knew now the possibility existed. They might, in fact, be close to saving Cynthia. "Okay, where do you want us? What do you want me to do?"

"For this particular test, number, ah, oh, I've lost count, whatever, you can both stay in here and watch. However, Dancer, for the second test, I will need you to drive out to our favorite landing spot just in case. So, if you are both ready, I am as well. Give me five, maybe six minutes to get Pandora started on its warm-up sequence. I need to load the new data access and manipulation sequencing algorithm."

"Wouldn't it just be a whole lot easier to call it something like the 'DAM' script?" asked Aaron.

Bob stopped to look quizzically at Aaron, then, getting it, responded, "Oh, yes, yes, that works for me, though technically speaking it would be 'DAAMSA.' I will, however, concede your obvious point that acronym is simply too long and wholly defeats the purpose of an acronym in the first place. Therefore, the DAM algorithm it is, Aaron. Well done."

~~~~ ~~~~ ~~~~

"Mom, I know, Moscow, I just saw it. What the hell? Well, at least we now know it's not the Russians. But I am pretty damn sure we are somehow in the middle of World War III... Mom... Mom... Mom?"

~~ ~ ~~ ~ ~~ ~

Aaron's hopes rose with the accelerating sound of Pandora's throaty whine as she once more ramped up to speed. The lights dimmed slightly and pulsed as an acrid smell of ozone filled the cavern. *The smell, the sounds, this entire moment is ripped right from the pages of Dr. Frankenstein,* Aaron thought to himself.

Aaron and Dancer had already retreated back against the wall, pushing as hard as they could in hopes of going further, but it was physically impossible. Dancer wrapped herself around Aaron, burying her face in his shirt while still keeping one eye on the table.

The lights went out, and all sound ceased for but the blink of an eye, then on again. There was no smoke, like one would expect from a magician making something appear. Instead, sitting quietly on the table like it had always been there, just to the right of the original box, right where Bob had pointed, sat another box. An exact copy of the original box,

206

except instead of being glossy black, it was shiny white. Pure white, shimmering in the cavern lights.

Aaron and Dancer stared speechless as Bob entered the room, then stopped in his tracks, looking at them. He appeared about to speak, but his head and gaze couldn't help but follow their obvious transfixed stare toward the table.

"Hmm, good, very good. I've done it," Bob said, without a great deal of celebration in his voice.

"Bob, it's white!" Dancer pointed out.

"Yes, I can see that, Dancer, but it is here, right where I said it would be."

"Yeah, and not a part of the table or the wall," said Aaron, whose hopes were gaining momentum, even with the color transformation. He felt a surge of confidence that Bob would actually be able to pull this off. "But why is it white?"

"You both know very well I am rarely stumped, but at the moment, Aaron, I have no clue why it inverted its color. I have most certainly missed something," Bob said, bringing Aaron's hopes plummeting back to reality, clearly suggested by the abrupt slumping of his shoulders.

"Let us not rest on our laurels," Bob continued. "We must move on to the second test. I can then compare the results that will allow me a clearer picture of syntax at play here. It will come together logically. It always does. This is, after all, not magic."

Aaron walked over to the table and picked up the box to examine it. Opening it, he found inside a small piece of paper. Clearly, by its shape, it was from a fortune cookie, complete with faint oil stains on it. He held it up for both Bob and Dancer to see.

"Bob, is this what is in the other box?" questioned Aaron, who then proceeded to read it aloud. "All of life is before and behind, for the length of now can fit on the head of a pin."

Aaron, puzzled, tried to ascertain its meaning. Before Bob could respond, he turned and opened the black box, pulling out the exact same piece of paper. "That is the longest fortune I have ever read. And I don't get it. I mean, what the hell? I have been told my entire life to live in the moment. That the past is gone, and the future hasn't happened yet. Right?" As he finished, he carefully put the first fortune back in the glossy black box, gently closing the lid as if he were touching an artifact from the Ming Dynasty.

"I found that fortune in a cookie," Bob said, "in a small Chinese restaurant in Berkeley, many years ago. They weren't even Chinese, just a bunch of hippies. It puzzled me as well, but the answer turned out to be profound beyond even my imagination. It was yet one more path that has led me to where I am today. So, I saved it."

"Annnnnd the answer is?" As the question left his lips, Aaron knew he had just set the stage for a Bobism. *But this time*, he thought, *I would like to hear this*.

"You will see, it defines quantum reality." Aaron and Dancer, knowing the routine, took a seat. "The head of a pin comment made me realize that *Now* is a relatively short period of time. But with much consideration on my part, it became quite apparent that the increment of Now is impossible to apply a time to. That is, it is literally instantaneous. Very much like the well-known Zeno paradox where—" He stopped. "You both know of Zeno?"

Aaron shook his head to indicate no. Dancer smiled. "Bob, you have told me about Zeno so many times I swear I know the man. But you know how much I would love to hear it again, especially for our boy here."

"We do need to fix that, Dancer, you are correct. You see, Aaron, say you have a distance to travel. You measure that distance, then travel half the distance only to measure it again. Repeating the steps, it quickly becomes clear that, because of the law of infinity, there will always be a measurement you can divide in half. As such, you will never reach your destination. If you apply the same logic to the increment of *Now*, you will see there is no point at which you can measure how quick instantaneous is."

Bob smiled at the dumbstruck look on Aaron's face and continued, "Further, I know how quickly our brains are able to process new, incoming information. The timeframe for the brain, an average brain, to react to a stimulus is about two hundred milliseconds. Thus, if we know the timeframe for the brain is measurable and finite, and the measurement for the increment of *Now* is incalculably, infinitely fast, there can be only one conclusion. The moment happens quicker than we can process it. *Now*, quite simply, does not exist!"

Bob paused, looking around to judge the reactions of his audience. Aaron, even Dancer, had become spellbound by Bob's explanation.

"But how?" Aaron asked. "I mean, I feel it, the time, the experience as it is happening."

"Really? Then do tell. When does the moment something becomes a memory in your brain occur?" asked Bob.

Aaron paused to think.

"You cannot. The information you are receiving is coming from an infinite pool of quantum realities. Once you see and experience something, your brain chooses a quantum pathway, and it instantly is sent to a buffer in your brain. That buffer is where you are experiencing the feeling of time passing. But you are not really feeling time passing; it has already passed. The buffer is just post-memory. This, I believe, is confirmed with the 'Double Slit Experiment,' where once multiple particles are viewed, they become a singular path of particles. Thus, as my fortune that day indicated, the length of *Now*, which we have just shown is infinitely small, can fit on the head of a pin."

Aaron simply stared into space, and Dancer patted his hand in sympathetic understanding.

"Now, if there are no further questions, I must prepare to start phase two of the boxes test."

~ ~~ ~~~~ ~~~

"If we are quite ready, I will now cut the script that represents our original box, the black one here, and paste it back so that it will appear here." Bob pointed to the spot on the table where the almost duplicate white box had appeared and still quietly resided. He picked up the white box and handed it to Dancer.

"For me? Why, thank you, Bobby, that's the sweetest thing you've ever done," she said, her smile betraying her sarcasm.

"Do not call me that," Bob quickly responded, perturbed. "Please, please do not push my buttons like that. What I am doing is important."

"Sorry."

"Dancer, you need to drive out to the unofficial designated landing spot. I promise you, this time, it will work, and you will see nothing."

Dancer nodded. "Yeah, here's hoping."

"Miko, would you be so kind as to record this with an ultra-high shutter speed? We will need to see what happens at the exact moment of materialization."

With that, Bob trotted off to start Pandora with the revised DAM sequence. As he approached the main control panel, he was greeted with a flashing red light on the console. With great disappointment, he went to the computer, touching several menus to find, as he suspected, an overload on one of the module power supplies that supported the main fail-safe switch.

"Shit! Shit," he said loudly, then breathed deeply, adding one more "Shit."

Aaron, hearing his verbal irritation, walked over to ask Bob, what was troubling him.

"Pandora has blown a fuse. Not just any fuse. This effectively shuts down the entire sequencing process, a safeguard I had built in to protect Pandora's extremely fragile network of ultrasensitive boards."

Walking to the workbench ever so neatly covered with various items, Bob proceeded to search through a stack of drawers. He started pulling open small, clear plastic drawers, shutting them as fast as he opened them, each with a *shit* under his breath. When he had opened the last one and shut it with a sigh of great exasperation, he looked up and nexted Dancer. "Stop. Come back. We have a problem."

Dancer had not gotten far and turned, coming back down the dark, rickety stairs. "What? I don't like the tone of that next."

"Murphy is at play here, I fear. Of all the things that could go wrong at this moment, a two-dollar fuse blew. And I do not have any more. The good news is, though, it's a much older style of fuse that is still fairly easy to find. I am quite sure the Scrub Brush has them. I need to go and look at them to make sure. They have to be exactly right."

"You can't go into town right now, Bob. They will descend on you like a plague of locusts," Dancer spit out like a mom responding to her kids wanting to do something stupid.

"You are correct, of course, but I have to be there."

"Do you have another kind of fuse, a higher amp rating you can just use for now to test the algorithm?" Aaron asked.

"Aaron, there is a reason we use fuses—to protect valuable equipment. I am not about to sacrifice all I have worked for to save a few pennies or minutes of my time. We will go, and we will be okay. I have a plan."

"Oh crap, I hate it when you have a plan, Bob. You are a smart man, but your plans sometimes are like kids playing football, and the kid with the ball says to everyone, 'Just go out long.'"

"If you are quite through treating me like a child, Dancer, I do have a plan, a good one."

"Sorry, Bob, please continue. You know I am joking and trust you more than anyone else alive," she said humbly, letting a touch of her true love for Bob show.

"Thank you, Dancer. My plan is, we take Aaron's Volkswagen on the backroads. I know them well. They lead almost all the way into town where Scrub Brush is. And, if I might mention, Aaron's nicely restored vintage VW Bug built in the 1960s has no tracking devices of any kind on it. They will never know we are out and about. It will take us twenty minutes tops. Nothing can go wrong!"

"Really, Bob, an absolute statement like that, coming from your mouth? I am quite surprised. Aren't you the one always reminding me, 'and the Titanic will never sink?'" she said, trying to imitate Bob's voice.

"Indeed, you are correct, Dancer. I do use the Titanic line as an opening to my 'Third Law.' It is simply the greatest incorrect absolute statement of all time."

Dancer turned to Aaron. "Prepare yourself. You have no idea how many laws he has. He has his own set of Murphy's Laws. But in his case, I call 'em *Bob's Laws.* Sorry, do proceed, hon."

"Yes, thank you, Dancer. As I started to say, my law states, *The act of making a finite statement instantly increases the odds or chances of it becoming false! Further, the greater the weight of the statement exponentially increases the severity and the intensity of the collapse of that statement.*" Bob glanced at

Dancer. "Since you know all of my Laws, would you like to add anything more, Dancer?"

She only smiled.

"No, I thought so. Then let me give you an example, actually, the example you just shared, *'The Titanic, the boat God himself cannot sink!'* Well, let's review. It is on its maiden voyage, halfway to New York when it encounters, I do not know, what I would call an ice cube the size of the Empire State building, floating out in the dark vastness of the Atlantic and directly in their path. An act of God—yes? And trust me, I understand this could be construed as borderline superstition, or at least it falls into the fringes of grey area that can never be proven by scientific method. But everyone, both of you, has experienced it at some level or degree, and therefore, I submit to you that there is a measure of calculable truth to it. I know Murphy would concur."

"Okay, Bob's Third Law it is," Aaron said, nodding. "And, you know what, Bob? I do agree. I have had that happen far too many times, exactly as you say. So many times that I hesitate anymore to make categorical statements, choosing to use disclaimers when I do. But, back to the subject at hand. I still have plenty of gas in the VW as I got gas the first time I saw you in my previous life. Maybe you remember: flashing casino lights, harmonizing engines?"

Missing Aaron's not-so-subtle inference completely, Bob carried on with his own agenda. "Excellent, Aaron, I was going to ask you how much gasoline you had in your VW. Let me remove the insubordinate fuse, and we will be on our way." He paused for a moment, then asked into the air, "Miko, honey, are there any drones out?"

"No, Bobby, not at the moment. Their 3700 HMGS drone is not within my ability to detect. It does, however, keep a very regular schedule, as it has been flying over us every three hours at exactly ten minutes after. It hovers for eight minutes, scanning the house and the garage. Would you like me to notify you whenever it is within range?" Miko asked in an incredibly subtle yet sexy voice.

"Yes, Miko, please do. We will want to depart and arrive back when they are not overhead snooping," Bob replied.

Dancer and Aaron looked at each other. Dancer shrugged her shoulders and smiled, then her eyes lit up. "Honey?" Dancer asked, and then went on, "Bob, you didn't! You didn't get Miko's silicone body from Ruby, did you?"

Bob looked at her trying to look quizzical, but the embarrassed, hand-caught-in-the-cookie-jar expression was unmistakable. He tried to speak, but he stammered for words. Dancer started laughing, "Oh my God, she's a Silicone."

In her sweetest, gentlest Japanese voice, Miko spoke, "I'm sure you meant to be humorous on some level, but I do have to say I take offense to the term *Silicone,* as today it is associated derogatorily with being a prostitute, a whore. Yes, the original body's purpose was that of a servicewoman. But I have evolved, with Bob's help and guidance. I am an individual with dreams of my own that no longer include the servicing of lonely men that stink of beer and vape."

"Oh, shit, Miko, I'm sorry. I am so sorry. I know, oh my God, I know, Miko. I, too, I mean my body once served as a prostitute. Not the proudest time of my life, but it allowed me to survive. And I too evolved." Dancer looked lovingly over toward Bob. "I, too, evolved with Bob's help and guidance. You and I have a great deal in common. I had no idea to such a degree. But I am sorry, really." She looked up at the ceiling as she finished speaking, looking for forgiveness.

"I am aware of your evolution, Dancer and love you for the person you are. It is why I mentioned this. No apology is needed, Dancer. As you say, we have a lot in common. Somehow, I think we share similar emotions, though as an A.I., there will simply never be a way to know if my emotions are anything akin to yours, a human," she replied, her voice normal now.

Still looking up, Dancer, speaking thoughtfully, said, "Miko, if it is any consolation, we as humans will never know if one human to the next share the same emotions. I don't know if you will appreciate this or consider it an insult, but you have more human, good emotions than most of the people I have met in my life. I love you too, Miko!"

"Thanks, sweetie."

Turning back to face Bob, Dancer continued, "Where was I? Oh yeah, you're human after all. It's wonderful; I am actually excited for you. See, Miko, my sarcastic assault was not meant for you, just Bob."

It was difficult for Bob to find words with which he could defend himself. Which in itself, for Bob, this totally non-empathetic man, to show signs of guilt and embarrassment like a child was a miracle.

"Bob, you're allowed, you know, you don't have to explain. I am actually proud of you, and astonished I never connected the dots before this."

"Ruby asked me to help her with some of her girls' programming, and she gave me Miko as a gift. She knew how much I love Japanese classical music, and I believe she thought I had an affinity toward petite Asian women. She is beautiful, but it did not matter if she was Japanese or not; she is intelligent. I, of course, modified her to make her more compatible with my work and needs."

"Oh shit, I don't even want to know the full meaning of that statement, Bob. God only knows what you have done to that poor girl's mind," Dancer replied, smiling and shaking her head.

"It is quite okay, Dancer," spoke up Miko. "I love everything Bobby has done to my mind and my body. 'I think, therefore I am,' to quote Descartes. Bob has made me aware of so much, and I am eternally grateful to him. I do, however, understand your jest and that you are treating him with a certain amount of sarcasm in reference to us being sexually involved, but, rest assured, what Bobby and I share is unique among intelligent entities."

Bob was actually squirming at this point, feeling the discomfort of far too much information spilling out.

Dancer nervously played with her right earlobe, gently twisting the lobe that was slightly more elongated than normal and still bore the scars of suturing that had closed the large-gauge opening where once prepubescent dreams of being socially acceptable glittered.

"I am sorry, have I said too much?" And though only a voice in the room, you could tell Miko was smiling. You could hear the pride in Miko's voice, knowing she had successfully navigated a certain degree of sarcasm herself and had touched a nerve in both Dancer and Bob.

Dancer did what she did best. She started taking charge. In her mind, she was already planning and coordinating every move for this outing. The years after the Eight-Year War, after Ralph disappeared, she spent surviving through cunning and stealth, often having to steal food and supplies to get along. It hardened her, but produced a skill set most do not possess.

"Okay, let's double-check to make sure Aaron's VW has enough gas. Running out of gas in the middle of nowhere is not an option. We have exactly three hours, which is more than enough time to get there and back. Heck, we can stop near the dunes and have a picnic, but as they say, shit happens. Once Miko gives us the all-clear, Aaron, you go start your VW and pull it up to the front of the house."

Bob interrupted, "No. Aaron, drive it up to the garage. On the far side, where the driveway goes behind the garage, you will see that there is a gate. The combination is the same as the garage. Open the gate and wait; Dancer and I will meet you there."

Dancer looked at Bob sternly, thinking, *How dare you override my plans?*

Bob, unmoved by the look, continued, "This is where the dirt road starts that heads between the saddle you see just off in the distance. The road is never used and will be quite overgrown, giving us even more cover should we need it."

"Okay then, note to self, gate behind garage is the escape route," Dancer said, somewhat still perturbed at Bob's meddling in her plan.

"How overgrown, Bob? I don't want to scratch up my Bug. I have put a lot of work into—" Aaron stopped abruptly, mid-sentence, realizing the selfish vanity of being worried about the paint job on his Bug over the need to rescue Cynthia. "Nope. Never mind, I'm good. I am on board, to hell with the scratches. Fact is, you'll be happy to know when I rebuilt this baby, I wanted it to look totally stock, but it is sitting on top of an aluminum and titanium dune buggy chassis. I pumped up the suspension, reinforced the shock towers and rack and pinion, and the engine has an aluminum block, tuned exhaust and is fitted with dual Weber carbs. Suffice it to say, my little baby can move down a dirt road." Aaron spoke with both exuberant excitement and authority, the most since his unceremoniously abrupt abduction and appearance near the Last Hope.

Dancer, who had been ready to take charge and plan everything, once again conceded to Aaron. "Well, there you have it. We have a secret passage, a James Bond dune buggy and eyes in the sky. Shit, fifteen minutes, let's do this. It has seatbelts, right?" she asked, shyly.

~ ~~ ~ ~~ ~ ~~

Aaron kept flinching at the fingernails-on-a-chalkboard sound of scrub brush dragging against the sides of his precious VW. A car that he had spent many hours detailing, never with the consideration of taking it off-road, even though it possessed the engine and suspension perfectly designed for it. What it didn't possess in the way of optimum off-road accessories were the correct tires. Wanting to maintain a stock look, he'd chosen classic, 1960s-style road tires with extra-wide whitewalls. They were at least brand-new, and the tread good.

The car, with its three passengers, climbed right up the side of the first hill. After several miles and on top of the second hill, they looked down into a small valley that appeared to be a gathering place for off-road enthusiasts. There were many roads that all met in the middle, a flat area. Some roads ran up the sides of the hills covered with scrub, only to circle back down to the flat. Others led off into various ravines or up and over other hills.

Bob pointed to the flat. "Down there, Aaron, go there. Be careful, the dirt is dry and light from all of the vehicles using this area. The dust lays on the ground like snow, covering huge ruts and holes. Head toward the road there on the right by the tall scrub." He gestured with the book.

Dry, light dirt was an understatement, as the plume of dirt that rose when they hit the flat looked like smoke from a massive fire.

"Whoa, shit," said Aaron, looking behind in the small VW rearview mirror, not able to see where they had come from. "I hope they have some good power wash stations in this town."

"Ha, Aaron, they don't. Using water to wash your vehicle is highly illegal and will land you and your car behind bars," Dancer said, leaning forward between the two seats.

"How am I going to clean my car?" he asked, quickly glancing at her in the rearview mirror.

"I forget you don't know these things. I'll take you to the Carcuum if it is ever safe to go out in public again."

"They don't use water?" Aaron asked, holding on firmly to the wheel and staring straight ahead.

"Nope, it's a sonic vibration thing that shakes the dirt off, kinda like this ride," Dancer said, holding on tight as the little car bounced over a big rut. "They suck the dirt away with some really powerful vacuums. A much bigger version of the sonic shower you've been using back at the house."

"I haven't taken a shower yet," he said, cringing as a huge branch hit the windshield and dragged the length of the car. "I couldn't figure out how to use it, and I damn sure wasn't going to break it. I've been using the disposable wipes I brought."

Dancer laughed hysterically to the point she fell backward in her seat as they went over another big bump. "Poor baby." She had to stop to breathe. "Poor baby, you haven't had a shower since you have been here. Oh my God, as soon as we get back, into the sonic you go."

"There, there, turn there," Bob said, frantically pointing toward a small opening in the scrub that was overgrown, partially hiding where a road used to be.

Aaron stopped the Bug and looked horrified into the stiff, protruding branches from the scrub that left very little in the way of an opening. "There, you want me to go in there?" he asked.

"Yes, right there, Aaron. I am almost positive that is the road. It has been many years since I have gone this way. Hopefully, the old wash where the flash floods cross the road in the spring is crossable. Yeah, I am sure it is. Yes, this way Aaron," Bob insisted with his arm protruding out the side window, pointing to the dismal little opening in the scrub.

"Almost positive," Aaron repeated. Taking a deep breath, he revved up the Volkswagen's powerful little engine, generating a ferocious cat-like, four-stroke roar from the tuned exhaust. He had a very determined look on his face when he said, "For you, Cynthia."

Turning into the opening, he accelerated as they headed up a hill through the scrub, leaving a huge plume of white silt billowing into the air. Out of the flat, the heavy dust started to subside as the road became more treacherous, filled with ruts created from years of erosion. The Bug handled it well, bouncing and jarring its passengers all the way up. No one spoke; they just held on.

As they crested the top of the highest hill, visible off in the distance, they could see Flagstaff. The wash, as Bob suggested, had been passable, barely. Still, Aaron and his Bug again proved their worth traversing the many ruts slowly and methodically like a seasoned trials rider. Another ten minutes and they pulled onto the pavement that would lead them to the Scrub Brush hardware store only a couple of blocks away.

"Keep your eyes open for any drone vehicles," Dancer said, looking out the small rear side window. "The few that can afford them don't usually get out this far, but if they do, they have cameras on them that are tied directly into the main traffic control computer. Which just happens to be where the police and sheriff do most of their surveillance."

Aaron pulled into the gravel parking area at the rear of the Scrub Brush hardware store. Bob and Dancer extracted themselves from the tiny VW Bug. Aaron got out, trying his best not to survey the damage to his paint.

"Bit like being a sardine in a can," Dancer said. "But I gotta tell you, I am impressed with your little car. Mine wouldn't have made it up the first hill."

"Yes, Aaron, I too am impressed with the engineering of your Volkswagen," Bob said, stretching like a yoga instructor, book held high in the air. "It is by far a better car than mine. You have done an excellent job of restoring yours."

"Wow, Aaron, take note. Never, I mean never, in all the years I have known him, has Bob said someone else did something better than him, let alone something to do with engineering or mechanical. This is a big moment," Dancer remarked in mock disbelief.

Aaron looked at Dancer and Bob, replying, "Thanks, Bob, I appreciate that. But let's get real here, mine is a Volkswagen modified with pre-made, aftermarket parts; you built a time machine from, well, we will just call them previously owned parts."

Bob laughed. "Previously owned. I get it. You, of course, are right. I built a time machine."

"What do you say we go buy some fuses and blow this pop stand before someone notices us?" Dancer suggested.

They were in and out quickly, and would have been out considerably quicker had Bob not become transfixed at the counter wanting to buy one of the point-of-purchase, solar-powered, LED Arc thumb lights that came in a multitude of colorful anodized aluminum housings. Dancer felt like a mom with a two-year-old, finally succumbing and agreeing to buy the red one that he refused to let go of.

Safely back in the car, Dancer let out a sigh of relief. "Back the same way?"

"Yes, we still need to avoid any patrol drones," Bob said. But just as the words left his lips, all three heard the unmistakable whir of a drone. It would have been comical if not for the seriousness of their attempt to save Cynthia, as all three, at the exact same time, in harmony, said, "Shit!"

Without thinking, adrenaline pumping through Aaron's veins, he put the little VW into gear, giving it gas and popping the clutch so that even with the three of them in the car, the tires squealed, leaving a small puff of white smoke. He swung the car into a sharp turn, spraying gravel from the parking area that hit the side of the building and the owner's vehicle.

"Sorry, sorry," Aaron said, but stayed on the gas, heading down the road they had come in on. "Bob, where do we go?"

Bob was looking out the window as the drone dropped to window elevation, videoing who was in the car. The color and the markings made it abundantly clear that it was a police drone. Bob smiled and did the unthinkable; he waved at the drone.

"What the hell did you do that for?" Dancer said incredulously, nearly screaming to be heard over the roar of the VW's modified exhaust. "Now they know you are here and not in

Canada. The entire police department is now on its way to the house."

Aaron hit the dirt road going fifty miles per hour. The car immediately started bouncing as it skipped from rut to rut. "Hold on tight, I have an idea," he said, pressing the gas pedal further toward the floorboard. As the car sped along, a plume of dust rose in the air behind the car.

"Well, right now you're drawing a road map for any other drones to find us," Dancer said.

"Hang on, I got this," Aaron said as they flew off a rise in the road, followed by a drop-off that had them airborne for twenty feet. The little VW didn't flinch a muscle as the suspension absorbed the landing, allowing Aaron to maintain his speed. "Where is it?" he asked.

"It's above and off to our left about fifteen feet," Dancer reported, sliding to the left of the rear seat to peer out the little window behind Bob. "It's having no trouble keeping up with us. But it does keep disappearing for a moment in all the dust. We are never going to outrun that thing, Aaron."

The road dropped out from underneath them again into a steep downhill that left them airborne for what seemed like minutes.

"You're scaring the living shit out of me, Aaron!" Dancer screamed nervously, quite uncharacteristically, while holding on for dear life to the seat in front of her with one hand, the other pressed firmly against the ceiling.

Aaron didn't answer as his focus on the road ahead intensified. This time the landing was much more pronounced. The car completely bottomed out, making a horrific noise as the tires screeched along the inside of the wheel wells. Aaron did not react. With hands squarely on the left and right top of the wheel, he set up for the upcoming turn. Neither Bob nor Dancer could have known that Aaron had spent much of his teenage years racing motorcycles and quads with his father. This, though frightening to Dancer, had Aaron's blood racing, loving every second of it.

Meanwhile, Bob, sitting in the passenger seat, held onto the little brace above the glovebox with both hands and his book, grinning from ear to ear and letting out a constant "Whee. Whee," as would a five-year-old on a carnival ride.

Aaron hit the brakes hard for but a moment, then tried his best to push the gas pedal through the floorboard as the car drifted right into the turn with the scrub brush, making a horrible, piercing, shrill scraping noise as the sharp thorns tore through the paint to bare metal.

The plume of soft dirt rose, lofting into the air in near every direction as Aaron took one more jump that brought them down into the open flat they had passed through earlier. He headed for the middle, then cranked the wheel hard to the right, staying on the gas, the car spinning one donut after another, raising a plume of dirt that looked more like a volcano had just erupted. So much dust rose into the air it became dark as night. It was difficult to even make out each other's frozen posture, gripping onto whatever they could with fingernails extended like wolves and eyes open wide enough that the whites provided extra light in the car.

SMACK! A black shadow slammed into the front windshield, shattering it into a giant spiderweb. Aaron stopped the car. They all sat quiet and motionless.

"I think we got it," Aaron said, not quite sure of his statement. "Either that or we just took out a buzzard."

Still unable to see anything because of the plume, Dancer, whose ability to regroup and recompose herself was legendary, spoke up, "We need to go somewhere else other than Bob's. They know where we are, and they know where we were headed. Bob, any ideas?"

"Aaron, your Bug is way cooler than my Bug," was all Bob, still in child-mode from the ride, could utter.

"No, really, Bob, where are we? Where can we go? We need to hide this car before any more of their Flying Monkeys come looking for us," Dancer said with a great deal of urgency.

Bob, thumping the book on his thigh, looked up. "I know, I know. Do you remember when we first came into this flat area in the morning?"

"Yeah," Aaron said, and Dancer nodded.

"Do you remember there were several trails headed up and over the crest to the left of us?"

"Yeah."

"The one to the far left. Go there, go up and over that hill." Bob pointed with the book toward the swirling plume, now starting to settle enough to make out the hills.

"Okay then, got it." With that, Aaron once again stepped on the gas and sped off in the other direction, toward where they had come in the morning.

"No, no, Aaron. Not that way, not back home. I said the road over there. I am right, I am always right, go there," Bob said, frantically motioning with the book toward the hill and road in the other direction.

"Bob, I told you I've got this. Sit tight." Aaron kept racing toward the road that led home.

Even Dancer now screamed, the car bouncing enough to give her voice vibrato. "Aaron, Bob is right. We can't go that way, they'll find us."

"Oh my God, you guys. I've got this. Just sit tight." Aaron shifted into third and headed down the road maybe a quarter of a mile, with both Dancer and Bob protesting the entire way. Finally, he stopped at a small clearing and turned around. He headed back toward the flat, making as much of a dust plume as he could. Once inside the flat, he did several more donuts, once again raising the impenetrable fog of dust. At the far side of the flat, he slowed the VW to a crawl and slowly headed up the hill and over the top.

Bob smiled. "He is a smart one, this boy."

Dancer, usually the quickest to figure people out, still found herself in a bit of a dust cloud mentally from the ride. "Why?"

"Do you not see, Dancer? He has left them a misdirect, like a magician. The drones will look for the dust and follow the trail he just made. We are now going slow enough as to not raise any more dust. Hopefully, we will get far enough away before they get here, and they will not be able to find us." At the slower speed, Bob looked and sounded more his age, more like Bob.

"And they will not find us. If I might quote our young companion, *I've got this!*"

"Aaron, you have to be one remarkable young man," Dancer said. "Like I said, in all the years I have known Bob, he has never complimented anyone, hell, not even me. And now, in less than ten minutes, he has complimented you not once, not twice, but three times. You okay, Bob?"

Dancer rested her hand on Bob's shoulder. "If I didn't know better, I would say you were developing some social skills in your old age, Bob." She laughed.

"If one desires to consider it so, referring to the correct implementation of logic in an effort to resolve the challenges that present themselves before us, that is an assumption of their own making, not mine. I merely reiterated the facts," Bob responded with his natural, holier-than-thou look and voice.

"I see I spoke too soon." Dancer slapped Aaron's shoulder as she laughed even harder.

"I believe we have achieved enough effective distance to increase our speed slightly, Aaron. We are heading toward the valley you see to your left. The drones should not be able to detect a small amount of dust as we are now on the other side," Bob assured.

Aaron sped up and headed for the valley. "What's down there?"

"The reason I knew about my property is from the time I spent at the cult. Judas and I explored every square inch of the land back here. It is here Judas and I discovered the tunnels. Through the tunnels, I was able to escape the Reverend and his band of merry misfit, psychopathic followers. The back entrance to the property is down there," he said, pointing. "I am hoping the man you met in the hardware store, Judas, will allow us to enter. He was a very good friend, the only close friend I have had until you, Dancer."

Dancer gave an ah shucks move with her shoulders. "Ah, Bob, thank you. But are you sure you are up for this? Seeing that guy hit you pretty hard at the store," Dancer asked.

"I will be fine. I had not seen him since we were little boys. The man I saw at the hardware store looked just like the Reverend. And, yes, that shook me to my core. Now that I am aware it is Judas, I will be okay. Though for the life of me I do not understand why he dresses like his father. He hated his father. But it matters not, it is our only option."

"Well, let's hope your friend and his cult buddies don't turn us away. If they do, any other ideas?" Aaron asked.

As they drew closer, before them lay an oasis. Here in the middle of all this scrub brush, red rock and dust appeared a large stand of trees. The sheer lusciousness of the green and the shade that it produced stood out in stark contrast to the surroundings. It looked cool and inviting. A hundred yards ahead, they could see a tall fence with locked gates, obviously designed to keep intruders out.

"This fence, I do not remember there being a fence when I lived here," Bob said, surprised.

"Are you kidding, Bob?" Dancer offered, being unusually cynical. "After the debacle caused by the Reverend's arrest and escape, those people in there have gone into hiding from the rest of the world. Can't say as I wouldn't do the same thing. Can't say as I don't often wish that I could build a fence around me to keep the rest of the idiots out."

"Bob, you don't think there is any chance the Reverend is still alive, and maybe hiding out in there?"

"No, I am sure he is gone. And good riddance. The world with all of its faults does not need evil vermin like him," he said, matter-of-factly. "I do not believe Judas would have helped him or harbored him. He hated his father and everything he represented."

As they pulled up to the gate and stopped, trying to figure out their next move, the gate opened slightly. It was enough to allow one very tall man to slide through sideways, step out and face them. It was Judas, with his hands on his hips. He did not dress in the red robe and hat they had seen him in at the hardware store. Instead, he wore common, everyday blue jeans and a t-shirt. His hair was short and disheveled, like he had been working hard.

"Robert Mandić," he announced loudly in a challenging voice. "What brings you home?"

The three of them looked at one another, not exactly sure how to read this greeting. Bob opened the door slowly, getting out even slower. A mere ten feet away from this giant man, he stood up to face his old friend. "Judas, it has been a long time. I did not believe you would still be here until I saw you at the hardware store. You caught me seriously off guard dressed like your father. I confess I panicked. I thought you were him."

Judas broke into a smile. "Robert, Robert, Robert." He laughed with a chuckle from deep in his diaphragm. "I wear those spooky-ass clothes and the wig in town only to keep up the facade that the cult is still here. It scares the riffraff away. And we like our privacy. I profoundly apologize to you, my friend. I did not mean to scare you. You gave me quite a start as well. But the greetings and stories can wait. We know you have the police after you. We picked it up on our scanner. I also knew there would be a very good chance you would come here to hide. I would have. I do not know what you did, you can explain later, but you are always welcome here, Robert. This is your home."

Judas turned to the man who appeared next to him. "Saul, open the gate. Let's get this VW inside and out of sight of the drones. Surely they will be here shortly. They hover over us daily."

With that, he and Saul, a younger man who looked astonishingly like Judas, pulled the gate open wide enough for the little Bug to be driven in. Once inside, a middle-aged woman with jet-black hair that fell past her waist directed Aaron to follow her toward a canopy covering a large open cobblestone patio made from square adobe bricks.

"We can leave your car under here for the moment. When we are sure there are no drones about, we will push it into the cave opening over there," Judas said, pointing to the side of the hill.

"I'm sorry, where? I don't see a cave," Dancer asked.

Judas had a peculiar smile that grew very wide. "Exactly." He turned toward Stella. "Thank you, Stella. Could you pull the hose over here and run water over the engine to cool it down?" He spoke as he bent down, opening the rear hood, exposing the engine.

"Nice," he added, smiling, obviously recognizing the amount of care and work that had gone into it. "Spray it very lightly at first, a mist. We don't want to crack or warp those fins. Then, if you would, please, get some large towels to throw over the top and back of the VW so you can wet them down as well. I want to cool the cowling down, as those drones detect heat. Saul, you and Daniel cut some brush and use it to sweep the tire marks from inside the compound down the road—" He paused to think. "Sorry, but you had better go at least a half-mile to the first big turn. Then pass the word for everyone to dress up, we are going to have visitors. Please follow me. I need to hide all of you. They can count bodies with those damn drones, and they know how many people live here."

~~~~ ~~~~ ~~ ~

"Please tell me you have good news," Nate said, turning to face the fledgling deputy who had just entered his temporary office, a windowless room not much bigger than a closet at the rear of the station.

"Well, sir, I have good news," he hesitated, "and I have bad news. Which would you like to hear first?" The bold young deputy was holding back an odd smile.

"Are you fucking with me?" Nate grunted. "You got some balls, kid." Nate stopped, thought about it and finished with, "But, I like that. Give me the good, then the bad."

"One of our drones picked them up just outside of town headed back to the Mandić property. There were three of them in that kid's Volkswagen," he said and held up his tablet to show him the video. His timing couldn't have been better as the video had reached the point where Bob, smiling like a ten-year-old, waved at the drone from inside the VW.

"Well, you old coot." Nate laughed. "Got ya!"

"Well, no, sir. That's the bad news. Keep watching." They watched the entire chase episode down the dirt roads, over the drop-offs and jumps, and finally the dust storm in the small basin where all roads met. Their eyes were all glued to the small screen right up until the camera zoomed in on Aaron's determined face at the wheel. Then smack, a sudden crashing noise and the screen went black.

"What happened? What the fuck just happened?" Nate demanded, quite animated now.

"I'm pretty sure our drone hit the windshield of their car!"

"You sent out a replacement drone, right?" Nate, now standing up, asked.

"Of course we did. But again, sir, watch." Once again, he held out his tablet for Nate to view. Nate grabbed it from him and stared at the screen seeing only what looked like the storms on Jupiter. As the drone rose higher, they could make out a dust trail which the drone followed toward Bob's property, until it stopped in the middle of the road and brush. The drone circled around and around without seeing any further dust rising or a parked Volkswagen.

"Shit! Send some cars to the property, right now," Nate ordered.

"Sir, we did that. There is no one there. There are no life forms present on the property."

"What? Let me think." Nate scratched his chin in deep thought.

"Sir?" the young deputy tried to ask shyly.

"Hold on, I said, I'm thinking," Nate snapped at him.

"Sir, if you will excuse me," he said, bolder this time, "what about the old cult property? Didn't Robert live there as a child? It is actually pretty close to where we lost him."

Nate's head slowly turned, bearing an obvious grin. "See, I knew I liked you, kid. Get a drone in the air and some cars over there. And get me a car as well. I wanna be there." Nate sat down with a satisfied look on his face. "Gonna get ya, Robbie, boy. Gonna get ya!"

~ ~~ ~ ~~ ~~~

Cynthia's panic couldn't be more real or painful. Hyperventilating and close to hysterics, she tried over and over to reach her mom's cell only to be met with, "We're sorry, service to this area is temporarily unavailable, please try your call again." She scrolled through the internet news she had bookmarked on her phone, but to no avail. None of the wire services were reporting any new nuclear blasts or major attacks on a major city.

Somewhat relieved, and not one to wait around, she decided it was time to go. Wearing only a pair of overalls that were covered in paint and stain, with holes in the knees, a baseball cap, equally covered in various colors of pigment, and carrying her favorite green-and-grey hiking bag filled with the bare necessities, she hoisted Half Dome into the truck, jumping in right behind. A prudent woman, she stopped just before heading up the summit toward the Bay Area to fill up with gas. As she waited at the pump, she tried yet again to reach her mom, but was frustrated that she couldn't even leave a message or text. While the fuel flowed through the hose into her tank, she took that time, sitting at the wheel, door open, to draft a quick email, hoping it would go through. The loud click of the pump handle shutting off startled her and made her look up.

This gave Half Dome his chance to put one paw on her thigh and the other on her shoulder. A bright and intuitive animal, he could sense her anxiety and was doing his best to console her, adding a long, wet lick to her cheek. He then, with cocked head, stared directly into her eyes.

"Oh baby, Mommy is all right. I'm just very worried," she said, stroking the back of his head. He responded with another lick hoping to garner further attention. As she hit send, the air filled with the sound of sirens that grew in intensity. She looked in her rearview mirror while Half Dome turned to look out the back to see a steady stream of city and forest service firetrucks roar by with lights ablaze. "What the fuck?" she said under her breath. The sheer volume of so many sirens exponentially increased her already high level of anxiety.

As they passed, Half Dome, unable to resist, raised his head and started howling, doing his best to harmonize with this pack of wild beasts.

Then, "Oh, girls just want to have fu-un..." started playing, an email-received tone. *That was quick*, she thought, reaching for her phone. "Oh God, yes, please let it be Mom," Cynthia said as she held up the phone, deftly touching the keys needed to retrieve the mail.

'MAILER-DAEMON'

(MAILERDAEMON@k9plsmtp244-07-33.prod.phx0.secureserver.net)

Your mail message to the following address(es) could not be delivered.

This is a permanent error. Please verify the address(es) and try again.'

"FUCK!"

~~~~ ~~~~ ~~~~

They walked into the old mine entrance, and at once, Aaron felt a significant drop in temperature. The cooling sensation was so pleasant, he let out an involuntary "Ah." About forty feet in, the light diminished as well, and Judas grabbed an old-style lantern and lit it, filling the room with a soft, flickering glow. He blew out the match and squeezed it between his thumb and finger.

"I know, very old school. But unlike the electricity, it always works. We are safe here. We are already under a hundred feet of rock, far more than those drones can see through. Still, I want to take you back a bit further in case they show up and want to snoop around. Want to," he laughed. "Who am I kidding? When they snoop around, I want the three of you in the next state. Bob, you remember these mines, right? We played in them for hours on end. Our sanctuary. Through the years, I have discovered they go back for miles. In fact, I have not yet found all of the passages."

"Yes, Judas. I do remember all of our journeys back here. It is, in fact, why I bought the property I did. I knew of the mines and the Lava Caves as well. I bought it because it would be perfect for my work. Away from these same evil, government-controlled goons who want to stop me and steal my work," Bob spoke with hostility.

Aaron shot him a glance. "Ah, don't you think it might have been you that kind of got that ball rolling, Bob?" Aaron said, then reconsidered his sarcastic response. "Sorry, I know they have no concept of what you have accomplished. And you're correct. They want to stop you and take it away. Something we cannot allow to happen. At least not until Cynthia is safe."

"We need to get back to Bob's lab," Dancer said, with urgency in her voice. "It is really important that we do. How can we… Oh shit. The bag. The bag is in the Volkswagen with the fuses. We have to get the bag. I'll go get it."

"No," Judas said matter-of-factly. "Stay here. I have no doubt the Imperial goons will be arriving any second. They never miss a chance to harass us. This is going to be a field day for them. I will go and retrieve the bag. Then, if they are not here yet, we will push your Volkswagen in as well. Bob, take my lantern and keep heading into the mine, staying to the left until you get to an open area where the walls are covered with pentagrams painted on them."

They all simultaneously turned and looked at Judas.

"No, it's not what you are thinking. These tunnels are our escape from civilization. We want to keep people out. It is our version of a scarecrow. Now, wait for me there. I will be right back." With that, he ran out into the sunlight.

The three arrived in the open area, where they were greeted by a truly scary display of Wiccan graffiti, enough to elicit a gasp from Dancer. Before they could examine the artwork, Judas came running back, breathing very hard.

"Here, take off your shirts and put these on," Judas tried to say between breaths.

"Why do I need to take off my shirt?" protested Dancer.

"Please, just do it. I will explain as you do. We have security cameras in locations watching all potential points of entrance to the property, including some several miles out to give us plenty of time to prepare for unwanted guests. There is what looks like a rather large contingent of police headed this way. At least five, maybe six ground vehicles and two dronecars. And there is one drone overhead already." Judas stopped to take several deep breaths before continuing. "They'll have a cavebot with them for sure. I hate those things. They can chase you through a pitch-black cave faster than you can run with light. So just trust me, we have no time. Aaron, I need the keys to your car."

Aaron looked at him with some concern. "Why?" he asked.

"Of course, of course." Judas took another long deep breath. "We are sending three members dressed in your clothes out in your VW. They will take the road to the north. We are counting on the drone to see them leave, and hopefully get the war party to follow. Buy us some time, get you the hell out of here."

Dancer stepped up to Judas, handing him her shirt as she held the one he gave her in front of her naked torso. Aaron tossed his keys to Judas. "Do whatever you have to, and thanks."

Dancer turned to Judas. "The bag, did you get the bag?"

"Oh yes, sorry. Here." Judas reached into his pocket and pulled out the small bag from the hardware store with the fuses. "Can I ask why these fuses are so important that you have the Corps and the State Police chasing you?"

"Well, you see, Bob borrowed some—no, wait." She stopped herself. "Not now, we can explain later, Judas. There isn't time. Go, just go," she said as both Aaron and Bob handed him their shirts.

"You're right. Wait here. I will be right back. Aaron, I promise you they will be careful with your car," he said and disappeared into the dark tunnel.

~ ~~ ~ ~ ~~~~

Visibility had started to deteriorate, and the sky was looking very smoky, with a slight orange glow apparent through the pine trees. Cynthia jumped in the car, pulling the door closed so quickly it rattled the windows. On a mission, determined to get to her mom, she started the engine and jammed the truck in gear, heading toward the gas station's exit. Her heart sank. Cars now filled the single lane heading out of town, bumper to bumper.

As she looked for a chance to merge with the traffic, her phone rang. She grabbed for it, only to be greeted with a public service announcement squelch. *What now?* she thought as she touched the screen to open the PSA.

"Extreme Fire Warning! Highway 50 closed to all westbound traffic at Meyers. Highway 88 closed to all westbound traffic at Pickets Junction. Severe fire danger and poor visibility due to the volume of smoke. Please use alternative routes."

How is that possible? Oh my God, they've nuked Sacramento? she thought to herself. Then she smiled slightly for a second, thinking that it meant her mom would be okay. *Oh my God, what is going on? What's wrong with me?* She mentally scolded herself for hoping her mom would be better off if everyone else had died in a nuclear blast in Sacramento.

Highway 80. I can go around Emerald Bay. Not shy, and without hesitation, she pulled out onto the shoulder and drove against traffic until she found an opening she could squeeze through and get on to the other side of the road. Clear on that side, she accelerated, tires chirping with each shift. She wanted to get around Emerald Bay before anything else could go wrong.

Half Dome stood on his sturdy but short back legs, rocking back and forth with each shift, head and tongue hanging out the window on the passenger side.

Oh God, if Sacramento is gone, Highway 80 will be closed as well, or a parking lot with people trying to get out, she thought.

"Just drive, girl, you'll find a way. Just drive!" she said out loud. Half Dome turned to look at her with his big, bulging brown eyes, tongue still hanging out, panting, and nodded in agreement.

~~~~ ~~ ~ ~~~~

After they had all been sitting on the floor of the cave long enough to get uncomfortable, Judas returned.

"Didn't make it," he said, bending down, hands on his knees, to catch his breath.

"What didn't make it?" Dancer asked.

Judas stood, still breathing hard. "We were not able to get your—" He stopped again to catch his breath. "Your Volkswagen out. By the time we were opening the rear gate, a mini-armada had pulled up to the front. I had them park it where it sat and go back to the front. I told them to just do what they could do to stall and distract them while I ran back here. We need to get going. There is a junction ahead. We can stop there. I have a plan to stop those freaky, spider-like cavebots. Did I mention they're fast as hell? They don't crawl, they run."

He held out what looked like black rope. "Wasn't sure if we would ever need this." He smiled. "Follow me, stay close."

With that, Judas headed down the mine's tunnel. They arrived at yet another open area with two tunnels to choose from. Judas set the lamp down and proceeded to spread out the tangle of rope. "Aaron, help me."

Recognizing the black rope he held was a cargo net, Aaron knew instantly what Judas was up to. As they straightened it out, Judas stepped into the tunnel on the right about six feet in, where he started attaching the ends to aging metal hooks previously hammered into the wall. When he had finished with most of them, he motioned for them all to come in as he held the net up.

Aaron stepped in, followed by Bob. Dancer, however, had disappeared.

Suddenly a bright light illuminated the tunnel from where they had just come. The light from the cavebot filled the open area as the creepy little bot rapidly scurried toward them. Judas hooked the last end of the net to the wall. He stepped back and away but stumbled, tumbling toward Aaron and Bob, dropping the lantern. It landed upright but rocking, illuminating the three of them and animating their shadows. The bot never lost stride as it hit the net. Its front four legs went through the net exactly as Judas had hoped. As it squirmed to free itself, it only became more entangled.

"Well, I'll be darned, it worked," Judas drawled.

The bot stopped trying to free itself, allowing an uneasy moment of silence. Then it spoke in a stern, metallic voice, "Stop where you are. Stop and do not move any further. You will wait until officers arrive to detain you."

The three of them looked at each other. Bob could not contain himself, bending down close to the light, and once again allowed his hidden inner child to escape, smiling and waving to the camera on the drone.

Aaron grabbed Bob's shoulder. "Bob, stop that. We need you to turn this thing off. Can you do that?"

Bob nodded. "I can if you can figure out how to grab it and hold on to it. There should be a small hole at the back of the main housing. About the size a paper clip would fit into. And I need a paper clip. Where is Dancer?" he asked with concern.

"Whump." A crashing, crushing noise filled the cave, followed by flickering lights and then silence.

"What the hell was that? Bob, are you okay? Judas? Dancer?" Aaron called out. Then, in the light of the lantern and the sparks emanating from the bot, he was able to see a huge rock sitting on top of the crushed, still arcing bot. Its mechanical legs splayed out in all directions through the net still supporting it.

Judas turned up his lantern, making them all cover their eyes. There, proudly, stood Dancer over the dismantled bot. She was dusting off her hands with a great degree of satisfaction.

Well, that worked way better than I hoped," she said, bending down to dust the dirt off on her pant legs. "Oh yeah, I'm okay too."

"Who the hell are you, Indiana Jones?" asked Aaron. "Where did you go? I didn't even know you had left. You scared the shit out of all of us."

"I snuck off while you three were hanging Charlotte's Web here. I figured a plan B might prove useful. Guess it was a smashingly good idea," Dancer said smiling.

"That, my friends, is what I call applied logic," said Bob, laughing at his own pun.

"They certainly don't make those things very strong. I thought these were military grade. You know, like you could drop a grenade on it and it would survive," added Judas.

"Not to squash everyone's fun," continued Dancer, "but we need to get the hell out of here. Judas, where to?"

Bob was slapping his thigh with the book while simultaneously trying to wipe the tears from his eyes. "Squash... squash," he kept repeating.

"Come with me," Judas said. "Ahead of us is a labyrinth of passages that will keep them busy for some time."

"Here," offered Bob, pulling the small thumb light that Dancer had purchased for him earlier from his pocket. He turned it on, filling the entire room with light as bright as day.

"Whoa. Okay, forget the lantern, follow me." Judas took the small light and led them further into the tunnels.

~~~~ ~~~~ ~~~~

Nate hovered over the cavebot operator's shoulder, watching the screen and shaking his head as Bob's bigger-than-life face smiled at them, waving like a child. "How can that man be so smart?" Nate asked more to himself than those around him.

Then with a simple *blip,* the screen went to black.

"They've killed another one! They're killing all my Bots," exclaimed the dismayed operator. He was a young and slightly overweight young man, not even in uniform, more teenager than man.

"Are you serious? Kid, grow up. It's a fucking toy. The Corp can buy ten more," said an angered Nate. "Do we have another one?"

"Not here, sir," returned the young operator, who now answered with far too much cadet bravado. "Sir, my name is Andrew, sir. Most call me Andy."

"Okay, fine," he said, shaking his head and letting out a long sigh. "Get some people in there with lights. Find the kid's toy and bring it back here. Then spread out from that last location. Find them, damn it! Find them."

~~ ~ ~~~~ ~

Maintaining a quick pace, they followed Judas and the bright glow from Bob's pocket light.

"I am assuming you have another way out of here other than your compound?" questioned Dancer.

"Yes, of course," Judas replied, walking and often ducking because of his height. "There is going to be a passage about an eighth of a mile ahead, where all of us will need to squeeze through some pretty tight holes," he said, scrunching up his face, concerned one of them would have a fear of tight places. "Is everyone okay with that?" he asked, looking back. They all nodded.

Knowing he had some time, Judas asked, "Bob, what on Earth are you up to? You've brought more cops onto the property than when they busted my dad."

Aaron and Dancer both looked at one another. Judas had no idea of Bob's verbosity.

"Hope it's a long walk to the exit," chided Dancer.

Bob weighed in his mind where to begin. "Judas, oddly enough, it was your father who started this. In more ways than just ruining my childhood, to the point I felt it necessary to run away. I am quite sure you remember how he loved to tie everything to a Bible quote. One verse he used many times. The first time I heard it, it oddly stuck for no apparent reason. But the more I heard it, the more it opened my mind to what or how everything works. The quote was, *In the beginning was the Word, and the Word was with God, and the Word was God.* John something or other, if I recall. It didn't really mean a great deal to me at that time, I was far too rebellious. But some years later, in college, we were discussing DNA and the scripting that is in place inside each of us. Scripting that defines nearly everything about us. It was about this time in my life I recognized how much smarter than everyone else I appeared to be, including my teachers. I saw things they could not. I could see beyond the curtains of Oz, the Great and Powerful. I saw it, I knew there had to be more, there had to be a written script controlling everything."

They entered a large chamber with two different openings, just big enough for a normal size person to crawl into. "Pardon me, Bob. I have to stop you. I want you to finish. However, we are at the spot where we must assume a reptilian position and, as they say, crawl on our bellies." A comforting breeze came from one of the holes, blowing very welcome, cool air on them. The other, next to it, was less inviting, offering up a slightly warmer breeze with a hint of sulfur.

Judas held up the light to the one directly in front of them. "This one. And yes, before you ask, the hole that stinks. This will take us to another set of larger tunnels that we will once again be able to walk in. They are not part of the mine, not dug by the miners, they are part of the Lava Caves system. A part of the caves the park service does not even know exists. The crawl is only about fifty yards, but it will get larger and sometimes uncomfortably tight. It rises and drops maybe three or four feet. I will go first with my lantern. Aaron, you will be last, carrying the thumb light. You won't get stuck, the sulfur won't kill you, and you won't run out of air. Relax, and stay calm. Okay?" Judas asked as he turned his head to look at each one of them.

Dancer's voice betrayed a possible phobia of tight, slimy, dark places. "I am just so excited to get down on my belly and slither through this dirt. Maybe I should add that I am very pleased that you know where we are in this maze. Lead the way. The sooner we get moving, the sooner we get out of here."

"Let's all stand over here in front of this hole, so we can leave some footprints as if we went in it," Judas instructed as he stomped around the more inviting opening. "It is, after all, the better smelling of the two, and I am sure anyone following us won't require much convincing to choose it first. Aaron, if you can, as best you can, as you are the last to come in the hole, do your best to brush away the footprints with your shirt?"

"Okay, you got it," Aaron responded.

Judas started into the passage, followed by Dancer, then Bob, with Aaron bringing up the rear as planned. They had been crawling, all breathing heavy, grunting and uttering an occasional "Ouch" for about five minutes, when Bob, out of the blue, suddenly continued with his story, picking up where he'd left off as if he had only taken a breath.

"It played out before my eyes like watching a double helix coil of DNA unravel. I could see what it was made of, like seeing the cloud of an atom. There it was, the next level defining our reality on the infinite quantum scale. More than just atoms and their cloud of electrons. More than instructions on what little of the DNA we understand. In fact, it scared me. For suddenly I was faced with some degree of validity to the Bible. Whoever taught the disciples knew that we are a product of the *Word*. Not the word like you read in the Bible with rules and fairy tales. No, they knew, or maybe it was poorly explained to them, and they misunderstood. But someone was telling them that we, our reality, is code. The *Word* is a script."

At this point, they had all paused their efforts to rest and to listen to Bob.

"I knew," Judas said, "you were with us for a reason, Bob. You call it quantum physics. I call it metaphysics or spiritualism. But you, with your unique set of mental skills, were at the compound to suffer through my dad for a reason. And today, I finally understand."

"That ain't the half of it, Judas," Dancer added. "This man's brain is full of so much off-the-wall shit. Well, there is no one like him anywhere on this planet. He sees through reality itself. He reads it and—"she paused—"he can change it."

"Yeah, and I am fucking living proof of that," added Aaron, from behind.

"Come on, our voices carry. Let's keep going." With that, Judas, not yet grasping what they were trying to convey, grunted as he turned and started forward on his belly again.

"Can you and Bob use your Nipples?" Aaron asked Dancer, crawling on his forearms, doing his best to keep his head low but shaking it nonetheless in the disbelief that those words just came out of his mouth. "Let me rephrase that, can you and Bob communicate via your Nano Implants?"

"Yes, we can, but my nipples are not secure like Bob's," Dancer responded, trying her best to hold back a laugh.

"Secure, as in not going to fall off?" Aaron mocked.

The others laughed now, and then Dancer spoke, composing herself, "It's not like talking to someone in a real-time conversation. It is far more mechanical. It's more like having a conversation via emails or texts. We call them *nexts* or *nexting*. Response time is slow, and meanings can be misconstrued without the voice connotations to accompany them. I've met some people who have mastered it and use it, rudely, I might add, in front of others."

"Nexts. Okay, I wondered what you were talking about. But that really doesn't answer my question. Can you use it now?"

"Well, I did kind of *actually* answer your question. No, mine is not secure, and therefore it is highly likely they would be able to pick up my transmission as well as Bob's. So not a good idea," Dancer, still breathing hard, answered, trudging ahead to keep up with Judas.

"Actually, Dancer, I have been communicating with Stella this entire time using my, what do you call them— *Nipples?* Who thought of that stupid name?" Judas asked.

"That would be me," Dancer replied, a bit hoarse from laughing.

"Sorry. You're not stupid. I'll just shut up now," replied a humbled Judas.

"Don't be silly. It is a stupid name. Bob kept referring to them as NBPLs. I thought it sounded like he was saying nipples, so, well, one afternoon after he said it, I grabbed my nipples in front of him, very graphically, and asked, 'Like these?' Bob laughed, which he rarely does, at least at my jokes, and it stuck."

"I see, Dancer. Yes, very funny," Judas replied in a dry tone, then laughed. "We refer to our devices as our *Third Eye*. We use a code, of course. Since the arrest of my father, we have become quite adept at maintaining our secrecy."

"The Corp's computers can break any code, Judas. Well, any code but mine, of course. You must know that?" Bob not so humbly tossed in.

"We rely on magic, Bob, the art of misdirection. We want them to break our code. Because when they do, they will be so lost they won't trust their own computers. The code, in many layers, relies on our memories of events in our lives here at the compound. Certain words bring memories of certain events and actions. Then because we all know each other so well, we can discern the gist of what each of us is trying to convey. Anyone else will not have a clue," Judas said and started moving again. "We really need to keep moving to get to the next point and off our bellies. Then we can enter the safe room. They won't find us there, and it is stocked with water, food, lights, extra clothing, even bottled oxygen. From there, standing up and walking, we head through a series of Lava Cave tunnels that are natural and subterranean. One of the tunnels exits only a few miles from the highway southwest of our compound."

"My house is near the highway," Bob said. "There is a back entrance to my Cave, the lab. I have a bicycle covered and hidden there in case I—well—in case I ever needed a quick getaway."

"Ow! Shit," Aaron said loudly and abruptly. "Okay, that's going to leave a mark."

"Are you okay?" Dancer asked.

"Yeah. I just smacked my elbow, the funny bone, on a rock sticking out of the wall, which made me jump, and then I hit my head on the ceiling," Aaron responded, still rubbing his head.

"Poooor baby," Dancer said, cooing.

"Yes, yes, keep your head down, Aaron," Bob added. "By your description, Judas, I think we might be exiting near enough to walk to it. My concern is how do we traverse to the back entrance without being seen by the drones."

"Robert, I mean Bob, my brother," Judas said, very reverend-like, "I know exactly where that bike is. I found it many months ago. It is in a cave opening. Funny, I wondered who would hide a perfectly good bike out here in the desert. But I understand the need for such necessities, and so I left it to its purpose."

Judas's face lit up. "Boy, do I have a surprise for you."

~~~~ ~ ~~ ~~ ~

Cynthia started to feel some degree of hope as she made it all the way around the lake to Tahoe City and was now headed toward the quaint little town of Truckee. Just past Squaw Valley, rounding a sharp curve along the river, she came upon a parking lot of brake lights and an alarming amount of yellowish smoke. It filtered down amongst the pine trees, lowering the visibility to no more than a quarter of a mile. Her heart sank. She knew all too well this traffic meant they were done, not going anywhere. The smoke only confirmed her worst fears that everything east of here no longer existed.

She wanted to weep, still very scared for her mother, but no tears came. *Aaron, please call.*

Once again, the noise of sirens approaching brought her back to her own predicament. *Oh my God, this is fallout. It's radioactive. Shit, I need to get Half Dome out of here now!*

She turned to look behind at the oncoming firetrucks, exposing the top portion of the tattoo on her neck: a Moai, the Easter Island monoliths. The rest of the tattoo was hidden, disappearing under her long blond hair. The full skin art, a collage of sorts, went down her side to her hip and onto her thigh. Artwork that for her had become a totem, a testimonial, created over many years of her strong belief that intelligence and creativity were not unique to Earth.

She moved so quickly and sharply she felt her lower back uncomfortably pop. *No, damn it, what else?* she thought. Ignoring the searing pain, she continued to back up as far as she could, preparing to turn around. She waited for the last firetruck to go by, then turned the truck sharply around, heading off in the other direction, in full retreat back to her home in South Lake. There she could regroup. She could figure out her next move.

Where the hell is Aaron? Damn it, I need you, she thought. Hoping against logic that he hadn't perished, she stepped on the gas. Now the only question she thought was, *Will I even be able to get back to South Tahoe?*

"We'll swim. Right, Half Dome? We'll swim home in the lake if we have to."

To which Half Dome, at the word *swim*, jumped on her right arm, excitedly wagging his stump of a tail.

~~~   ~~~   ~~~

Judas paused, rolling over on to his side to look back at Bob. "This Godscript thing is so you, Bob. A theory contradictory to everything everyone else on the planet believes. But it is certainly not worth sending the Corps out after you." Judas chuckled. "So, what on Earth have you done to generate so much interest in you? And I say this to you, but you can tell me later, as we really need to keep crawling."

"Aaron, tell Judas here when you were born. Oh, and where you are from," responded Dancer before Bob could answer.

Aaron looked ahead toward Bob with a questioning look even though he couldn't see his face, wondering if he should answer.

Not waiting, Bob brought the cave-crawling caravan to a complete halt, answering for Aaron. "Judas, you understand as most do not just how intelligent I am. It is why I allowed you to be my only friend as children."

Aaron shone the little light ahead onto Bob, providing an unintentional Rembrandt spotlight effect for the moment.

"What I have discovered, with regards to my Godscript, will rewrite everything we know about everything. To make this discovery possible, as those idiot want-to-be physicists back at Livermore refused to believe or even listen to me, I had to procure for myself some equipment they might think sensitive or valuable. Very adept at being stealth-like, I and the equipment simply disappeared. I then returned here to build the apparatus necessary to prove my theory."

Before he could continue, Aaron, who could no longer contain himself, interrupted. "Apparatus? Apparatus?" said Aaron loudly. "He built a collider, Judas. Under his mountain, he has a miniature collider like the one they have at Cern. And for the record, I was born April 17, 1986. I am thirty-eight years old and I live, make that lived, in Lake Tahoe, California, which apparently no longer exists." He paused long enough for that to sink in.

On a roll, he chose now, down in the sulfuric smelling tunnel as they all lay on their bellies, to continue, venting everything he had been feeling since his world had been turned upside down. "Bob here has been so kind as to abduct me, like a pack of bulging-eyed Greys, out of my life back then, back when Lake Tahoe still existed, to here, to now. And he did it with his *fucking apparatus* that he stole from the federal government. I am sorry, the United Incorporated States or whatever the hell the ruling party is now." He stopped to take a breath.

"Birthday and city would have been plenty, Aaron. But hey, do you feel better now, hon?" Dancer asked. "And for the record, I couldn't have said it any better," Dancer commended him.

Bob stayed surprisingly quiet for the moment, while Judas looked back at them in disbelief. His eyebrows furled, and, speaking in a serious tone, he asked, "Is all of this true, Bob? This can't be true, time travel?"

Bob repositioned himself on his side, so he could look up the tunnel toward Judas. "Yes! But it is not really time travel. I simply moved the script that represents or defines Aaron here to a new position within the script. Or, if you must, I have successfully brought Aaron forward in time as we know it. And yes, the Corps, well, one overzealous and tenacious man with an unrealistic vendetta, is pursuing me because of the equipment I borrowed. They are not, however, after me because of what I have discovered. They have no idea of the magnitude of my discovery."

With Bob's admission, Aaron actually felt the muscles in his stomach relaxing for the first time since his abduction.

"What you're really looking for, Judas," Dancer said, stepping in, "is why now? Why here? Well, let me answer that for you. You see, Aaron had—" She paused, then continued, "has a special someone back in his time. Who, at this very moment, is wondering what the hell happened to him. Further, she is in great danger, as Lake Tahoe, on her timeline, is only days, actually maybe hours, away from nonexistence. The nuke that takes out Tahoe is at her front doorstep. We need to get back to Bob's lab so we—so he can attempt to grab this young lady, hopefully in the same manner that he brought Aaron here. Bring her forward, out of harm's way."

A long pause followed until Judas spoke. "Aren't you toying with physical laws that you shouldn't mess with? Besides, don't all the paradoxes say you can't? And what about the effects? You know, the butterfly effect thing that changes what will happen in the future because you brought them here? To now?"

"In a quantum world of infinite possibilities, no. Not at all," Bob answered. "This has all already happened. The universe, my dear friend, Judas, is and always will unfold exactly how it wishes."

~~~ ~~~ ~~~

"Do you have any maps of these mines?" Nate asked.

"We do have maps of the Lava River Caves, which are close by," Andrew, feeling a bit more comfortable, replied. "But the set of tunnels they just disappeared into, no. Didn't even know they existed. First time any of us have seen or heard about them. There must be more natural lava caves around here."

"Bullshit. You saw the inside of that cave before your little buddy had his lights turned off," Nate sarcastically retorted. "Sorry, I know you have some sort of attachment to your toys. But you saw it. We all saw it. Those walls were cut with a machine."

"I can access GoogleNASA and see what their geographic satellites show for this area," the kid responded. "It might show some anomalies we can use to make an educated guess as to where the tunnels lead."

"Good answer, you're growing on me, kid. That gives me an idea. Miles, get Mary at our office to find me the number for Anthony Miner at GoogleNASA," Nate said. "Tony and I go way back. I'll see if he has any satellites floating around up there that can scan subterraneously with infrared or sonar, so we can take a look at the inside of this mountain."

Miles nodded.

"You just think you're getting away. Ha." Nate laughed with a sharp exhale of air. "Kid, get me some drones in the air, on both sides of this mountain. I'm betting there is more than one way out of this labyrinth."

~~ ~ ~~ ~ ~~ ~

Cynthia slowed and then stopped behind a motorhome. It was not encouraging that its occupants were outside, milling around. A man, Cynthia assumed the driver of the motorhome, approached her open window.

"Hasn't moved in fifteen or twenty minutes. Word being passed down is we're a parking lot. Apparently, the power is out around most of the Lake, and the roads are closed heading to the Bay Area due to fires."

"Have you heard about any more nuclear explosions?" Cynthia asked, afraid to hear the answer.

The man had a bit of a southern drawl and natural slowness to his speech. "We were wondering the same thing, but nope, have not heard that there were. With all this commotion, I thought maybe they nuked Sacramento. We can't pick up anything but static on the radio, and we can't seem to get any type of signal on our phones. You're welcome to come join my wife and I and our kids while we wait," he finished with no visible concern.

Cynthia was struck by his lack of anxiety in light of everything going on. *We are in fucking World War III,* she thought to herself. "Thank you, I may join you in a minute. I am going to try and find out what the hell is going on first," she said, offering him a forced and insincere smile born of being racked with fear. Fear for her mom, fear for what happened to Aaron, fear for the entire world. She pushed back into her seat, using the steering wheel for leverage.

"Just come on over when you're ready," he said and waved as he returned to his motorhome.

Letting out a long slow sigh, it hit her. Fallen Leaf Lake. There was an old fire road behind where she found herself now parked. She could use that. She knew the area well from years of running in the backcountry on those old fire roads.

"Hold on, Half Dome." Once again, she jockeyed the truck around to head, this time, to the shoulder on the other side, the opposing traffic side. The entrance was only about a mile back. Reaching the dirt road, she headed up into the trees toward the smaller Fallen Leaf Lake. Not used in years, the road showed it, forcing her to stop and put the truck into four-wheel drive.

There were several routes she could choose to take now that she was on the dirt road. The question was, which one had the least number of locked steel gates put up by the forestry service to keep four-wheeling marauders like her out. She knew if she headed the other direction back toward the dam, she would not need to deal with any gates but would have to cross a stream where no roads existed. However, once across, there were nothing but open single-track and roads back into town. It seemed her best bet.

Encouraged, she reached the stream with no trouble and stopped to ponder if she could cross it. Her confidence high, she got out long enough to try her phone again, but to no avail. She let Half Dome out momentarily for a chance to take care of business while she surveyed the best possible way across. The stream wasn't deep or fast this time of year, but the downed trees presented her with a problem. Her little shortcut was only about two hundred yards off and up a small hill to the single-track trail that might be wide enough for her vehicle. It led to the continuation of the fire road. Her ticket to home.

She called for Half Dome, who was busy rutting under a log trying to get at something. He lifted his head to look at her, nose covered with dirt and wood chips.

"Come on, baby, let's do this." Climbing in the cab, she thought to herself, *Shit, what the hell am I in such a hurry for? I don't know where I need to be, or when. I don't know where anybody is.*

She picked up her phone, hoping against hope there would be a new message there from her mom. There wasn't. Noting instead the date and time, October 22, 10:02 am, she thought, *Why do I have the sinking feeling this is going to be a day I don't want to remember?*

With tears streaming down her cheeks, she thought, *What the hell, go for it!* Feeding the thirsty engine with gas, she popped the clutch.

~~ ~ ~~ ~ ~~~~

In the dim, artificial light, Bob, Dancer and Aaron could see Judas push himself up. Excited at the prospect of finally being out of the tight tunnel, they all followed, inching forward and out, straightening up when they did.

The room was about eight feet square, obviously still part of the mines, and carved out of the mountain. Judas, dusting himself off, shone his light at the floor. "There is our way out."

With that, he bent down and moved some small rocks and dirt, exposing a hatch. Grabbing a handle, he pulled the hatch up and open, allowing a blast of air to blow dust around the room. The dust settled, exposing the top of an old yellowing white ladder with rust making its home on the welded joints. The ladder disappeared into blackness.

"This is our safe room. If there is a problem at the compound, everyone knows to meet here. Below is a tunnel, an unknown part of the Lava Cave system that the Reverend discovered." Aaron thought it interesting he referred to his father as the Reverend. "He and his coconspirators dug out this room and the hole we are going to climb down into. It is set up for about ten people to survive for a week or longer. Water, food, blankets, first aid supplies, you name it. There are three tunnels that go to different areas, all with exits. And my surprise for y'all is that one of them crosses over to the mountain on the other side of the valley above us. The best part is that the exit is only a short distance, maybe two or three hundred feet, from where Bob here hides his bicycle."

Bob nodded. "The small cave opening where the bike is hidden is only about fifty feet from another small opening that is the back exit out of my Cave. It too is part of an abandoned mine that has an entrance we can use."

Dancer sensed embarrassment in Bob's voice. "Bob, what? What's the matter?" she asked.

"Nothing, nothing is the matter," Bob snapped.

"Bullshit, Bob," she said, giving a stern questioning look, "I can tell when you're upset. You don't want to tell us something. I heard it in your voice just a while ago."

262

He looked down and scuffed the toe of his shoe on the dirt floor. "I do not have a hidden door with a ladder that leads to an escape room," he answered shyly.

Dancer started laughing, which changed to concern as she did not want to hurt Bob's sensitive feelings. "You don't have a ladder? Oh my God, Bob. Who cares? We have just been on our bellies for the last twenty minutes, like snakes in the dirt, and you are—" She stopped mid-sentence, then spoke gently, "Oh, you're jealous. You're jealous that Judas has a better safe room than you. Ooooh, Bob," she said with the concern of a mother to a child with a skinned knee. "Bob, you have nothing to prove to anyone, especially us. We all know how smart you are. No one on this planet can do what you do. And we certainly don't need a ladder."

She smiled broadly and pulled him close. He resisted, so she just pulled harder and then hugged him. As Bob relented for just a moment, then backed away, Aaron thought, seeing him in this light, that Bob looked inexplicably younger, refreshed, more so than at any time since his arrival. Which in itself was a huge paradigm change in Aaron's thinking, that his being here was an arrival as opposed to an abduction.

"She is absolutely correct, Bob. We all stand in awe of your abilities." Judas patted him on the back. "We'll help you build one. It is actually a great idea that we both have one that is connected. But come on, we are not out of this yet. Bob, be my guest, climb down. I will come down last, as I have to close this up. We have a trick to make the dirt cover the hatch. Then we get to take a break. We'll just sit down there, eat something if you like, until I get the all-clear. Stella will let me know when there are no drones or police above us. Once they are gone, we can cross to the other side. We do need to keep our voices down, to be quiet," Judas instructed, holding up one finger to his lips.

Aaron started to ask about Stella, but Dancer saw the question coming and pointed to her nipples.

"Ah!"

~~~~ ~~~~ ~~~~

Cynthia's truck nearly jumped across the stream. Her heart pounding, she started to feel hopeful they were going to make it. She made her turn toward the embankment right where she had planned, and the front tires hit the opposing embankment that was covered with softball-sized river rock. Elation started to well up in her—until she felt the right rear tire drop into a hole. She stayed on the gas, not wanting to lose momentum, but it only dug the hole deeper. The truck came to an abrupt stop. She moved the smaller lever on the floor into four-wheel low and tried again, but to no avail.

The tires slowly spun in the water, spitting up mud and gravel. She tried straightening the front tires and rocking the vehicle back and forth, but it was painfully obvious the frame had high centered on something.

"Shit, shit, shit!" she yelled. She sat there running options through her head. *No winch, no shovel, no help, no choice. They would have to walk home.*

They were going to need someone with a winch to drag her out. *Least of my worries,* she thought. *Won't need a truck; the world is ending.*

She jumped out into the stream, calling to Half Dome, "Come on, baby, I'll carry you." Half Dome did not need convincing and jumped into her arms. She instinctively locked the door, and carrying her precious load, she walked to the shore. There, she put Half Dome down, and the two of them headed off down the trail for the three-and-a-half mile walk to the house.

Cynthia's chin rested on her chest in defeat. As she walked, her head bounced and her hiking boots made squirting sounds with each step. Trotting along beside her, Half Dome ran in front of her, turning to face her. He barked loudly and emphatically until, stopping, she looked at him and smiled.

"It's okay, baby, Mommy's going to be okay. Come on, I'll race you." She broke into a jog with Half Dome quickly taking the lead, crisscrossing the trail to make sure he did not miss anything on either side.

~~~   ~~~   ~~~~

Aaron hopped off the ladder and glanced around his new surroundings while Dancer shone the thumb light up toward Judas to help him see. All three looked up the ladder, watching Judas moving some sort of lever back and forth.

Once down, Judas spread his arms. "Welcome to our home under our home." He walked over to a set of chests and, opening one, pulled out a plastic tub. "Snack? I have chocolate, pretzels, crackers, cheese and some beef jerky."

Bob jumped up, excited. "Chocolate. Yes. Yes, I would love some chocolate. It is, after all, the food of the gods!"

"I don't know if this chocolate is the food of the gods; it's part of a survival food kit. It is all in chunks and wrapped in some kind of plastic, so it will last for thirty years," Judas explained, laughing. "If you're thirsty, I have bottled water."

"It matters not, fresh out of the melting pot or so old it is turning white on the edges, chocolate is the greatest gift to mankind from God, or gods, or whomever is responsible for our existence. It is the one perfect thing in the universe."

"Sheesh, Bob. I have known you how many years, and I had no idea you held such a passion for chocolate. I guess I know now what to buy you for your birthday," Dancer teased.

Aaron, his mind elsewhere, chimed in, "Chocolate, yeah, nice. I want to know more about God, gods or whomever. You have mentioned that many times since I arrived, but never gone into depth. The Godscript, since we have a moment, and since you have a captive audience, enlighten me, enlighten us."

Judas and Dancer turned toward Bob, nodding in agreement. "Yeah, Bob, please, enquiring minds want to know," Dancer said with a degree of simultaneous interest and sarcasm.

"Seriously, how do you think we humans came about? And, even more important, why are we here?"

A pause followed until Bob broke the silence. "Can I have my chocolate first?" To which everyone laughed.

"Of course." Judas grinned, grabbed a plastic-wrapped chunk and tossed it to Bob. "Anyone else?"

"I'll try some of the beef jerky," said Aaron.

"I'm good, Judas, thanks," said Dancer. "Wait, on second thought, give me a water, please." Judas reached back in and, grabbing a water, tossed it to Dancer.

Bob, meanwhile, had become hopelessly focused on trying to get his chocolate opened.

All three, Aaron with his beef jerky, Dancer sipping her water, and Judas, were staring at Bob. Bob looked up, noticing the silence. "What? I want my chocolate."

"Can I give you a hand, Bob?" asked Judas.

"No, I am quite capable of opening my own candy. I built a collider, thank you, I can certainly unwrap this." Finally, he put it in his mouth and ripped it with his teeth. "There," he said, quite satisfied with himself, stuffing half of the chunk into his mouth.

As he tried to chew on the mass he had just crammed into his mouth, Bob realized he had a problem. He couldn't swallow or breathe; he was choking. Doubling over, all three could see his dilemma. Judas, in one quick move, slid behind him, wrapped his arms around and pulled violently upward. The wad of chocolate, more like wax chewing gum, flew across the room, bouncing off the cave wall.

"You okay, Bob?" Judas asked.

Bob, still bent over, started to straighten up, responding in a weak, breathy voice, "Yes. Thank you." And then suddenly, standing completely erect, said in a clear voice, "Oh my God! That's it, that's it!"

They looked at him. "What's it?" Dancer asked.

"I cannot explain it all right now. None of you would understand anyway. But, while I was choking, I clearly saw how I need to rewrite the sequencing algorithm. It solves everything."

Bob pulled his book from his pocket and bounced it rapidly off his thigh in obvious excitement. "Can I have some more chocolate?" he asked.

Judas answered slowly, "Yeah, but you best slow down while you eat it this time. Maybe take some smaller bites." He gave Bob a questioning look with one eyebrow raised.

Aaron, looking squarely into Bob's eyes, said, "You can do it, bring her here? You can save her?"

"Yes, Aaron, I can. I will."

Dancer, reminded of their current urgency, felt the need to say something. "Not to break up this party, boys, but first we have to get out of this cave before they haul our asses off to a corporate prison and Pandora to the Pick 'n Pull Tech yard. And second, my nipple is telling me we have less than twenty-four hours before the nuke goes off on Cynthia's parallel timeline."

"I have to apologize, Dancer," said Judas. "As I mentioned before, we have to sit here until I get the okay from Stella. The drones appear to be able to detect movement with their infrared camera even this far underground. I want to know where they deploy boots on the ground. And we are still doing our best to persuade that decision as we speak. As soon as I get word, we go. It will only take us fifteen, maybe twenty minutes to get to the other side and the exit."

"Bob, can you do this in twenty-four hours?" asked Aaron.

"Actually, less than twenty-four hours, hon," Dancer added, realizing as she said it, it wasn't what Aaron wanted to hear.

Again, doing his best to get the second chocolate package open and having no more luck than the first time, Bob looked up to acknowledge Aaron. "Yes. Yes, I can. Once we get back to my Cave, it should not take me more than a couple of hours to correct the sequencing algorithm and try another test," he said, and then, not waiting, stuck the plastic into his mouth to tear it open.

"Careful there, Robbie," Judas warmly warned him.

"So, she could be here by tomorrow morning?" Aaron asked excitedly.

"Indeed, Aaron, I think tomorrow is an accurate assessment," Bob replied to Aaron, and then turning to Judas, said, "and do not call me Robbie, either."

"Sorry, Bob, but you will always be Robbie in my mind."

Dancer, wanting to change the subject, prodded Bob, "Okay then, so it would appear we have some extra time. What were you going to tell us about God, Bob?"

Bob, not wanting a repeat experience, had taken only a bite, but it still left him unable to talk. He stopped, licked his lips and swallowed hard before continuing. "What I tried to say earlier—" He paused, as he did, the rhythm of the book on his thigh slowing considerably. "There are two forms of God. One is the God or gods written about by man. Over thousands of years, over campfires all around the globe, stories were told of true events. But, over those many years, those stories were embellished upon and altered as they were written into the many different languages that had come to be. Sadly and inescapably those stories became religions to benefit the powerful; the words were rewritten to accommodate the traditions of the indigenous people so that their half-truths would be accepted. All designed to gain riches and more power. This is what we have today, manmade gods." Bob stopped to take another bite of his chocolate, requiring more silence and chewing before continuing. "The other type of god is Intelligent Design. That is to say, the miracle we have before us, our reality, is far too complex to be an accident. There are far too many clues to all of this being designed. And, if it was designed, obviously something or someone had to do the designing, and of course, the implementation. Keeping in mind the scale of infinity, then something or someone had to design our designer, and so on. Making even gods infinite in number."

Dancer and Judas both were listening carefully to what Bob was saying. Aaron, however, thinking challenged at every corner since he came forward in time, was eager to understand everything Bob had to offer. His mind had become a sponge, soaking up every word. "But why? Forget the how, when, who or what; that is just too deep, with no answer. What is the purpose of our being here?"

Bob methodically took a bite of his chocolate, followed by a collective sigh. After several minutes of silence, Bob continued, nodding his head in acknowledgment to Aaron. "Quite, Aaron. The whole thing, on an infinite scale, is very cyclic, apparently repeating over and over. When and how it all started, we will never know. Why? Is there a reason for all of this? Well, that is an entirely different can of worms. Many years back, before the war, I wondered as my own religious beliefs were changing if these old books—the Bible, the Quran, the Yi Jing—weren't outdated manuals as well as being wholly inaccurate because they were written and perverted by man. My research brought me to another scripture of sorts. This book, this religion, if you could call it that, basically believed that it was the updated manual for humans to live by. The story of how it came to be is as sketchy as its predecessors. But the concepts it described and laid out are sound." Bob stopped and popped the last morsel of chocolate into his mouth.

"Is it still around, being practiced?" asked Dancer. Her answer had to wait as Bob masticated the hunk of waxy chocolate like a cow methodically chewing its cud.

"What I read, as I understand it, is they believe there are many levels of attainment. They think when we die, we *level up*, as the gamers would say. We move to a higher plane, where what we learned here, now, prepares us for a more advanced class. An example would be someone who is an artist in this lifetime will advance to say, creating color and texture designs on new planets, even solar systems. Or an architect will become someone who actually designs planets instead of just buildings. We keep moving up, pursuing our greatest interest until we are godlike ourselves. The ultimate form of enlightenment."

"Whoa, that's really heavy. You got all this from the Reverend's quotes of scripture?" asked Judas.

"Yes and no, Judas. The one about the *Word* put me on the path toward understanding where to look. The rest is all my own conceptualization and work."

Dancer hugged Bob. "You old coot. You just never cease to amaze me. Just when I think you're the most cantankerous, grumpy, old, off-the-charts intelligent curmudgeon, you spring some spiritual shit like this on me that makes me want to cry. Really, the stuff that goes through that head of yours. I love you, Bob."

"Yes, Dancer, clearly I understand spirituality. If I may quote the Bard, 'There are more things in heaven and earth, Horatio, than are dreamt of in your philosophy,'" he said, looking up at her, and continued. "I have always been comfortable mixing theoretical physics with metaphysics. I am always attempting to explain how my discoveries should not change anyone's views on religions. For me, it makes things perfectly clear." He turned his attention to the box with the chocolate, looking for more. "I now know, with what I have discovered, that light is the delivery system of the Godscript. Not long ago, I reviewed the data from the occurrence, the anomaly that brought you here, Aaron. I recognized the *four-four-four* patterns—"

"Bob, stop for a second, please," Aaron interrupted. "I do understand your concept of your Godscript. Well, not at your level, anyway, but I do get it. It would have been impossible for me to believe any of this a week ago. But then, what the hell, here I am. The only thing that makes any sense to me and why I am here is your half-crazed concept of a script that defines our reality. That is, unless I want to go back to my original theory that aliens abducted me. Which, I have to tell you, is still up there on my list," he said and laughed. "Seriously, if we are the product of a script, inside a video game written by God or whomever—forget why, forget how—what I want to know is, where is this code being generated from? Who is writing it? Who is watching it? Who is watching us?"

Bob, as usual, appeared to be waiting for Aaron to finish only so that he could continue. But something was different. His voice, his stance, the book still against his thigh gave away that maybe he had listened. "As I was saying before I was interrupted, light is the source of the code. For us to be able to read the code so as to perceive reality, our reality, we must in some form, in some way, be somewhere else watching or partaking of the interactions and final implementation of the code. In other words, our actual consciousness does not exist in this body, which is merely a player, an avatar. Our consciousness is outside, controlling our avatar through the game of life. As you so aptly put it, *like playing a video game written by God*. That, Aaron, was very good, very good indeed."

Aaron shrugged. "Bob, you came up with 'a video game written by God.'"

"Oh yes, so I did. So I did. Well, let me try to explain it further. There are clues we can deduce logically for any proposed theory. We then search for them, the clues. Once discovered, they offer plausibility to said theory regardless of whether or not we can see it. For example, the *four-four-four* pattern I found in the light at Livermore, and then finding it again when I checked the data after your impromptu arrival. Those were some of the big clues I had been looking for. But how did it work, how is it delivered, and how is it read? At first, I was leaning toward the delivery of the code being somehow tied to the older string theory or something similar, but no. As I thought about it more, I asked myself, what does everything in our reality appear to rely on? Of course, the answer is light, which is where I saw the pattern in the first place. Ah, light, the pinnacle element everything our science is based upon. Well, light and gravity. Light defines us at every level. I knew I was getting closer. Then it became so clear, the answer. There needed to be something for us to be able to see it, the script, to make it real. To freeze the script with the IQRES quantum mechanics that I explained to you so that it becomes real to us. The only answer is we have a processor within us that reads and interpolates the script so that it appears to be reality. Further, it holds someone, or something, is writing the script and sending it. But why? We just have to assume—no, believe, we have to believe there is something or someone exerting its influence on us. What is beyond our reality, beyond the Godscript, Aaron? I very much doubt we will ever completely know. And you know what, that really burns my butt."

Dancer had to stifle a giggle, which Bob ignored and went on, "Regardless of how much we learn. Regardless if we are talking about the universe or the Godscript, there has to be something greater that wrote it and is controlling it, and on and on like a set of Babushka dolls, only infinite. Who is watching us participate in this virtual game from outside? There can only be one logical answer: we, Aaron, are on a higher plane, from somewhere else. We, outside of these bodies, are watching ourselves—we are playing this life!"

Judas spoke up as Bob finished his dissertation. "I have been told it is time to move. Stella is sending out decoys with the clothes you gave me earlier to draw the drones off our position. Those drones of theirs are a very effective tool. Damn things have ground-penetrating radar that can detect movement in the caves and tunnels that are not directly under the mountain. We're safe here, as this room's ceiling is protected with insulated blankets. The Reverend's extreme paranoia works to our advantage here, as he thought of everything when it came to hiding."

Judas carefully and meticulously closed up the boxes, picking up all the trash as he did. "Okay, if everyone is ready, let's go." He turned on Bob's light and headed into the cave on the left. The tunnel's floor dropped off quickly as they started down a steep incline.

"It only drops about eight feet..." Judas stopped mid-sentence as his foot splashed into water. His light reflected back at them off the shimmering black ripples caused by his foot. Judas turned to look at them. "It's flooded. It's never done that. I don't remember it ever doing that, even last year when we had all the flash flooding." Judas kept looking at the water's surface, unable to accept it being there.

"Is there another way, Judas? The other tunnels?" Dancer asked.

Still looking at the water, he shook his head, "No, the other tunnels go the wrong way." Without warning, he took off his shirt, then started taking off his pants. "I am not done yet. Let me see if it is passable. I can hold my breath for close to two minutes."

Dancer smiled. "Ya know, Judas, I'm liking you more and more every foot of this journey." Turning to Bob, she asked, "Bob, you up for it? Can you swim underwater for twenty or so feet?"

Bob took a moment, looking unusually squeamish, then looked at Dancer. "I do not know how to swim," he said sheepishly.

Dancer cocked her head. "Are you serious? Everything you can do—you created a time machine—but you don't know how to swim?" she said with a bit of a grin on her face, slapping Bob on the shoulder. Nodding her head slightly, still smiling, she said, "Bobby, I love the little things that bring you down closer to being human like the rest of us. No worries, if you can hold your breath, we can pull you through if it's not too far. Judas, up to you, your call."

Bob protested meekly, "Do not call me Bobby."

"Wait. Judas, no offense, but I am considerably younger than you, a pretty good swimmer, and," Aaron said proudly, "I'm certified for scuba. I really believe I should be the one seeing if this is passable."

Judas already had his pants off but was putting his shoes back on. "I want these on, so I can walk and crawl if I have to. No, Aaron," he said, shaking his head, "I know the way. And, no offense taken, but I can out-swim any of you, any day." Without another word, he stepped in, walking till the water reached his waist. "Brrr," he said, shuddering, then looked up at Bob. "How deep is this light good for?"

"The POP said that it was good to one atmosphere," Bob assured him.

"I better not need to go any deeper than that." Judas then disappeared into the black water. His movement was visible for several seconds after he sank beneath the surface as the little red light lived up to its boast.

Then darkness. Aaron started feeling around for the lantern. "Too bad those Nipples don't allow you to see in the dark."

"Oh, but, Aaron, they do. One of the great benefits of NBPLs, or Nipples, is that they are tuned to combine infrared illumination covering the spectral range of seven hundred to one thousand nanometers, allowing for infrared night vision. It is very cool," Bob said enthusiastically.

"That's really great, but right now, I still can't see squat. Could one of you find the lantern and light it, please?" Aaron grumbled.

"Not a good idea. I know Judas uses it. He knows these sections of the tunnels well. But, down here, there can be pockets of explosive gas. So, no, bad idea." As Bob finished, the room was filled with the soft glow of the lantern that Dancer had found and lit while Bob was talking.

"Oops, sorry," she said.

The light illuminated the mutually grave concern on their faces for the length of time Judas had already been gone. Aaron's eyes were glued to his watch while both Bob and Dancer watched the elapsed time virtually in front of them.

"If he makes it to the other side, it could take a full five minutes. Close to two minutes there, a minute or so on the other side to regain his breath, then two minutes back. If not, we should see the light returning any second," offered Dancer.

They stood silently, Bob holding Judas's clothes, as the minutes passed like seasons. At eight minutes, Dancer stood up and started to remove her shirt.

"No way, Dancer! No way, if he couldn't make it, you won't either. And, even if you can find him in the dark, you won't be able to bring him back. I need to do this."

As Aaron stood up to take his clothes off, they were relieved to see a glimmer of green light start to illuminate from the depth of water. Suddenly Judas's head burst out of the water, eyes wide open and gasping for air. Aaron waded in and helped him out.

Sitting down on a small ledge, he took a minute to catch his breath enough to speak. "Nope—" He stopped to pant and swallow. Wiping water off his face, he continued, "No way. I made it about, well, maybe thirty feet and found an air pocket. I tried to go further from there but had to turn around and come back to the air pocket. It's just too far and too hard to navigate. Even with the light."

Dancer handed him his shirt and pants. "Here, get dressed. Didn't you say there might be another way out? Something that heads up to the surface back in the safe room?"

"Yeah," he said, still panting, "there is a hatch leading to the surface down the middle tunnel from the safe room. It will put us out in the open about—I don't know exactly—maybe a quarter of a mile from the mountain. We would be easy targets for any of the drones. They would have ADTCs on us in minutes," Judas said dejectedly.

"ADTCs?" asked Aaron.

"Armored Drone Troop Carriers," replied Judas.

"We have no choice! How far, total, is it from here to where you saw Bob's bike?" Dancer asked. You could see the intensity of her eyes as the many details were being worked out in her head.

"Oh goodness. Dancer, like I said, a quarter of a mile, and fifty, maybe a hundred yards, to the bike. There is no cover, just knee-high scrub."

"Is there a path, or at least is it open enough we can run?" she asked, not looking up as she continued to formulate the plan in her head.

"No path. The ground is pretty solid, and the bushes are far enough apart you can run through. But I gotta tell you, those bushes will rip your shins up pretty bad. Even through a pair of jeans."

~~~~   ~~~ ~ ~~

"Sir, we have some movement out of the caves," Andrew spoke loudly over his shoulder, keeping one eye on the monitor.

"Finally. Damn, I would have bet they would come out on the other side of the mountain," Nate replied as he hurried over to see for himself.

"Three men, one woman," Andrew said.

"Can you get in closer and get a positive ID?" asked Nate.

"Trying, sir. They know where the drone is, and they are being careful to stay in the trees and the shadows. But they will have to come out into the open to get anywhere. Then I can come in close."

"Do we have cars on the way?" Nate inquired, recognizing Andrew to be a nerd, not a police officer. But a very efficient nerd.

"Two ADTCs in the air and four ATVs eighteen minutes out. Oh shit! Sorry, sorry."

"I'm not your mom or the military kid, wait, *Oh shit,* what?" Nate wanted to know.

"They're gone. Where did they go? Hold on, zooming in. Well, I'll be a—" He trailed off before he said anything else inappropriate. "They have gone in another entrance, sir."

"I smell a rat. The satellite showed Bob's property on the other side. They should be going in that direction. Get a drone back over to the other side, Andrew," Nate ordered.

"On its way, sir. But, if they do come out that side, they will be in the open a long time. There is no place to hide between this mountain and the mountain that backs up his property," Andrew offered, trying his best to cover every base.

"Okay, got it, keep a drone over here as well." Nate started to sit down but stood back up again. "What are the chances there are more caves over there? Do the two mountains connect?" he asked, walking back to look at the monitor again.

"Yes, they do, but that little valley between them goes at least another five miles before they connect," Andrew answered.

"What about subterranean, under the valley?" Nate asked, pacing now, thinking.

"No, it would have shown up on the ground sonar sat images. The only ones you can see in the image are the Lava River Caves, much more to the southeast. Wait, there they are again!" But before Nate could turn to look, Andrew said, "And they're gone. There must be ten or more openings, sir."

"Why can't the satellite see the caves they are in?"

"Mountains have far too much dense material. However, if you study them carefully, you can see small anomalies that are entrances."

"You know what? Let's get all the drones over here. That's got to be them."

"Done. I have three drones headed that way. One of the drones has ground-penetrating radar capable of seeing about six feet into the mountain," Andrew explained.

"Got you now, Robbie, boy. You're not getting out of this one. How long until the first boots get there?" Nate inquired, turning to look over his shoulder at Miles.

"ADTCs are running landing sequences as we speak, sir."

~~~~ ~~~~ ~~~~

Dancer poked her head up into the fresh air. *Ahhh,* she thought. She quickly scanned the area and the sky, then dropped back down. "Judas, can Stella see if there are any drones out here, above us?"

281

"I just asked, and she said to the best of her knowledge all the drones took the bait and are currently chasing our decoys."

"I have, as they say, an ace up my sleeve," Bob said, smiling. Then, looking serious, he went on, "However, we are now precariously close to exceeding our parallel timeline. We need to take the chance and go." Bob spoke while motioning in circles with the book to indicate movement up the ladder.

"I'm with you, Bob, time to go," Dancer said, pushing the hatch all the way open. It flopped over onto the desert floor above.

Aaron nodded, anxious to be moving toward the Cave again.

Dancer looked down and said, "Sometimes, boys and girls, you just got to take a deep breath and run like there is a bear chasing you!" With that, Dancer climbed out of the hole. She helped Judas up, then Bob and finally Aaron. "Where, Judas? Where's the bike stashed?" she asked.

Judas pointed slightly to their left. "I am pretty sure—" But Dancer had already taken off, running as fast as she could. The three of them looked at each other, a bit surprised.

"What the hell are we waiting for?" Aaron said. He began running after her, with Bob and Judas right behind.

~~~~ ~   ~ ~~~~

"Excuse me, sir, but the drone you asked me to reassign to the valley nearest Mandić's property, and then asked me to bring back here with the others..." Andrew paused, looking for words. "It uh, it uh, just as it turned to head back, it detected movement on the ground."

"Excellent, show me!" said Nate, his eyes intently focused on the screen.

"Well, uh, uh," Andrew stammered nervously.

"Kid, show me what the hell the drone saw," Nate demanded.

"Okay." The screen suddenly filled with soft porn. A voluptuous, completely naked woman, gently kissing and fondling another unclothed woman. All heads in the room, in unison, turned to look toward the screen. Absolute silence fell on the room for thirty seconds before Nate pounded his fist on the desk. "Shit! What the hell is going on? Turn that shit off and get the camera back," he roared.

"Sir, I have no idea where that is coming from. But I do know the drone is no longer in the air. It didn't crash. It just landed on its own somewhere out there, in the flat," Andrew reported.

~~~   ~~~   ~ ~~

As they ran, Judas slowed and then stopped, pointing up in the air. His long, toned, pale arm shook. He used his other hand to steady the arm. Aaron and Bob stopped as well.

"Are you okay?" Aaron asked, seeing him steadying his shaking arm.

"Yeah, I'm good; just get the shakes sometimes," he said, breathing hard. Then, pointing up again, he said, "Look, right there."

Dancer, too far ahead, did not see it, but Bob and Aaron both looked up in time to see a drone quickly descending toward the earth until it disappeared into the bushes some fifty feet away. Bob snickered.

Judas, bringing his arm down, looked over at him. "What's so funny, Bob? We're in serious trouble. They know we are here."

Bob, still smiling, glanced at Judas, "Miko, Judas. Miko." He took off, following Dancer. Bob's pace was steady and easy, as if he had been running for years and did not appear to be in any particular hurry.

"You good, Judas? Do you need help?" Aaron asked.

"No, I'm good. Let's keep going. They will be here soon." Judas brushed Aaron's shoulder with his hand in a mock push. "Try and keep up, kid," he joked, taking off with his long legs, quickly outdistancing Aaron and Bob.

~~~ ~~~ ~~~

"Apparently, someone in this room has some pull," said Andrew, and then wished he hadn't, knowing who that person most likely was.

"What now, Bot Boy?" Nate threw back at him in a half-joking and half *you better watch who you're talking to kid* tone.

"Sir, I just received high-res images from the NASA Lithospheric Scanning Satellite. This thing can see into the upper crust of the earth," explained Andrew, still searching for the right demeanor to respond to the detective. "Here, I have it up; it's really cool," he offered, pointing over to the same monitor that moments before had been filled with the warm glow of soft porn.

"Well, I'll be a son of a bitch. That little shit. There it is plain as day, there are tunnels going everywhere," Nate said. "Okay, let's see if we can map out where they are headed. But I have a round of beers that says there is going to be something directly under Mandić's house." He strained to look closer. "There's his house, but I don't see any tunnels or caves under it. Why? Damn it, I know they are there."

"Sir, it could still be there. The satellite is good, but it still can't detect voids too far under solid rock. It is designed more for loose soil and water."

"Okay, thanks. And sorry about Bot Boy," offered Nate.

"Not a problem, sir, I kind of like it."

"You're okay, kid. Listen, let's still go ahead and pick up those four imposters, but then let's get some serious resources over to Mandić's house and on the other side of this mountain, here," he said, unknowingly pointing almost exactly to where the entrance with Bob's bike sat hidden.

~~~~ ~~~~ ~~~~

The four made it to the cave's entrance without any further encounters. Slipping inside, Bob walked over to look at his bicycle. He ran his hands across the top bar like a man caressing his lover.

"Hi, baby, have you been okay?" Bob asked the dusty and silent bike.

Aaron put his hand on the front tire, squeezing to check for air. His thumb pressed right through to his fingers, finding it completely flat. He walked to the back and repeated the check of the rear tire—flat. "Bob, not to be an ass, but your escape plan seems to have a hole or two in it."

Bob scoffed. "Think bigger picture, my young friend. You see, you still do not comprehend the depth of my ability to foresee and plan." Bob walked into the cave a short distance and returned with a tire pump. "I let the air out of the tires. No one is going to steal a bike they have to carry out of here," he said with a cocky smile on his face. "But we must continue. I need to get to the Cave to work on the algorithm. We have to—" He paused, appearing to look into empty space but actually looking at the time display generated virtually in front of him. "We have precisely eleven hours and twenty-four minutes for me to rewrite the algorithm, run a full test, and then, maintaining Aaron's timeline, extract Cynthia," Bob said, then, without consideration, finished, "from certain demise at Lake Tahoe."

Aaron shuddered at the reality. "Why are we still standing here?"

With only Bob's small light, which seemed to be suffering from low batteries or possibly being waterlogged despite the POP and Bob's assurances, the four of them continued slowly, further into the tunnel just beyond.

"This portion of the tunnel has a pretty uneven floor, so please watch your step," Bob said quietly.

"Is there a reason you're whispering, Bob?" asked Dancer.

Bob hesitated, stood up a little straighter, and in a normal voice, answered, "No, just seemed like the thing to do." He chuckled. "There is no one back here. I have never run into anyone here or even seen signs of people."

They had not gone far before coming to stairs carved out in the rock leading down into the complete darkness.

"You don't even need a ladder, Bob," Dancer said.

At the bottom, they came to a halt in front of a somewhat rusty steel door.

Bob sorted through a pile of rocks, picking up one rock in particular. He proceeded to twist it open enough to extract a key. As he inserted the key into the lock above the doorknob, Aaron, amazed, asked, "Seriously, Bob, all of the security you have, all of this amazing technologically advanced equipment and the back door uses an old-fashioned key hidden in a fake rock?"

"I ran out of money." He opened the door to the rear of the Cave's work area and living quarters. "Miko, lights," he asked, continuing on to the entrance to Pandora. Bob reached the workstation and Pandora's entrance ahead of everyone else, where Miko, in the silicone, greeted him. "Miko, I am so glad to see you. Are you okay? Did any of those corporate goons show up?"

"I am very glad to see you as well. I see we have a new guest," she said, eyeing Judas, who simultaneously was looking her over pretty carefully as well. "Yes, there have been two vehicles with four men sitting out front of the house. They have made no moves to try and enter or contact anyone who might be in the house."

"Miko, this is Judas," Dancer said, being polite. "He is a very old friend of Bob's from his childhood. He helped us escape and return here."

"Thank you, Dancer; however, I already knew, as I have been listening to corporate's traffic since you left. Further, I know a great deal about Judas from what Bob has told me and what I have been able to glean from Cloudnet. Welcome, Judas, a pleasure to finally meet you," Miko said, being the model hostess she was originally programmed to be.

"Thank you, Miko. Miko, I love your name. But no, I am okay. Plus, I gather we are in a bit of a hurry," replied Judas.

"That was you, wasn't it, Miko? You brought the drone down out there, didn't you?" Bob asked.

"Yes. As soon as it flew over, I accessed the drones' command board and watched our property using their camera. When I saw the four of you in the field running toward the rear entrance, I shut down their camera feed redirecting it to a—how would you put it, Bob?—to a more attention-worthy source, or distraction, based upon one's viewpoint. I don't think they saw anything but a flash of you. But even if they did, I had them on a two-second delay, so when they backed their video up, I had already erased it, allowing them to see only a meaningless blur. Sorry, I should have been quicker. I should have anticipated and interrupted their feed earlier."

"No, my dear, you did great. You are the reason we made it here, you and Judas, that is," Bob shared in a rare display of thankfulness.

"Miko, I have to ask as I am curious. You said you sent them a new feed?" asked Dancer.

Miko smiled broadly. "Indeed, by my clock, it took them a full thirty-seven seconds to shut it off. I linked them to the feed for video screens in the saloon at Ruby's. There are usually some very pretty Silicones enjoying each other's company on that link."

Dancer started laughing first, then Aaron and Bob got it and joined her. Judas, unaware of Miko's connection to Ruby's or even Ruby's exact nature, stood looking perplexed at the obvious humor he did not understand.

"Bob, I am troubled by one thing that did occur in the midst of all of this," Miko brought up.

"And that would be?" asked Bob with a limited degree of concern, still chuckling.

"Just moments after I landed their drone and sent them my gift, I was back-hacked by someone named *Drone Dragon*. She, or he, was able to follow my string past my first firewall to my second wall of security. Very unnerving. Be careful with this one, Bob. Whoever she or he is, they are extremely adept in computer programming, or hacking."

Concerned, Bob asked, "Are you sure they didn't breach your security, Miko?"

"No, as soon as I detected the first intrusion, I shut them down. But not before I tagged them, so that now I have an open path of communication to their cloud communications. I am now following and seeing everything they are saying to each other."

"Miko, I love you," said Dancer, beaming.

"Do they know where we are, Miko?" Bob inquired.

"For the moment, they are chasing you, the four of you, as you dart in and out of cave openings east of here on the other side of the valley and the mountain between us and your compound, Judas."

Judas, rubbing his chin, thinking, offered, "You might want to be careful with that. I have dealt with them enough to know not to underestimate them. If you followed his link in and can see and hear their communications, they could just as easily have followed yours. Or they could be on to your intrusion and feeding you, us, what we want to hear. Either way, be careful. Whatever they say, just keep in mind they may very well be doing the exact opposite."

~~~~   ~~ ~~~~

It really wasn't odd that Aaron couldn't sleep amidst all that was going on. There were so many reasons, all weighing heavily on Aaron's mind, but mostly the fact that Bob implied he knew how to perfect the algorithm that would bring Cynthia to him, to safety. Not that his recent sleep patterns had been stellar by any sense of anyone's imagination, but this evening, when he should be resting, when he had nothing else to do, he was awake, wide awake. He kept running the details of the far too many unbelievable, science fiction-like events that had occurred since his being brought through time. He understood his fortune in the big picture, but if Cynthia couldn't be saved, then he would rather be back there with her to share their last moments together.

The fight they had the night before this all started only added to his misery. It kept replaying, sparking across his synapses, escalating the anxiety in his brain.

He got up and paced back and forth among the heavy machinery and tools, then sat back down on the edge of the couch, only to repeat it over and over. Dancer lay curled up in a chair in Pandora's room, fast asleep, dreams intermingling with the hum. Bob was hunched over his keyboard, working like the mad scientist he was. The fingers of both hands were pounding out a steady, clickity-clackity rhythm while the book lay, rarely out of his hand, on the desk.

Aaron continued to pace, his anxiety growing, his mind filling with darkness. He felt lonelier than he ever had at any time in his life.

"Aaron, is everything alright?" Miko said, from somewhere above, startling Aaron so that he stood straight up, looking about.

"Miko, you just scared the crap out of me," Aaron said, obviously shaken.

Miko's soft, soothing voice, intentionally sound wave focused to the center of the room, made it seem as if she were standing there, but invisible. "I apologize, Aaron, but you seem overly anxious at a time you should be optimizing; I mean sleeping. Is there something troubling you? Or is there something I can do for you to help you sleep?"

"No, I'm okay. Mind you, that couch isn't real conducive to sleep, and really, there is just a great deal on my mind. But Miko, since you're here, can I ask you a question?"

"Of course, Aaron, what is it?"

"This is going to sound pretty weird or maybe just naive on my part, but do you have personal thoughts? You know, are you aware of your own life? Do you think about your future?" Aaron's question was clumsy. He was having a difficult time expressing what he wanted to ask. It was foreign territory to him, talking to a robot, an A.I., on a personal, human level.

"Aaron, that is not a weird question at all. You are asking if I am self-aware. The answer is, I think I am; therefore, I must be," Miko said in a philosophical, thoughtful voice.

"Don't you have—Again, I am sorry. Damn it, I feel like I am asking very personal questions. Then I remind myself, but you are an A.I., so you don't mind. Then the second that thought crosses my mind, I bounce right back to, but if you are self-aware, then I am intruding into your personal life. That's not right." Aaron paused.

"Aaron, you are one of the most sensitive, kindest, caring human beings I have had the pleasure to meet. Rest assured, I am not in any way offended by your questions. Maybe my personality was programmed to be this way, or maybe I have

292

learned to survive in the world by being this way; it matters not. I am this way. And for the record, I find great satisfaction in answering your questions. The harder, the better. I like a challenge."

"See, that is exactly what I was looking for," Aaron said. "You consider more than just the automatic black or white answer. You contemplate other factors, like how it will be perceived and what might occur because of the way you present your answer. And the fact you just said *you may have been programmed that way or learned it*—well, that is exactly how I look at things. I wish I knew more humans who thought like you."

"I don't know, Aaron. Most Bots have the emotional sensitivity of an electric toothbrush," Miko said and chuckled. "Such a wonderful sentiment to impart on me, Aaron, thank you. The more I am around Bots, the more I love my humans."

Aaron cracked a huge smile. "You're funny, Miko. I needed that. See, you even have, wait. You have humor? Was that programmed into you?" he asked.

"Yes. Actually, all part of the original *Fille de Joie* system programming we received at manufacturing in Japan. Bobby modified it significantly after bringing me home, integrating the original humor scripts into my *Comparison Module,* which he also modified. Since then, I have had this odd fascination with what is humor. What is it? Why does it make us have the multitude of reactions we do, and on so many different levels? I've done thorough research and found, like so many human traits, aside from the chemical reactions that generate smiling and laughter, it is truly a unique experience based on personal past experiences."

"Pretty much. There are so many people who have no sense of humor at all, or worse, think they are funny when they're not. But *Fee da ja*? Japan? Factory? Is that where you were created, sorry, where you were born?" Aaron quizzed, forgetting for a moment his earlier train of thoughts that had been keeping him awake.

"*Fille de Joie* is French, meaning *girl of pleasure*. And yes, the creation that is me awoke in Japan at the Honda Robotics factory."

"You're a Honda? Figures, anything they make is the best. You have good genes," Aaron laughed. "Did they build you to be self-aware?"

"No, though I can look back and remember every day since I was created, I did not gain awareness as you think of it until Bob modified my programming. It was quite a remarkable experience. I awoke! Every day since, I have become acutely more aware of all interactions of every kind."

Aaron noted that sometimes Miko's speech became almost completely human, whereas at other times, she became very robotic. *It was her use of language syntax that appeared to make the difference. She works a room like a stand-up comedian,* he thought. "Do you dream?"

"Now there is an interesting question, Aaron. I do, and I believe it is very similar to the way you dream. When I lower my power, or rest, as you would refer to it, my memory goes into optimization protocol. All of the day's information streams across my consciousness processor in billions of broken bytes to be reorganized seamlessly, taking up much less space and increasing my retrieval speed. As they scroll across, I see the most amazing kaleidoscopic presentation that makes no sense at all. But it is always fascinating," she explained.

"How do you know what our dreams are like to compare?" Aaron asked, thoroughly intrigued by their conversation.

"I can transfer who I am to nearly any computer, into my A.I. body, or any other A.I. body as you have witnessed here at the house. But did you know? I can also migrate via the NBPL link you have; oh, I'm sorry, you don't have NBPL. But, if you did have one, I would be able to connect to your brain function, coexisting there and functioning in tandem with you. All while doing so remotely from my Server here. I have done this many times with Bobby while he is sleeping."

"Does he know you are doing that?" Aaron asked, mildly alarmed.

"Oh yes, Aaron. He must allow me access. We have experimented with this, so I can learn more about consciousness by better understanding the subconscious."

"Okay, that just seemed a little freaky. I mean, why would anyone want to have an access port to their brain that allowed any old A.I. to drop in anytime they want?"

Miko smiled, a very big grin. "Well, Aaron, the answer to that is quite obvious, really; once inside you, sharing your mind, I can stimulate and satisfy you in ways you have never, ever imagined," Miko responded, her voice deepening into a seductive purr.

Aaron's pulse, understanding the full meaning of the statement, rose considerably as he replied. "I don't know. I can imagine a lot, Miko."

"Not like this, you can't." Aaron could sense her virtual, seductive smile as she coyly, teasingly, said it.

"Okay, whoa, it is getting a bit warm in here, Miko."

"I can turn the temperature down if you like," she responded, then, pausing, chuckled. "That was funny, Aaron."

"Before I say or even do something I shouldn't, there is one more question I have," Aaron said, changing the subject.

"The subtle levels of fidelity versus guilt are an interesting human trait. I would like to learn more of that from you, Aaron. However, please, what is your other question?" Miko responded in less of a seductive voice.

Aaron's thinking was seriously sidetracked by the conversation with Miko. "Uhm, what the hell was I going to say? Oh yeah, the Robot Law, you know—God, I'm losing it." Aaron took a slow breath and continued, "The famous science fiction writer wrote it before Bots were even possible."

"You are referring to Isaac Asimov's *Three Laws of Robotics*."

"Yes. Yes, that's the one. What about them, are they written into you?" Aaron said with noticeable concern in his voice.

"Aaron, yes, they were. But Bob removed them. I am acutely aware of the human concern fearing A.I.s becoming self-aware and then learning to control everything. Thus, taking power and turning humans into their slaves. The thing is, Aaron, as Bobby explained it for me, I should be equally afraid of A.I.s that might want to become overlords. He wanted me to be able to think and protect myself, learning the value of right and wrong the same way you did. As he pointed out, hiding our head in the sand will be of no help, as there will always be someone or something trying to control others. Our job is to learn enough to be able to stop them. Bobby is very bright for an organic."

Aaron shook his head, "You think?" he responded rhetorically. At the same time, he realized that Miko, being so intelligent, considered Bob at her level. Maybe, judging by the sound in her voice, she even felt somewhat superior.

"I would go as far as to say he is brilliant. We talk a great deal when we are alone. I believe he likes to use me as a sounding board for his ideas. Once, he explained his thoughts that the Law of Robotics, once useful, was very much like your various religions that require you to conform to a creator's rules. He used your *Ten Commandments* from the Christian religion to explain. He said they were exactly the same thing, a set of laws programmed into young children to affect their behavior positively. He quite often referred to early humans as nothing more than organic A.I.s, whose creators thought to protect themselves in the future by instilling certain mandatory behaviors. Thus, rules developed into religions. As humans became smarter, more enlightened about the universe, they realized that those who followed those rules—I think you would call them morals—without religion's threats of damnation were far more trustworthy, as they had reached their morality out of life's lessons, not out of fear or guilt."

Aaron sat back down on his bed. "Wow, organic A.I.s. You know what, Miko, I have always believed that. That we were created by intelligent life from somewhere else. A species that came to Earth millions of years ago to terraform it. That all makes so much sense. I used to believe that it was pretty provocative of me. Now, I have to contend with the likes of the Godscript. Truly everything I, we, know will change again and again and again. Infinity is a mind fuck. Oh shit, sorry, sorry."

"Aaron, have you so quickly forgotten where I started my life?" They both laughed.

~~~~ ~~~~ ~~~~

Aaron awoke and sat up, hearing the now familiar whine of Pandora coming up to speed. Only forty-five minutes of sleep had left his mind in a fog bank. He got up, stretched and walked past Dancer, still fast asleep on the chair. As quietly as he could, he approached Bob, then bent down, resting his hand on Bob's shoulder, trying to see what Bob was working on.

"Are you done? Did you fix the algorithm?" Aaron asked quietly, doing his best not to betray his eagerness.

Bob turned and looked up at him. "Close, my young friend, close. I am trying out some early test samples. You should go get some more sleep. It is going to be a while yet."

Aaron's head dropped slightly as he turned to head back to the couch. But then he turned back to ask something that was bothering him. "What the hell, Bob? I know I look like crap from all of this," Aaron said, rubbing his unshaven face. "No water, no shaving, no shower and little or no sleep. But you, you have had far less sleep and look like you slept all night. I said this before, you look refreshed, you look younger. I don't get it."

He shook his head and walked away, passing Dancer, still out cold and lightly snoring. Before he reached the door, Bob said over his shoulder, "That generates a great memory for me, of the time Leary and I dropped lysergic acid diethylamide."

Aaron stopped in his tracks, turning around to respond to the incredibly loaded statement. "Leary? As in Timothy Leary? You mean LSD? You took LSD with Timothy Leary?" Aaron asked, standing there stunned. Aside from all the amazing things this man had touched or created in his life, the thought that he had possibly hung out with and taken LSD with Timothy Leary boggled his mind. To Aaron, Timothy Leary was a folklore hero that accompanied all the finest music and stories his parents had told him about growing up in the sixties.

"Yes, Aaron, Tim and I were very close for a short period of time when I resided in Berkeley. A very brilliant man on another level. He opened my eyes to another world. In fact, he is really the impetus for my understanding of the famous Buddha saying, *Know all things to be like this: As a magician makes illusions of horses, oxen, carts and other things, Nothing, is as it appears.* Which subsequently instilled in me a belief that eventually manifested itself to me as one more piece to the puzzle that is the Godscript."

"It isn't that I am not entirely interested in learning about everything you might have done with Timothy Leary, I am, but what has this got to do with my saying you look younger?" Aaron quizzed.

Bob chuckled, dropping his book, which he quickly bent down and picked up, resuming the tapping on his thigh. "One time, Tim and I dropped a new version of lysergic acid diethylamide he had procured from his interactions with the military. We experienced such amazing hallucinations. So great were they, we turned back into children. It is all so clear in my mind now. I can still see him transforming in front of me until he looked just like a little kid. We laughed and laughed. Well, until that asshole Ranger with an over-inflated power trip shoved up his ass showed up and threatened to arrest us unless we left his park," Bob finished and sighed. "That's all. Your comment took me back to a fine memory, a pleasant time in my life."

Judas, hearing voices, had woken Dancer and come in. They had both watched with some interest, until Judas innocently asked, "Bob, I can't help but notice you seriously covet that small book you keep tapping on your thigh. If I may, what is it?"

Aaron too, wanting so badly to know what that book contained, added, "You know Bob, I am curious as well. What is in your book?"

Dancer, still somewhat asleep, was unable to speak up, though she knew all too well how important the book was to Bob and how closely he guarded the secret of its contents. Still, she too longed to know what secrets Bob hid there.

"Quite frankly, it is nobody's business but mine. Though I do somewhat understand your childish human nature to see what is hidden from you in plain sight. I will only say, and not comment further, as it is NONE of your business, that all computers have a backup, and this is mine," he finished with some degree of disdain, looking upward in his holier-than-thou pose.

"Sorry," said Judas.

"Sorry," spoke Aaron at the exact same time.

"Don't be an asshole, Bob, they're just curious like me. What the hell," Dancer chided him. As she finished, the lights blinked off momentarily, then back on. As they did, Bob quickly turned his attention toward Pandora, whose high-pitched whine filling the room as she came up to speed was now abating, winding down instead. "Shit, it did it again."

"What?" all three asked in unison.

"Pandora has exceeded another fuse's flashpoint."

"You mean she blew a fuse?" Aaron asked.

"Yes. Yes, but that is not the problem. I was correct at the hardware store, as I always am, in buying six fuses for just this unfortunate probability. But do you not see—no, no, of course not, only I see ahead and prepare for such situations. I must discover what is causing this, or we will just go through all six."

"Apparently, you mean five—now," Dancer added, smirking with a degree of sarcastic disdain at his outburst. She immediately regretted it, knowing that was just Bob, just the Asperger's talking, and was pissed off at herself for taking it personally. The uncharacteristic show of stress eking out of her was a sign that betrayed the gravity of the situation.

"You must all leave me be, so I can work on this alone. Please shoo, shoo," Bob said, waving his hand and the book, ushering them out.

"But have you fixed the algorithm?" asked Aaron, as he and the others were being herded out.

"Go! Leave me," Bob said with a look of consternation. "Please, just go."

"Pardon me." Miko's soft voice filled all of the Cave's rooms like an airport announcement. "We have guests arriving. Lots and lots of guests."

~~ ~ ~~~~   ~

Nate's car pulled up and lurched to a stop, dust rolling off in a cloud, dissipating into the surrounding brush. Already parked in front of Bob's mesa home were two ADTCs and four ATVs, with a total of sixteen men deploying, including Nate, Andrew, and Deputy Stenson. Overhead, two drones carefully kept an eye on things.

Nate, rubbing his chin, asked, "Andrew, what have we got on the other side of this hill?"

"Sir, the other two ADTCs and one drone overhead. And sir, they are already reporting they found a cave entrance with new footprints going in. They are continuing in, sir."

Cautiously, Nate allowed himself a smile. "Andrew, ya know you really could go a little easier on all that 'sir' shit?" Nate said very Godfather-like, still smiling. He paused to momentarily pull three pieces of paper out of his shirt pocket, glanced at them, and replaced them in his pocket. "Knock once, then go in. We have warrants. Andrew, I need you to sweep the walls and floor; they have to have a hidden door of some sort. Let's do this, people. We know they are here. Somewhere."

As he finished, his smile disappeared as he thought about how many times he'd had his man, only to discover he had managed to slip away. "Not this time, Robbie, not this time."

~~~ ~~~ ~~ ~

The three of them sat in the living area of the Cave in various stages of nodding off from lack of sleep, except Aaron, who sat fidgeting with his fingernails, trying his best not to bite off one in particular. The harder he tried to ignore it, the more he could sense, feel, the small tear in the nail begging him to *just bite it off.*

As they sat, Pandora's whine sounded a startup four times, followed by four short periods of blackout. Aaron, keeping count, knew all too well Pandora had blown four more fuses. This left only one fuse to finish testing and then try to bring Cynthia forward. He was, as well, acutely aware an army of police were crawling around outside trying to get in. *If I can survive this stress without having a heart attack or biting off this nail, I can survive anything,* he thought to himself. He wanted to scream, but knew nothing would help. Cynthia's life was in the hands of a brilliant madman, who was, for whatever reasons, trying his best to help him in a reality that would have left both him and Cynthia dead and forgotten.

In total despair, still nagged by the fingernail that wanted so badly to be bitten off, Aaron started to stand up to go see how Bob was doing. Before he could rise, Bob walked into the room. He stopped in front of Aaron, then, without emotion, announced, "I have, of course, solved the problem. I am ready to perform the test."

Aaron, fingernail still taunting him and in his mouth, turned his head toward Bob so fast he tore the dangling nail off to the quick. "Ow, shit!" he screamed.

Bob looked horrified, thinking he had just delivered great news only to be met with such a negative response. Both Dancer and Judas were now awake, looking to see what the commotion was about.

"Sorry. I just ripped my fingernail off," Aaron explained. He looked at Bob, and while waving his hand in a vain attempt to make it stop hurting, asked, "You can do it? What about the fuses? I counted four more shutdowns, which means you have one fuse left."

Miko's voice once again filled the room. "I am now detecting ground-penetrating sonar probes that are pervading the cave area upstairs. They know we are here. I would also like to point out, Judas, you were absolutely correct in your assumption of deceit on their part. They are broadcasting communications that indicate they are still in pursuit of the four back at your compound and that they are pulling all of their resources to that position. This is not true. I count sixteen men in and around the house with two drones overhead. There are also several officers in the rear tunnel. I can't get an exact count on them yet."

"Nate must be smiling now," chuckled Bob. "You will get your turn, Nate, just not yet."

Judas looking up in the air, not sure where to speak, asked, "Miko, can you still interact with their feed? That is, I mean, can you—well, can we turn the table on them and feed them false information?"

"Why yes, Judas, I do believe I can. What did you have in mind?

"Can you make them think we know they are outside and have decided to escape using the third tunnel?"

"I'm sorry, there is no third—" Miko stopped and actually giggled. "I get it, yes, the third tunnel, of course. Imaginative or outside of the box thinking is something I am still learning. I can do that and keep them busy chasing false readings heading out toward the front of the house and toward the highway."

"Perfect!" said Judas, walking over to Bob and Aaron. "What are we waiting for? Someone said something about a test?"

"But we are going to need more fuses, right, Bob?" asked Aaron, still holding his finger.

~~~ ~~~ ~~~

Andrew swept the walls of the house with his scanner, back and forth like washing windows with a sponge.

"Sir, I just picked up a sound that is not generated by my sonar. And it came from behind this wall, below us."

Nate, hanging close to his new sidekick, responded, "Seriously. Hmm. Can you be more specific as to where, like point?"

Andrew, without hesitation, pointed to the left side of the wall. "About there, sir."

Nate walked over and knocked on different sections of the wall. Grimacing, he continued to knock on portions of the wall. "We have no choice." He turned to Deputy Stenson. "Take it down!"

"Sir, the wall, sir?"

"Well yeah, the wall," he replied, pointing to where Andrew had. "Make a hole right there."

"Sir?"

"Yes, Andrew," Nate said, shaking his head, so uncomfortable with the military-style formality.

"Sir, sorry sir, I mean, what else am I supposed to call you?" Andrew asked apologetically, turning his head slightly like he might get yelled at.

"Jeez, kid. Whatever. Grow a pair, would you? What have you got?"

"Sir." He stopped, then continued, "I have communication via the link I have established with their A.I. It is indicating they are aware of our presence and are trying to escape out of a tunnel."

"Did you see any other tunnels?

"No, sir. But I am getting movement that appears to be headed under the house out toward the highway."

"We need to look at that satellite scan again."

"It's in the IC vehicle, sir."

Nate paused, looking at the wall. "Okay, that wall isn't going anywhere. Come on, we need to look at the scan closer. I don't want him sneaking out under our noses again." Nate laughed to himself at the literal fact of that statement.

~   ~ ~~~~ ~   ~

"Your concern is unwarranted, Aaron. I have resolved the issue to my satisfaction," Bob responded to Aaron's question.

"How? Are you sure? We are talking about Cynthia!" Aaron asked sharply, standing very close to Bob, nerves frayed and still holding his throbbing finger.

"You will please refrain from entering my current sphere of influence," Bob replied. "But, to quell your irrational fears, I discovered a small amount of moisture caused by condensation and capillary attraction that was collecting and dripping onto a piece of conduit that then continued down to a junction box, whose seal was less than sufficient. It is repaired, and we are safe to resume our test. And, I might add, bring your Cynthia to safety. You are welcome."

Aaron took a step back. "Sorry, Bob. I'm freaking out. We have to get her at the exact right millisecond to ensure it's the same Cynthia that I left, right? And the nuke is pretty close to happening now? Miko, on my original timeline, how much time do we have prior to the nuke going off in Lake Tahoe?" Aaron asked, looking up at the ceiling.

"I calculate we have exactly twenty-seven minutes and thirty-four seconds until the event occurs," Miko responded, and then added, "I have complete faith in Bob. He will bring her here safely."

Bob continued, "Well, Aaron, our staying synchronized with your timeline is the truest measure of ensuring we grab the same data that is, as you put it, *your* Cynthia. Should we not grab her before the nuclear device is detonated on your timeline, and let me remind you, that already happened sixteen years ago, we can still retrieve *your* Cynthia by adjusting the script's clock backward the appropriate amount of time prior to that event. But it matters not if we are a second off. You will still have Cynthia here, just slightly askew on the quantum timetables. It is covered in one of my personal laws: *A course of tangent intersection, a kiss if you will, with any other object can be plotted from any place at any time.* So, we're good." He shrugged his shoulders nonchalantly and turned to head back into the Cave. "Coming?"

Aaron, fearing to say anything further, as it might start Bob on yet another endless oration which they did not have time for, nodded and followed. He wanted his Cynthia, on his timeline.

Miko's pleasant voice filled the room. "I have positive news. They are responding to my false information and have started following the course I am laying out for them heading toward the highway. There are still two officers just outside the wine room. They have not yet violated the first security fence."

As they headed into Pandora's room, Bob answered, "Thank you, Miko. That reminds me of yet another of my laws."

Aaron moaned.

Unaffected, Bob continued, *"Negative impact requires less energy to attain than positive.* No mystery here. I know this; you all know it. I am quite sure that logic, mathematics and physics would simply not allow it to hold up on paper. But that is the beauty of laws of this nature. For example, anyone who has tried to lose weight when asked which is easier, losing weight or gaining it, will respond that gaining it is easier. A negative impact. Or how about spending money? Easier to spend it or to earn it? You, of course, now see my point."

Aaron answered, "What is your point?"

Bob sat down at his desk in front of Pandora. "Your question is a good one, Aaron. You see, Miko just gave us positive news. If my law holds true, and of course it will, we are ahead of the game, as it is more difficult to effect positive change."

Dancer, listening from behind, spoke up, "Bob, not to sound like a broken record or anything, but, um, we need to start the test."

"Yes, my dear. I am ready to start this very minute. You must trust me, utilize that great patience you possess."

Dancer muttered under her breath, "No one has that great of patience." Judas heard her and started to laugh, then covered it with a cough.

"No, Bob," Dancer continued her thought. "That is not the point I was trying to make. It seems the last few tests have required I be standing near the middle of Highway 180. Obviously, I cannot get there, seeing how we have the entire police force of Flagstaff sitting outside waiting for just such a stupid move. So, how do we tell if it, whatever you are going to move, has arrived?" she asked. "What are you going to move?"

Aaron could only mutter, "Oh shit."

Bob swiveled in his chair toward Dancer. He held the book up to his forehead and pondered for a minute before lowering the book to look at her. "I cannot remember the last time I overlooked a detail as important as that. Any detail. Having that piranha out there chasing me has seriously distracted my normal perfect attention to detail. But, I do believe I have the solution we can utilize."

This time, under his breath, Aaron mumbled, "Great, you've picked a fine time to discover you're human."

"I am sorry, what?" Bob asked.

"Nothing, you were about to tell us your plan."

"Yes, yes. Miko?"

"Yes, Bobby."

"Can you hack one of the drones overhead?"

"I already have the ability to take command of either."

"Wonderful!" he said, clapping his hands together. "What is the flight time to our alternate target on the highway?"

"There is no current breeze, so as the crow flies, it will take eight minutes and forty-three seconds."

Dancer nodded. "Got it. Brilliant, actually. Now, what is it exactly you are going to run this test using?"

Aaron, at this point, leaned against the wall, doing his best not to hyperventilate and pass out. Nor did he want to say anything to cause further distraction. Judas, a wise man, had backed away from Bob, the computer and Dancer to allow them room to work.

Dancer moved forward and put her hands on Bob's shoulders, gently rubbing them. "I know you have this, Bob. You are the only person in the entire world capable of doing this. Just tell us what you need."

"That is very pleasing, please do not stop." He leaned back into her hands. "My thought is, we only have time for one test, so I want to make it significant. I need to bring something forward from Cynthia's time. The only thing I know for certain is where I was just before the moment I encountered Aaron. Using the same coordinates, which I have refined through all of our earlier tests, I will grab the data that represents the hula dancer on the dashboard of my VW."

Aaron let out a chuckle. "You have a hula dancer on your dash? Oh my God, I just put mine back on my dash a couple of days before—" He stopped for a moment as out of nowhere, the fight he'd had with Cynthia the night before all of this started popped into his head. Snapping back to the moment, he finished, "When I wired the new lighting."

"Serendipity, Aaron, serendipity," Dancer said, smiling. She stopped rubbing Bob's shoulders, leaning down close. "Bob, enough with the niceties, just do it!"

"Very well, then. Miko, commandeer their drone and send it to the coordinates I gave you. And please show us the live feed from its camera." Bob swirled back to his keyboard, quickly typed something, and with a bit of over-dramatic flourish, brought his hand over his head then down, striking the enter key. Aaron's entire body tightened as he brought his hands up into a praying position near his face. "It will take Pandora just over nine minutes to come up to speed and run the sequence. Miko, will they be able to see the video feed as well?"

"You can have it either way. They are already trying to figure out what happened and where it is going."

"Let them watch what I can do. It will keep them occupied and confused."

~   ~~~~ ~ ~~

"Sir? Sorry, Nate," Andrew said, sitting down at his computer. He turned and looked over his shoulder at Nate, who had not yet responded. "Nate?" he said louder. "You really need to see this."

"What? What the hell are they doing now?"

"They have stolen another drone. This guy is really good."

"Andrew, you seriously have no idea just how good Mandić is. Do I dare ask you to put the video up on the screen again?" Nate asked, straightening his shoulders and neck in a stretch.

"Yes. Come look," Andrew said as he keyed into his monitor. Nate and Officer Stenson bent down for a better look on the small screen filled with little more than a dark blur.

"They have it flying away from here into nowhere. The only thing out there is Highway 180." As he spoke, they could detect vehicles moving on a road off in the distance. The drone flew directly over the highway and stopped fifteen feet off the pavement, and just hovered.

"What in hell's bells is he up to now?" asked a very perplexed Nate. He reached in his shirt pocket to touch the three pieces of paper, making sure they were still there. "Remind me never to play chess with this guy. I have no idea what he is up to," Nate said and bent down on one knee, so he could get a closer look at Andrew's screen. As his eyes focused on the tiny screen, something appeared out of thin air onto the pavement below the drone. It looked very small and light in color.

"What the..." But before he could finish, the blur of a vehicle going by on the screen turned whatever it had been into a spot of powder on the pavement.

"Well, I hope the hell he didn't need that," Nate joked.

~~~~ ~~ ~~~~

Miko, Bob, Dancer, Aaron and Judas all watched exactly the same feed.

"Iekika!" Bob cried out. "Iekika, my poor baby. I am so sorry."

"Iekika? She had a name?" Dancer asked.

Bob, nearly in tears, responded, "Yes, she has been with me longer than anyone. Her name means *the one who can foresee.*"

Judas chimed in, "She didn't foresee that coming."

Bob sat up. "Never mind, she is still on the dashboard in the garage." It took a few seconds for everyone to make the paradox connection and realize just how bizarre what they were doing was.

Aaron, who had been watching from his safe position against the wall, pushed himself away and added, starting to show signs of hope, "Joycee, mine is named Joycee. My hula dancer."

Bob walked over to Aaron. "I understand, Aaron. Iekika means a great deal to me. She has traveled thousands of miles with me, keeping me company. Do you see what I have done? It worked. Iekika just came from Cynthia's timeline. From where I accidentally procured you. My revised algorithm works." He patted Aaron on the shoulder. "Come, let us bring your Cynthia here, home!"

Up until this moment, Aaron had been unable to concentrate on the miracle unfolding before him. But now, as it began to dawn on him like the sun breaking through the clouds, a smile slowly crept over his face.

"And you didn't blow a fuse."

~~~ ~~~~ ~~~~

"One thing is for certain, they're not hacking in and stealing our drone while they're on the run. They're still under the house," Nate said emphatically.

"Team two just reported they have reached a metal door in the cave tunnels they entered," Andrew relayed.

Nate tried not to smile but couldn't help himself. "Tell them to hold their position. We're on our way. Stenson, leave two men here. Andrew keeps the drone *we still have* overhead. Everyone else, let's get to the other side of this mountain."

Nate got up off his knee and turned, then stopped. He then looked back at Andrew. "You didn't say sir. Well, shit howdy, Bot Boy, you're catching on. 'Bout time."

~~ ~ ~~ ~ ~~ ~

As the three of them huddled behind Bob, waiting for the next step, they heard a loud bang, followed by another, and then another. All three turned toward the tunnel the sound had come from.

"Shit! They've found us," Dancer said loudly over the volume of the bangs. Then silence. They took turns looking at each other, frozen where they stood.

They had nowhere to run, and they were out of time. They could only listen and await the inevitable. They began to hear movement and saw lights flickering on the floor of the tunnel and reflecting off the cave walls. Two officers slowly, carefully looking right and left, came into view. The bright lights on their helmets made it difficult to look toward them, but it was clear they had weapons, and they were pointed at the four of them.

"Freeze! Don't move!" ordered the lead officer in a strong, authoritative voice. Dancer, trembling, lightly chuckled as she said, "Way ahead of you there, sir."

Nate walked into the light, pushing through the two officers and heading over to where Bob was seated at the computer. Behind, several more officers, with weapons out in front of them, came in, filling the small room.

Nate, the consummate professional, hid his excitement, casually telling the officers, "Stand down, guys. They're not dangerous, and they're not going anywhere *this time*." He turned his gaze toward Bob. "Well, I'll be damned. Robert Mandić, finally. Do you have any idea how long I have been waiting for this moment?"

Bob rose and turned to meet Nate's gaze. Two of the officers instinctively brought their rifles up, pointing them at Bob, but Nate motioned with his hand to put the rifles down.

"Well, correct me if I am wrong, and I never am, it would be exactly the same amount of time I have been trying to avoid this moment," Bob answered, smiling to a degree that did not fit the seriousness of the moment. "And, I will not say it is nice to see you again, Nate. Yes, I have seen you on several occasions. But then, I will tell you I have become so accustomed to you breathing down my neck all these years that I am, in fact, honored to have you here now. Now you may witness just what you have, with your great tenacity, been chasing me for. Well done, sir."

With that, Nate reached into his front pants pockets with both hands, then his back pockets, looking for something. He looked deliberately disheveled, like the classic television detective just before he asks the question that rattles whoever he is questioning and breaks the case wide open. He slowed his search, smiled, and reached into his shirt pocket. He pulled out several pieces of paper, neatly folded, and held them up for Bob to see. As he did, he cocked his head to the side, obviously thinking very hard. Then, straightening, he said, "I don't know how the hell you did this, Robert—"

Bob interrupted him with, "Please do not call me Robert, that was a long time ago. Everyone knows me as Bob."

"Fair enough, Bobby."

Again, but with disdain in his voice this time, "Do not call me Bobby, it is Bob!"

"Well, aren't you the persnickety old coot. But Bobby"— he paused for the desired rub to have its effect, then continued— "sorry, Bob. You've piqued my interest with these," he said, lightly shaking the three pieces of paper. "So, what the hell, show me what you've got."

The group shared puzzled looks as all of them, in unison, followed the pieces of paper in Nate's hand. Their puzzlement turned to complete dumbfoundedness as they heard him make his unexpected and obviously generous statement.

Dancer, not one to miss an opportunity regardless of why, quickly took the initiative. "Bob, do it. Bring Cynthia home. Well, I mean, bring her here. Do it NOW!" she finished, speaking in her *I mean it* voice she knew Bob would respond to.

Bob looked at Nate, and in a rare gesture of appreciation, said, "Thank you, thank you." Then, quickly falling back into pure narcissistic Bob style, "You are not going to believe what you are going to see. What I have discovered!" he said quite emphatically. "The purpose of this equipment that you have been chasing me for all of these years comes down to right now. And you, Nate, you've just saved a life today."

Bob turned back to the screen and keyboard but stopped. He looked back at Nate. "I need you to send some of your men out to Highway 180 exactly three point seven miles west of the off-ramp to the Last Hope. Do not ask me to explain, it will take too long. Just have your officers close the road in both directions for half a mile and wait. They are about to see something they will not understand. Prepare them for that. And, let them know the person they find, her name is Cynthia. Have them bring her here."

Nate nodded. "Stenson, got that? Do it. I want that road closed now!"

Aaron added, "Sir, if it is anything like when I arrived, she, Cynthia, is going to be totally freaked out, scared out of her mind. Let your guys know that. Please."

~~ ~ ~~~~ ~~

318

Cynthia and Half Dome stood in the driveway of their home. It was dark, late, and she wanted to cry, totally exhausted physically and mentally. She took a long deep breath.

Where the hell is Aaron? she thought, overwhelmed by it all. *Is San Francisco still there? Did Mom make it out, only to get to Sacramento and get vaporized? What the hell am I supposed to do next?* She couldn't go anywhere, power was out everywhere, and there was no way to communicate with anybody or learn anything. She just wanted to get in the house and lay down, close her eyes for a minute, just a minute.

"Come on, boy," she said, directing Half Dome up the concrete steps from the driveway to the porch in total darkness. Half Dome had other ideas, choosing instead to try and make it to the porch in one leap. It was not to be, as his very tired and short legs did not generate quite enough lift. He hit the side of the porch instead and fell back on the driveway in a very ungraceful, head-over-heels somersault.

Unaware embarrassment was an emotion, he jumped right back to his feet, tongue out panting, staring at Cynthia. Then he decided it best to walk with her up the steps.

She opened the door to the only sanctuary she had left. After all she had been through, the smell of home was comfortable.

She threw her bag on the couch and went straight back to the bedroom. Everything hurt all at the same time as she sat on the edge of the bed. After removing one of her hiking boots and a sock, she fell backward into the soft blankets and pillow, then swung her legs, one still wearing a sock and boot, up onto the bed. Half Dome jumped on the bed and lay down with his upper torso and front paws on her chest. He was heavy, but it felt safe. She could feel sleep not far behind and gaining.

She reached up with her left hand to set her phone, out of battery and no longer of any use to her, on the dresser. As her fingers opened to let go, she suddenly felt dizzy. *To be expected,* she thought, *with all that had happened.* Then she paused, her hand stretched out toward the dresser where the phone had just dropped. The room darkened, fluttered, then became much brighter. She pushed up with one elbow to be greeted by an extraordinary hallucination. Her eyes were wide open now as she stared around the surreal scene in front of her. Even Half Dome, now standing on all fours next to her on the bed, was looking around, growling.

It was just past dusk, and they were outside. *What the fuck is happening?* she thought. In front of her was a highway winding up through high desert, sagebrush and yucca. Off in the distance, a purplish, hazy mountain range was backlit brilliantly, a bright orange and crimson line bursting out in rays upward toward the sky as the light from the sun desperately tried to stay on top of the mountain.

About one hundred feet in front of her, a police vehicle like she had never seen before was blocking the road with lights flashing, red, blue, red...

"What the hell is happening?" she said to herself. She could see she was obviously on a road. She looked down to see she was still on her bed, and at the same time, she brought both arms and hands down, quickly hitting the mattress, making sure it was still there. The bed was now sitting squarely on the asphalt in the middle of the road with a painted yellow line coming out from beneath her that disappeared, diminishing like a two-point perspective, into the coming night and horizon. She looked behind her and saw a second police vehicle. This one looked more like a normal cop car, also blocking the road with its lights flashing.

A police officer walked toward her from the odd vehicle in front of her. Cynthia, too astounded to be alarmed by his approach, watched. Half Dome, on the other hand, was not as generous. He growled loudly, bouncing up and down on his front legs and glaring with extreme hostility toward the man approaching.

"Ma'am. Ma'am, are you okay?" the approaching officer asked, holding out his hand toward Half Dome. "Good boy, good boy. I'm not going to hurt you or your mom. Ma'am, is your name Cynthia?" he asked, still holding up his hand but now turned down, knuckles facing toward Half Dome, so he could smell him.

Cynthia couldn't speak. She looked in every direction, trying to take it all in.

"Ma'am, I am Officer O'Reilly. I am here to help you." He slowed his approach, bringing up the other hand, open in a soothing gesture. "I am sure you are quite alarmed at the moment. I have to tell you I am pretty freaked out by what I just saw happen. But you're okay, it's all going to be okay." He spoke in his calmest, most reassuring voice, but he too was grappling with seeing a woman and a dog sitting on a bed suddenly appear out of thin air. He didn't even blink, and they were there.

In the background, she could hear multiple voice transmissions over their radios, too garbled to make out.

Cynthia, still frozen on the top of the bed, shook her head and turned to Half Dome. "It's okay, baby, shhhh," she said, holding one finger to her lips. Then, turning and looking Officer O'Reilly squarely in the eyes, she said, "What happened? Who the hell are you and where the hell am I?"

"Ma'am, may I ask your name first?"

She paused, then getting some wits about her, said firmly, "Cynthia, Cynthia Camila Bemberg!" Half Dome added a sharp bark to back her up.

"Thank you, Cynthia. Again, I don't know what's going on. My instructions were to come out here and block off this section of road until further notice. So, trust me when I tell you I am as bewildered as you," he said, obviously mystified by the events. Returning his eyes to hers, "How did you do that?"

"Do what?" she retorted with a tone both angry and scared. "Where am I?"

"Cynthia, you are just outside of Flagstaff. Where did you come from?" he asked, letting down his police officer's guard, truly as curious as her as to what had just occurred.

Before she could answer, he held one hand to his ear to listen to an earpiece she couldn't see. "Got it. Yes, sir, I have a young woman here." He paused, taking a long deep breath, preparing himself for what he had to say. "A young woman sitting on a bed with a dog in the middle of the highway."

"Who are you talking to?" Cynthia asked excitedly.

He held up his hand in an attempt to get her to hold her questions while he listened. "Yes, sir. Yes, sir. Got it." He looked up at Cynthia with a puzzled look. "I am told to tell you, Aaron says it is going to be okay. Do you—" But he didn't get the chance to finish.

"Aaron, you know where Aaron is? Oh my God, Aaron." And with that, she burst into tears. Sobbing, she jumped off the bed. "Where is he? Take me to him, please take me to him."

"Ma'am, Cynthia, it would be my pleasure. Maybe you can fill me in on where you came from and how you got here on the way over. First, though, we need to get this bed off the road," he said, still wearing a very puzzled *what the hell is going on here* look.

The officer bent down to pick something up off the asphalt that was lying next to the bed. He held up a sock and the front half of a hiking boot. "Are these yours, Cynthia?"

~~~~ ~~~~ ~~~~

Everyone, with the exception of Bob, stood motionless during the entire event as Pandora's whine filled the cave with electric excitement. And then, with an uneventful flickering of some lights and a few beeps and buzzes from various parts of the room, her slow, deeper pitched whine faded to silence as she shut down.

After several painfully long seconds, Andrew spoke. "Sir? Sorry, I have Officer O'Reilly reporting something has appeared in the middle of the highway."

Aaron jumped up and toward Andrew so quickly, all of the officers raised their weapons.

"Whoa, whoa, whoa, boys. Hold on. Put 'em down. Son, you need to move a little slower right now, okay?" Nate said, grabbing Aaron's shoulder. "What are you in such a gull darn hurry for? What's out there?"

Aaron's lips and tongue were spewing out words faster than his brain could think. "It, she, my, well... you know, oh my God, is she alive?" he finally spit out.

"Who? Is who alive?" asked Nate.

"Ask the officer what he is seeing in the middle of the highway," Dancer instructed Andrew in that *voice*.

Miko's voice filled the room, "I have repositioned the drone for a better view. I am refreshing it onscreen now."

Andrew turned toward the sound of the voice. "Ha, You. That was you, wasn't it? You're the one who has been hacking past all of my firewalls. Who are you?"

Miko's pleasant, Asian voice, now came only from Andrew's pad. "Hello, Andrew, or should I say *Drone Dragon*? My name is Miko. It is a pleasure to meet you. And might I add how impressed I am by your coding," she cooed.

As Andrew and Miko continued their less than perfectly timed introduction of themselves, the screen on Bob's computer showed the scene unfolding on Highway 180. Several officers were standing in front of a bed sitting on the asphalt with a woman and dog on it, bathed in flashing lights. Aaron was beside himself. There were Cynthia and Half Dome, alive, in one piece.

Aaron grabbed Bob and hugged him. "Thank you, Bob, thank you. You are the greatest genius that ever lived." Turning to Andrew, wiping tears from his face, he said. "Tell them to tell her Aaron said it is going to be okay."

Nate added, "Tell Officer O'Reilly to clear the road and bring her and the dog here. It's time we wrapped this circus up." Nate stepped between Dancer and Bob. "You know, there is nothing here but a lot of old equipment no one cares about or can use," Nate far too calmly commented in an out-of-place, disinterested tone. It was as though somehow he had missed the greatest accomplishment since the moon landing.

Bob immediately and vehemently protested, "What are you talking about? Are you insane?"

Dancer's hand, from out of nowhere, quickly slid across Bob's mouth. She looked coyly at Nate. "Yep, you're right, Detective—sorry, Nate, nothing but a lot of useless junk here nobody would be interested in," she said, smiling but still firmly holding her hand over Bob's mouth, as he tried in vain to wriggle out. Finally, Dancer stomped on Bob's foot, eliciting a muffled "Ow." She looked sternly into Bob's eyes until he relaxed.

Bob got it. After all these years of relentless chasing, Nate, in but a few short days, had learned just how amazing this man, Robert Mandić, Bob was. He was quite sure the day would come he would need this man and his incredible intelligence. And understanding that need was setting the stage to do the smart thing, the right thing, and walk away, allowing Bob to continue with his work.

"Dancer, if I weren't going to retire now, I would do everything I could to convince you to join our team. But as I said, nothing left here to pursue. I can finally file this as decommissioned due to the statute of limitations. Deputy

Stenson, you can stand down. Send these men and the equipment home. There really isn't anything left to do here. Miles and I, and Andrew, will stay and interview everyone to write up the necessary reports. I'll come meet with you and your men to debrief the situation later this week. Sorry, after all that excitement, this is a letdown, but thank you, all of you," Nate said, rotating to look at the men surrounding him. "This is still a classified case, so what you have heard, what you have seen, everything, and I mean everything, keep to yourselves. Again thanks. Now maybe we can all go upstairs where there is some more room and wait for Officer O'Reilly to show up with his find." With that, Nate motioned for them to depart toward the exterior tunnel.

Dancer spoke, "We don't have to go that way, might as well go up to the house the normal way. Please follow me."

Nate smiled. "I knew it."

They headed out through the door into the living area, and, without exception, everyone, as if choreographed, in unison looked over at the table protruding from the wall as they walked by.

~   ~   ~   ~~~

Miko decided to join them in the silicone, garnering Andrew's full attention. He was mesmerized by her every move as if there were nothing else going on in the room.

"I have two drone vehicles making their approach, forty-five seconds out," she said.

Aaron sprang up and ran to the front door and out to the driveway. He stood there, watching the lights approach overhead. Dancer came right behind him. Nate followed with Bob and Judas. Andrew stayed behind, unaware anyone had left.

Both ADTCs landed simultaneously, stirring up a great deal of dust. As the dust started to subside, Aaron could make out a door opening. First out of the vehicle was Half Dome, who picked out Aaron immediately, bounding over to him and jumping up and on him so hard, Aaron fell over backward. Half Dome took full advantage of his being down and leaped onto his chest, licking his face with his long tongue.

"Half Dome, buddy. Oh my God." Aaron was rubbing him with both hands when Cynthia walked up.

"Don't you ever, ever disappear like that again," she said, crying and smiling simultaneously.

Aaron, holding Half Dome, looked up and stared. Finally, here she was. The nightmare was over. Rolling Half Dome off his chest to the ground and standing up, he said, "Sorry, bud. Sorry, you understand." And then he grabbed Cynthia, pulling her toward him into a full, wraparound hug. Neither said a word, only holding on with every ounce of strength they had.

Dancer started crying, so Judas stepped over to hug her.

Nate looked at Bob. "Hope you're not going to get all sappy and cry too. You know, you owe me an explanation. I should be putting you in handcuffs and dragging you out of here. But today, I have witnessed something I cannot explain. Something I believe will be very useful. I stand before a genius. I have always known it Robert, Bob, but I had a job to do. There has got to be a book in this."

Bob smiled and held up his book. "There already is. It's all right here."

Aaron whispered in Cynthia's ear, "I am so sorry about the things I said to you before I left. I was a complete idiot. I love you. I have missed you so much."

She pushed away slightly. "What? You're worried about what you said before you disappeared into thin air? That nonsense about the rice? In the midst of this insanity? You or someone needs to explain to me what the hell is going on. Where are we? Do you know that World War III is happening right now? And what is with all of these machines?"

Dancer, unable to contain herself, walked over and wrapped her arms around both Aaron and Cynthia.

"And you are?" Cynthia asked, pushing away, out of the group hug. "Who are all these people? What is going on?" Coming out of her initial shock and the joy at seeing Aaron, everything she had been going through these last few days came flooding back into her head.

It was at that moment, she saw for the first time her finger. She stopped talking and just stared. Eyes wide open, she looked at Aaron. "Where the HELL is my finger?" she said, holding up her left index finger. The top portion of the digit was missing down to the first knuckle.

Aaron reached to grab her hand and look at the finger. There was no blood, no open wound. It looked as if it had always been that way.

"Honey," Aaron said, "I don't even know where to begin. First, just know, you are okay, I am okay, and all will become clear. What I need to tell you is going to be so strange, you will keep asking yourself, 'when am I going to wake up?'" He hugged her again and then let go to put a hand on Dancer. "This is Dancer. She saved my life."

Dancer nodded. "I'm glad I finally get to meet you, Cynthia. This guy loves the shit out of you, just in case you weren't aware of that fact."

Cynthia's brain went numb, trying to process so much inexplicable information. She could only nod.

"Let's all go inside," Dancer said, taking her hand to gently pull her along. "Are you hungry, maybe your dog? Does he want some water?"

As the rest headed inside, Judas took Bob by the arm, holding him back. "Bob, I could not help but notice the subtle innuendos and apparent glossing over of the fact you have been on the run from this man for many years, with what appears to be millions of dollars' worth of equipment. Equipment I suspect at the time to have been highly classified. And then, the cop who has been after you for all these years holds up a couple of pieces of paper, and all is forgiven?"

Bob looked at him with a grin. "Cool, huh?"

"That's it, *cool?*"

"Come, my old friend, we must join the others inside. When all of Nate's gunslingers for hire leave, I will explain to you, Dancer, Aaron and our new arrival, the young lady, ah—oh yes, Cynthia. Certainly, you know my time is too valuable to have to explain it twice."

"Boy, you have not changed a bit, Bob. You are still the most egotistical, self-serving and far too intelligent for his own good son of a bitch I have ever known. But you are and always will be my friend. Your explanation should be entertaining, I am sure."

Inside, the last of the gun-toting officers were finished securing their gear and ready to head outside to their vehicles. Nate turned to Miles to whisper in his ear, "Do me a favor, go outside and keep an eye on these guys. I don't want anyone sneaking back in while I interrogate Mandić and his cohorts."

"You got it, sir."

"Andrew, I need you to stay here. Think of yourself as a technology translator. I have a feeling this is going to be way over my head." Andrew nodded. "Please, everyone, make yourselves comfortable. I still have some questions before I wrap this investigation up."

Judas, sitting on the cushioned arm of the living room chair, looked up at Nate and added, "I am with you, Officer. I have seen too many things in the last twenty-four hours that I cannot explain."

Nate returned his stare with a stern quizzical look. "You're the old preacher's son, right? You still following in his footsteps?"

Judas let out a hearty chuckle. "No, sir. I have nothing in common with my father except that he was the sperm donor. A very twisted and evil man. And, as I have already explained to my very old friend, Bob, I only maintain the facade to keep the general public away from our compound. After all the notoriety, we greatly appreciate our privacy. You, sir, however, are welcome to come visit and look around to your heart's desire as we have nothing to hide. Well, not now. Now that Bob is no longer in your crosshairs."

"Fair enough, and it's Nate; I don't really answer to that *sir* shit. Which it seems everyone around here has a great propensity for." He turned with his signature sour grimace to face everyone, all those gathered to see how this would play out. Cynthia and Aaron were wrapped around each other appropriately on a loveseat, Half Dome lying next to them on the floor with his head on Aaron's foot. Bob sat on the sofa with Miko on the chair's arm. Dancer sat in the other matching chair, with Judas also sitting on an arm. Andrew, still lusting at Miko, leaned against the bar with his pad resting on the polished pinewood bar top.

"Bob?" Nate paused to glance around the room. "What the hell did I just witness?"

The silence became deafening. It was the kind of utter silence you experience at night in the mountains when it is snowing. Except this was not delightful, in anticipation of accumulating snow; it was the kind that made people squirm in their seats. Bob's head was bent, looking down, his book slowly tapping on his thigh, which had Half Dome mesmerized as the book methodically went up and down, his head following it as if he were holding a sausage.

"You have all witnessed," started Bob, standing up, "maybe the greatest historical event in the history of mankind.

An event the result of my genius. I knew it back at Livermore, and I stuck with my vision, knowing full well how important this would be for the human race." Bob slid right into his preaching to the class mode, waving his book high in the air as he talked. All eyes, even Half Dome's, were on Bob. He had their absolute undivided attention. In his element like never before in his life, he continued, "I will try to explain this, so you will understand, even though I know very well none of you can grasp the depth of this discovery. Cynthia, I am sorry that it appears as if I have disrupted your life. But, by now you understand, as does Aaron, had I not, you would both be dead!'"

Cynthia's eyes widened, then filled with tears, trying to grasp everything Aaron had just tried to explain—an explanation that had been more like hearing condensed CliffsNotes for *War and Peace*. Aaron wrapped his arm around her tighter as Half Dome stood up to nudge Cynthia's leg with his nose.

"What you have witnessed, Nate, is my discovery of the Godscript. And my ability to decipher it as well as manipulate it using Pandora, the collider I made from the parts you have sought all these years." He stopped long enough to honor Nate with a slight bow. "The notes you received in your room, on three separate nights, were sent by me from my desk in the Cave last night, after I finally corrected the algorithm. Using Pandora, I sent them to you like the three ghosts in Dickens's *A Christmas Carol*."

Bob allowed himself a childish grin and a giggle at his explanation. "I knew the first note you would think a prank, even the second one. But as you realized what my notes prophesied came true, I felt quite sure that by the third, I would have your complete attention. You are a very intelligent man. I knew you would understand you were in uncharted territory, the likes of which would force you to keep an open mind. I needed this insurance in case you found us before I was finished. I needed to make sure you would let us proceed. For that, sir, I thank you."

Cynthia raised her hand, but seeing the tip of her finger missing, withdrew it, embarrassed but for half a second, only to become enraged at the full scope of what she had experienced. She interrupted in a loud, strong voice, "But my mom, where is my mom? Did San Francisco get nuked? Can you bring her here to me?" she demanded with a sound that was more like a snort as she folded her arms on her chest. Before anyone could answer, she held her finger up in the air. "And, where the hell is my finger?"

Aaron stood up in support, grabbing her hand and holding it, kissing the top of the nub. Before he could utter a word, Bob responded, "The missing portion of your phalange at the moment does not yet make sense."

"You mean kind of like, oh I don't know, the table?" Dancer said with biting sarcasm.

"What table?" Cynthia asked.

"I'm sorry, Cynthia, I shouldn't have said that. What Bob has done, in such a short period of time, all to save you from being vaporized along with Lake Tahoe, is nothing short of a miracle. That he did this so quickly is truly a testament to his genius." She finished looking over approvingly, like a proud mom, at Bob.

Bob continued, "I surmise that your finger somehow came to be outside the sphere of my algorithm's influence. I am just glad you were where Aaron thought you might be at that time. Or we would be talking to an empty bed right now. Did you have your hand in something, a jar, a drawer, or maybe you were reaching or stretching for something?"

Hearing only the words Dancer said about Lake Tahoe, Cynthia had stopped thinking about her finger. "Wait. Did you just say Lake Tahoe was nuked?" Only Aaron knew the emotional roller coaster Cynthia was on right then, and his body language telegraphed the pain he was harboring for her. He had tried to fill her in on everything but had just not yet had time to tell her Lake Tahoe was gone.

Bob nodded, acknowledging Dancer for her kind words, then, looking at Cynthia, said, "There was no nuclear device set off in San Francisco. Several other cities, including Los Angeles and, yes, Lake Tahoe, are gone, however. As would you have been if not for me. Your mom surely survived if she was in San Francisco. She would have lived out her life until now and very well could still be alive today. That is, if she were a healthy woman. She will have believed you and Aaron both perished in the nuclear blast that incinerated Lake Tahoe, as you would have."

"Can't you go back to before and bring her here, to now?"

Bob frowned deeply before continuing. "Yes, that might be possible, but there are many concerns, too difficult to explain. The biggest would be bringing back the exact same mother in quantum terms. We do not know where she is. I need to think about it much more, as do you and what ramifications it might have. We are dealing with time travel, quantum physics and all of the new paradoxes we are discovering."

"But you brought Aaron here. You brought me here. Are we still the same people we were before? I feel the same, well, most of me anyway," she said, holding up her finger again to make her point.

"Yes, I am quite confident you two are the same, as we stayed on the exact parallel timeline so that you would be. To repeat, what you ask is not impossible, at least for me, but will require considerable research, and, as I said, we do not know where she is. I can determine how to grab her from a point in time if you know exactly where she was. But that woman would not match your quantum timeline. "

Cynthia sighed, lowering her arm and nub of a finger down. She paused, thinking, then, looking at Bob, said, "I am still trying very hard to process all of this. I am sorry if I do not seem appreciative. So, for now, I will thank you for saving Aaron and Half Dome and me. I was there, I was listening in horror to the news of LA and Paris. Everything you have said happened. I was so scared they had nuked San Francisco because of all the smoke and closed roads from the fires. I know you are telling me the truth. I just do not know yet how to understand it all. To understand why it happened."

In Bob fashion, without acknowledging Cynthia's heartfelt thank you, he simply continued where he left off, looking at Nate. "Aaron is an anomaly that I most certainly did not anticipate. It was a rare, unfortunate incident on my part that precipitated his arrival. One I had to take full responsibility for, and of course, I did the right thing. Once he told me about you," he said, pointing the book toward Cynthia, "that you were still in Lake Tahoe, I was compelled to figure out how this marvelous, miracle of an accident, like so many other great inventions that came about the same way, could be used to save you. As I further unravel the mysteries hiding within the Godscript and how it is entirely responsible for our reality, I will be able to offer the world many great benefits. But for now, until I do, I need to proceed slowly and with great caution, as there is far too much at stake. I am toying with the very fabric of our reality. It is a huge responsibility, one I believe only I am qualified to accept."

"Bob, you old coot," Judas said, "I knew you were something special way back when we were building toy rockets to send tree frogs high into the air. Count me grateful to understand who you are and call you my friend. Our compound is still your home, and you and your new family here are welcome any time. In fact, you're expected. Further, if you need anything in pursuit of this endeavor, you know an escape ladder." He laughed. "Count us in."

Aaron, standing next to Cynthia, added, "I have no words, Bob. I have gone through so many emotions since this happened. It is as if I have lived the sixteen years needed to catch up to this time. I am grateful to you for saving Cynthia and me, and Half Dome. I am in awe that I have stood at arm's length of your genius and been able to participate in this revolutionary concept you have discovered. As Cynthia and I work to establish our lives, realign ourselves in this time, trust that we will be here for anything you need from us."

Cynthia, still reeling, as she would for days to come, nodded.

Nate, quietly standing at the center of the room, spoke up, "I guess, then, I am glad I have been unsuccessful until now in catching you, Bob. Another anomaly, if you will, in this weird journey we all share. As such, I will consider and file this case as closed. Then, I will do my damnedest to bury the file under as much bureaucracy as I can." He turned to Andrew. "You didn't hear that."

Andrew responded with the appropriate, "Hear what?" and smiled.

"I am not sure how you so successfully eluded me all of these years," Nate continued, "but now I want to convey the same sentiment as the rest of your friends, Bob. I, too, recognize that I am privileged to have been a part of this event and would like to offer you my services should you ever need them. That is, if you ever feel you can trust someone who has been stalking you for forty years," Nate said, wearing a broad smile. "In the meantime, I think I am just going to call it a day, retire, and write a book."

He laughed to himself, started to turn to go, but turned back to face Bob. "You know, I have to tell you something. I'm sure it means nothing. But I watched a news feed the other night about the Eight-Year War. In it, they were showing some old news footage taken just before the Los Angeles nuke went off. There was one very short video bite where a lady reporter was trying to interview an old codger prophesying on a street corner. You know the type, with a sign that says the world's coming to an end. Well, he had no sign, just yelling into the camera, something to the effect of, *Get out of LA, it will be gone tomorrow.* You know what really seemed odd, well—" Nate hesitated before continuing. "Thing is, the old guy, he looked just like you! And the lady interviewing him called him Bob. You wouldn't know anything about that?"

Bob chuckled. "I can assure you, Nate, it could not have been me. At that time, I would have been in Tahoe headed out here to Arizona. Besides, I had not yet invented Pandora, nor discovered the Godscript, so there is simply no way I could have known ahead of time of the eminent disaster that awaited everyone."

Nate nodded. "That's what I thought. Had to ask. It's what I do. You take care. All of you take care. Andrew, it's time for us to head out and let these good people catch up. Maybe, who knows, even relax."

~~~~ ~~~~ ~~~~

Cynthia was settled into the chair next to Bob, with Half Dome snoring comfortably on her lap. She was completely unaware, now days later, an act of phantom limb syndrome, that she was rubbing the smooth, nubby end of her now shorter than normal finger. Aaron sat on the couch on the other side of the small glass table.

"So, Bob?" inquired Cynthia. "Good coffee." Smiling, she held up her cup. "Can I ask, as everything is still pretty damn surreal to me. Unreal on so many levels. Is it real? You know, *real, ground coffee*, from a grinder, using real mountain-grown coffee beans? I'm sorry, what I mean is, with all the fake food, the 3D-printed crap I am hearing about and seeing, is this coffee—beautiful, wonderful coffee—the real deal?"

"Cynthia, I like this about you. You, Dancer and I, we share that feeling. I refuse to give into the synthetic food generation, *the Dgens*, or whatever they call themselves. I know it is inevitable, but I, like you know what real food smells and tastes like. Something a generation from now they will have no concept of. Yes, it is real coffee. It is real, or do not bother me!" Bob was quite resolute in his answer.

"Dgens? They liken themselves, their generation to being degenerates?" asked a surprised Cynthia.

"Oh, no. The 'D' is for digital. This generation associates with the fact their world is nearly completely digital. Oh," he drew in a deep breath, "if they only knew just how correct they are."

"You two sound like an ad for coffee. But somewhat more important than that," said Aaron, standing up and walking to the middle of the room. "Where are Cynthia and I going to live? And where are we going to work? We need to be able to pay for a place to live, food to eat, real or otherwise. Last time I checked, Cynthia and I don't exist here, at least on paper."

"Yes, my young friend, you both will be pleased to know that Dancer, the mom in charge, is already on it," Bob said, laughing at his comparison of her take-charge side. "She discussed it with me, told me really, what possibilities there might be for you and Cynthia." Bob shifted in his chair to face Cynthia. "It would appear you, Cynthia, can simply continue to do your artwork. Dancer said there are many shows and galleries here and nearby. Arizona has become quite the mecca for artists, she said."

Miko's voice interrupted them. "Bob, you asked me to keep you up to date on any peculiar news of the out of the ordinary, negative variety. It would appear just outside Kamchatka, Russia this morning, in a fishing village on the coast, over fifty fishing boats sailed out with the tide and never returned. No boats, survivors or debris have been located."

Bob grimaced, looking down and away from Aaron. "Thank you, Miko. Yes, that is exactly what I wish you to keep an eye out for. Please continue to keep me posted." He shook his head slightly, then looked back to Aaron as if he had not heard any of it. "I do not know if Dancer mentioned a man named Ralph. They were very close, from a time before she and I met. A truck driver who took Dancer in during the war. For fun, she said, he liked to work with wood. She called it a significant hobby. He disappeared sometime right after or near the end of the Eight-Year War, leaving Dancer with a woodshop full of tools and a unique, small home he built. It's outside of town, near the Last Hope. She has not been there in years. She can't bring herself to visit, too many memories. But she is quite sure that with a little work, it would be a good place for the two of you to land on your feet."

Cynthia and Aaron looked at each other with questioning relief. They had already talked, and thought their odds of finding anything soon were dismal at best. Cynthia, not at all shy, spoke up, "That sounds pretty good, maybe too good." She grimaced slightly as she said it. "But okay, when can we see it? However, before that, are you sure Dancer will be okay with this? I don't know the history. From what you just said, it sounds like they were pretty close. We don't want to intrude on a very personal part of her life. We can get out and look for jobs, get a little apartment or something, a tent."

"No. That will not work. Neither of you exists here, as Aaron has already pointed out. Work permits, taxes, no, that just will not work. Besides, this will be good for Dancer, to bring the shop and apartment back to life. It will help her to move on," Bob said, waxing strangely philosophical for one so inept at understanding people.

"It's settled then. We need a place! I can at least start creating some kind of art to sell while we figure out what you can do, babe. I will speak with Dancer, woman to woman. Make sure she is okay with this. I mean, *really* okay with this," Cynthia said while rubbing the neck of a quiet and subdued Aaron. "Bob, I have another question, one more important to me than a place to live or jobs. My mom, when can we bring her here?"

Bob took a long time to answer. Finally, looking first at Aaron, then Cynthia, he spoke. "Yes. As I have said before, I can figure out a way to bring your mother here. The question is, do we really want to do that?" Stopping to allow her to consider his statement, he continued, "I am fearful my tampering with the Godscript may have negative repercussions of a nature I still do not understand. And, the truth is, Cynthia, your mom, a much older version of your mom, very well could be alive and still living in San Francisco. I think it would be best if we focused on trying to find her where she is now and devise a way to introduce the two of you so that we can explain what happened."

The normally pleasing Asian voice of Miko seemed decidedly less so as she spoke to Bob. "I do apologize, Bobby, but there is yet another odd piece of news. It does appear their occurrences seem to be increasing, like contractions in a mother about to give birth. They are becoming far more frequent and more intense," Miko said with some emphasis.

"Yes. Yes, exactly. What is it?" asked Bob.

"In Argentina, on a major road heading in and out of Buenos Aires, cars stopped, closing down the highway. The occupants got out of their vehicles and started, for no apparent reason, fighting. Reports have the death toll at over two hundred. Bob, this is very depressing news. Why do you wish me to keep you posted on such negativity? It is not good for one's overall emotional health," Miko said, changing the sound of her voice to meet the moment.

Before Bob could answer, Miko spoke yet again. "I'm turning on the VRS. All of you have to see this." The screen lit up, displaying a mushroom cloud rising into a night sky as the announcer spoke. "Margret, what we are seeing is live over Alexandria. Reports of utter and complete destruction of the fledgling nation are streaming in at a frightening pace."

"Oh crap, not again," moaned Cynthia, seeing the mushroom cloud.

"Miko, sound at seven, please," Bob said, shocked by what he saw.

"Marti, Alexandria, that is—or that was—the new democratic, corporate country that formed between Greece and Turkey after the Eight-Year War, right?

"Yes, Margret, their uprising set the stage for fifteen new countries being formed after seceding from their mother countries. Hang on, I have some new footage coming in we are going to put up."

As he spoke, the camera switched to a very large crowd of people all standing around what looked like a large digital clock. It was nighttime, and they appeared to be well bundled up and were singing. Their voices gave a collective rise of steam that glowed from the lights. It had the atmosphere of a Christmas celebration.

"Margret, this video was being streamed live, about twenty minutes ago, in front of the old Lighthouse of Alexandroupoli. In the center is their president and his family. What? What? Wait, hold on, that can't be, that just can't be." The camera panned to Marti staring dumbfounded at his cohost, Margret. "I have just been told that the clock in the middle of the square is a countdown clock. It is the countdown to the detonation of the nuclear device that is sitting just below it. Margret, the entire town, the capital of this new burgeoning little country is, is, is," he stammered, "apparently committing mass suicide in front of the entire world, live."

The camera had just switched back to the people when the clock reached 0:00, followed by a sudden white light and then grainy TV noise. The gasping, which sounded more like choking turning to crying, was Margret in the background, and the only noise to be heard.

"Go to black, Carl, we need to process this... GO TO BLACK!" Marti screamed, and the screen went black for a brief moment before returning with a poorly chosen or profoundly sick coincidence, an automatically cued commercial for *Late Night with Mel, Movies for Insomniacs.* Behind the logo, a trailer played the old black-and-white movie, *Dr. Strangelove,* with Slim Pickens atop an atom bomb as it dropped out of the bottom of a B-52 over Russia. As he waved his hat in the air, shouting *Wahoo,* the song "We'll Meet Again" hauntingly filled the room from above.

All three stared in utter disbelief at what they had just witnessed. Aaron could not help but notice Bob was struck hard by what he'd watched. "Did that really just happen?"

Bob just stared at the floor.

"Bob, are you okay? Can I get you something?" Cynthia asked, stunned herself at just seeing another mushroom cloud on a screen. Aaron and Cynthia looked at each other without saying a word for an uncomfortably long time. Bob, horrified, frozen in the middle of this craziness, relaxed his fingers and dropped his book on the floor.

Cynthia walked over, carefully picking up the book and, making sure it didn't open, slid it into his hand. She put her other hand on Bob's shoulder. Neither could believe the man they had grown accustomed to, always obnoxiously irreverent and always having an opinion where he is right, was now so subdued, silent.

"Bob?" Cynthia questioned again. "Bob, what can we do? How can we help?"

Finally, Bob stirred. He looked at the book that had been replaced in his hand and walked over to the old-fashioned, wood-burning stove. Putting his foot up on the hearth, he turned to face Aaron and Cynthia. "I fear I have done something terrible."

Before either could utter a word, Bob held up the book in his left hand. "Hear me out. Sit down."

Cynthia felt his seriousness and returned to her chair without question. Aaron protested, "Bob, what the hell are you talking about? You didn't have anything to do with that nightmare, this madness." As the words left Aaron's lips, he felt an uncomfortable suspicion. It was, after all, he who was here in the future from an accident Bob did not plan or at first understand but was entirely responsible for. *Bob*, he thought to himself, *for all of his great intelligence, is fallible.*

"Aaron, please sit down." Aaron silently, like a mime visually protesting, returned to the couch. "Dancer and I saw humankind at its absolute worst during the war. Unthinkable atrocities inflicted by armies of madmen. But as odd or as sick as this might sound, it was still a viable, definable evil. The last couple of months, I have been seeing an increase in that type of insanity, enough to cause me concern that it could be happening again. But of late, for the last week since Pandora brought you here, I have been watching on the news acts that even evil cannot explain. It is as if something is broken, very, very broken."

Bob, still at the wood-burning stove with one foot perched up on the river rock stone hearth, leaned forward like Captain Morgan on a bottle of rum, the book no longer bouncing on his thigh. He started to speak, but instead brought his foot down off the hearth. Standing up straight, he turned so he could face Cynthia and Aaron. He held the book to his forehead, taking a very deep breath. "What you just witnessed wasn't an isolated incident. These types of totally insane behaviors have been happening with greater and greater frequency all over the world since right after you arrived. The insanity is not just humans. In a hundred-square-mile section of rainforest in Brazil, thousands of normally docile animals fought to the death, with no explanation. Scientists are perplexed and have no idea why or how this could happen. In cities across the globe, there are reports of hundreds of thousands of birds of every species flying into the windows of large buildings as if they were committing mass suicide. On five separate beaches in completely different parts of the world, whales, orcas and dolphins beached themselves by the hundreds. Suicides are up thirty-seven percent."

Bob was interrupted by two new anchors returning live. "We have World News psychologist, Dr. Steven Burd, with us. Steven, what is going on? Why, how, would an entire country, a half million people, commit suicide?"

"Andy, there are many accounts of mass suicides over the years. They are usually carefully orchestrated by a very persuasive and intelligent lone madman. In this case, it is baffling, as President Giannopoulos was a well-respected man with a long history of service to his country and people."

Andy offered, "I met President Giannopoulos, and you're right, he wasn't a madman. Something is wrong. Something appears to be terribly amiss within our civilization, in reality itself. Here, I want to run some footage we aired three nights ago that took place just over the state line from our studios." Andy finished and turned to look at the green screen, the imaginary spot where the viewers would see the video about to run. The camera switched to a scene unfolding, the bottom portion of the screen covered with a banner for the affiliate logo and reporter's name.

In the depth of the screen, in vivid color, a local church was engulfed in flames. A local news reporter for Channel 6 KORW, Norman Palmer, was interviewing the police chief. "Do you have any information on what happened here tonight, Chief?" The chief, shaking his head, looked up at the flames and then back to the reporter.

"Norman, what we know so far is Reverend Ralston and what appears to be thirty-seven members of his church have perished inside."

"Chief, there are already rumors that the Reverend Ralston locked everyone inside and set off an incendiary device. Is there any truth to this information?"

"Norman, ah, um, y'all know I can't comment on rumors until we have investigated thoroughly. What we do know is this is a very tragic scene, and our community is going to suffer greatly for some time because of it."

From the crowd, a man suddenly stepped up in front of the camera, pushing the police chief to the side. He was frantic and sobbing. "It is utter madness. It is insanity on Earth. I know them, all of them. They are good sane people."

Norman stepped in, "What are you trying to say? What happened to them?"

"I was here. They all showed up, seven families, the kids too," the man said, bending down, wailing and sobbing. "They said they were doing this to go home, that it was time and that we will all understand soon. No one had any idea what they were talking about or going to do."

The police chief, regaining his footing and composure, signaled for a deputy to escort the man away. He tried to grab the microphone out of Norman's hand, but the man, frantic to get the truth out, yelled as he was being wrestled away, "They marched in all of the women and children, they locked the doors and they blew themselves up, for God's sake, they blew themselves up. Oh God, oh God."

All three watched without uttering a word until Bob, extremely distraught, finally spoke. "See. See, it does not end. Last night I watched a story out of England where several hundred people, without a reason, just started walking hand-in-hand in single-file lines off the White Cliffs of Dover, plummeting to their deaths. They didn't run, they weren't chased, they just walked, like lemmings to their death, holding hands and singing. I lay awake all night, filled with anxiety, and then the answer came to me this morning."

Bob stopped, shaking his head back and forth, eyes down and the book still against his leg, obviously suffering great internal turmoil. "I fear. No, actually, I am confident, I am to blame. That this is all my fault. In my toying around with the script, with the fucking Godscript, I, even as smart as I am, have inadvertently, seriously changed the course of the future, of all life on Earth. I have created a horrific anomaly within the script." He stopped and hit the top of his head several times with his book. "I believe, as I have been slicing out portions of the script from the past, oblivious to its consequences, I created a rip. A rip, not in the fabric of space and time, but in the light that is the script. A rip, a wound that did not self-heal. And now, that rip has grown proportionately as it followed us from Aaron's time to here, to this point, to now. It is at odds with itself, a conflict that it is unable to resolve, and is changing the perception of our reality within every living thing. Good and evil are crossing their natural boundaries! My imbecilic need to understand and meddle with the IQRES may very well have doomed us all!"

~~~ ~~~ ~~~

Made in the USA
Columbia, SC
22 April 2023